Novels by
**C. S. Friedman**
available from DAW Books

*The Outworlds*
THIS ALIEN SHORE
THIS VIRTUAL NIGHT

*The Coldfire Trilogy*
BLACK SUN RISING
WHEN TRUE NIGHT FALLS
CROWN OF SHADOWS

*The Magister Trilogy*
FEAST OF SOULS
WINGS OF WRATH
LEGACY OF KINGS

*The Dreamwalker Chronicles*
DREAMWALKER
DREAMSEEKER
DREAMWEAVER

THE MADNESS SEASON

IN CONQUEST BORN
THE WILDING

# C. S. FRIEDMAN

# THIS VIRTUAL NIGHT

## DAW BOOKS, INC.
**DONALD A. WOLLHEIM, FOUNDER**

1745 Broadway, New York, NY 10019

**ELIZABETH R. WOLLHEIM**
**SHEILA E. GILBERT**
**PUBLISHERS**

www.dawbooks.com

For Linda Coleman and Roderick Smith, who reminded me that there is light beyond the darkness.

And for Caleb. Just because.

# Acknowledgments

As always, I am deeply indebted to my beta readers, whose insights and criticisms helped shape this book: Carl Cipra, Jennifer Eastman, David Walddon, David Williams, Zsusy Sanford, and Linda Gilbert. Some of them went above and beyond the call of duty on this one, and I am very grateful.

Thanks to Larry Friedman, Kim Dobson, Carmen C. Clark, and my editor Betsy Wollheim, for their support throughout the writing period. And to Betsy and my agent, Russ Galen, for maintaining faith in me during my unproductive stretch, when I was struggling to have faith in myself.

Thanks to Marylou Capes-Platt for her meticulous editorial work, Adam Auerbach for his beautiful new cover designs for both *This Virtual Night* and *This Alien Shore*, and Joshua Starr for his assistance in . . . well, a little bit of everything.

Special thanks to Steve Anderson for his help with high-tech weapons research. Sometimes there is one thing you really really REALLY have to get right, and it helps to have someone who knows the subject and can communicate it so well.

Lastly, thanks to Linda Coleman and Roderick Smith, who met me at one of the lowest, darkest moments of my life, and helped me get back on track. Words do not exist that can ever thank them enough.

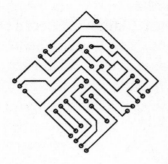

WHEREAS the Hausman Drive offered humanity the stars, allowing Earth to colonize planets throughout the galaxy

WHEREAS it exacted a terrible price for that freedom, altering the DNA of all who used it, so that their children no longer appeared human, causing the drive to be abandoned

WHEREAS Earth, fearful of contagion, severed all contact with its mutated descendants, and through that act of cowardice plunged its colonies into the darkness of Isolation

WHEREAS Guera's discovery of the ainniq offered a new means of crossing vast distances, so that the survivors of Isolation could be rescued, and a Second Age of interstellar civilization begun

AND WHEREAS only Gueran outpilots, by virtue of their particular Hausman mutation, can navigate the ainniq safely, thus granting them a natural monopoly over transport and commerce between the human worlds

WE ACKNOWLEDGE Guera's unique and daunting responsibility in the arena of human affairs, and therefore establish a central governing organization called the AIN-NIQ GUILD to facilitate and guide the reunification of humankind. It is tasked with establishing a code of Common Law that will protect all humans equally, regardless of their outward shape, variation, or capacity. It will seek out the lost colonies of Earth and invite them to be part of humanity's new deep space community. And it will invite the inhabitants of Earth to join their cousins in deep space, while recognizing that ancient angers are slow to fade, and the assimilation of Terrans into our new civilization will be a challenge for all concerned.

*Preamble to the Founding Charter of the Ainniq Guild*

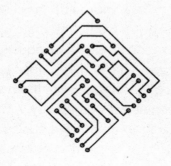

To control perception is to control reality.

MICAH BELLO
"Deconstructing Reality: A Post-Immersive
Perspective" *(Journal of Virtual Technology,
Vol. 427, No. 5)*

# HARMONY NODE
# HARMONY STATION

**T**HE DRAGONS were out in force tonight.

Ramiro tried to keep to shadows as he moved, but the narrow stone corridor didn't offer a lot of cover, and the flickering light from torches set high on the walls kept shadows constantly moving. Which meant that the evasive maneuvers they'd used to avoid the Citadel's reptilian guards aboveground wouldn't work here. If any dragons crossed their path while they were down in the labyrinth, the two of them were done for.

"Should be coming up soon," Van whispered nervously. He glanced down at the crumpled parchment map in his hand. "Any minute now."

*You've been saying that for an hour,* Ramiro thought.

The labyrinth was ancient, a maze of tunnels whose masonry had been degraded by centuries of rainwater seeping from above; the floor was littered with fragments of fallen brick, making walking treacherous. As they picked their way carefully over the rubble, Ramiro was acutely aware of the tons of earth poised overhead, held at bay by nothing more than rotting mortar and a prayer. *How does the gaming program do that?* he wondered. The virt software that was controlling his sensory input could add anything to the environment that a person could touch, taste, hear, or see, but what physical experience conjured such a sense of claustrophobia? What tangible sensations translated into *dread*?

*God,* he thought, *I love Dobson games.*

"You okay?" Van put a hand on his shoulder and squeezed. Ramiro could feel his friend's fingers trembling, though whether from excitement or fear it was hard to say. Intellectually a person might understand that a virt couldn't hurt anyone—it only provided the illusion of being hurt—but it was possible for a player to get so wrapped up in the story that he forgot such fine details. The resulting adrenaline rush was very real—as was the pain that the virt would feed into their brainware if they were injured in this fantasy realm. And fear of *that* was totally rational.

"Yeah," he lied. "Keep going."

They hadn't expected so many dragon guards to be on duty. True, any they ran into down here would likely be in human form—a necessary adaptation within the labyrinth—but that didn't make the creatures any less dangerous. Dragons could breathe fire even when they were transformed, and a fireball in these narrow tunnels was on the list of things Ramiro would like not to run into. But the fact that so many dragons were present confirmed that this place was important, right? That was a good thing.

Suddenly Van grabbed Ramiro's arm, jerking him to a halt. "Incoming," he whispered. Ramiro knew enough to trust his friend's instincts—Van had an almost supernatural ability to anticipate in-game threats—so he looked around for cover. But there was nothing. The tunnel was too narrow, its walls too smooth. If a dragon guard showed up now they were dead.

Then: "There!" Van cried, pointing ahead. Squinting, Ramiro saw nothing at first, but then the flickering shadows seemed to resolve into a deeper black shape on one wall. An opening of some kind? Whatever it was, it was the only option besides standing there and looking stupid. They ran toward it, leather armor creaking and weapons jangling with every step. Ramiro's heart lurched with every sound, but that couldn't be helped. When you were loaded down with this much gear you couldn't run quietly.

Dobson games were great on detail.

The dark space was indeed a crumbling archway. Thank God! Maybe it would lead to a chamber where they could hide, or even better, a side tunnel that would allow them to get the hell out of here. Ramiro skidded on rubble as he tried to make the turn, and he had to grab onto the side of the arch to steady himself. A quick look behind him confirmed that no enemies had shown up yet. Jesus Christ, they might really make it! He turned back to the dark space, wondering what kind of chamber or tunnel they were about to take shelter in—

Only there was no chamber. No tunnel. Just a mound of rubble from floor to ceiling, where the tunnel had collapsed long ago. Despairing, Ramiro knew there was no way the two of them could clear it in time.

Shit.

He could hear footsteps coming from behind them now, chillingly alien in their rhythm. *Scritch-scritch-THUMP* . . . *scritch scritch THUMP*. Talons on stone. Heart pounding, he pressed back as far as he could into what little space they had, drawing his short sword as he did so. The weapon had a dragonslayer amulet embedded in the hilt, so in theory he was ready to fight such a creature, but he'd bought the charm from a sorcerer who wasn't exactly reputable, so whether it would work or not was anyone's guess. He wasn't anxious to test it.

Then the dragon came into sight. It was a monstrous, hulking beast—half reptile, half human, and so tall that its crested head scraped against the ceiling as it walked. Its eyes glowed red with demonic power, and Ramiro knew that if a warrior looked into those eyes, or engaged the dragon in any way, he would die, instantly and forever. The concept was terrifying, but it was also a relief; the visceral panic that he'd experienced at the sight of the creature began to subside.

It was an NP, a non-player. Some mundane person had just happened to pass by the place where they were gaming, so the virt had used him as set dressing. The burning red eyes were a warning not to engage with him, since he would not have a clue about what was going on. Ramiro watched, breathing heavily, as the dragon passed by without noticing them. Of course it did. Now that Ramiro had seen its eyes, he would expect it to do nothing else.

That was another thing Ramiro loved about Dobson games. They wove any necessary restrictions right into the narrative, so you could stay immersed in the story. Another virt might have just slapped a cautionary symbol on the hulking figure to warn players to keep away, or maybe rendered it in black and white (an especially tacky solution), but Dobson had turned the warning itself into part of their story, giving them an in-character reason not to engage the creature. Genius.

Of course, that was only necessary because station rules prohibited multi-player virts in public spaces. If you confronted a passing stranger as though he were a dragon he might report you to the authorities, and then you could wind up in serious trouble. Ramiro didn't understand why that was necessary—was anyone really getting hurt?—but for now the prohibition was an inconvenience the gaming industry just had to accommodate.

As soon as the dragon was gone they edged back out into the main tunnel and started forward again. Soon they came to the place where their map said an entrance to the inner labyrinth would be located: the final stage of their journey. The heavy wooden door that barred their way was coated in cave-slime, but they could tell that there were inscribed runes beneath it. As Van used his sleeve to wipe slime away, Ramiro could not help but wonder at how many runes there were. It seemed oddly excessive.

On an impulse, he paused the game program. He wanted to see where they really were.

Stone walls morphed into plasteel panels. Flickering torchlight was replaced by the steady glow of lighting strips. The decaying tunnel was now a service conduit, streamlined and pristine. Wow. No matter how many times he dealt with reality-overlay programs, the suddenness of the transition always shocked him.

"Got it!" Van exclaimed. His mock-medieval garb was gone now, replaced by a gray no-G jumpsuit with many cargo pockets. Ramiro saw that the spell-chest tucked under his arm was real, though the mundane version wasn't nearly as ornate as the one Van had picked up in the virt. That was . . . odd. A game that could control all your senses, make you see or feel anything it wanted to, had no need for physical props. Yet apparently the box of magical artifacts had one.

As for the door itself, it had morphed into an oval-shaped portal with a high-pressure vacuum seal around the edge, flanked by a security panel. Clearly whatever part of the station the two of them had wandered into, it was a place that gamers didn't belong. That too was odd. Normally a virt would never lead them into restricted territory. But maybe that was a perk of playing with a master programmer's son. Maybe Van had convinced his father to give them access to parts of the station where mere mortals were not allowed to go.

Maybe.

Ramiro watched Van trace the runes with his fingers, muttering an incantation to give the motion power. As his fingers passed over the security sensor its light switched from red to green. Probably reading his fingerprints. "We're in!" Van exulted, then he stepped back quickly. Ramiro reactivated his virt just in time to see the massive wooden door swinging in their direction, and moved out of the way.

"You sure we should go in there?" Ramiro asked. Something about the situation felt wrong. Just . . . wrong. It bothered him that he didn't know why.

"After coming all this way? Hell yeah!"

The doorway gave them access to a tunnel even darker and narrower than the one they'd been in. Here there were no torches, so Ramiro turned up the flame on his oil lantern to light the way. Flickering amber light played along the strands of ancient spider webs, dancing in the breeze from their passing. The hollow drip-drip of water somewhere in the distance hinted at a vast empty space up ahead. Now and then Ramiro thought he saw gleaming eyes in the darkness, but if anything was out there, it chose not to show itself. Thank God.

Eventually the tunnel disgorged into a cavern whose ceiling was lost in shadow high overhead. The part that they could see was a good twenty yards across. Directly opposite them was a stone sarcophagus with figures of demons carved into its base; the columns surrounding it were decorated with matching images. In the flickering lamplight it looked as if a room full of tiny devils were dancing.

For a moment the two of them just stood frozen, wonder and fear slowly giving way to elation. This was what they had come for, the prize they'd been gaming so long to find. It was hard to absorb that they'd finally succeeded.

"Stay here and stand guard," Van whispered as he started toward the sarcophagus. The place seemed to demand whispering.

Ten days: that's how long it had taken them. Ten days of skipping out on work and blowing off family obligations and not answering messages from friends, so they could focus exclusively on this quest. And in the end their dedication had paid off. There were other teams running the same virt—Ramiro and Van had crossed paths with a few of them—but the undisturbed layer of dirt on this floor suggested that his team was the first to find its way here. Which meant that whatever sorcerous swag was in that sarcophagus was theirs to claim.

*This'll send us to the top of the leaderboards for sure.*

Ramiro watched as Van opened his spell-chest and began to remove items from it, arranging them on top of the sarcophagus: amulets, herb bundles, tiny parchment scrolls . . . all the stuff they'd spent the last ten days collecting. The placement of each piece had to be perfect, Ramiro knew, and he watched as Van placed them, adjusted them, stepped back to study them, and then reached out to adjust them again. He turned some pieces around and flipped others over, and then started combining them, stacking them like checkers, one on top of the other. At one point he pressed two items together and rotated them, as if he was screwing one into the other. Ramiro's brow furrowed as he watched. Van was the team's sorcerer, and it was his job to know how such artifacts worked, but the game they were playing didn't usually require motions like that for activation.

*Are they real props too?* Ramiro wondered suddenly. Normally he'd have assumed they weren't, but the box had been real, right? So maybe the magical items were as well.

He hesitated, then visualized the pause icon again. Suddenly the game was gone, and in its place was a large mechanical room. There were switches and valves and pipes and data screens all over the place, and the sarcophagus turned out to be a control console. *Red ring: Oxygen,* one screen read. In the game that had been a picture of a demon. *Red ring: Pressure.* More demons. *Green ring: CO2.*

They were in Environmental Control.

Life support.

*No game should have given us access to such a place,* Ramiro thought. Suddenly the sense of wrongness was overwhelming. Fear was stirring inside him—real fear, not the fake gaming stuff. "Van!" he called out. His voice was shaking. "Pause the game! Look around!" His voice echoed from the cavern walls, filling the chamber with his fear.

But Van was too wrapped up in arranging his magical items to listen. He did really have props for them, Ramiro noted, but not simple physical markers. Each one was a small device of some kind, and as Van connected them to one another, tiny lights blinked in acknowledgment. The game was directing him to assemble something.

"Van!" Ramiro yelled. He could hear the panic in his own voice. "Stop it! Stop putting those damn things together! Listen to me!"

But Van didn't respond. Ramiro could have been a ghost for all his words mattered.

*Maybe he can't hear me,* he thought suddenly. *Maybe the game is keeping him from hearing me.* But why would it do that? What purpose could it possibly serve?

Deep within his brain, a primal voice urged him to flee. *Run! Run as far and as fast as you can! Don't wait! Go now!*

But he couldn't leave Van behind. Not if there was real danger here.

He sprinted toward the console, meaning to break apart the strange device before it could do anything. But even as he did so Van threw up his hands triumphantly and stepped back, and Ramiro knew that in the virt the sarcophagus was probably cracking open. On top of the console, the small device blinked and beeped. Too late. Ramiro was too late! One by one the red lights on the device were turning green, while behind the thing, in the real world, security screens displayed various elements of environmental control: *oxygen, pressure, circulation, air quality.*

All the services that human beings needed to stay alive on a space station.

Then whiteness exploded, consumed him, melted him. A roar like a thousand ships' engines filled the room, then was gone. He was aware of being thrown back into the wall, but felt no impact. What little was left of his body was no longer capable of sensation.

Then the world was gone.

Both worlds were gone.

**GAME OVER**

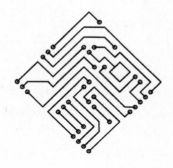

## SAKUNA

That which was forgotten, the *sakuna* remembers.

That which was lost, the *sakuna* seeks.

That which was divided, the *sakuna* reunites.

*KAJA: An Outworlder's Guide to the Gueran*
*Social Contract, Volume 1: Signs of the Guild*

# GUERA NODE
# TIANANMEN STATION

THERE WERE five suns hanging over Ru's head. White suns, identical in size, evenly spaced, as if they marked the points of an unseen pentagram.

Strange.

Dimly she remembered that one should not stare at suns. She tried to look away, but her motor control wasn't back yet, and she couldn't turn her head. She closed her eyes, but the suns blazed crimson on the insides of her eyelids, mocking the effort.

*Outrider Gaya?*

The words buzzed in her ears like insects; if she could have moved her arm she would have swatted at them. Slowly the fog of stasis was lifting, sensation seeping back into her body. She was aware of tender bruises where the contacts of the stim suit were still attached to her skin, soreness in her throat where the respiratory tube had been, and an itching deep, deep within her flesh, beyond any hope of scratching. They were familiar discomforts, and she welcomed them as a sign that she was coming out of stasis properly.

Still the voices buzzed in her ears.

*Is she awake?*

*I saw her eyes open for a moment.*

*Ru? Ru Gaya? Are you awake?*

Proxima Five had insects that could mimic human speech. Maybe that's where she was.

*Readings say yes.*

*Ru. Respond if you can hear me. It's important.*

Slowly she opened her eyes again. This time the suns resolved into the lights of an examining room. Still very bright. Painful to look at. She uncurled her fingers and felt the hard shell of the stasis pod beneath her hands. Why was she still in the pod, if she wasn't on her ship?

Then memories enveloped her.

*Screaming voices coming closer: alien voices, hate-filled voices. The words are foreign but the bloodlust behind them is clear. The lander is only a few yards ahead of them and she and Tully run toward the ramp, desperate to make it before their pursuers catch up to them.*

*Suddenly Tully gasps and goes down. As she reaches out to grab him she sees there is a slender metal dart sticking out of his leg. Cursing, she drags him forward those last few feet. Up the ramp. Through the hatch. Darts strike the ship as the door whisks shut behind them, but one dart makes it through in time. It misses Ru by inches, hits the far wall, and clatters to the floor. Its tip, black with poison, gleams in the dim emergency lighting.*

*Shit.*

*Tully is moaning in pain, and she knows that if there is poison on his dart he can die if she doesn't tend to him. But if she doesn't get the lander off this damn planet they will both die for sure. She can hear a distant banging on the hull as she sprints for the navigator's console. "Hang on," she mutters, as she forces the lander to skip half the steps of its launch protocol. The engines roar to life and suddenly the banging ceases; no doubt the locals are running for cover. Good. Good. Her hands dance feverishly over the console. As soon as the seals are confirmed they can get the hell off this benighted rock—*

Something sharp stabbed her arm. INJECTION, her wellseeker

informed her, red words scrolling brightly across her field of vision. DA-MASOL. The drug started burning away the last of the stasis fog, scattering her planetary memories. The room around her was coming into focus now, as were four people flanking her open stasis pod, two male and two female. All Gueran, from the look of them. Guild, most likely. The room itself was stark, white, sterile. Some kind of medical facility?

"What happened?" she gasped. "Where am I?" Then the post-stasis sickness hit, and she leaned over the side of the pod and vomited. Someone had put a container by the side of her pod, and she aimed for it as best she could. Small cleaner bots whirred into action, racing to clean up the mess that had missed the target.

When she was done she just hung there for a moment, draped over the edge of the pod, trying to catch her breath. Damn. Normally she wasn't *this* sick when she woke up. What the hell was going on?

"Vital signs normalizing," a woman's voice said.

She pushed herself up to a sitting position. The stim suit made it hard to move, but the thin tubes of fluid that had cushioned her flesh for years were starting to empty now, and each passing minute made motion easier. "Where the hell am I?"

"Tiananmen Station." The man who was speaking was wearing a medical tunic and a headset with two golden snakes spiraling around its central band, reminiscent of a caduceus. "Your ship was damaged. Our scouts caught up with you outside Omarus Node."

Omarus Node. But that hadn't been on their route—

Ru shut her eyes. *Shit.*

"I'm Medic First Class, Evan Chase. I was asked to oversee your awakening, in case the stasis pod had been compromised." A pause. "Can you tell me your name and number?"

"Ruisa Gaya. Birthworld Guera. Outrider First Class." Reciting the data had no purpose other than to verify that her mind was functioning well enough for her to . . . well, recite data . . . but the ritual nature of it helped her focus her mind back in the real world, and in that sense it was comforting. "License Number 108-A-59923." Then she leaned over the pail and vomited again. Nothing but green fluid came up, the last residue of the stuff the stasis program had been pumping into her system for years now. It felt like she'd been asleep for three hundred.

Someone handed her a towel and she used it to wipe her mouth clean. Meanwhile the four people watching her were suspiciously silent. They were probably using their headsets to net a private conversation, which to her mind was pretty damn rude. "What's up?" she demanded.

"Tull Syng isn't in his pod," one of the women said. "There's a note about a neurotoxin in his med log, but no body."

Full memory returned then, and with it a wave of knife-edged guilt. "I buried him in space," she muttered. "It was what he wanted."

"You should have brought him back. We need blood and tissue samples to verify the cause of death—"

"And you'll find them in biostorage," Ru said testily. "I do know how to do my job." She shook her head sharply. "They hit him with something as we were leaving. Some kind of metal dart. That's in storage now. And I took samples of every part of Tully that I thought you might want to look at."

By the time the autopilot had taken over, and she was finally able to tend to Tully, his skin was a ghastly gray and he was struggling to breathe. She had managed to get him into the med pod and assigned all the ship's free resources to saving him, but it was too late. The neurotoxin on the dart had done irreparable damage. For three days she'd hovered over him while the medical programs struggled to stabilize him, cursing her own helplessness. Then he'd exhaled his final wheezing breath, followed by a cold and terrible silence. There was nothing to do after that but weep, curse, and deal with his body appropriately. "He told me he wanted to be buried in space," she said. "So I honored that."

*Bury me in space,* Tully had begged. *Otherwise, they might find out. . . .* He didn't finish the sentence, but she understood. There were some parts of his life a man wanted to keep private, even in death.

Slowly she swung her legs over the side of the pod, eased herself onto her feet, and tested her balance. It wasn't good, but it was within the normal parameters of stasis recovery. Returning to full function after years of suspended animation wasn't easy. "Am I free to go?"

"We need to run some tests," Chase said. "Given the extension of the stasis period—"

Ru's eyes narrowed. "The *what*?"

"Your ship was damaged during launch. It went off course while you and Outrider Tull were in suspension, and missed its scheduled return. The stasis program rebooted automatically—"

"How long?" Ru demanded. "I was on a three-year mission. How long was I gone?"

"Twenty years." Was that pity in his voice? "The Guild had to wait until your ship got into range before it could initiate recovery. I'm sorry."

*Twenty years. Holy shit.* Ru shut her eyes for a moment, fighting the urge to be sick again. If there was one scenario all outriders feared, it was that somewhere in the darkness between the worlds their ship would fail them, and they would hurtle forever through the endless night, neither fully alive nor dead, with no hope of rescue. This time the Guild had rescued her, but barely. Maybe next time she wouldn't be so lucky. "The ship?" It took effort to force the words out. "What about my ship?"

"Under repair. All the data's in here." The woman took a small clear chip out of her pocket and handed it to her. Ru looked around for her headset, but nothing was visible in the stark white room other than medical equipment. What did they expect her to do, eat the chip and absorb its contents?

Doctor Chase tapped on one of the walls and a white drawer slid forward. Inside was Ru's simple crescent-shaped headset, resting on a neat pile of her clothing. Her smaller personal possessions were next to it, mixed in with her partner's. She had to turn away for a moment as a wave of guilt came over her.

*I'm sorry, Tully. I should have known it was too dangerous. I should have stopped you.*

"We won't keep you long," Chase promised. "The Guild just wants to make sure no biological functions were compromised by your long sleep."

Ru's first instinct was to protest that she didn't need any help, but then a wave of exhaustion overcame her. It might have been twenty E-years since she had consigned her partner's body to space, but she'd slept through most of that. To her body and mind, it felt like it had happened yesterday.

*My partner's dead. My ship is damaged. The mission was a failure. I almost didn't make it back. Now here I am, seventeen years behind schedule. So where am I rushing off to?* She sighed. *I'll bet my time-share is occupied.*

"What the hell," she muttered.

If the Guild wanted her to get an official certificate of health before she left here, then that's what was going to happen. No one denied the Guild anything. She spread her arms like a martyr awaiting crucifixion and told them, "Do your worst."

*I'm sorry, Tully. Whatever universe your soul is in now . . . please forgive me.*

**S**he paid for a private cab to Red Sector. She probably shouldn't have— God alone knew what seventeen years of automatic rent payments had done to her savings—but she wasn't in the mood to deal with public transportation right now.

Twenty years, this time.

Twenty fucking years.

Shit.

She hadn't put her headset on yet. It was in her lap, ready to serve as interface between her brainware and the outside world, but she couldn't bring herself to activate it. During the mission it would have done nothing more than give her access to the ship's private database, its innernet. But she was in the domain of the outernet now, and the minute she connected to it her brain would be flooded with public data. Semi-sentient ads for services, networks, gadgets, resorts . . . each one designed to analyze a person's likes and dislikes and craft images designed to entice her into performing the desired action. Her adblockers were twenty years out of date, so the minute she connected to the outernet she was going to get blitzed by two decades' worth of crap. Not something to look forward to.

She did put her wellseeker through its paces, and it checked out her bodily functions one by one, offering to adjust any chemical balance that didn't seem quite right. Given that she'd just been inspected top to toe by the Guild's medics, such an inspection wasn't really necessary, but the familiar medicinal murmur was comforting.

FATIGUE LEVEL 4, it informed her at the end, letters scrolling red across her field of vision. STIMULANT DESIRED?

She visualized a cartoon hand making a thumbs-down gesture. NO.

Ironic, wasn't it, that sleeping for seventeen years could leave a person so tired? But she knew that what her body craved now was not sleep, but *normalcy*. It wanted to run her through the natural stages of sleep at its own pace, her muscles completely relaxed, her lungs drawing in air and then releasing it without the help of a respirator. There was no way to explain to someone who hadn't experienced extended stasis how pleasurable—and emotionally necessary—that first natural sleep was.

*Soon,* she promised herself. *Soon.*

Soon, too, she would have to report to her Guild masters for debriefing. That prospect was considerably less appealing. The thought of sitting in front of a panel of Gueran authorities and answering their questions echoed the disciplinary courts of her youth, reminding her that though she enjoyed considerable autonomy during her missions, her lords and masters on Guera still called the shots. But there was no point in cursing a contract with the Devil after you'd signed it.

Hopefully the Guild would pay for her ship's repairs. If not . . . well then, she wasn't going anywhere for a while.

The foyer of the timeshare complex was crowded as always, full of businessmen in faux silk suits, commuting politicians, migrant station workers, and of course, outriders. It wasn't the most luxurious apartment complex on the ring, but it was in a decent neighborhood and the internal security was tight, so it stayed busy.

She didn't recognize anyone. She barely even recognized the lobby, given how drastically it had been redecorated since last she was here. That's what happened when you slept for twenty years. It made for an odd sense of disconnection, as if nothing about her was real. Occupational hazard. You either got over it or you quit outriding.

The man behind the desk (she thought it was a man, but with some Variants it was hard to tell) nodded a polite greeting. He had three long fingers on each hand, and when he rested them on the desk it gave him a bird-like aspect. If Ru had been connected to the outernet she probably would have called up information on his sourceworld, just out of curiosity, but since her headset was still not activated she just smiled back and said, "Ru Gaya."

He stared into space for a microsecond as his headset accessed the necessary records. There were blue stalks rising from his head, but she couldn't tell if they were natural or part of his headset. "Welcome back, Outrider Gaya." His brow furrowed slightly. "You are . . . later than expected."

"Seventeen years, yeah, I know." She shrugged. The motion irritated her stasis bruises and made her wince. "Sorry about that. Is my suite available?"

Another microsecond of unfocused staring. "Currently yes, but it's assigned to Outrider Pasador and his partner beginning on the tenth. . . ."

"I'll be gone by then. Or I'll work something out with him."

"Good enough, then." He ran a gangly bird finger across a screen in front of him. "Please relax in the lobby while I have bots prepare the suite." He cocked his head slightly, which set his blue stalks quivering. "Next time, if you call when you dock, I can have your apartment ready by the time you get here."

"I know," she said shortly. "Stuff came up."

She went to find a chair that suited her Terran-style physique. The only one available was next to a bunch of young girls who were giggling and whispering and pointing at an empty spot in the middle of the room as if there were something there. They were probably hooked up to a shared universe game. No doubt in their heads the lobby looked like a tropical beach, or a magical palace with dancing cutlery, or something else suitably silly. Role-playing virts had been prohibited in public spaces last time Ru was here, but if gamers were subtle enough they could usually go undetected. These girls weren't being subtle, though, and the opulent headset that one of them was wearing, adorned with crystalline butterflies on wires that tinkled each time a movement of her head set them bouncing, was hardly inconspicuous. Maybe the laws had changed in the last twenty years. Overdecorated headsets seemed to be the fashion of the moment, and as Ru looked about the room she saw many that were—to her eyes at least—excessive. One woman had a stylized golden vulture perched on her head, its wings sweeping down around her ears; another wore a scale model of a waystation, its inner ring fitted around her head and two others magnetically suspended above it; yet another wore a crown of graduated spikes that splayed out from her head like sunbeams. Ru vaguely remembered having seen something like that in a picture of an ancient Earth statue. Yet all those headsets—large and small, modest and decadent, tasteful and bizarre—did the same thing in the end, serving as interface between the brainware inside a person's head and the ocean of data outside it.

Hers still wasn't turned on.

The girls had become quite loud, and one of them suddenly got up and ran toward the door, barreling into a woman in a glossy pink jumpsuit. Immersed in her game, the girl hadn't even seen her. A seven-foot tall Frisian in a security uniform approached, spoke to her harshly, then addressed the other girls. Ru couldn't hear what he was saying, but his intent was clear. They argued with him for a few minutes, but in the end he sternly ushered them out. *They should be glad he's not reporting them,* she thought, as the sound of tinkling butterflies faded in the distance.

"Outrider Gaya." It was the receptionist. "Your suite is ready."

She nodded her appreciation and headed toward the tube at the back of the lobby. From there it was a short trip to the front door of her timeshare, which opened of its own accord at her approach. A new feature.

The apartment looked exactly like it had the day she'd left for her last assignment. Her furniture was positioned normally, the art monitors were displaying her favorite paintings, and even the robe she'd left thrown across the sofa was in exactly the same position that it had been when she left. Never mind that an hour ago all her possessions had been packed in a storage crate and tucked away somewhere in the depths of the station; the staging bots had arranged everything to perfection, making it seem like she just left the suite yesterday. It was an illusion, to be sure, but a comforting illusion, and she stood in the doorway for a minute, letting the familiarity of the place seep into her, soothing her spirit. All other things might change—*had* changed—but this, her territory, remained constant.

She adjusted the wall color to a soothing blue and walked over to the shelf unit where her colonial artifacts were displayed. A statue of a six-armed god from Hadrian Four, a fertility carving from Acer Six, a scarf of New Tuscan silk that changed color in response to her emotion . . . there was an item from every Variant race she had helped rescue from Isolation, given to her by grateful peoples. What she had no mementos from were the colonies that had failed to adapt when Earth first cut off contact with them, or—far worse—had destroyed themselves when their Hausman mutations began to surface. The only living colonies the outriders ever found were those whose inhabitants had made their peace with the concept of mass mutation, and whose gene pool had stabilized to reflect a few dominant traits. Everywhere else there was only emptiness, alien landscapes that had long since swallowed up the bones of Earth's abandoned children.

Reaching into her bag, Ru took out the one keepsake of Tully's that she had claimed as a memento. It was an opulent glass phallus with a rainbow of colors swirling in its depths and a series of hash-marks etched around the base. She knew that each mark represented an intimate encounter between her partner and some newly discovered class of Variant. Xenophilia was his secret pleasure and his weakness, and ultimately it had cost him his life.

*I will never forget you,* she promised his spirit.

In the washroom she took a good look at herself for the first time. There was a small purple bruise marking each place where a stim suit contact had been attached, but otherwise she looked much the same as she had before stasis. Her color was healthy, her olive skin smooth and taut, her muscles weak but not atrophied. Apparently the stim suit had done its job maintaining her physical state. Her copper-brown hair was a disheveled mess, the short bob crusted with bits of dried gel from the suit, but that was only to be expected. Rebirth was messy.

She took a hot shower, reveling in the wasted water—a luxury one didn't have on small ships—then headed into the bedroom unit that the bots had connected to the suite and stretched out on the bed, wearing nothing but her headset. Soothing smells wafted into the room, triggered by her weight on the mattress. Post-stasis weariness enveloped her like a warm cocoon.

Home.

She reached up a hand to her headset, hesitated a moment, then turned it on. *Might as well get this over with.* Shutting her eyes, she imagined she could feel her brainware detecting the headset's presence, checking its credentials, and establishing the necessary protocols. That, too, was an illusion. The processor that perched spider-like inside her brain was no more detectable to her conscious senses than her natural brain matter was.

A field of twinkling stars appeared as the headset tested its visual

programming. Then those disappeared, and bright white letters on a
field of midnight blue took their place.

WELCOME BACK, RU GAYA.
THERE ARE 102,345 UPDATES AWAITING DOWNLOAD.
YOU HAVE 1,395,092 UNREAD MESSAGES.
ACTION?

With a groan she turned over on her side, and she was asleep before the headset asked again.

Any act intended to compromise the integrity of a space station should be considered not only an assault upon that station, but an offense against humanity itself. The perpetrator should find in us no leniency, no sympathy, and no refuge. In this all the outworlds are united, Common Law and Independent alike, for humanity cannot colonize deep space unless the structures that protect human life are considered sacrosanct.

ELIMANI SINJARA
*Beyond Barriers: Ten Principles of Governance*
*That Transcend Political Boundaries*

# HARMONY NODE
# TRIDAC STATION

**M**ICAH WAS drawing with pencil and paper. It would have been more efficient to use a stylus and screen, but he took pleasure in the exotic sensations that the ancient tools engendered. The subtle vibrations in his fingers as the tip of his pencil rubbed across the paper, leaving behind a trail of microscopic grit. The heady sense of waste as he destroyed what had once been part of a living tree, for nothing more than a momentary indulgence. Primitive, perverse pleasure. He could imagine his distant human ancestors sitting around a fire on the plains of Terran Africa, writing just the same way.

Never mind that the 'paper' was really plastic and he'd had to pay an arm and a leg to have it textured properly. Or that he'd positioned a graphics screen underneath the paper to record the pattern of his pencil strokes, so if he erased a detail—itself a messy process that drove the cleaning bots crazy—a copy of the original would remain in storage. It was the illusion that mattered.

He was deep into his work when a monster suddenly appeared. It was an ugly, ill-proportioned creature with the wings of a dragon, the legs of a horse, and three reptilian heads that spurted fire as they writhed against the lighting panels in the ceiling. The flesh was translucent, so Micah could still see his work schedule displayed on the screen behind it. That only added to its ugliness.

He calmly took note of the monster, then returned to his work. "What do you want, Ron?" He visualized the icon that would transmit the sound of his words to the person who had sent him the image. "I'm busy."

The monster resolved into a human shape, flat and cartoon-like but recognizable. "How did you know it was me?"

"Because you're the only one who sends me visuals without getting permission first. What's up?"

"I was checking to see if you were in. I'll stop by."

Micah opened his mouth to respond, but before he could make a sound the image disappeared.

That was odd.

Ron Demeter normally preferred to stay in his studio, relying upon netted images to communicate. If he was willing to actually leave his room and walk down three whole corridors and a staircase just to talk to Micah, something important must be up. Curious, Micah put his pencil aside in its velvet-lined collector-edition case and waited. It did feel good to take a break; his hand was getting cramped from having to control the pressure on the ancient writing instrument. Did early Terran writers have some kind of special exercise regimen for their hands to prevent such discomfort? He would have to research it.

A short time later the portal pinged. Micah gestured it open and Ron entered. He was Terran, of course—as was nearly everyone on this station other than Micah—and his impossibly blond hair brushed the top of the doorway as he entered. "You alone?"

Micah spread his hands melodramatically. "As you see."

"I mean, *really* alone?"

*So we're going to act like we're running a spy game. Okay.* He directed his headset to sever all connections to outside systems. Ron waited in silence, one foot tapping impatiently on the floor. Such an overt sign of anxiety was unlike him. "All right," Micah said at last. "We're isolated. Now can I ask what all this melodrama is about?"

Ron looked around the room suspiciously, as if checking it for hidden eavesdroppers. At last he seemed satisfied. "Dragonslayer was your baby, wasn't it?"

"If you mean, was I part of the twenty-person project team that developed that game—my primary job being to keep everyone else from wandering off on tangents? Yes, I suppose you could say it was mine. Why?"

"You heard about the explosion on Harmony Station?"

He shrugged. "Just the basics. I haven't been following offstation news much these days. Some kind of accident, yes?"

"Actually, they're thinking it was sabotage. A deliberate attempt to damage the life support systems."

"Shit. Seriously? No, I hadn't heard that." Given that everyone in the outworlds was dependent on artificial life support systems for survival, there was no worse crime in the eyes of the Guerans than to attack one. And no limit to the punishment that might be meted out to someone who tried. "Is everyone okay?"

"Yeah. Air quality in that ring will be affected for at least another hundred hours, and I hear it's cold as hell in some sectors, but the backup systems got online fast enough to prevent any casualties. Other than the two who were responsible for the whole mess. There was barely enough left of them to identify." He drew in a deep breath. "Micah . . . the guys who did it were playing Dragonslayer."

He exhaled sharply. "That's not possible."

"Whether they were actually role-playing at the time is anyone's guess. But they were at least streaming the game. That's been verified."

"Dragonslayer has locational restrictions built in. It would have directed them away from that part of the station, and if they insisted on going into restricted space the game would have shut down. I should know. I coded that failsafe myself."

"Yeah, well, I guess it didn't work very well, because I'm telling you, investigators checked the guys' activity logs, and it looks like they were running the game when they died."

He exhaled sharply. "Ron, it's just not possible—"

"Just listen to me, okay?" He glanced back nervously at the door. "They're going to be inspecting the Dragonslayer code. *Your* code. They want to find out how the game might be tied to all this." His expression tightened. "Did you put a back door in that program, Micah? Some way that you could sneak in new code after the game was inspected and released? I'm told all designers do that. They hate to give up control of their work. If so—" He held up a hand quickly. "Don't tell me. I don't want to know. I just came to warn you. Tridac's going through that code line by line, right now. And if they find anything suspicious—anything at all—they're going to start asking you questions, and you'd better have answers ready."

A chill ran through Micah. "*Tridac* is doing the investigating?"

"That's right."

"Not Dobson?"

Ron shook his head.

"You sure?"

"Would I have come here if I wasn't?"

Shit. Tridac was a Terran corporation, a monstrous company whose influence stretched across the outworlds like an unholy web. Normally it relied upon local subsidiaries such as Dobson Games to oversee its day to day business, but if the mothercorp was pulling rank this time and handling the investigation itself, that suggested they didn't trust Dobson's people. And Micah was one of those people.

*This is terrorism we're talking about,* he reminded himself. If Guera decided that Tridac was responsible for the explosion on Harmony, it would cut off the company's transit rights. Oh, Tridac's people would still be able to travel to neighboring stations, but transportation between nodes—the intersections of the ainniq which defined deep space territories—required a Gueran pilot. No company as vast as Tridac Enterprises could function properly if the Guerans refused to transport its goods and people from one node to another. Micah could just imagine the other megacorps descending upon Tridac's stranded holdings like vultures on a corpse. No, the megacorp would be desperate to find out what had happened on Harmony before the Guild did, and woe betide any virt designer who bore even a faint scent of guilt.

"They won't find anything that leads to me." He was trying to sound more confident than he felt. Yeah, he'd inserted a few special surprises into the game—all designers did that—but nothing that should cause him trouble if they found them. Nothing that he could remember, anyway.

*Even if I did do something Tridac would have issue with, there's no way to fix it now. The game is active on too many worlds. It would take an army of sniffers to find every copy.*

Suddenly the room felt very warm. PULSE INCREASING, his wellseeker observed. ACTION? He hesitated, then flashed the icon for NOT NOW.

"Look," Ron said. "You didn't have anything to do with the explosion. Right?"

He muttered, "Right."

"So there's nothing to worry about. Just think about what kinds of questions they might ask, and be ready."

*Yeah,* Micah thought, *on a regular Guild station that might be enough. But as long as we're on this station we're subject to Earth Corporate Law, which isn't known for either justice or compassion. And Earth has no love for Variants.*

Seeing the look on his face, Ron sighed. "I'm sorry to have to bring you such lousy news. I just thought you should know."

Micah forced himself to nod. "Hey, I appreciate the warning. Really."

"Let's talk about something else, okay? What are you working on?" Ron walked over to the desk and looked down at Micah's drawing. He frowned. "Looks like a pile of shit."

With a sigh, Micah turned the drawing toward him. *Be grateful for the distraction,* he told himself. "It *is* a pile of shit. I'm trying to decide what insects to add to it, to increase the revulsion factor." He picked up a game chip and offered it to Ron. "Here, try this."

Ron raised an eyebrow as he inserted the chip into his headset. Micah triggered the connection that would allow him to share its feed, and a moment later the translucent image of a dead animal appeared. Its flesh was so decayed that one couldn't tell what species it had originally belonged to, and the stink of putrefaction that arose from it was so powerful, so nauseating, that Ron instinctively put his hand over his mouth to keep from gagging. After a moment he turned away from the image, and though he didn't actually vomit, he looked like he was about to.

Then the virtual image disappeared, and with it the noxious smell. When Ron turned back, his face was two shades paler than before.

Ron shook his head. "Jesus, man. You could have warned me."

Micah grinned. "Pfft. No fun in that."

"I thought you couldn't code smells into a virt?"

"You can. It's just hellishly difficult. Smells don't map neatly onto the cortex or resolve into a simple wave form, so they're harder to manipulate. Most designers just don't bother with them. But I've got a theory . . ." He hesitated. "Tell me, what did you feel when you saw that?"

"It stank like bloody hell."

"No, that's what you *smelled*. But what did you *feel*?"

Ron thought about it for a moment. "Disgust. I felt . . . disgust. Revulsion."

"The emotion. Not a physical sensation?"

"That's right."

"Smell is rooted in the limbic system. That's the same part of the brain that governs our most primitive emotions—fear, aggression, lust, hunger, despair—and also memories. So I'm thinking, if I can identify specific smells that trigger those responses, and figure out how to code them into a virt—"

Ron's eyes widened. "You'd be able to trigger specific emotions."

"*Real* emotions. Not the usual suspension-of-disbelief crap but a genuine visceral response. Which means that gamers running from

Dobson monsters would experience actual fear, as if their lives were really in danger! Imagine what that would be like! Imagine what kind of an edge it would give to the company if we could successfully bring that to market."

Ron was silent for a moment. It was certainly not the enthusiastic response that Micah had expected. "Put this away for now," Ron said quietly. "Just for a while. Go work on something else."

"But you don't get it. This is cutting edge stuff. The first person to establish a fully functional olfactory model will go down in the history books. It'll usher in a whole new generation of virt technology—"

"I *get* it. I do. Game designers will be able to manipulate human emotions. That's one step away from manipulating human thoughts, right?"

Micah's smile faded. "I don't know if I'd go that far—"

"Because you understand the limits of the technology. As do I. But a corporate investigator might not be so well educated. He'll come here looking for a link between Dragonslayer and the incident on Harmony, and when he finds out that one of our designers has been experimenting with mind control . . . what conclusion do you think he might draw?"

A chill ran through Micah. "It's not mind control—"

"Technicalities. Tridac will have to blame someone for this, if only to preserve their stock value. If they can't find the real perpetrator, but know you've been experimenting with mind control . . ." He let the words trail off suggestively. "Put this away for now. Please. Delete all your working files from Dobson's network. You can leave the stuff on scent coding; that's a reasonable project for any designer to be working on. But for God's sake, anything that talks about direct manipulation of human emotion . . . wipe the system clean of it. For your own protection."

Micah wanted to argue with him, to protest that things couldn't possibly be that bad, that there was no need for him to abandon the work that had so consumed him. But he couldn't. Because deep inside he knew his friend was right. If Tridac learned about Micah's current research, there was no telling what it might do. "Yeah." His tone was bitter. "That's probably best."

Ron handed him back the game chip. "I never saw this. I don't know what you're working on. We never had this conversation."

"Never." Micah's voice was distant, hollow. "And I don't know anything about the investigation."

"Best that way," Ron agreed. He hesitated. "I'll let you get back to work . . ."

"Yeah." Micah's tone was bitter. "I've got a lot I have to do." *A lot of work I have to destroy.*

He watched in silence as Ron left the room, waiting until the doors closed behind him. Then he picked up the pencil case and hurled it against the wall with all his might. His custom-made pencil went flying, its precious mock-graphite lead snapping as it hit the floor.

*Fuck* Tridac!

It was him against corporate security. Him and his files. Him and his code. Him and the paradigm-shattering research that could have launched him into the history books forever. Only now that would all have to wait. Maybe a short while. Maybe forever.

*They'll find the perpetrator,* he told himself. *Then everything will go back to normal.*

With a sigh, he started making a mental list of all the files he was going to have to delete.

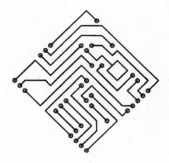

Society requires boundaries. Boundaries require common understanding.

How shall we seek commonality, after rejecting the concept of mental conformity?

BELLA AGINCOURT
*New Horizons: Birth of a Social Contract*

# GUERA
# (MEMORY)

"**R**UISA. COME in."

Executive Lifestyle Counselor Ian Cyprus put aside the tablet he had been reading and offered her a smile that looked surprisingly genuine. He was a lean man with a ruddy, sun-kissed complexion—aggressively healthy—and cleanly defined muscles running down both forearms. Not what she'd expected by a long shot, but it was a nice change from the career bureaucrats she'd been dealing with. The kaja pattern painted on his face in fine black lines was the *nantana*, symbol of a personality type that Ru neither liked nor trusted. *Nantana* were always trying to discover things you weren't ready to reveal, reading your face and body posture like others might read a book. Some *nantana* were so good at it that the mere twitch of an eyelash or the subtlest change in vocal pattern might lay bare one's most guarded secrets. She always felt naked around them.

She nodded him a terse greeting. "Hey." She had painted the *raj* on her own face, an edgy, aggressive kaja that suggested she had a low tolerance for bullshit. She liked the way it looked on her, its sharp black lines accenting her high cheekbones and the natural angularity of her face. Around the edges of the main design she'd added a hint of *kita*, which was a token gesture of respect to his authority. *I acknowledge your rank*, the combination said, *but I'll give you less trouble if you're direct with me.* It was a deliberate counter to the *nantana's* love of social banter, and she waited to see how he would respond to it.

His eyes unfocused for a split second; no doubt he was visualizing the icons that would bring up her psych file. She watched as his eyes tracked a few lines of unseen text, after which he nodded and sat back down behind his desk. She took a moment to look around the office. It was a large room, simply but tastefully decorated in muted tones of blue and amber, and the art on the walls was appealing but aesthetically unchallenging. Clearly whoever designed it had wanted people to focus on conversation rather than décor. In seeming opposition to that intent, however, one whole side wall was transparent, a vast window looking out upon the heart of the city. The view was impressive, but she hadn't come here to admire the scenery. She forced her attention back to Cyprus.

He was watching her, of course. *Nantana* were always watching you. He waved her toward a chair, his air of friendliness polished and perfect as he said, "Have a seat, Ruisa. Or would you prefer some refreshment first? There's food and drink." He indicated a side table, where several pitchers of colorful liquid and a platter of decorative snack food were on display. She shook her head and sat, wary of his genial manner. This wasn't the kind of reception she'd expected, to be sure. *You can spend an E-month in detention,* the judge had told her, *or meet with a lifestyle counselor and have that sentence reduced to three days.* "I'm good." Even to her that sounded curt, so she added, "Thanks."

STRESS INDEX RISING, her wellseeker warned her, scrolling the message in bright letters across her field of vision. ACTION?

NO, she visualized stubbornly. She knew that the wellseeker could release enough sedative into her bloodstream to dull her into a stupor, but what was the point? This guy knew who she was. More important, he knew *what* she was. Smiling at him like a drugged idiot wasn't going to make this meeting go any better.

He studied her for a moment in silence, then said, "You know why you're here."

She shrugged stiffly. "I crashed a singler."

"Someone else's singler."

"Yeah."

"Which you stole."

She couldn't stop a smile from appearing. "Sorry about that."

His eyes narrowed. "This isn't a joke, Ruisa. You're in a lot of trouble."

The smile faded. She nodded solemnly. Three nights in a detention facility had blunted the edge of her usual defiance by a bit. But only a bit.

"This isn't the first time one of your little *adventures* has ended in disaster, is it? But this time people got hurt. There was major property damage."

"I really am sorry," she said, this time with a hint of genuine regret in her voice.

"You can't go on like this. You know that."

A muscle along her jaw tightened. She said nothing.

"I'm here to help you find a better way. One that won't put other people at risk." He paused meaningfully. "Or you."

"Meds, you mean." She said it between gritted teeth.

"That's one option."

"Tried them. Not my thing. Thanks so much for the offer, though." She'd greeted adulthood by trying out all the drugs that could alter her neural patterns, making her brain function more like what the Terrans had once called "normal." The law required she do that much, so that she would fully understand her medical options. Great. Message received. Now she knew what kinds of adjustments were possible, and, like many Guerans, she'd chosen to return to her natural state, rather than live in a state of perpetual falsehood. It was other people who had issue with her Variation.

"You know that drug therapy can be fine-tuned," he said. "It need have no more effect than you want."

"I *tried* it," she said harshly. "And yeah, the meds shut down all the cravings that were getting me into trouble. No more hunger for novelty. No more aching for the kind of rush that you only get when you risk something real. No more feeling like the mundane, predictable world is smothering you, and you need to escape it at any cost. The only problem is, those cravings are *part* of me. Why should I deny my nature? Aren't our mental differences supposed to be strengths, rather than weaknesses? Why can't Guera accept who I am, instead of demanding that I change?"

If she'd expected the question to fluster him, it failed. Calmly he gestured toward the window. "Look out there, Ruisa. What do you see?"

She twisted around and looked. Beyond the courthouse gardens that surrounded this building was the Gueran capital city: gleaming spires, sweeping walkways, mirrored skyscrapers that reflected the shifting clouds overhead, giving buildings the illusion of motion. It was beautiful and impressive, and on another day she might have appreciated the view, but she couldn't see how it was remotely relevant to her situation. "A city," she said, turning back to him.

"Yes. A city." He paused. "Think about what it took to build that city, Ruisa. Think about what it takes to keep it functioning, on a planet where no two people view reality the same way. Think of the monumental effort we must expend as a society to achieve the kind of stability that makes great cities possible, when every member of our population is alien in mindset to every other."

She stiffened slightly. "So . . . I'm a threat to Guera's stability. Is that your point?"

The brief flash of frustration she saw in his eyes was perversely pleasing. "My *point* is that society must have rules. Gueran society more than any other, given the challenges we have to deal with on a daily basis. Else there will be chaos."

Her cheek twitched nervously. Where the hell was this conversation headed? "Yeah, that's me. Ruisa Tours, Mistress of Chaos."

STRESS LEVEL YELLOWZONED, her wellseeker warned. ACTION?

SHUT UP, she growled mentally.

He sighed. "This is the third time you've been picked up on charges of reckless public endangerment. Each incident has been more extreme than the last. If you don't get your hunger for stimulation under control, it's going to drive you to an early grave. And maybe others with you. You know that can't be allowed. Your right to self-expression ends when it threatens the welfare of others."

"So that's it, then." She folded her arms tightly across her chest. "You're going to force me to medicate. That's why I'm here now, right? So you can tell me that." She snorted. "So much for personal autonomy."

"No one's going to force you to do anything, other than make a necessary decision about your future. You're legally an adult now, so that choice is due anyway." He leaned forward slightly. "Ru, do you want to be part of Gueran society? If so, then you need to accept the responsibility that comes with it. Or would you rather go your own way, free from all our rules and restrictions? That's a legitimate choice. Guera will support you in it. Just not here."

For a moment she was speechless. "Are you saying . . . Guera would *banish* me?"

"I'm saying you have several possible paths open to you," he said evenly. "Some might involve leaving this planet."

She bit her lip, determined to hide the wave of fear that had suddenly come over her. STRESS INDEX REDZONED, her wellseeker warned. ACTION? She hesitated, then visualized ADJUST and allowed it to feed a few drops of sedative into her bloodstream. Just a few. Calm flowed into her veins, muting the edge of her fear without quite banishing it. The tightness in her chest loosened just a bit. "What about the benefits of my Variation? Isn't that what we're taught in school, that every cognitive mode can be viewed as a gift? Sure sounds to me like mine is being rejected."

He chuckled softly. "What kind of mindset do you think drove humans to brave the wilderness of Earth, with nothing more than primitive weapons and a prayer? Or commit themselves to storm-tossed seas with no knowledge of what lay on the other side? What makes humans want to climb a mountain so high that its peak can barely sustain life, or risk the lethal pressure of the deep sea, just to see what lives there? They had your spark. Your restlessness. The first man to set foot on Earth's moon was driven by that same restlessness, as were the Hausman colonists, and later the first outpilots. Without that spark—that *hunger*— humanity could never have gained the stars." He leaned forward intently. "None of those people could have tolerated a mundane life, Ru. Waking up every morning to a predictable routine, facing a future without novelty or risk, suffocated by the sheer triviality of their daily existence . . . they couldn't have accepted it any more than you can."

She got up and turned away from him, wanting a moment of relief from his piercing gaze. "There's no unexplored wilderness anymore." Her tone was bitter. "The colony worlds were all mapped and terraformed long ago. The outworld stations are human constructs, every nut and bolt and circuit documented." She looked back at him. "There are no more great seas to cross in search of the unknown, Counselor. No storms to brave, not knowing what will be left when they pass." *Why do you tell me about things I can never have?* The thought was an ache inside her. *It only makes the situation worse.*

"Ruisa." The easy smile had faded now, replaced by a more serious expression. "If that's the kind of life you want—embracing your hunger rather than trying to deny it—I can help you find it a proper outlet." A pause. "It is my job, you know."

"But not on Guera," she muttered.

"Probably not," he agreed.

*Banishment.* You could dress it up in all sorts of fancy words, but that's what he was talking about. She didn't fit in here, so her people wanted her to leave. Bitterness clogged her throat; she had to clear it before she could talk again. She looked back at him. "I have family here. Friends."

"Guera's only six months' travel from the nearest ainniq. You can come back and visit whenever you want."

*Yeah, but as an outsider. No longer part of this world.*

She walked to the window; it allowed her to hide her expression from his *nantana* scrutiny while she gazed out at the city. So ordered.

So perfect. Had she ever fit in here? *Could* she ever fit in? Maybe not. But Guera was her home. Abandoning it would be like losing a piece of her soul. She rubbed her hands on her thighs to still their trembling.

*You won't have this city—or any other part of Guera—if you go on like you've been doing. You'll have the inside of a cell in a cognitive readjustment center, and those look the same on every world. Either way, the freedom of Guera will be lost to you. Is it better to give that up now of your own volition, for some positive purpose, or wait until it's forcibly taken from you?*

With a sigh she lowered her head. "All right," she muttered. She would never forgive her people for making this choice necessary. Never. "Tell me what you think my options are. I'll at least hear you out."

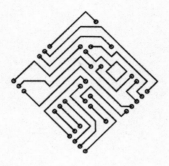

We may share the outworlds with Terrans, but the barriers that divide us will always be there. Long after they stop referring to Variants as non-humans, the visceral belief that we are exactly that will still persist, denying our common roots. It is part of their fiber, their spiritual substance. How then shall we establish trust between us?

ALYS KUMEN
*Galactic Currents*

# HARMONY NODE
# TRIDAC STATION

*T*HERE'S NOTHING *here.*

Micah had studied the game code for so long that his eyes were starting to glaze over. Thus far he'd discovered two secret narrative pathways and five practical jokes that people on his team had inserted without his permission. He was annoyed, but hardly surprised. Other than the one with the naked dancing girls (or boys, depending on the sexuality of the viewer), none of them were of concern to him. Tridac's investigators wouldn't even give them a second glance.

There was nothing in the game code that even hinted at the story behind the attack on Harmony Station. Nothing.

Leaning back in his chair, he rubbed his eyes with a weary hand. He hadn't slept well since Ron's visit, and was starting to pay the price. Now and then he would catch himself dozing off as a particularly tedious section of code scrolled before his eyes. How often should he review the same sections? He couldn't stop searching, because Tridac wouldn't stop searching. The megacorp *had* to find some flaw in the code that they could blame for the event on Harmony, so they could make a show of "fixing the problem." And if they couldn't find any code that had been tampered with, they might well manufacture some. A sacrificial lamb would have to be chosen. Someone who could be discovered, blamed, and punished, so the Ainniq Guild was satisfied the matter had been dealt with. Never mind whether that person was really guilty or not. Micah had no doubt that Tridac would frame an innocent coder if that would get them off the Guild's shit list. Terran corporations were ruthlessly pragmatic.

They were also ruthlessly Terran.

Stretching out his arms in front of him, he gazed at the brown stripes and whorls that ran down their length, contrasting against his otherwise pale skin. Normally he kept his sleeves rolled down, hiding most of his markings from view. The ones on the sides of his face weren't as easily hidden, but he had a collection of exotic headsets that drew attention away from them, and maybe people who were ignorant of his Variation would think the markings were nothing more than makeup. He hated having to worry about such things—indeed, he had been assured by his superiors that there was no need to worry—but so many Terrans distrusted Variants that it seemed the wisest course.

Which made him an ideal scapegoat.

*Focus, Micah.*

Someone was logging his power usage; he'd discovered it while changing the settings on his apartment's climate control. He couldn't even guess why someone would want to do that, but the timing made it suspect. He'd also discovered that his immediate superior was reviewing his work files—not exactly a crime, but not business-as-usual either. Sometimes when he left his office he had the sense that someone was watching him, though he could never catch anyone actually doing it. Was that paranoia, or something real?

*Focus on the work. . . .*

If the terrorists had really been running Dragonslayer they wouldn't even have seen the real life support center, much less been able to interact with it. So how could they have set off an explosion there? Not to mention, the virt was supposed to go into sleep mode as soon as a player entered a restricted area. It shouldn't have been running at all in that location. But Dobson had a record of the two guys inloading the final quest segment right before the explosion. So they were definitely playing in a restricted area. How was that even possible? The longer he searched for answers, the more questions he seemed to have.

With a weary sigh he leaned forward on the desk, resting his head in his hands. He must be missing something. Some vital clue that would make all these conflicting elements come together. But it wasn't in the game code. He was convinced of that.

A sudden knock on the door startled him. "What?" The proximity sensor should have alerted him that someone was approaching. Had he been so wrapped up in his thoughts that he hadn't heard it? "Who is it?" He waited for the door to relay a response, but there was none. Great. He was going to have to check the settings again. Why couldn't the damn thing just work like it was supposed to? He started to get up—

Suddenly the door gave way with explosive force, and two men in chitinous black armor rushed him. For a moment he was frozen in place, too stunned to respond, then he stumbled backward, trying to get away from them. As he did he grabbed the chair and shoved it in front of him, hoping to slow them down a bit. It was all he could think to do. Desperately he looked around the room for something he could use in self-defense—anything! But though the far wall was hung with dozens of weapons—display models from his game—they were too far out of reach.

Then one of the men yanked the chair out of the way while the other slammed into Micah, shoulder first, driving him into the desk. Equipment crashed noisily to the floor as the first man grabbed him by the arm, twisting it behind his back so hard that the pain was blinding. The other grabbed him by the hair, and together they began to drag him across the room. He struggled wildly, like a beast in a trap, but to no avail. They were stronger than he was and faster than he was, and they were clearly trained for this kind of confrontation. All he was trained to do was sit behind a desk and design imaginary fistfights.

He opened his mouth to scream for help, but then he saw the red Tridac insignia on one man's collar, and the sound froze in his throat.

They had come for him. That's what this was. Tridac was going to accuse him of altering Dragonslayer. Who would help him if that were the case? No one who lived on this station, that was for sure. He was at the mercy of corporate justice now.

They dragged him out into the hallway, only it wasn't a hallway anymore: it was a mouth now, armed with glistening fangs above and below, and the floor was its tongue. The men clearly meant to feed him to it—

He woke up.

Shaken, he raised his head from the table. His headset was askew, and he pushed it back into position. The desk was still in place. All his equipment was still on it. His heart was pounding so hard he felt as if a rib were about to snap, but his arm no longer hurt.

SYSTEMIC STRESS DETECTED, his wellseeker informed him. RED ZONE. ACTION? He drew in a deep breath, then visualized the icon that would release a bit of sedative into his veins.

A dream. That's all it was. A fucking dream.

His friends had advised him not to take this job, he remembered. *Terran corporations don't operate by Common Law. If anything goes wrong out there, you'll have no legal protection.* But Dobson Games had made it clear that station residence was a condition of employment. For security, they'd claimed. In the end he had chosen to accept the risk in order to work with some of the best designers in the virtual immersion industry. Not to mention gain access to Dobson's state-of-the-art equipment for his own research. Given some of the ideas he wanted to explore, that was no small thing.

Now all that was at risk.

He visualized the symbol that would connect him to the station's innernet. Menu icons scrolled into his field of vision, and he looked for the one that would open the master archives. He needed to review Corporate Law so he knew exactly what his rights were. Could Tridac really send thugs after him, like they'd done in his dream? Or was he protected by due process, as he would be on the waystation? He needed to know, if for no other purpose than to banish his nightmares.

He found the icon. He started to activate it—

And stopped.

If he accessed those files, he realized suddenly, he would leave behind a data trail. What if whoever was spying on him checked his innernet activity? They would know he had been researching his rights. Would an innocent man do that?

He took his headset off. The menu icons faded from his vision.

*I have to get away from here.*

The docking ring was crowded as always, its private facilities teeming with uniformed stewards waiting to fawn over traveling executives, its public spaces just plain damn crowded. In the lobby of Public Transportation Center Five, row after row of people sat in the waiting area, most of them leaning back in their chairs as if asleep, their eyes flickering back and forth beneath half-closed lids as they focused on the digitized vista of their choice. All of them were terramorphs, of course, identical in shape to Earth's first spacefarers. In Terran parlance, "they looked human." No matter how long Micah worked on Tridac Station, he never got used to the eerie uniformity of its population.

He wandered up to the registration desk with what he intended to be a casual saunter, though it lost some panache in the lo-G setting. In truth his heart was pounding, and if any of the security cams focused on him were taking biological readings, they would detect it. Or maybe a real person was watching him. There were so many people here that anything was possible.

*Just pretend you're not worried. This is a normal booking. A weekend's jaunt.*

The clerk was a woman with a corona of blazing red hair. Ruddy freckles suggested her coloring was natural. "Can I help you, Micah Bello?"

Startled, he realized she must have run a facial recognition check as he'd approached her station. Of course. That was just part of her job, and of no significance whatsoever. "I'd like to book a pod to Harmony."

"Singler, doubler, or multi?"

"Singler."

"For how long?"

"Just the weekend."

Her gaze turned inward as she accessed the necessary files. If Micah's wellseeker notifications had still been active they would probably be blazing all the symptoms of his anxiety across his visual field, but the system had gotten so annoying that he'd finally put it into sleep mode. *I'll have to detect my own stress*, he thought dryly. *Just like an Earth primitive.*

The woman's brow furrowed. "I see you've already booked a singler on the fifteenth. Do you want to reschedule that?"

"No. I'll still need that. Today is just to meet up with an old friend who's passing through the node." Even to his own ears that didn't sound convincing, so he added, "The fifteenth is for a convention on Harmony. Ethan Hephaestus will be presenting a paper on stimulus overload in immersion coding. . . ." Now he was talking too much. It didn't sound natural. He shut up.

He'd figured that if Tridac thought he intended to flee the station they might take action to prevent it. By booking a later flight he was assuring them there was no rush. Now, hopefully, they would not be paying as close attention to his movements, and if he could move quickly enough—unexpectedly enough—he might get off this benighted station before anyone realized what he intended.

"I have an MKJ47 available," the woman said, then added apologetically, "It's the budget model."

"That's fine. That's fine. Bill it to my account." Oops. What if someone was watching that account? Should he have paid cash? Too late now. *God, I really suck at this spy stuff.*

The MKJ47 lent new meaning to the phrase "budget model." Its narrow entrance was just big enough for him to squeeze through, and inside the pod there was barely enough room for the evac equipment, a piss station, and a single chair that had seen better days. All of it was sized for Earth humans, and none of it looked adjustable. Leave it to the Terrans to produce a vehicle no one but a Terran could fly.

He stowed his bag in a small chamber under the seat and strapped himself in, then watched as the pod went through its automated pre-flight routine. His registered flight plan appeared on the forward display monitor, a smooth arc from Tridac to Harmony, just far enough from the median route to avoid most other traffic. Five hours of travel time in all. What few manual controls the pod had were on an emergency panel folded away into the ceiling; Micah pulled it down briefly to familiarize himself with their layout, then locked the panel back in place. In all his years he'd never needed to steer a pod himself and hoped he would never have to.

Then the outer door closed, the inner door did likewise, and a faint hiss could be heard as environmental controls took over. The main display flashed confirmation that all systems were functioning properly, and then, with stomach-lurching abruptness, the pod jerked free of its mooring, and headed toward the launch queue. Not exactly the smoothest exit, but he didn't care. As long as he was moving in the right direction he was happy.

He set the viewscreen to give him a 360 view of surrounding space. If anyone on Tridac wanted to keep him from leaving they'd have to make their move soon. But no one approached the ship, and soon enough his MKJ47 was at the head of the line. And then . . . launch. The blackness of space folded around the tiny singler and the mooring lights of the station swiftly faded behind him. One hundred miles out. Two. He was so on edge that he had to remind himself to breathe. Three hundred miles—

LEAVING TRIDAC CORPORATE TERRITORY, the viewscreen proclaimed. ENTERING COMMON LAW SPACE. ETA HARMONY STATION: 4.95 E-HOURS.

With a sigh he expelled his last tortured breath. He'd made it! Whatever happened now, it would happen under Common Law. He had *rights* again.

Mentally exhausted, he leaned back into the padded chair and shut his eyes for a moment, drinking in the solitude. Then he called up a design file to work on. Not his sensory research, of course. Those files were safely tucked away in his brainware in read-only format; he would have to outload them to another system to do any real editing. Instead he called up the setting files for his current project and started reviewing the visual elements in his Viking mead hall virt. It was relaxing to focus on the mundane facets of his job: adding more smoke to the fire, repositioning snowdrifts, tweaking the phase of Earth's moon until it shed just the right amount of light on the outdoor scenes. He decided to go with a full moon, and wondered if he should alter the gravity profile to reflect its presence. Earth's moon was powerful enough to shift whole oceans, so surely it had some effect on human beings.

How frightening it must have been for Earth's primitives, knowing themselves at the mercy of nature! Their gravity was dictated by ancient rocks hurtling through space rather than the ordered science of man-made stations; their world wracked by wind-storms and rain-storms and dust-storms and ice-storms and fires. He loved natural planetary settings for their emotive potential, but God knows he would never want to live in one.

ALERT

The warning appeared in his field of vision, a jarring incongruity in his Viking longhouse. He paused his work and looked at the display screen. **MANDATORY COURSE ADJUSTMENT**, the pod was telling him. **PLEASE CONFIRM.**

"Data," he ordered.

A tri-D map appeared in front of the screen, with Tridac Station at one end of the display and Harmony Station at the other. Between them a webwork of fine lines stretched across the starscape, some connecting the two stations, some heading offscreen to unseen destinations. Each line represented the registered flight plan of a ship currently in transit, and there were so many of them along the main route that it was a miracle none of those ships ever collided. But their passage was a delicate dance, perfectly orchestrated by the ships' autopilots, in constant communication with one another. No two ships would ever cross the same point at the same time.

But: INTERSECTION IMMINENT, his pod was warning him. Two of the lines were highlighted. One, in red, he recognized as his own flight plan; the other, in blue, was coming from Harmony. The ships themselves were still many miles apart, but Micah's autopilot had projected both flight paths and determined they would intersect if someone did not adjust his course. A green line appeared on the screen, indicating the detour it was recommending. That would add twelve minutes to Micah's flight, but if the alternative was colliding with another vehicle, what choice did he have? The other ship was a larger vessel, and would expect Micah to get out of its way. The hierarchical dance of autopilot travel.

"Fine," he said. "Confirmed."

The green line turned red as his original course disappeared from the screen. Good enough. He turned his attention back to the virt, studying the array of foods laid out for feasting. It was all pretty basic. Maybe he should add something seasonal for the history buffs to notice. He sent out a query for information on seasonal foods in the Viking era, then cursed himself for being an idiot. Of course there was no response. They'd left Tridac's innernet behind and weren't within range of the outernet yet.

ALERT. MANDATORY COURSE ADJUSTMENT. PLEASE CONFIRM.

"Say what?" he muttered. "We did that already."

But it was a different ship this time. This one was farther away than the first, but apparently Micah's autopilot was convinced that it, too, was a navigational threat. This time the detour would cost him seventeen minutes. But what choice did he have? Short of taking control of the pod and flying it himself, this was the only way to get where he was going. "Confirmed," he growled.

This time he didn't go right back to work. He ordered the pod to keep the transit display active, and he watched as the web shifted and pulsed, strands rearranging themselves like fairy filaments in a breeze.

**ALERT. MANDATORY COURSE ADJUSTMENT. PLEASE CONFIRM.**

Damn it to hell! Not another one!

Was this because he was flying an MKJ47, a ship so pitifully small that everyone in outspace expected him to just get out of their way? The proposed new flight path was a full seven degrees off course, which would turn him away from Harmony altogether. That was unacceptable.

He called up data on the new ship. The owner was unknown. The call sign was one he didn't recognize.

**CONFIRM NEW FLIGHT PLAN,** the autopilot pressed.

He turned on the comm. "ACKER502A-85, this is MKJ47-9A. Your current trajectory conflicts with our registered flight plan. Over."

No answer.

"ACKER502A-85, please adjust your course. Over."

Still no response.

**CONFIRM NEW FLIGHT PLAN,** the pod insisted.

"Yeah," he muttered, because there was no other choice. "Confirmed."

This time the adjustment was sharp enough that his body was pressed sideways against the safety harness for a moment. He was going to have to find a safe path around this last asshole before he could head toward Harmony again. He ordered the autopilot to display his options.

**ALERT. MANDATORY COURSE ADJUSTMENT. PLEASE CONFIRM.**

He stared at the display in disbelief. Apparently the first ship *had* shifted course. Right into his new flight path. What the hell was going on?

Maybe they were playing traffic games, competing to see who could force the greatest change to Micah's course from the greatest distance. He'd never played that game himself but he knew that there were people who did, usually spoiled brats who had the keycodes to their family's vehicle and way too much time on their hands. For a moment he considered putting his pod on manual and seeing how these guys dealt with a good old-fashioned game of *chicken*, but better sense prevailed. This was a vehicle designed for dull, uneventful, *automatic* transportation, and he could well discover in the midst of maneuvering that he had overestimated its capacity to dodge obstacles.

CONFIRM, the pod pressed.

The new course it was proposing would be twenty degrees off true, a major detour. That was not acceptable. He suggested another detour that would get him back on course sooner, but the autopilot told him that one, too, was blocked. And then another. Was this all just a coincidence, caused by the heavy traffic? Or were there more ships interfering with him than he'd realized, spread out in just the right pattern to frustrate his efforts—anticipating where his autopilot would want to go, blocking those exact paths? It was a paranoid thought, but he couldn't shake it.

He expanded the transit display, projecting his current course onto it along with a query for possible course adjustments. It turned out those damned ships had cut off most of his options, including all the routes that led to Harmony. A chill ran through him as he saw where the available ones would take him.

Nowhere.

He was headed toward open space now, a sector that had no stations, no habitat, not even a supply depot. The paranoid demon in his brain whispered that the ships had driven him this way with a chessmaster's brilliance, positioning themselves so that his autopilot would *expect* them to get in the way and would take preemptive action to avoid them. And if they kept it up he soon would be forced to fly into the endless darkness. Emptiness without refuge. Eventually he would run out of fuel, while they, in their larger ships, would have enough to get them home. And then there he would be, entombed in darkness, swallowed by the fate all outworlders feared. . . .

*Who's paranoid now, Micah?*

This was no childish game. Those ships had *purpose*. But who would want him to disappear into the barrens of space? Tridac wouldn't want him dead, would they? They still needed to question him, right? Unless they already knew who screwed with Dragonslayer, and wanted to protect that person. What better way than to provide a different scapegoat, whom the Guild would never be able to question?

A new kind of fear took root inside him: a visceral sensation, cold and nauseating. This was real fear, he thought with wonder. Not the gaming simulacrum he invoked with his carefully scripted illusions, but raw survival instinct, the gut-wrenching terror of an organism staring into the face of Death. It was a horrifying sensation, but it was also perversely fascinating, and even as he reached out and pulled down the manual control panel with shaking hands, his mind was cataloging all those sensations, storing them away for future reference. *A game designer to the end,* he thought bitterly.

The manual controls couldn't be manipulated by brainware; he had to actually use his hands. It took him three tries to get the pod to accept his security codes—damn those MKJ47 protocols!—but finally the autopilot surrendered control to him. He would still need the ship's navigator to calculate possible flight paths, but he could make his own decision now about which one to follow. And if he chose one that swung a bit too close to one of these assholes' ships, and forced it to veer off course . . . well, that would serve it right.

*I could call for help,* he thought. But what was he supposed to say to Transit Authority when they answered him? *There are some ships interfering with my flight path, and I think it may reflect a deliberate effort to herd me into the empty depths of space . . . no, I don't know who they are . . . well, they're still pretty far away, so I'm just speculating about their intentions . . . I understand, I'll get back to you when I have more concrete data.*

He pulled the shuttle into a sharp angle, hoping the sudden move would take his pursuers by surprise. It bought him a few precious seconds, which he used to swing around the far end of the traffic stream.

There was a group of freighters off his stern, and if he could slip in between them he would be safe from any further interference; anything that got in their way would be forced to yield the right of way. But it turned out there was another small ship on his tail, closer than the others. Damn it, how many of them were there? Even the smallest one could run circles around his MKJ47. Why the hell hadn't he upgraded when he had the chance?

He turned again, cutting sharply across the flight path of a tourist shuttle and a corporate transport, trying to escape his new pursuer. Warnings appeared on his screen, some of them formal requests for course correction, others less polite. GET OUT OF THE WAY, YOU AS-SHOLE!!! He pulled his craft into a tight curve to slip between two small pods, no doubt sending their autopilots into conniptions. If he managed to survive this mess he'd likely be spending his next year in traffic court.

*Which would be on Harmony, so that's fine by me.*

By the time he swung back toward the convoy the new pursuit craft had positioned itself directly between him and the freighters. For a moment he was tempted to fly straight toward it—*let's see who flinches first!*—but he knew his MKJ47 didn't have the power or maneuverability he would need to pull that off without getting himself killed. Fuck. He was sweating now, and because he'd turned off his wellseeker he couldn't adjust his stress level. Sweat dripped into his eyes while he tried another sudden course change, and then another. Smaller ships veered out of his way, traffic parting for him like the Red Sea. Maybe his crazy flight path made their autopilots think the MKJ47 was out of control. *Get away from the crazy person!* He laughed, but the sound was tinged with fear.

One of his pursuers was heading straight toward him now, trying to force him out of the main traffic stream. He tried to maneuver around it, but that ran him into a cluster of school transports. Cursing under his breath, he pulled out of the main traffic lanes and headed toward the darkness of space once more. He wasn't going to make it to Harmony, that much was clear. Did he have any other options? He expanded the navigational display until the nearest stations were visible. And yeah, there was one he could probably get to safely.

Tridac Station.

Maybe that was their plan all along—not to drive him into empty space, but to force him back into the arms of his employers. If so, that was the one place he sure as hell wasn't going. His hands trembled on the touchscreen as he tried to come up with a way out of this mess. But his fuel reserves were starting to run low due to all the high-speed maneuvering, and he was starting to get warnings about it on his screen. IMMEDIATE DOCKING RECOMMENDED. Tridac was the only berth he could get to in time . . . no, wait. There was one more. A small research station called Shenshido was within range. Information on it should be in the pod's database. He fed the name to his ship and waited a few endless seconds for it to find the right file.

SHENSHIDO STATION, HARMONY NODE
RESEARCH FACILITY/CLASS ONE HABITAT
CONSTRUCTED BY SHIDO CORPORATION '070–'073
REGISTERED INDEPENDENT UNDER TERRAN CORPORATE
    LAW IN '074
MANAGEMENT TRANSFERRED TO CONSORTIUM OF
    TERRAN CORPORATIONS '113
CURRENT USE *UNKNOWN*
POPULATION *UNKNOWN*
EXTERNAL SECURITY CLASS 8S
INTERNAL SECURITY CLASS *UNKNOWN*

Management by Terran corporations. That would include Tridac, but also its fiercest competitors. If Micah could make contact with one of the other megacorps before Tridac got to him, they might grant him sanctuary, if only to frustrate their rival. The chaos of corporate politics which Micah had always despised might yet prove his salvation.

Carefully he set a course back toward Tridac, plotting a wide arc that would swing him close by Shenshido. Hopefully his pursuers wouldn't realize what he intended until it was too late for them to inter-fere. They seemed to be falling behind him now, perhaps content with his choice of direction, perhaps just loath to leave the traffic stream. For as long as they were surrounded by other vehicles their coordina-tion was masked; once they were out in the open, Transit Authority might take note of their activity.

Micah wiped sweat out of his eyes and tried to relax, but there was no way his racing heart was going to settle down on its own. He brought his wellseeker back online and had it feed a trickle of anxiety medica-tion into his bloodstream. Not too much—he didn't want his mental reflexes dulled—but even a few drops offered welcome relief. The knot in his chest loosened a bit, and his breathing became less tortured. The fear was still present, but no longer smothering him. Thank God for modern medicine.

It took him half an hour to get within range of Shenshido. His pur-suers were far behind him now, but he knew that if he turned back to-ward Harmony they'd be ready to block the way again. No matter. He had other plans now. For the first time since going off course he felt a spark of hope.

He was close enough now to get a good image of Shenshido, so he ordered the ship to put that on his main screen. As it came up, he stared at it in disbelief, then slammed his fist into the console, cursing in frustration.

Even with Shenshido's minimal exterior lighting, he could see that the station was in ruins. The docking ring was little more than a skele-ton, struts sticking out from its shell like the bones of some half-devoured beast. He could see multi-legged maintenance bots poised here and there on the wreckage, waiting for the orders that would set them in motion, like insects on a corpse. The station core was in slightly better shape, but there was no sign of human activity. Hell, the station should be demanding his ID by now, or giving him instructions for ap-proach, or . . . something. But there was no signal on any wavelength.

AGITATION DETECTED, his wellseeker warned.

What the hell was he supposed to do now? Even if he wanted to enter the station, the mooring bays were in such disrepair that they probably wouldn't seal properly. And if Micah didn't get official clearance to dock, the station would treat him as a hostile entity. Was it armed? With an independent station you never knew. People who made up their own rules didn't have to respect common protocol.

*Tridac would let you dock,* he reminded himself. *You could always take your chances with them.*

*Yeah. Right.*

He altered course to bring him closer to Shenshido. The move would alert his pursuers to the fact that he wasn't really headed toward Tridac, but that couldn't be helped. Would they respond immediately? Or wait to see what he did? He prayed feverishly for the latter as he began to circle the station, searching for any place where he could dock safely. If he'd been flying a more sophisticated ship there might have been more options, but the MKJ47 was just a transit pod, designed to go from point A to point B, autodocking at both ends. It didn't have the adaptability needed for more creative solutions.

Something on the surface of the station moved.

He turned his attention to that spot, magnifying the display so he could see it more clearly. One of the maintenance bots had apparently shifted position, drawing its arms in beneath it. Then there was a flicker of movement some distance away from it: another bot making the same adjustment. A third followed. All the bots that he passed over were shifting position, creating a mechanical wave that rippled across the ring's surface behind him. He'd designed too many games with warning signs just like that to ignore the threat it implied, and he pulled his pod up sharply, hoping to get away before the strange robotic dance beneath him turned into something worse.

Too late.

One of the bots shot up from the station, heading straight toward him. Another followed. And then a third. Long silver legs trailed behind them like squid tentacles as they streamed through the darkness, more and more bots joining the swarm, until the display screen was full of them. He tried to get the pod to fly faster, but by the time full acceleration kicked in the first bots had reached him. One struck his ship with enough force that he could feel the control console vibrate beneath his hands, and his external cams showed it splayed out across his hull like some unholy starfish, slender arms clinging to whatever crevices were available. Then another joined it, and a third, and a fourth, and a fifth. . . . For a few precious seconds he stared at the screen in horror, heart pounding, not knowing how to respond. Then he tried some sharp maneuvers to . . . what, shake them off? The MKJ47 wasn't built for that kind of action, and the starfish clung to it effortlessly though every twist and turn. Maybe if he got further away from the station they would lose the signal that was guiding them and turn back. He urged the singler to maximum velocity, setting a course away from the damaged ring. But the bots held on tight. There were so many of them now! They covered his entire hull, arms interlocking in a complex lacework. How could there have been so many of them on the station without him noticing?

*You thought they were just maintenance bots, not worthy of your attention.*

Suddenly there was a grinding sound at the front of the pod. Shit. Were they trying to break in?

HEART RATE REDZONED, his wellseeker warned. BP RED-ZONED. ADJUST? "Shut the fuck up," he growled. He tried to visualize the icon that would turn the wellseeker off again, but it was hard to focus on anything other than the sounds now coming from different sections of his hull; they must be trying to cut their way through from all angles. If they broke into the pilot's chamber while he was unsuited he wouldn't stand a chance.

He struggled to unstrap himself from his seat, but his hands were trembling so badly it was hard to manage. Finally he got free and pushed himself toward the rear of the pod. There the evac was waiting, its frame a gaping maw. For a moment he hesitated, knowing that once he committed to evacuation his odds of survival were slim. But if he stayed here his death was certain. Grabbing the evac frame, he pulled himself into position in the center of it, trying to remember the proper order of steps from his safety training. Feet onto the shoe blocks. Hands into the waiting gloves. Head pressed back to trigger the evac program. Suddenly there were robotic arms coming at him from every direction, and it took all his self-control to remain totally still as they wrapped a pressure suit around him, lowered a helmet over his head, strapped an oxygen pack and jet frame onto his back, and sealed every seam. CONFIRM EVACUATION? the system asked when it was done, projecting the letters across the inside of his visor. At the far end of the pod the hull was beginning to twist, as if some giant hand were crushing it. The navigational display sputtered and went dark. Sparks shot across the chamber as the main lights went out. "Confirm!" he gasped.

Gas rushed into the pressurizing channels in his suit, squeezing him so tightly that he couldn't draw a breath. Then the emergency lock behind him opened and the vacuum of space sucked him out, along with a swarm of small objects torn free from their holders. He was spinning in the darkness, and the station was above him, then below him, then above him, below him . . . He fought back nausea as his stabilizers finally kicked in, and the small directional jets built into his suit stopped his rotation. Stars and space swam around him for a few seconds more, and as they finally settled he twisted around to look for his ship.

The bots were dismembering it. A few of them had extruded vast silver nets as fine as spider silk, which they were using to gather up the segments that others had cut loose. A pair of bots flew around the dissection site, a net stretched between them, probably looking for smaller bits that might have floated away.

Shit.

They were coming around the far end of the wreckage now; any moment their sensors would detect him. He had to get out of their search range, fast. He triggered a short burst of propulsion to thrust him backward, praying that the jet spurts coming from the bots themselves would mask the energy expenditure. He dared no more. With agonizing slowness he drifted away from the wreck, while the pair with the net rounded its far end and turned toward him. Then suddenly there was a flash of light, so bright that it triggered his suit's defense mechanism. His visor went opaque, blinding him. Darkness filled his suit, thick and stifling, making it hard to breathe. What were the bots doing now? Had they noticed him? He was helpless to do anything to save himself. Panic welled up inside him—

And as suddenly as it had darkened, his visor cleared. He drew a long, shaky breath, and struggled to get his bearings. The light must have been from some kind of explosion, because all that remained of the ship now was an expanding cloud of small fragments; the bots were flying around crazily, trying to gather them all. That took attention away from him, but as soon as they'd netted all the visible pieces they would probably do a final scan of surrounding space, to see if they'd missed anything. He might be beyond their range in a physical sense, but his suit's energy signature would blaze like a star to that inspection. He was going to have to shut down everything if he wanted to remain unnoticed.

Including his life support.

While the bots chased down the last fragments of his ship, he reactivated his wellseeker and let it release a bit of sedative into his blood stream, taking the edge off his panic. Then he waited, heart pounding, as they gathered up the last of the fragments of his dismembered ship. Most of the bots were turning back toward Shenshido, but a particularly large one began a circuit of the debris field, its sensors turned outward. Clearly it was searching for outliers. Micah drew in one last deep breath, and—

*Now.*

No more air. No more thrumming of the suit's pressure system. He had no clue what was supposed to happen to a human body when a suit's pressure failed, but probably he'd suffocate from lack of oxygen before that became an issue. He watched in silence as the mechanical eye of the bot turned in his direction. Stared right at him.

Then it turned away.

He brought his life support back online, then drew in a deep, deep breath of air. The bots were all heading toward Shenshido now, their nets and their booty trailing behind them as they accelerated into the darkness. One by one he lost sight of them.

And then he was alone. Unharmed, but utterly alone. Floating in the darkness with an evac suit, a six-hour supply of oxygen, and not much else. No one was around to attack him, but no one was around to help him, either. The suit's propulsion could get him back to Shenshido, but were there people there? By the time he arrived the attack bots would be back in place, waiting for their next target to approach. Would a lone man in an evacuation suit qualify, or was he small enough to slip past their sensors?

It didn't matter. There was nowhere else to go.

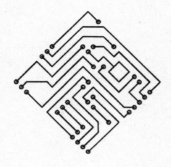

## NANTANA

The tapestry is eternal, without beginning or end. Its threads are so tightly interwoven that the eye must struggle to focus on any one of them. Its colors are so enmeshed one must labor to discern the greater pattern.

The *nantana* can see each thread. It can identify each pattern. It knows, with instinctive certainty, where the addition or removal of a colored strand might alter the tapestry's shape, or its color, or its purpose.

Sometimes it moves a thread, for amusement.

Sometimes it has purpose.

Sometimes it merely watches.

*KAJA: An Outworlder's Guide to the Gueran*
*Social Contract, Volume 2: Signs of the Soul*

# GUERA NODE
# TIANANMEN STATION

THE DEBRIEFING was no better or worse than usual in terms of protocol, but the atmosphere was considerably more solemn. There were four Guerans sitting opposite Ru instead of the usual two, but given that she'd lost a partner, that was to be expected. They wanted extra *nantana* present to interpret her expressions and her posture and the pattern of her fidgeting, adding their observations to the report she had already filed. The only one of the four she knew was a man named Tye Jericho, who had apparently been promoted since their last meeting. How many of her debriefings had he overseen, now? Three? Four? The lavender bangs brushed back over his scarlet headset seemed to be begging for chromatic rescue. But his was a friendly face, and that saved her from having to recite the details of Tully's death to a crowd of total strangers.

There was a time in her life when she would never have allowed anyone to study her like this. It made her feel like a laboratory animal, poked and prodded with knife-edged words while dispassionate scientists muttered profound things like "Hmmm" and "That's interesting." But she knew this was the price she had to pay to explore new worlds and discover lost civilizations, so she endured. It was harder than usual with Tully absent, though. His empty chair was a painful reminder that she had lost not only a partner but a friend, and even an occasional lover. Once or twice she had to stop talking while she struggled to compose herself; the *nantana* no doubt took mental notes about her state of mind while they waited. What was considered "normal" when you were mourning a partner whose relationship with you had been so intimate, so complex?

She did manage to get through the interview without revealing the real cause of Tully's death, which was a small victory. There was no reason anyone had to know that it was Tully's unwise choice of a sex partner that had caused the official First Contact strategy on Proxima 5 to explode. Apparently having sex with a woman in the priestly caste was punishable by death, if that woman didn't seek her gods' approval first. Jericho helped with that, redirecting the interview when it strayed in an unseemly direction. Why? Did he know that there were outriders who considered sexual experimentation to be one of their job benefits, who competed to see which one of them could rack up the most "first contact" experiences? If so, he didn't say anything about it, for which she was grateful

Thanks to Jericho, she never had to reveal that detail. Thanks to him, the meeting ended without her feeling angry, or anxious, or upset— her usual responses to administrative rituals like this. She nodded a curt farewell to her interrogators and headed for the exit. Her mission was officially done now, and the Guild no longer had any right to tell her where to go or what to do. At least until she signed on for her next job.

There was a bar in the outer ring that had a drink with her name on it. The sooner she got to it the better.

The Lucifer Club was gone.

Standing in the middle of the crowded promenade, Ru stared at the place where it had once been. PROMETHEUS CLUB, the sign said now. Same location, same storefront design, even the same font for the title—but a different name. So was it the same franchise? Lucifer's whole selling point was that it never changed, so the thought that it might have done so, even in such a small detail, was disconcerting.

A sensor light flashed briefly overhead as she approached the entrance, acknowledging that the club's guest program had identified her. No doubt it was streaming her personal data to the staff right now. The familiar protocol soothed her nerves a bit, and when the doors parted she saw that the inside of the club was indeed the same as always. The floor plan, the lighting, the décor, even the music playing softly in the background were exactly the same as they had been twenty years ago, the last time she'd visited, and the time before that, and the time before that, *ad infinitum*. Worlds might change while an outrider slept, fashion and culture might race headlong into the future during her cold stasis sleep, but the Lucifer Club was always the same. Always home.

Except for the name.

There was a Runyat behind the polished wooden bar. Ru had never seen him before, but he nodded to her as if she were a regular. "Welcome back, Outrider Gaya." His arms were bare, no doubt to show off their snake-like patterning. "The usual?"

She nodded. "Please."

She flashed a quick query to the outernet to access his name and public profile, so she could address him as if they knew one another. The illusion of intimacy was the heart and soul of the Lucifer experience. *Treat each guest as if they had been there yesterday.*

The drink that he handed her was clear blue with a minty aroma. "Blue galaxy, sans salt." Then he offered her a small data chip. "Newly updated."

"Thank you, Basil." She slid the chip into her headset but didn't activate it. "If I may ask . . ." She glanced toward the portal. "What's with the name change?"

The bartender sighed. "There was a digital virus making the rounds a while back. Nasty thing. At first it only targeted Guild pilots, but then it started mutating into more destructive forms. Took them a good three years to hunt down every last version of it."

"Ah, let me guess . . . they named it Lucifer?"

The bartender nodded. "People came here thinking there was some kind of connection. I'm not sure what they imagined that would be, but we started getting some really weird types in here. I mean, think about the kind of person who would find a bar appealing because it was named after malware. So in the end, management decided the old name had to go. The rest is all the same, though, I promise you."

*And the myth is similar enough*, Ru thought. *Prometheus, bringer of knowledge to humankind, tortured for eternity.* "Thank you." She took a sip from her drink and looked around the club.

"If you need anything more," he said, "let me know."

"Of course."

The main floor was dominated by a restaurant, moody in color and dimly lit by faux-candles. That had been the style back when the Lucifer Club was founded, and so it would remain the style forever. A few tables were occupied, and she spotted one or two other outriders. Even if they had not been wearing the *sakuna* kaja—the symbol of their profession—she could tell they were outriders by the way they looked around the room: eyes yearning for some unseen comfort, souls strangely disconnected from everything around them. Experts had written volumes about the psychological effect of long-term stasis, but no outsider could truly understand what it was like to exist in a universe that was different every time you returned to it. This club, with its artificial familiarity, was a psychological lifeline.

As she headed toward the back of the room she spotted an outrider she knew. There were three Belial twins perched on high stools opposite him, bald heads and half-bare breasts gleaming in the candlelight as they flirted in eerie unison. Outrider groupies. Tully had enjoyed such attention, but Ru found it distasteful; as she nodded briefly to her colleagues she tried to avoid the groupies' fetishistic gazes, so they would not address her.

*In their eyes you are a romantic figure*, she reminded herself. *Fearless explorer, discoverer of lost worlds, rescuer of civilizations. Such types have always been the object of lust.*

That didn't make it any less creepy.

In the back of the club were smaller, more private spaces, and she chose a shadowy alcove as far away from the other patrons as possible. There she settled into a chair, shut her eyes, and activated the bartender's chip.

WELCOME TO THE PROMETHEUS OUTRIDER PORTAL.
PLEASE ENTER YOUR LICENSE NUMBER TO PROCEED.

She was about to do that when an image suddenly appeared in her field of vision: a flock of animated birds trailing a banner behind them: HAI KAWAII! Annoyed, Ru directed her headset to block the image and anything like it. Advertising was one thing she didn't miss when she was on a mission. She focused again on the task at hand, visualizing each letter and number of her outrider license and letting her headset transmit the images to the club's private innernet.

OUTRIDER STATUS CONFIRMED.

Now she could access the club's private databank, and with it the records she needed to bring herself up to speed: not cold, clinical historical files gathered from the outernet, but notes recorded by outriders themselves. Here was the history her comrades felt she would need to know, regarding the events that had made them feel the most lost when they returned home. The most displaced. Here was a list of references that had become part of popular culture while she was gone, recorded by those who understood how ignorance of common phrases could hinder communication. And here was social criticism, as well—brief, dry commentary on a changing world, as seen through the eyes of those who were perpetual outsiders. She added her own to the bottom of one thread.

ARE OVERSIZED HEADSETS A REQUIREMENT NOW? I'VE
SEEN SOME SO UNWIELDY I WONDER HOW THE
WEARERS STAND UPRIGHT. IT'S JUST A TECH DEVICE,

PEOPLE. IT'S OKAY IF YOURS ISN'T A UNIQUE FASHION STATEMENT.

The birds returned. HAI KAWAII! She swatted at them reflexively, cursing under her breath. Damn advertisements!

"You need to update your adblocker."

Annoyed, she looked up to see who was talking to her, invading her private time.

Tye Jericho.

She stared at him for a moment, part of her wanting to berate him for the interruption, another part—the far larger part—aware that she owed him for his support in the debriefing. Finally she sighed, accepting the inevitable. "So tell me, what the hell is 'Hai Kawaii'?"

"Advertising slogan for a fast food franchise. Very aggressive in their marketing. If they spent half as much money on food quality as they do on hacking adblockers, they'd probably be a Fortune 10,000 company by now." He nodded toward a nearby chair that matched her own. "May I?"

Her eyes narrowed. "I'm not feeling especially social."

"That's fine. I'm here on business, not to socialize."

"You couldn't have talked to me about it while we were still at Guild headquarters?"

A corner of his mouth twitched. "Some conversations aren't suitable for Guild headquarters."

His face was an impassive mask, impossible to read—as always—but the fact that he had launched directly into business was a gesture of good will. Two *nantana* would be having a very different conversation. Finally she sighed. *What the hell. It's not like there's somewhere else I need to be.* She gestured for him to take a nearby chair. As soon as he sat down a servobot rolled up to the table, carrying a blood-red drink with a multi-colored sprig sticking out of the top. Jericho must have ordered it when he arrived.

"All right." She took a deep drink from her own glass. The mild Frisian narcotic always helped her unwind after a mission. "So what's so important that you had to follow me all the way out here to talk about it?"

"Call it a job offer."

An eyebrow rose slightly. "I already have a job. Unless you know something about my employment status that I don't."

"I know that your ship is being repaired, and it'll be some time before you can take on a new assignment. So right now, you're unemployed."

*And I need to find a new partner before I can go out again. That'll be a lot harder than getting my ship repaired.* "So you thought I might be, what . . . bored?"

There was a hint of a smile. "Restless, perhaps. Or curious about how much it would pay. There could be a lot of money involved."

"I need quality downtime more than I need a freelance assignment." She waved her free hand. "But go on, I'm listening."

For a moment he just looked at her. It was a *nantana* gaze—piercing, invasive. She stared back defiantly. At last he asked, "What do you know about the incident on Harmony?"

"You mean the explosion?" She shrugged. "Basic details. No one seems to know very much." *Except for the Ainniq Guild. They always know more than they let on.* "Two people tried to blow up Harmony's environmental control center. Since they blew themselves up in the process, no one knows why, or even who they were." She raised an eyebrow. "Or have they figured that out now?"

"The motives are still unknown. Medtechs think they may have been moddies, but there's no way to tell for sure."

"Not enough of their brains left intact to study, I'd imagine."

"Exactly."

She took another drink. The Frisian narcotic was starting to work its magic in her veins: everything in the room was a little quieter, a little softer, a little less irritating. "Look, this is all very interesting, but what does it have to do with me?"

"The Guild believes they have identified traces of their last communications. Most involved an MPV—multi-player virt—that they were running. Maybe significant, maybe not. But they were also in contact with an independent station in the node."

"Independent, meaning not subject to Common Law? So you would need their permission to investigate further."

He nodded.

"Still not seeing my role in this, sorry."

"What if I said the signal came from Shenshido Station?"

"I'd answer that I don't have a clue what that is."

"A small research station. The company that built it went under about a decade ago. Some kind of corporate war back on Earth. Shenshido wound up ownerless, effectively abandoned."

She chuckled. "And I'm guessing it lasted a whole day before scavengers picked it apart."

"They tried. Neighboring stations joined forces and drove them off. Possibly the only time Terran corporations have agreed on anything. In theory they all have access to Shenshido's research facilities, but no one seems to be using the place."

"Not valuable enough to need, but too valuable to discard."

"Precisely."

"So . . . what? You think the two on Harmony were taking orders from someone there?"

"It's possible. We don't know anything about what's going on inside that station. It's also possible some other party bounced a signal off it. It's been done before."

"I'd expect the station would have a record of that."

"It probably does. It also has a board of corporate masters who have made it very clear that Gueran authority is not recognized there, and no Guild agent will be allowed to set foot on the station to investigate. We can communicate our concerns, they said, and they will investigate and let us know what they find."

She snorted. "Yeah, right."

"You see the dilemma."

"You need someone who isn't a Guild agent to go out there. Someone you know and trust—" Suddenly she realized where all this was heading. "Ah, shit, Jericho. Tell me you aren't about to ask what I think you are."

"Like you said. We need someone who can go out there and take a look around. Someone they won't connect to the Guild."

"I work for the Guild."

"Only when on assignment. Technically you're a mercenary."

"Yeah, and I'm sure that'll make a big difference to whoever tried to blow up a waystation." She took another drink. The glass was almost empty now, but suddenly her buzz was insufficient; she would need a refill before this conversation was over. "You think if you hire an outsider they'll give that person station access?"

He said nothing.

She put her drink down, slowly. "Jericho . . ."

"I need you to investigate a crime that the masters of Shenshido might be involved in. Or at least have knowledge of. Asking permission for that would tip our hand." He leaned forward. "You're a professional observer, Ru. Trained to assess alien locations and peoples. That's exactly the skill set needed here. And you're used to functioning without the outernet. That's equally important. Shenshido may not have a functioning innernet. Few others could handle that kind of environment for long."

"Yeah, well, that's all very flattering, but even I can't sneak onto a space station. As soon as an airlock opens, someone knows you're there."

"I agree. You'd have to have a good cover story to explain your presence."

"Like what? *I was bored between jobs, so I just thought I'd swing by an abandoned station and have a look around?*" She laughed shortly. "I'm guessing that won't work."

Again that *nantana* gaze: intense, disconcerting. "The assignment interests you?"

"I haven't said no yet."

He reached into his tunic, pulled out a small black billfold, and handed it to her. Inside were an ID card, a data chip, a cash chit, and a license. She pulled the last one out and looked at it. "Bounty hunter," she muttered. "Hell, that actually could work . . ."

"The license identifies you as an independent agent, answering to no one. The cover story gives you an excuse to go anywhere, following rumors that your quarry took refuge there. It gives you a good reason to look around the station . . . and it gives them no reason to think you are connected to any other party."

"Like the Guild."

"Like the Guild."

She turned the ID card over in her fingers, studying it. "So let me get this straight. You want me to adopt a false identity, lie my way into an independent station, and search for evidence of Terran involvement in a terrorist act, all while I'm not protected by Common Law, or by the Guild." She looked up sharply. "I'm guessing this is off the books as far as the Guild is concerned."

"No one but me knows about this. And it needs to stay that way."

"So no backup. No rescue if things go south. Just me." She exhaled in a hiss. "And you think I would agree to do this . . . why? For the money?"

"What would you rather do instead? Hang out in a bar while you wait for your ship to be repaired? Kill time in mundane pursuits? I hear Paradise has an impressive shopping mall. Or you could just relax, maybe read a good book. A few dozen good books. Maybe a hundred, if your repairs take long enough. You've got nothing else to do while you wait." He leaned forward in his chair, his gaze intense. "How long before boredom drives you to do something foolish, just because you need to do *something*? I'm offering you novelty, risk, and reward. Don't tell me it isn't tempting."

She whistled softly. "Someone's been reading my psych file."

"Someone didn't have to read your psych file. Someone has known you long enough to understand your nature, and to know that you're perfect for this job. And that it's perfect for you."

She knew that he was playing her, and that made her hackles rise. But there was no denying that the bait was tempting. "Tell me about the money. With the understanding that I haven't agreed to anything yet."

"Ten thousand creds from me. There's also a reward of a hundred thousand that the Guild has offered, for any information leading to the identification and arrest of those responsible for the Harmony incident. Bring back anything useful, and I'll make sure you qualify."

She laughed. "Yeah. No. That's not how it works. You'd need to pay me fifty thousand for this job, half of it up front, plus five thousand per diem." She waved off any possible objection. "Think about what you're asking me to do—and the risk involved—before you make me a counteroffer that kills my enthusiasm."

Silence. Then: "All right."

"Now tell me about their security."

"Anti-scav, mostly. If you go in with a valid ID and follow normal docking protocols there should be no problem."

"*Should* be." Her eyes narrowed slightly. "You don't *know*."

"Our most recent data on Shenshido is two years old. That's one of the reasons we need you to go out there."

She exhaled heavily. "I'll need my ship."

"I can supply one. Along with any supplies required."

"My lander is operational. Only the mothership was damaged. I'll just have to get the skimmer released from cold dock . . . I assume you can help with that."

"I can get you something bigger. Faster."

"I'm taking my skimmer."

"It would—"

"This is isn't open to negotiation, Jericho." Her voice was firm.

"May I ask why?"

For a moment she hesitated. Then: *What the hell. He probably knows already.* "Because it's armed, and your ship won't be."

The look of surprise in his eyes made it clear that he hadn't known. "I've seen the schematics for your skimmer. There are no armaments on it."

"Yes," she agreed. "That is correct. There are no armaments on the schematics of my skimmer." She paused. "Is that a problem for you?"

His mouth tightened, but he shook his head.

"We get the job done. That's what the Guild cares about, right?"

"So what about this job? Are you in?"

She leaned back in her chair. "Transfer twenty-five thousand credits to my account. I'll leave for Harmony when it's confirmed."

Emotion flickered briefly in his eyes. Relief? *He wasn't sure he could win me over,* she realized. *And he didn't have a good plan B. Damn! I could have charged him more.* "I'll see to it as soon as I leave here," he said.

"Which leaves only one question . . ."

He raised an eyebrow.

"You said it's important for the Guild not to know about this. Why?"

For a long moment he hesitated. How much was he willing to tell her about the Guild's internal workings? That question was almost as interesting as the assignment itself. "We sent two investigators a while back," he said at last. "Dedicated men. When they came back they were . . . less dedicated."

"Meaning?"

"Someone got to them. Convinced them this project didn't need to be a priority. At least that's what it looks like. Granted, the change in attitude was subtle, but it was . . . disturbing."

She said it quietly: "You don't trust your own people."

"Let's just say I'd like to keep this project between us, for now." He put his drink down. "I'll go see to that transfer."

He started to get up to leave, but she waved for him to wait. "Who owns the station, Jericho?"

"I told you. There's a board of representatives—"

"That's who *manages* it. I'm asking who *owns* it. If it's an independent station, that means one political entity had to take responsibility for it. Guera wouldn't have approved the status otherwise."

His eyes unfocused for a moment as he turned his attention inward. Probably netting a query to Guild Headquarters.

"Tridac Enterprises," he said.

She leaned back in her chair and watched as he left the club, turning the bounty hunter license over in her hand, wondering what kind of mess she had just gotten herself into.

Of course, not knowing was half the fun.

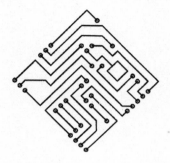

We can replicate the trappings of fear. We can set the stage for it, provide props for it, craft terrifying stories to inspire it. But we cannot replicate fear itself.

That must come from within.

MICAH BELLO
*Crafting Nightmares (presented at Virtcon LVIII)*

# HARMONY NODE
# SHENSHIDO STATION

**T**HE DARKNESS around Micah was thick and suffocating. Intellectually, he knew that was just an illusion—fear distorting his senses—but the knowledge couldn't banish his queasiness. Nor could the many tiny points of light in the distance, coming from stars and nearby stations, not strong enough to illuminate anything. One of them was Shenshido. One of them was Tridac. One of them, barely visible from here, would be Harmony. He switched on his helm light, but its outward beam was swallowed up instantly by the darkness. In this dust-free environment such light was intangible, invisible, uncomforting. The evac suit squeezed his body tightly, its embrace claustrophobic; its coolant pulsed against his skin as it channeled excess body heat away.

He wasn't normally the kind of person who cried under stress, but if one was going to do that, this was as good a setting as one could get for it.

He turned his wellseeker back on and it offered him a dose of sedative, but after a moment's uncertainty he said no. There was only so much of any one drug stored inside his body, and he might be heading into a situation where he would need a lot more of that one. Then the wellseeker starting scrolling information on his current physical and emotional state in front of his eyes, and he shut it off so that he could see the stars and stations clearly.

So peaceful. So cold.

*Concentrate, Micah. You've only got six hours of air left. Get your shit together.*

He brought the suit's navigation program online and programmed a course for Shenshido. The suit took a few seconds to digest the order, then fired the small navigation jets in perfect sequence to turn him around, precisely 180 degrees. Jesus. He'd been facing in the wrong direction. For some reason that struck him as perversely funny, a final absurd blow struck by an unfeeling universe. He even laughed briefly, though the sound was hollow.

Then the jets fired again and there was a brief feeling of acceleration, after which . . . nothing. He could not feel any movement, and the darkness immediately surrounding him was featureless. How did he even know he was moving? He focused on his anger at Tridac, his raw indignation that after years of loyal service he should be treated like this. For a few precious minutes it drowned out the fear, allowing him to think clearly.

If he made it to Shenshido, he would have to deal with the bots again. What was it, exactly, that they were programmed to respond to? Obviously the approach of an unknown ship, but what else? If he could avoid triggering their defense programming, maybe he could slip past them. *How would one program such bots?* He approached the problem like a gaming puzzle, to make it seem less overwhelming. *Say that their job was to repel or destroy unwelcome visitors. Such visitors would have to come in a ship, right? But how would a security program distinguish enemy ships from local maintenance bots? Not everything that flies near a station is a threat.* Shutting his eyes, he tried to concentrate. When that accomplished nothing, he called up the spaceship stats from one of his games and started scrolling through them, looking for some key element that would distinguish enemy vessels from maintenance bots. *The energy signature of a ship would be higher,* he realized. *A maintenance bot only needs enough power to cruise around a station and do minor tasks. It could run on a simple battery. A ship has to have engines large enough and powerful enough to maneuver at high speeds during long voyages. The energy signature would be completely different, as would the nature of its exhaust.*

That made sense to him. It would certainly work in a game. But would the tiny jets attached to the evac suit allow him to pass as a bot? He wouldn't know until he tested the idea.

As he approached the station, he ordered his suit to reduce his speed to almost nothing. Maybe if he drifted into range of the bots slowly enough, without firing his jets at all, he wouldn't trigger any response. The downside of that plan was that he wasn't going to be able to slow down again before hitting the station, so whatever speed he chose now, that would be his speed upon impact. Minimal. Absolutely minimal. With agonizing slowness he drifted toward the docking ring, studying its shadows intently, searching for any sign of the bots. Not until he was nearly upon it was he able to spot one. There: perched on the edge of a broken airlock, its tentacle-like arms curling under the edge. Now that he had found one, he was able to spot others. All quiescent, thus far. God willing, his theory about how they functioned was correct.

Then one of them started to move, and his heart nearly stopped. It rose slowly, then turned in his direction, until he was staring directly into its sensor array. One vast malevolent eye, studying him. Suddenly he was acutely aware of all the noise he was making: motor whirring inside his suit, respirator hissing, blood roaring in his ears like an ocean. Intellectually he knew that the bot couldn't hear any of that, but his fear was not a thing born of intellect, and he found himself holding his breath, as if air rasping in his lungs would be one sound too many.

But whatever the eye saw in him was deemed acceptable, and the bot settled back into its waiting position. He exhaled in relief. Maybe he would make it to the station after all.

Suddenly something struck him in the side—a hard, flat object that slid along his body like a knife blade, catching on the ridges of his suit and threatening to rip the whole thing open. In panic he reached out in that direction and pushed himself away from it. For an instant he could see what it was: a strip of plasteel that had peeled loose from the station, jutting out into the darkness like a scythe. He'd underestimated its size from a distance, and been so fixated by the bots as he got closer that he hadn't seen it coming at him. Then it was gone, as the force of his response sent him tumbling head over heels into the empty space between the rings. The station spun wildly around him, its core rising and falling in his field of vision like a moon gone mad. Each time it passed it seemed larger, closer. There was no way for him to stop himself from crashing into it unless he let the suit stabilize him, but that meant using the jets—

*You don't have a choice. Just do it. Now!*

He triggered the emergency control and felt the jets kick in, countering his motion with short, sharp bursts, hard enough to jar his teeth. Gradually his motion was stabilized, then slowed to almost nothing. His head was still spinning and he felt sick, but at least his movement was under control. He looked back toward the docking ring, dreading the sight of an army of hostile squid bots heading toward him. But whatever their threshold for threat detection was, he apparently had not crossed it.

The closest part of the station was a strut connecting the rings, so he dared one final spurt to move himself in that direction, praying that the bots would continue to ignore him. Twenty yards. Ten. There was a row of shallow rungs running the length of the strut, intended for human repair crews, and as he neared it he reached out as far as he could, determined to grab one. For a moment he thought he was too far away, but then the tips of his fingers brushed one of the rungs, and he made a last desperate stretch and closed his hand around it. A moment later he was jerked to a stop, and though the force of it nearly pulled his arm out of its socket, he held on. A deep trembling ran through his body, half physical relief and half emotional exhaustion. This was the first solid object he'd been in contact with since his ship was destroyed, and the moment was overwhelming.

This part of the station wasn't as badly damaged as the docking ring, but there were a few places where its outer shell had been compromised. Not too far away was a tear he might fit through, so he pulled himself hand over hand in that direction. Eventually he had to leave the rungs behind, but there were enough irregularities in the strut's surface for him to grab onto, now that he wasn't hurtling pell-mell through space. And his hands were much steadier now.

The opening turned out to be smaller than expected. He might have been able to get through with the evac suit on, but with air tanks and navigational jets strapped to his back he'd never make it. Frustrated, he looked around to find a better way in, but there wasn't one. If he wanted a bigger opening he'd have to return to the docking ring and face off against the bots.

*I won't need the jets inside,* he told himself. But it was still unnerving to detach the life-saving framework from his suit and wriggle his way out of it. Apparently that unnerved his suit, too; a bright red warning flashed across his visor as the frame finally came loose. **ALERT! NAVIGATION CONTROL DISCONNECTED!** He tried to maneuver the jet frame through the opening without him in it, but it was the wrong size and shape for that, so he finally hooked the whole assembly to one of the rungs. First rule of survival: never discard anything useful. How many times had he punished players for forgetting that?

He still couldn't squeeze through the opening due to his oxygen supply, but he was damned if he was going to disconnect *that*. At last he managed to loosen its harness just enough to give him some slack, and he was able to push his tank through the opening, then follow it. The rough edges of the plasteel scraped against his suit as he squeezed through, but all he could do was pray that nothing would tear.

Nothing did.

Inside was a transit tube with no vehicles in sight. There were no interior lights, so he turned the helmet lamp back on, then re-tightened his oxygen harness as he took a look around. The dark circular tunnel was too long for his light to illuminate much, but something at the far end was reflecting it. Hopefully some kind of pressure seal. If so, there might still be a viable atmosphere beyond that point.

Pulling himself hand over hand along a guide cord, he headed that way. The tube was narrow, dark, and claustrophobic, but compared to where he'd been for the last few hours it seemed a veritable paradise. When he got to the end he saw that yes, there was an emergency hatch, shut tight. The control panel had settings for atmosphere and G-field; hopefully everything was all still operative. When he tried to open it the door didn't respond, but he'd designed enough space stations for game settings that it took little effort to find the emergency override. The door opened halfway and then stopped, but that was good enough. As he squeezed through the opening he could feel a slight tug coming from the direction of the core, no doubt the ring's G-field leaking through. The airlock beyond had one other exit, in the far wall; he headed over to it, oriented himself according to the large red arrow on the wall—feet *down*, head *up*—and threw the large manual switch that was labeled *exit*.

*Please work please work pleasepleaseplease work . . .*

For a moment nothing happened. Then the hatch behind him jerked closed, and he imagined he could hear its seals snapping shut. Was there a hissing sound as air filled the chamber? He'd never had his helmet off inside an airlock so he didn't know. A few seconds later the station's G-field hit him, not in a gradual adjustment like a fully functional G-lock should provide, but suddenly. Every limb of his body weighed a ton, and his legs nearly collapsed beneath the crushing weight of his torso. Just for an instant. A moment later the shock of the transition faded, but his legs were still strained. His evac gear weighed more than he'd expected.

A moment later the exit slid open, revealing a lightless space. There was no welcoming committee, human or mechanical, nor any indication of where he was. *Well, if there's anyone inside the station, they must know I'm here by now.* Finally he took a deep breath and stepped across the threshold. Lights came on, illuminating a small waiting room with benches along the walls—all of them designed for Terrans, of course—and an archway beyond, leading to some larger space. According to his suit's readout the air was thin but breathable. Good enough.

He reached up to remove his helmet, fumbling with the seal because of the heavy gloves. Finally he managed to get it off, and air, fresh air, flowed across his face. Never in his whole life had any sensation been so pleasurable. For a moment he just stood there, savoring it. Then the soft hiss of oxygen reminded him he was far from done. He pulled off his gloves, then wriggled out of the harness that held his oxygen in place. He thought he heard a hose somewhere tear loose, but who cared? A suit like this could only be used once. He pulled off his gloves and split open the suit that had been sealed around him, peeling the damn thing off him like the skin of a fruit. The clothing that had been compressed underneath it was damp from sweat, and his hair was soaked. He took his headset off for a moment and shook his head like a dog, scattering salty droplets everywhere.

Still no sign of any people or bots.

He salvaged what few survival tools the suit's outer pouch contained—medical supplies, a small plasteel tool with a dozen different tips folded into it, several tubes of high-calorie food paste and fortified water—and loaded them into his pockets. He propped the empty suit up on one of the benches, then looked toward the archway. "Hello? Anyone there?" No one answered. He said it louder. Still no one answered. He headed toward it.

Beyond it was a large chamber whose lights came on as he entered. It was circular in shape, with small kiosks set along the walls. Each one had its own name and design. *Vast Repast* had pastries displayed above a mock-wooden counter. *King Knosh* had a giant bagel with a smiling face on it. *Taste of Kawaii* had a pink storefront with cartoon kittens all over it; they'd been still when the lights first came on, but as he approached they began to dance a tango across the marquis. Music was playing somewhere, and different music was playing somewhere else. The melodies clashed.

A food court. He was in a goddamn food court!

It seemed so utterly absurd, given his circumstances, that he just started laughing. The sound was half fear and half relief, and once it started he couldn't stop. All the tension of the last few hours came pouring out of him, and with it a few tears. A food court! Well, he was safe now, for sure! Hell, he could even get a sandwich if he wanted!

After a while the laughter subsided and his mood settled. Closing his eyes, he flashed a query to the station's innernet. If all this tech was working properly, hopefully that would be, too. There was a pause, and then:

SHENSHIDO GATEWAY. CORPORATE ID OR GUEST?

*Yes!* GUEST, he told it. He held his breath.

APPROVED.

Now, in theory, the whole of Shenshido was at his fingertips. He spent a few minutes getting the hang of the interface, then called up plans of the station. What he received wasn't terribly detailed—you probably needed a corporate ID to get more than the basics—but it was good enough for now. He called up a map of the inner ring, noted his location on it, and studied what was around him. Mostly shopping and residential facilities, which was standard for a corporate station; Terrans liked to separate their living quarters from their work space.

Then, about ten minutes' walk from the food court, he saw a label that made his heart skip a beat: COM CENTER.

Thus far the station's automated facilities had proven functional. If the communications center was as well, he could send out a call for help. Then it wouldn't even matter if anyone else was on this damn station. For the first time since leaving Tridac he felt his spirits lift. He started toward the com center, then stopped. Was it gaming instinct kicking in, or did things just seem too easy? He headed over to a kiosk selling travel supplies, climbed over the counter, and looked for food. All those shelves were empty, but he saw a rack of backpacks hanging on the back wall and took one of those, stowing his tools inside. "Sorry," he muttered to the shop's absent owner. "I'll send you money when I get home."

Suddenly there was a scratching sound from across the room. He froze, looking around for the source. But the food court was silent once more. After a minute he vaulted back over the counter and headed toward the exits, but he kept looking back over his shoulder, just to make sure nothing was following him.

Nothing was.

The station grew darker as he hiked to the com center, and also grew dirtier. Whatever bots maintained the food court clearly had less interest in the housing section. There was actually dust in a few places—dust!—and some damage near the base of the wall. A few scratches, a few stains, nothing truly ominous, just odd. He couldn't think of what would leave marks like that.

Once he thought he heard the scratching sound again, but though he froze for several long minutes, looking in every direction, there was no hint of where it was coming from.

At last he reached the promised land. *Communications Center*, the sign over the door said. As he approached it the panels split open, admitting him to—

*Hell.*

He stood in the doorway just looking at the place, so shocked that for a moment he was unable to process what he was seeing. Then details came into focus: Screens shattered. Consoles gutted. Wires tangled and knotted like intoxicated snakes.

All gone. Deliberately destroyed.

Slowly he walked into the room, picking his way carefully across fallen conduits, over fragments of console housing, past bits of stuffing that someone had ripped from a padded chair. He searched for some remnant of equipment that he could work with, but there was nothing. Whoever had destroyed this place had known what he was doing.

Coldness settled in his heart. The brief spark of hope vanished. And he heard the scratching again, this time from just outside the doorway. Just for a moment, and then it was gone. The hall outside seemed darker than he remembered. Were the lights fading? What if the power on the station was failing? There was no other exit from the room, which meant that he could brave the doorway, with all its myste-rious noises, or wait here until the station died around him. There was no third option. Breath held, he listened for some other sound from the mysterious presence, but there was only silence. Finally he walked toward the door. Nothing attacked him. He hesitated, trembling, then edged out just far enough to look around the threshold. Nothing was there. Sighing in relief, he put his hand on the door frame and lowered his head, meaning to rest until his pounding heart slowed to its normal rhythm. But there was something odd under his fingertips, that drew his gaze upward again. Long scratches, like the ones he'd seen in the corridor. Several, in parallel. He ran his fingers down them, feeling how deeply they were etched, and shivered.

Your average corporate flunky wouldn't know what they were. The low-level techs who had manned this com center wouldn't recognize them. But he did. He'd designed too many fantasy games not to. And they were spread out as wide as his hand, placed as high as his shoulder. Whatever had made them was as tall as he was, and probably larger.

Claw marks.

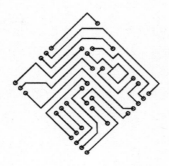

If we wish to colonize deep space, then our first step must be to cast aside everything we think we know about designing space stations. The ones built in the past, huddled close to life-giving stars, were nothing like what we need now. Our new stations will have no sun to draw upon for power. They will have no planets to provide them with raw materials. Everything needed to build and maintain them will have to be harvested from distant star systems and imported across vast distances. The logistics will be daunting. The expense will be immense. Raw mass will take on a value that transcends its form; items that were once considered garbage may become valuable commodities.

Until we find a practical solution to this problem, deep space settlement can never be more than a fantasy.

SOLAN GETTYSBURG
*The Deep Space Paradox (Gueran Archives,
Tiananmen Station)*

# STAR V-1020-10XC
# (50 YEARS PREVIOUS)

IT WAS time.

The harvester's call had gone out months ago, summoning her children back to her. From the clouds of a gas giant they came, wisps of methane trailing behind them; from above the molten seas of the innermost planet they came, their overheated wings fading in the chill of open space; from the belt of asteroids they came, samples trailing behind them like the segments of a vast insect. Some had harvested enough mass that it was hard for them to accelerate, which is why she had given them so much time to get back to her. It also gave the service bots time to organize the deliveries that had already been made, so that not a single inch of space would be wasted.

It had taken her years to get to this system, and years more to fulfill her mission here. It would take her years to get home.

Time meant nothing to her.

She cruised the skies above an alien sun, buffeted by its solar winds, feeding on its light. Sometimes she passed close enough to a planet that her vast wings cast a shadow upon the ground, as if a monstrous bird were circling overhead. Then she returned to the darkness again, to drink in more of the star's radiation and prepare for her return. She had enough power stored to fuel the trip back to Harmony, and enough raw mass to build an entire station once she got there. Crystals and metals and gases and ice filled her hold, and even some organics: anything that her programming told her might be of value to humans. This solar system had been a rich one, and her children had done their jobs well.

If she had been human, she would have been proud of her performance. Since she was merely a mechanical construct—albeit an unusually adaptable one—she simply felt *complete*.

The last of her children were arriving now, and they drew in their wings as they approached, so that they could squeeze into the narrow berths along her hull. Soon they would surrender their autonomy, and be absorbed into the ship's greater digital intelligence. The harvester would be complete once more.

At last it was done. She ran an inventory application to make sure all her parts and programs were accounted for, then spread her wings wide—miles wide—to catch the solar winds and bind them to her purpose. A sudden flare from the star's surface licked at her rear engines as she began to accelerate, then was gone. A human poet might have suggested that the star was saying goodbye.

Light years in the distance, Harmony Node was waiting.

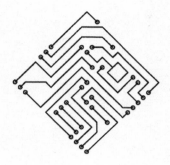

What folly, to think that a machine created by humans could have the power to strip its makers' children of humanity!

NUY CHENGARA
*The Hausman Delusion*

# HARMONY NODE
# INSHIP: ARTEMIS

**T**HE AINNIQ was eerily beautiful. A sliver of space that did not look like space, alive with shadows the mind could not identify. A flaw in a black jewel, catching the light unexpectedly—then disappearing from view as the angle changed, equally unexpectedly. Colors that had no name shimmered within its depths; shadows that required no light pulsed up and down its length. The universe had been fractured in its first nano-seconds of birth, space-time wounded beyond hope of healing, and the Guerans had learned to navigate those wounds as one might the rivers of a great world, or the veins of a body. Entering the ainniq, a ship might defy the usual limits of space and time; skipped along its edge at just the right angle, a signal might cross the galaxy in less than a lifetime.

Traveling through the ainniq, one might also be devoured by the unique predators that called it home.

Ru gazed at her main viewscreen as she strapped herself into her au-tochair, watching the ainniq until the bulk of the outship blocked it from her view. As always, it inspired a sense of visceral awe, even humility. Here was a danger she dared not face on her own, far beyond the bounds of normal human recklessness. Beyond that darkling gateway were creatures that the human mind could not fathom and the human eye could not see, creatures whose flesh was the stuff of space itself. Only Guerans with Pilot's Syndrome could see them clearly, and even that was not always enough to avoid them. Some outships never returned.

Then the bay of the outship closed around Ru's vessel and the ainniq was gone. With a sigh she loaded the theta-sleep program into her headset and leaned back in the autochair. Waking brains called to the dragons of outspace, so only people who were needed to pilot the outship would be conscious during its passage. That was fine with her. Danger was an elixir she was normally hard pressed to resist, but this was a threat beyond her ken. Her Variation might make her impulsive, even reckless, but it did not make her suicidal.

She slept.

Harmony Node. The name was a joke. Maybe even a deliberate joke. Guildfolk were not incapable of humor, though it was usually of a dark and ironic sort. This would certainly qualify.

The node was located in a region of space with nothing of any special interest to humankind: no habitable planets, no lost colonies, not even a star system within convenient distance that might be farmed for supplies. If not for the presence of the ainniq it wouldn't even have been given a name. But there were ainniq here, two of them, and where they merged a fork was visible, providing a landmark for outpilot navigation. That was enough to merit human development. Like ancient sailors who had established a base of operations anywhere they found a viable harbor, the Guild established settlements wherever its outpilots could surface safely. In this case, that meant in the middle of nowhere.

Why the place had drawn so many Terran corporations was anyone's guess. Maybe they liked the idea of a node that did not have a Variant world associated with it. Or maybe one of them had moved here for that reason, and then others had followed in its wake, hungry to spy on a rival, sabotage competing projects, or maybe just fulfill the

old Earth adage: *Keep your friends close and your enemies closer.*
Back home, Terran megacorps waged war like ancient nation-states,
and while such behavior wasn't tolerated in the outworlds, Terran hostilities had a way of infecting more civilized cultures. Perhaps it was
just as well that seven of the nine Terran stations in Harmony had ne-
gotiated for independent status, setting them apart from the rest of outworld society.

But there was a price for that. Security surrounding the independent stations was complicated and often inefficient, which attracted other
types of entrepreneurs: black marketeers, scavengers, smugglers of both
digital and material goods, even pirates. The outer sectors were as close
to a lawless frontier as one might find in the outworlds.

What better name for such a place than Harmony?

ALERT: APPROACHING SHENSHIDO CORPORATE
TERRITORY. LEAVING ALLIED SPACE. TERRAN
CORPORATE LAW WILL APPLY.

Ru closed her reading program and opened a com link to the
station.

THIS IS SKIMMER ARTEMIS, REQUESTING PERMISSION
TO DOCK. ID SKM411-AD72-11A. PLEASE ASSIGN
APPROACH PATH.

There was no response.
She sent the message again.
Still silence.

The station was visible on her screen now, a spherical core with two
coplanar rings. Classic Terran design. It wasn't very large, but given
that its purpose was research rather than luxury living, the size seemed
appropriate.

She transmitted her message again just to make sure the security
programs were aware of her. If Jericho was right, their awareness would

protect her from the station's automated defense. If he was wrong . . . well, things could go downhill very fast.

She was approaching the outer ring now, and Jericho had not exaggerated the problem: the thing had been ripped to pieces. Her practiced eye picked out elements of backstory: long cuts where scavengers had tried to remove materials, sections seared by assault weapons, craters and tears where high-velocity objects had smashed into the station's shell. The space surrounding must have been strewn with debris at one time. Had Shenshido gathered all that up, or did Tridac swing by periodically to take care of housekeeping? Or had scavs hung around the periphery of battle like vultures, hungry to claim any scraps that drifted outside Shenshido's defense zone?

**ALERT: ENTERING SHENSHIDO CORPORATE TERRITORY.**
**TERRAN CORPORATE LAW APPLIES.**

She was close enough now to get a good look at the station, and her ship fed data into her brainware while she studied it. That was yet another reason she'd wanted to use her own skimmer. Part of an outrider's job was to evaluate colonies from a distance, so her skimmer was loaded with software designed for that purpose. As she approached the outer ring her ship noted the presence of spider bots, highlighting them on her display and providing her with hard data regarding their function. But she didn't need data to know how dangerous they were. The warring moons of Oberon Nine had used similar bots, and she had no desire to tangle with them again. She sent out her call sign again, just to make sure whatever AI was running those things knew that she was legit.

*Easy, boys. No scavs here, just a licensed bounty hunter.* Again there was no answer, but by now she didn't expect one. Either Shenshido was uninhabited, or there was some reason its inhabitants weren't answering her.

It was time to find out which.

She watched the spider bots closely as the skimmer searched the outer ring for a safe place to dock. Apparently there wasn't any. Most of the mooring sites had been ripped open or blown to bits, and the few that remained didn't look stable enough for her liking. The last thing she needed on this crazy assignment was for an airlock to blow while she was in it. She turned the skimmer inward, to search for a suitable site on the inner ring, or perhaps on the station proper—

—and three of the spiders lifted suddenly from the station's surface, heading straight toward her.

Her heart skipped a beat, but she did nothing. The skimmer was designed to function in a planetary atmosphere, so it had a more substantial outer shell than the spiders were used to; it was also streamlined to reduce drag, so there were few edges for them to grab onto. If these three attacked, she might have enough time to shake them off before others joined the fray. Right now her best bet was to continue on her course as a legitimate visitor would do, following Jericho's instructions to the letter, sending out all the signals one would expect from a regular transport vessel. If he was right about how they operated, that would be enough to hold them at bay. But damn, they were hard to ignore! Tully and she had nearly gotten killed in the Oberon system.

The three came close and circled the skimmer once, twice, three times. Apparently whatever they saw satisfied them, for they finally returned to their perches. She exhaled loudly in relief. Apparently Jericho had been right about how to deal with them.

She pulled the skimmer into orbit between the inner ring and the core, so its sensors could search both surfaces for a viable entrance. Various anomalies were displayed for her to evaluate, some of them downright bizarre. In one place she found a jet suit that had been tethered to a strut like an abandoned pet; what sense did that make? Surely anyone with a brain would strap on his nav jets before he exited the station, not after. But not far from that, the ship located a small emergency hatch on the core itself, probably designed for human maintenance crews. Hopefully there was some kind of maintenance facility inside, tied to the station's global systems.

She directed the skimmer to position itself so that her own escape hatch was directly over it. It had no mooring seal, but that wasn't a problem; the skimmer was equipped to adapt to whatever kind of tech it encountered. Compared to some of what Tully and she had dealt with, this was hardly even a challenge. An expandable tunnel extended from her own skimmer to the structural ring surrounding the maintenance hatch, adapting itself to fit the ring and establish an airtight seal. A short time later the ship told her SEAL CONFIRMED.

Now the big question: to arm, or not to arm? It was best not to look belligerent when confronting unknown agents, and she knew that anything she carried on her could be detected by the station's security. But this was hardly a casual visit. And besides, she was supposed to be a bounty hunter, wasn't she? It might look suspicious if she wasn't carrying *something.*

She decided on a compromise, and chose a few of her more subtle options. A coat lined with safeskin. A set of taze rings. A collapsible shock rod. After some consideration, she added a shock pistol to the collection. It was small enough to fit into an outer pocket, and unlike the other choices, wouldn't require her to be close to an opponent. The rest she left behind. Anything that might damage Shenshido or release toxic substances into its air supply was not likely to be tolerated by its masters. Of course, she had her usual folding blades and a coil of razor wire hidden in her boot soles: not easy supplies to get to in an emergency, but unlikely to be discovered by hostile parties. The blade had gotten her and Tully out of some tight spots in the past.

Tully . . . She sighed. How she wished he was present to share this adventure with her! And not only because she could use the backup. She missed his wit, his energy, even his annoying quirks. She'd brought his most prized memento along with her, to remind her of him, and though the colorful glass phallus looked ridiculous strapped into the pilot's chair, it was oddly comforting. As though his spirit was still with her, ready to have sex with any new Variant race they came across.

She stuffed some additional emergency supplies into her outer pockets, then headed over to the skimmer's escape hatch and pulled it open. A few feet below her, the status readout on the station's hatch proclaimed that the temperature, pressure, and air composition inside the station were within acceptable human parameters. Good. She unsealed the small hatch, hesitated for a moment, then pulled it open. A small ladder led down into darkness. It was far from inviting, but at this point anything that wasn't going to attack her was acceptable. She ordered the skimmer into lockdown, then began to climb down through the opening. As soon as her head cleared the hatch's frame, it closed automatically behind her.

She was in.

The lights hadn't come on, so she was left hanging in cave-blackness. Not a good start. But as she called up the icon that would trigger the emergency light on her headset, overheads finally flickered on, revealing the stark gray walls of a very small airlock. Big enough for one person with standard gear, maybe two people at most, but no more. She climbed down to the floor of the lock and positioned herself in front of the inner hatch, staring directly into the sensors that would be taking her measure. "Open lock," she ordered. For a moment she thought it wasn't going to respond; then it unsealed, revealing a small staging room with a narrow door at the far end. Tools and pressure garments festooned the wall like holiday ornaments—which confirmed her guess about this being a maintenance facility—but there were no people anywhere. She took a moment to listen for any sound of human activity before she started across the room. Nothing. The place was as still as a morgue.

*Now I am officially breaking and entering*, she mused.

Beyond the staging room was some kind of engineering center, filled with monitors and consoles and conduits, its walls lined with cabinets whose contents she could not begin to guess at. She inspected a few of the work stations, but none of them had what she needed, so she kept looking. A network node overhead blinked at her, indicating that the station's innernet was operating, but she didn't trust it enough to let it connect to her brainware. At least not until she knew what had happened to all the people here.

Finally she found a small office with a floor-to-ceiling bank of security monitors, and she sat down at the main desk and activated the manual controls. A map of the station was easy to summon up, though it was far from detailed. The two uppermost levels of the station core were mostly offices and meeting rooms, with a few interconnected labs. The levels below were unmarked, save for titles spaced evenly around the station: *Biome 1, Biome 2a, Biome 2b* . . . this place must have been a biological research station once. What if some disease had gotten out of control and killed everyone? Could that explain why there wasn't a person in sight? For a brief moment she questioned the wisdom of her visit. Then curiosity crowded out her unease, as always. The danger was perversely invigorating.

She copied the map onto a chip, then decided to take a look at Shenshido's transit log. The system wouldn't let her into its secure files, but she managed to access a summary of activity that was part of the public record, and scrolled through the data from two years back, when Shenshido had first gone dark. If something odd had happened on the station, that might be reflected in its traffic patterns. But there was nothing out of the ordinary: no grand convoy coming in to assist the station, no organized evacuation going out. Shenshido had descended quietly into silence.

*That means most of the people who were working here probably never left,* she thought. *Are they dead, or . . . what?*

She finally closed the transit files and called up the data that Jericho had asked for: Shenshido's communication history. He'd given her a program that would gather the information he needed, so she loaded that and watched as data scrolled across the screen. In theory, it would reveal what signals had come in to Shenshido around the date of the Harmony explosion, and hopefully where they came from. But she wasn't adept enough at interpreting such data to know if she was collecting what he needed. She would have to deliver it to find out.

*If he shares that much with me,* she thought bitterly. *Once I deliver what he wants, he'll likely shut me out again, like Guild folk always do. They're happy to use us, but they don't see us as equals.* A flicker of ancient resentment stirred in the recesses of her brain, and she had to force her thoughts away from it. *He's always treated you decently,* she reminded herself.

When Jericho's program had accessed and recorded everything it could, she tucked the chip back into her headset and called up the map for her own use. Information on what had happened to the people here would be valuable to Jericho, so she would take a look around and see what more she could gather.

She left the engineering complex to explore the rest of the station. Hallway after hallway. Room after room. The further she went, the more eerie it seemed that there were no signs of trouble anywhere. Every automatic system was functioning perfectly. Lights came on when she entered a room and shut off when she left. The data stations she found in a few offices were operational, but passcoded. She searched a dozen offices and meeting rooms, tested a dozen computers, opened the cabinets in a dozen labs, looking for some kind of clue. She did find one room where some furniture had been broken up, and it looked like there were pieces missing, but there was no way to tell what they were without reassembling everything.

Finally, exasperated, she decided to try the labs on the next level down. She used the map to locate the nearest staircase and headed toward it, nearly tripping over a floor-scrubbing bot along the way.

The ambush came without warning. Projectiles suddenly flew at her from both sides of the hall: long, sharp rods that shot out of the air vents and slammed into her armored coat. Arms, shoulders, torso. The safeskin solidified momentarily as each rod hit, preventing it from piercing through to her flesh, but that did nothing to lessen their momentum. Projectiles battered her body like hammers as she fell back, trying to get out of the line of fire. Then one of them struck low on her leg, beneath the hem of her coat, and she could feel it bite deeply into her leg. An arrow. Shit. What were arrows doing here? At least there were no more of them coming at her; whatever trap she'd triggered seemed to be limited to a single volley. She started to back away from the area, watching the walls as she did so, wary of any other openings that might harbor weapons. Then she hit the bot again and stumbled, nearly falling. But no. Wait. There was no bot there. She'd stumbled over nothing.

*Shit.*

Her right foot was numb now, and coldness was rapidly spreading up her leg. What the hell had been on that arrow? She tried to pull her pistol out of her pocket, but it took all her concentration just to close her fingers around the grip and pull it out. Then her legs collapsed beneath her, and she fell to her knees in the middle of the hallway. *Get up!* a desperate inner voice urged her. *Get out of here!* But whatever poison had been on the arrow was too powerful; fiber by fiber, her muscles were giving up the fight.

They came then, rushing at her from doorways and intersections nearby, half a dozen humans in worn jumpsuits, primitive weapons in their hands. Knives. Spears. Bludgeons. She tried to lift her arm to fire at one of them, but the limb wouldn't obey her. Spots were swimming before her eyes. *I'm going to die now.* The thought was oddly distant, like it belonged to someone else. *This is what dying feels like.*

Someone was standing over her with an axe. A fucking axe. He looked like an illustration from a vid game. She wondered if she would feel the bite of his weapon, or if she had become too numb for that.

"STOP!"

The man with the axe hesitated. The label on his shirt said *Cisco Tech*, Ru noted. A company name. What a strange thing to notice when one was about to die.

"Stop!" the voice repeated.

She blinked as footsteps approached her, trying to fight off the darkness that was closing in. A man crouched down by her side: weathered skin, black hair streaked with gray, a short beard to match, and cruel eyes. Such cruel eyes. His headset was black and coarse in texture—faux wrought iron—and shaped like the hand of a great clawed beast, talon-tips framing his face. He stared at her for a minute and then reached out and grabbed the collar of her coat and pulled it down, so that the lining was visible. "Safeskin! There's no safeskin on this station. Where did you get this?"

She wanted to push him away, but her body would no longer obey her commands at all. It was getting hard to breathe. She had no strength to talk.

"You're from the outside," he challenged her.

Somehow she found her voice. "Yes."

"You have a ship?"

Even in her drug-addled state she was alert to the danger lurking behind the question. She managed to shake her head. "Dropped me off . . ."

"But they'll come back for you, yes?"

She didn't know what answer would keep her safe, so she said nothing.

The man stood. The others kept their distance from him, she noticed. Out of respect, or fear? There was something about him that made her skin crawl. "We bring her back with us," he announced.

"But Ivar." It was a woman's voice. "If she's one of them—"

"*We bring her back.*" He glared for a moment to see if there would be any further protest, then nodded toward Ru. "Rollo, you carry her. Be careful. She has value."

*Value*, Ru thought numbly. *I have value.* Someone pulled her up from the ground, but her legs were a million miles away. *Maybe today is not my time to die.*

Then darkness swept that final thought away, and all was silence.

We are the beasts in the night, stalking the Terran camp-fire. We are the voices in the darkness, whispering things no Terran wants to hear. We are the eternal Other, feared and reviled, and no flowery words or diplomatic platitudes will ever change that.

*(Excerpt from a propaganda 'cast of the Haus-man League. Author unknown.)*

# HARMONY NODE
# TRIDAC STATION

*BEHOLD THE outworlds*, Khatry thought, as he gazed out into the galactic darkness. No sun blazing in the heavens, to provide warmth and light. No planet or moon within view. No band of orbiting habitats, so densely clustered that one could barely catch sight of the Earth between them. Just the blackness of space, punctuated by space stations so distant that their external lighting could barely be seen from his observation deck.

Emptiness was good, Khatry mused. Emptiness had potential. Space with nothing in it was space that a man could develop however he liked.

There were times when the CEO of Tridac Enterprises (Harmony Division) missed Earth. But there were more times when he didn't—times when he gazed out upon the vast expanse of unclaimed space and felt a sense of primal awe. His ancestors had experienced that same awe, gazing up at the night sky from the plains of Africa. They had assigned names to the darkness, and made offerings to it. To them the stars were spirits, guides in the night, whose favor must be courted and whose wrath must be feared. Little did they know that someday the heavens would lose their magic, as a multitude of man-made satellites brightened the night sky, outshining distant suns.

The ancient spirits were dead now. Their temples had been claimed by more modern gods, whose prophecies were voiced as *Terms and Conditions*. He, Victor Khatry, Earthborn, was their priest.

A soft chime alerted him to an incoming message. "Receive," he commanded.

A holo of his personal secretary appeared in the center of the room. Through its translucent substance he could still see the stars. "Jack Grimm is here to see you, sir."

He nodded. "Send him in." As the image of the secretary faded, he said, "End display." The stars surrounding him vanished, the room brightened, and the features of his office became visible once more. In its center was a sleek wooden desk he'd had shipped in from Earth, back when he first arrived, and everything else was designed around it. The desk was made of real wood, not a synthetic. Never mind that it had cost him a small fortune to bribe the Terran authorities to allow native wood to leave the home system, and a second small fortune to ship it here. Ancient kings had thrones made of gold and silver; Division CEOs had desks made of real wood. The message was the same.

Grimm looked like one would expect a man with that name to look, harsh and dour. Khatry disliked him, but he knew he was good at what he did and would keep quiet about the things that mattered. "You have something to report?"

"Just wanted to tell you, Bello's done with. Killed by security bots from Shenshido. He triggered them himself, so none of my people had to get involved. No one will be able to trace this back to us. Or to Tridac."

"So he took the bait."

Grimm snorted. "Fled like the boogeyman was after him." He grinned crookedly. "Which it was, in a manner of speaking."

"You've seen the body."

The grin faded. "There's no body. Ship's converter overloaded during the attack, the whole thing blew—anything as fragile as human flesh, I figure was vaporized."

"You *figure*." Khatry's tone was chill. "I prefer certainty."

"The spiders scanned for life support after the explosion, found nothing. No human could survive out there without it. He won't be troubling you again."

*He never troubled me before*, Khatry thought. *He was just in the wrong place at the wrong time. A fatted calf who wandered too close to the altar.* "And the evidence?"

"The spiders delivered all the debris to me, but a lot was lost in the explosion. What do you want done with the stuff we've got?"

"Make sure all identifying marks are gone, then deliver it to our scav contact."

He nodded. "And the message on the gift card should be . . . ?"

He considered. "Tell him I would be pleased if his people stayed clear of Shenshido for a while."

The crooked grin returned. "I doubt he's planning a return trip. Their last visit didn't go so well."

"Feel free to remind them of that." When Grimm didn't move he said, "Is there something else?"

"Sir . . . this may be above my pay grade . . . but what's up with Shenshido? Shouldn't someone be repairing it? Or dismantling it? Or . . . something? I got a look at the place while I was out there. It's a fucking wreck."

There was a moment of silence. Then: "That is indeed above your pay grade."

Grimm's jaw tightened, but he bowed his head in assent. "As you wish."

"Any other questions?"

"No. I'll see the wreckage is disposed of properly." He bowed his head again, managing to convey both respect and arrogance. *What a piece of work he is*, Khatry thought as he watched Grimm swagger out. *But a useful one. For now.*

"Resume display," he commanded, and the stars returned.

In truth, he had no idea why Shenshido was being handled this way. Someone at the top of the Tridac hierarchy had decided that the station should not be dismantled, repaired, or allowed to fall into the hands of a rival company, and had sent Khatry instructions to that effect. While orders direct from Earth were something no CEO in the field dared ignore, it seemed a criminal waste of resources to him. He'd inspected Shenshido right after the big scav attack—to assess the damage—and thought the place still had potential. Certainly it should be used for *something*. But the triple-encrypted, no-reply orders made it clear his superiors thought otherwise, and didn't want to discuss the matter with him. *Hear and obey,* he thought bitterly. But that was price you paid when you served a megacorp. At least until you rose high enough in the company's hierarchy to earn a seat on the Terran Board.

A paneled office. That's what he would buy himself, when he got that far.

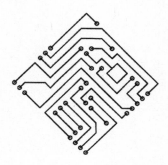

What price must we pay, for inviting this new technology into our brains? What losses must we suffer, for compromising the integrity of the human soul? What dangers must we face, unimaginable to past generations, because we in our arrogance have seen fit to create them?

MAXWELL ONEGIN
*Think Again!* (Historical Archives, Hellsgate Station)

# HARMONY NODE
# SHENSHIDO STATION

**T**HE LIGHTS flickered intermittently as Micah headed back toward the food court, and one time they went out for several long seconds, making his heart lurch in panic. He activated the flashlight on his headset. When the lights came back on it was still visible, as a narrow beam of glowing dust motes that swirled in the air currents like insects. He tried to stay focused on that, and on where he needed to go next, and not think about the claw marks he'd seen. But it was impossible.

*Something* had destroyed a whole room full of equipment, digging its claws deep into a plasteel wall. He didn't know of any human Variation with claws that large, so it must be some kind of beast. Even now it might be picking up Micah's scent, tracking him through the flickering darkness. Hunting him. Hopefully he could get off this damn ring and put some kind of barrier between him and it before it caught up with him.

When he got back to the food court it was darker than he remembered, with a patina of grime on the walls and floor and an atmosphere of imminent decay. Had he been so ecstatic to reach a place of safety, when he'd first arrived, that he hadn't noticed how dismal the place looked? Even the air seemed different now: colder, clammier. Maybe the life support systems faltered when the lights went out. If so, a longer period of darkness could be deadly.

*Just focus on getting off this ring. Don't think about anything else.*

As he passed the lock he'd come in through, he hesitated. He'd planned on leaving his evac gear here, but was that really a good idea? If the station's life support failed . . .

*Then I'm going to die anyway,* he thought grimly. *A near-empty oxygen tank won't save me. Best to travel light.*

A sudden scraping sound from behind made him jump. A high-pitched, nerve-jangling sound: claws on tile? He looked around the food court, desperate to discover the source, but saw nothing. *Easy, Micah. You're almost at the exit. Stay focused.* The tube that led inward toward the core was positioned behind the one he'd arrived in; wouldn't it be great if the former were fully functional, and a transport pod was waiting inside it to whisk him away? But no such luck. When he finally reached the tube he wanted, the door didn't open as he approached. While he struggled to work the manual override controls, he heard the high-pitched scraping sound again. Closer this time. *Stay focused, Micah.* His hands were shaking, but he knew that his only hope of getting away from the source of the noise was to make it into the tube. Finally the door parted, revealing a dark and empty space. There was a maintenance ladder to one side of the entrance; as he swung himself over to it, he hit the control that would shut the door behind him, praying nothing would follow him through at the last moment. Nothing did. The door closed with a soft hiss, leaving him with only his headlight to see by.

He clung to the ladder for a moment, giving his pounding heart a chance to settle. For the moment, at least, he was safe. The climb down to the station was a long one, and he was already exhausted. He passed a transport pod at one point, a cylindrical capsule that had once carried commuters from the core to the ring and back again, now frozen in mid-journey. There was just enough space between the pod and the wall for him to squeeze past. Down, down into darkness he continued, until the ladder ended and once more there was a floor beneath his feet. He held his breath and strained to hear any hint of movement overhead. But all was silent. The beast that had ravaged the outer ring hadn't followed him.

When he exited the tube the lights came on automatically, but dimly, perhaps at half-strength, revealing a small waiting room. The dust that danced in the thin beam of his headlamp was thicker than it should have been in the filtered air of a space station; life support systems might be working here, but they weren't working well. He looked around the room, noting half a dozen static chairs and a water outlet. Nothing else. He headed to the outlet and took a deep drink, then squeezed a few inches of food paste out of one of his tubes. *Cheesecake,* the label said. It tasted vile, but getting some food into his stomach made him feel a little better.

He called up his map of the station, to see what his options were. Most of this section was taken up with offices and small labs, but there was a large complex not too far away that was labeled *Engineering.* Perhaps some kind of control center. If there were still any people on this station they might well be there, and if not, maybe Micah could find some working communication equipment. The thought of being able to call for help imbued him with new energy, and he fixed the map in the corner of his field of vision so that he could see it as he walked.

Empty. The station was so empty. It was a different kind of emptiness than in the ring, where one could imagine the human exodus was recent. The emptiness here felt . . . ancient. Absolute. As if he was hiking through a place humanity had forgotten.

But though humans were gone, other forms of life had apparently prospered. He saw several vents with dark vines protruding from them; one was low enough on the wall that he could take a closer look at it. He queried the innernet about it, but got no useful data. He prodded one of the vines, to see if it had the resilience of a living plant, and his fingers came away with a sticky black substance on them. He started to wipe it off on his shirt, then thought better of it, and wiped his hand on the wall instead. The parallel streaks he left behind were eerily similar to the claw-marks in the outer ring.

What the hell was this stuff, and how did it get into the ducts? The map indicated there were biological reserves on the lower levels, but those should have been sealed off. Especially if the station was used for scientific experiments. A sudden chill ran through him. What if the dust that was dancing in the beam of his light was organic? What if an experiment on the lower levels had gone wrong, releasing biological toxins into the air? That might explain why there were no people here. Though if they'd all died at once, there should be bodies lying around. And if it killed them one by one, over time, why hadn't they called for help? He fumbled for the first aid kit in his pack to see if it contained a filter mask in it, but no such luck. Whatever was in the air here, he was going to have to keep breathing it.

He continued down the corridor. More and more vines appeared, hanging down from the ceiling in thick clumps; he had to duck to get past some of them. Black tangles clustered in corners, around the edges of vents and doorways, underneath lighting strips. The further he went, the more of the corridor they filled. Soon he would have to start clearing them out of the way if he wanted to keep going. Given the mystery gunk he'd just rubbed off his hand, he wasn't anxious to make contact with any of the vines again.

Then he turned a corner and stopped short. Stared. And cursed.

The corridor ahead was completely blocked by vines, so thickly tangled that he could barely see the vents they protruded from. There was no way to proceed any further along this route unless he cut his way through with his utility knife. Like a primitive hacking his way through a jungle, only the short blade of his emergency knife would take hours to clear a path. He needed a fucking machete.

*You can find a way around it*, he told himself. But whatever these organics were, they seemed to be clustered in the very section he wanted to enter; the odds were good that even if he could find another approach to the engineering section, that, too, would be blocked.

"Fuck," he muttered. Then he yelled at the vines, pouring all his frustration and his despair into the cry: "FUCK YOU!"

The mass quivered.

He stepped back quickly, pulling the knife from his pocket. But the vines were still, now. Had he imagined the movement? Was he so tired that he was starting to see things? He looked around for some small object he could use to test the vines, but of course in the middle of a station corridor there was nothing. He started rummaging through his pockets for something expendable, and found the half-empty tube of cheesecake paste. Just heavy enough. He held it in his hand for a moment, studying the curtain of vines in front of him, then threw it with all his might at what looked like the thinnest spot. Maybe if it broke through, he could get a sense of how far down the hall this obstruction went.

But it didn't go through. It hit the vines and hung there in mid-air, a ghostly white intruder trapped in a black web. After a few seconds it began to slide down, drops of gelatinous sap slicking its bright plastic surface. In a distant part of his brain Micah understood why that image repelled him—he'd once presented a paper on *The Emotive Power of Gelatinous Textures in Virtual Settings*—but his response was visceral, and treating the cause as an intellectual exercise didn't help.

A vine moved.

With a gasp, he took a step backward. A tip of one vine beneath the food tube was curling upward, shaping itself around it. As the tube slid into its embrace the vine tightened, wrapping around it like a hungry python—

Micah turned and ran. The whole world was full of black vines, and once he nearly ran face first into a web of them. Another time he nearly tripped over a clump on the floor. Were they all moving now? Would they reach for him if he stumbled? He used the map in his head, retracing his path from before, praying that whatever the hell those things were, they stayed rooted in place. When he reached the waiting room he hesitated . . . but what was he going to do, go back upstairs and face the beast? He ran across the room and beyond it, into a part of the station he hadn't seen before. The halls were free of organics—thank

God!—and he ran until he could run no more, then stopped, doubling over as he gasped for breath. When breathing became less of a struggle, he visualized the icon that would activate his wellseeker. It greeted him by scrolling bright red warnings in the corner of his visual field, listing all the biological systems that were off kilter, but he ignored those and just told it to give him a small dose of sedative. A few seconds later he could feel his muscles begin to relax, and the fear eased its death grip on him.

When he had his strength back he started walking again. He figured he would put a little more distance between him and the vine, and then look for a place to rest. At one point he saw a dark branch on the floor ahead of him and his heart sank, but as he edged carefully closer he saw that it was not a vine like the others, just a piece of a long stick that had been broken in half. He picked it up, then found another piece that was clearly its mate. One had a pointed tip, stained black; an arrow? There were dark spots on the floor near where it had been lying, but in the dim lighting he couldn't tell if that was blood or just grime. Who would use such a primitive weapon in a space station?

Suddenly he heard a rustling sound: the movement of clothing? He gripped the sharp half of the arrow in one hand and pulled out his utility knife with the other, aware that neither was ideal for combat, but what the hell else was he supposed to do?

A dark shadow moved into the hallway, about ten yards ahead of him. Too far for his headlamp to illuminate details, other than its human shape. "Off!" it demanded. The voice was male, deep-timbered, and in another setting might have been intimidating, but Micah was so glad to see another human being that all he felt was elation. It took him a moment to realize what the man wanted; when he did he reached up and turned the headlamp off, so that it was no longer shining straight into the man's eyes. Now Micah could be seen.

Slowly the figure approached. He was a tall man, Terran in appearance, with harsh, angular features and a stark silver headset. A breastplate made of layered strips of gray plasteel covered the chest portion of his jumpsuit like an insect carapace, and bracers of the same material were strapped around his lower arms. Makeshift armor? There was a weapon in his hand, pistol-shaped but with a two-pronged tip. He kept it pointed at Micah as he approached, dark eyes taking his measure, up and down. "Who the fuck are you?"

"Micah Bello. My ship malfunctioned and crashed while docking . . . I've been looking for people . . ."

The man held out his hand. After a moment Micah realized what he wanted, and handed him the arrow. The man looked it over, studying the tip in particular. Then he glanced at the floor, at the dark spattering that might or might not be blood; his weapon was still pointing at Micah's heart.

"Who are you?" Micah asked.

"Jamal." The man finally lowered his weapon. "My name is Jamal." He tapped a small device that was affixed to his ear. "Serjit . . . you there?" He waited a moment, listening. "I'm in sector five. There was some kind of combat here . . . looks like blood on the floor. One arrow left behind. Are we missing anyone?" Another pause. "Well, let's make sure of it. And put the patrols on alert. If the exos are hunting in this sector now, we need to be ready for them. Meanwhile," he scowled at Micah, "I've got an unidentified person here. Claims he's a shipwreck. Ship's gone." A longer pause. "No, Variant."

"Sarkassan," Micah offered.

"Says he's Sarkassan." A pause. "No, not exo. At least far as I can see. Certainly isn't acting exo." A pause. "You want me to bring him in?" Another pause, then dryly: "He's pointing a utility knife at me. I assume if he had anything bigger I'd be looking at it."

Whatever response he got seemed to end the conversation. He focused his attention on Micah again. "Serjit says I can bring you in to meet the others. Expect to be interrogated when you get there. Standard operating procedure." He snorted. "Well, no, not *standard*. It's not every day we come across an outsider." A corner of his mouth twitched. "Unless you'd rather hang out here, wait for the exos to find you."

"What are exos?"

He snorted. "Some experiment down in Bio went bad, and now the station's full of the mutated bastards. Sometimes they eat the people they catch." He held up the arrow. "This is one of theirs. The black on the tip is probably poison. Primitive but effective. And the owner is probably still nearby." He nodded down the corridor, the way he had come. "We should move before he comes back. Unless you feel like fighting."

"I'm good," Micah said quickly. He had a thousand more questions, but this obviously wasn't the time or the place to be asking them.

As he fell in beside his new guide he gripped his small knife tightly, watching the shadows closely for *exos*. Whatever the fuck they were.

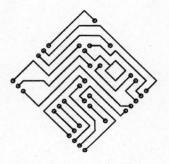

The concept of "Us versus Them" is deeply ingrained in the human psyche. It echoes our primitive roots, a time when loyalty to the tribe could make the difference between living and dying. It's as powerful a driving instinct as the need for food, and sex, and—if properly manipulated—can provide a compelling story dynamic.

MICAH BELLO
*Crafting Nightmares (presented at Virtcon LVIII)*

# HARMONY NODE
# SHENSHIDO STATION

**W**HEN RU first woke up she thought the sky was real. It was bluer than Guera's sky—bluer than any sky she'd ever seen—and the crisp color would have been quite pleasing had her head not been pounding. Slowly her vision came into focus, and the reality of the sky became clear. Maybe if there had been only one sun she might have been fooled a bit longer, but the row of neatly spaced sun lamps arching across a dome-shaped ceiling high overhead gave the game away.

All of which she could see because she was in a primitive hut that had no roof, just an open framework with a rolled-up tarp at one end.

SYSTEM SUMMARY, she prompted her wellseeker. A moment later, biological readings began to scroll down the left side of her visual field. Her biostats weren't ideal, but considering she'd just recovered from a dose of poison that could have killed her, they were reassuring. She let the wellseeker feed her something to quiet her headache, and a moment later the pounding subsided.

With effort, she pushed herself up to a sitting position. Every inch of her body hurt and her muscular response was slow, but everything

was responsive; whatever toxin had knocked her out hadn't disconnected any vital circuits.

The hut she was in was small, and apparently designed by someone
who lacked any skill in hut-making. The walls were constructed of half-
trimmed tree branches bound together with mismatched ropes and
ties: braided strips of plastic, twisted vines, strips of cloth, even a few
thin chains. And of course, the highlight of the entire design was its
lack of roof. The furniture was mismatched as well, chairs and table
and a narrow chest of drawers made from different synthetic materials,
each piece looking like it had been salvaged from a different low-rent
office. The cot she was lying on was a study in salvage art, the frame of
a rolling cart topped with a webwork of mismatched plastic strips.
*PROPERTY OF LAB 5* was printed on one of them, *KEEP OUT* on
another. As an outrider, she recognized the significance of the haphazard construction. The owners did not intend to stay in this place. It was
important for them to believe they would not have to stay here. This
ramshackle place was a cry of defiance.

But where was *here*?

She reached into her pocket to check for her weapons, only to discover that she had no pockets. Or coat, for that matter. Someone must
have removed her outer clothing while she was unconscious, along with
every item she'd been carrying. Not good. The only things she still had
on were her boots, her jumpsuit, her headset—they would have needed
a passkey to release the maglocks on that—and her rings. She was surprised about the rings, but evidently whoever had stripped her of all
her other gear didn't realize what they were. And the heels of her boots
didn't look like they'd been opened, which meant the tools in there
were safe as well. After a moment's consideration, she decided to leave
them hidden for now, in case someone was watching.

One leg of her jumpsuit had been rolled up, revealing a clearflesh
dressing where the arrow had struck her. The area under it was sore but
didn't have the telltale tenderness of an infection. She rolled down the
jumpsuit leg and swung her feet over the side of the makeshift cot.
Standing up turned out to be harder than expected. For a moment the

hut swam around her, and she had to grab the nearest wall for support while she waited for her vision to settle. Finally, when she thought she could move without throwing up, she began to inch her way to the only visible exit, a narrow opening with a tarp hung across it. Doorway to the unknown. The thought brought a rush of excitement. Novelty, as always, was a heady elixir.

She pushed the makeshift curtain aside.

The hut was in a small clearing, surrounded by a forest of sorts. Tall blue trees were spaced around the periphery with unnatural regularity, patches of shrubbery evenly spaced between them. Not the sort of thing one expected to find on a space station. There was a person present, sitting in a plastic office chair, watching her as she stepped down from the threshold: the man who had saved her. Now that her vision was clear she could see that his clawed headset was shaped to fit over two bony crests arching back over his skull from brow to nape. His clothing had probably been black once, but time and wear had reduced his jumpsuit and flight jacket to a mottled gray. The soles of his heavily scuffed boots were thick enough to contain mag plates, and his wide belt had utility rings hanging from it, both standard accessories in a no-G environment. Most ships these days had some kind of grav net, so the fact that he was outfitted to travel without one was . . . interesting.

Her possessions were laid out on a small table beside him. Coat, shock rod, and all the basic supplies from her pockets, neatly arranged for inspection. Her ID wallet lay open, next to a flask of amber-colored fluid and a rack of empty test tubes. The shock gun, however, was gone.

"Up at last," he observed gruffly.

She rubbed her forehead, trying to massage away the last of the ache. "Where am I?"

"Biome Five. My personal haven, such as it is. You're goddamn lucky to be alive, girl." He nodded toward her coat. "That's grade-A armor you had on. Without it . . ." He shook his head and made a tsk-tsk noise. She started toward the table, but he raised a hand to warn her back. "Not yet . . . let's see, what's your name?" He peered at her ID. "Ru? Bounty hunter, fourth class. Okay, let's have a little chat first, bounty hunter fourth class Ru. I go by Ivar. And you're welcome for saving your life, by the way."

She stared at him for a moment, briefly contemplating which she'd rather do more: grab for her weapons or smack him in his arrogant face. Neither was likely to improve the situation, so she just muttered, "Thank you."

He took up one of the test tubes, poured some of the amber liquid into it, and offered it to her. After a moment she took it and sniffed it. Alcohol of some type. Strong. Wary of being drugged, she pretend-sipped it as he returned to his office chair. He waved her toward a fallen tree trunk. "Please, hunter Ru. Sit."

She would have preferred to stand, but her legs still felt weak, so she lowered herself down onto the rough bark, trying to look stronger than she felt. "Are we still on Shenshido?"

"*Everyone's* still on Shenshido. For two years now. That's kind of the point." He poured himself a vial of the yellow stuff.

"What happened here?"

"Let's just say if there is a God, he fucked this place over good." He swallowed his test tube's contents in a single long gulp and winced.

"And the atheist explanation?"

"Idiots upstairs were playing with something they shouldn't have, and it bit them on the ass. At least that's the story I was given. I'm not a scientist myself, so this is all second hand." He poured himself another drink as he talked. "People in one of the main labs went crazy. Got violent. The few that weren't affected fled from the crazy ones. Some fled the station, but they didn't make it far. Or maybe they did make it, but never told anyone in the outside world what was going on here." He paused. "Or maybe no one in the outside world gives a fuck what happens here. Communications are out, so once the last ships left, everyone else here was fucked."

*The communications equipment in the engineering center looked functional enough when I was there,* she thought. Granted, she hadn't tried to contact any other stations, but still. Something in his story wasn't adding up.

"You said a ship would be coming for you," he said. There was an edge to his tone now, cold and hungry. "That seems a strange arrangement. I'd think you'd want it docked here, ready to go."

"The docking ring's a mess," she said. That part was certainly true. She didn't trust him enough to tell him the rest of it—that she was here alone and her ship was moored to the station, unguarded. Never mind that if he got to it he wouldn't be able to get through her security; it was what he might do to get to it that worried her. "My pilot didn't trust the mooring options, so he offered to keep her in a holding pattern until I found our target."

"And did you?"

"Not yet." She shrugged. "Some leads pan out, some don't."

"He's dangerous, this guy?"

"Killed a few members of his family. Bloody mess." She looked at the test tube in her hand. What the hell. She really could use a drink. The alcohol tasted acidic, and it burned her throat going down though it felt good spreading through her veins. She closed her eyes for a moment, savoring the sensation.

"You can call the ship back when you're ready to leave? Or what? Is there some kind of schedule you set up?"

*Too curious*, she thought. The echo of desperation in his voice wasn't an issue—if he'd really been stuck on this crazy station for two years, what else would one expect?—but there was something else there, a darkness behind the words, that made her doubly wary. *You'd hijack my ship if you could, I'll bet. Fly off and leave me here, stranded with the others.* It was just a feeling, but years of outriding had taught her to trust her feelings. "We made arrangements," she hedged.

"And I suppose when you get home you'll tell the Guild what happened here? So they can send out a rescue team?"

Was that what she would do? Tridac owned the place and should be in charge of rescuing anyone stranded here. But would they do that? Or would they find it cheaper and easier to just cleanse the place, making the whole problem go away? If the scientists here had been working on any kind of secret project, the latter seemed more likely. If she told the Guild first, instead, Shenshido's situation would at least become part of the public record. Tridac would no longer be able to act in the shadows, and fear of negative publicity might save some lives. "That seems the best way to go."

He leaned forward intently. "And what if someone wanted to get off the station before they arrived?"

Her eyes narrowed. "Meaning what?"

"Meaning, I'm sure there's room on your ship for at least one other person. Meaning, if you take me with you when you leave, I'll make it worth your while. Cash, contraband, labor debt. Name your poison."

"You know that I work for law enforcement," she said quietly.

"I know that you're working for them *now*. One job." He poured himself another drink. "You're a mercenary, same as me. And don't worry, there's no price on my head. Check it out, if you want. I'll wait." He leaned back in his chair again, drinking from his test tube as he gave her a moment to access the innernet. Was that a bluff? An independent station was unlikely to have up-to-date records from Gueran law enforcement, so even if she couldn't find anything in its files that mentioned Ivar, that didn't mean anything. She bluffed back, staring into space for a moment as if she were communing with the station's data system; let him worry about what she might discover.

"Whatever they're paying you for this job," he said finally, interrupting her fake reverie, "I'll pay you ten times that much to take me with you to wherever you're going, and drop me off first thing."

"And the other people here?"

He shrugged. "A few more days of waiting won't kill them."

*So much for group loyalty. What's your connection to them?* She was burning with questions, but sensed that if she interrogated him too directly he might shut down. *What are you so afraid of, that you need to get away before the rescue team arrives?* His offer of labor debt in payment—slaves—suggested some pretty dark dealings, and blatant interrogation might rub him the wrong way. And she needed his help. The station map didn't distinguish between the various sections of the lower levels, so without someone's help she wasn't going to be able to get back to her ship. Hell, she couldn't even find a flight of stairs, other than by walking around randomly and searching.

"Let me think about it," she said carefully.

He didn't look pleased by her response, nor did he look surprised. A man who traded in contraband and slaves was probably used to people not trusting him. "Well. I suppose with that said, it's time you met the others."

*About time.* "Can I get my gear back first?"

He considered for a moment, then nodded toward the table. She put her coat back on and stowed all her accessories where they belonged, piece by piece, while he watched.

"My gun?" she asked.

"Consider it the cost of being rescued."

She opened her mouth to protest . . . but hell, he had saved her life. Fair was fair.

He led her to a path that cut through the forest. Most of the trees and brush were evenly spaced—obviously planted—but now and then she saw dense thickets of brush flanking the path. Probably blinds. "You expecting an attack?" she asked.

He shrugged. "Crazies haven't come down here yet. If they do, they'll get more than they bargained for."

Soon human voices were audible, and the path disgorged them into an open field, maybe half a mile across. In its center was a stockade of rough-hewn timber, easily twice Ru's height, surrounded by neatly ordered gardens. There were several people working those gardens, dressed in lab uniforms with short-sleeved shirts and drawstring pants in a dull blue-gray. They looked up when they heard people approaching, and tensed at the sight of Ru. How long had it been since they had last seen a stranger? The nearest ones backed away nervously as Ivar led her toward the compound's gate. God alone knew what they thought she was capable of.

Inside the compound, small huts were huddled together in groups, narrow paths wending between them. A few larger shelters stood apart from the others, and Ivar directed her toward one of those. The whole place looked primitive, but that didn't surprise her. She'd seen enough worlds in the course of her outrider duties to know that even the most advanced colony could devolve to a primitive state, if circumstances warranted. And here they clearly had.

*Upstairs there's a station full of clean modern rooms,* she thought. *The inner ring is probably full of vacant apartments. Why did they come down here, instead of claiming some of that space?*

The house Ivar led her to had a real wooden door, clearly a luxury here. He knocked on it.

"Come in," a woman's voice said from within.

The interior lacked the rummage-sale quality of Ivar's abode, though the roof was the same open framework. A table, several chairs, a bed, and a chest had been hewn from natural wood, and there were even a few decorative pieces on the walls. On a table Ru saw pieces of pottery, rustic in design, and the small rug on the floor looked handcrafted. If the message of Ivar's hut had been *Fuck it, I'm not staying here!* the message of this one was, *Well, if I'm stuck here, I'm going to make the best of it.*

A tall red-headed woman stood as they entered. Like everyone else here she was dressed in lab clothes, but she'd torn the sleeves off to reveal smoothly muscled arms with colorful tattoos. Thorned roses on one arm, a dragon on the other.

Ivar nodded respectfully to her. "This is Ru Gaya, the one we found upstairs." He looked at Ru. "This is Zevi, chief of the Seventh Collective."

Ru bowed her head slightly, as he had done. "Honored."

There was a moment of silence as Zevi looked her over. Her gaze rested briefly on the places on Ru's body where weapons might be hidden. "Ivar vouches for you," she said at last.

"I'm grateful for that."

"He says you're an independent. Bounty hunter."

Ru nodded. "That's right."

"So you have a ship."

"It wasn't able to dock." Maybe someday she would trust someone here enough to tell them the truth. "It'll be coming back for me later."

Zevi's eyes narrowed. "You understand our situation here?"

"Enough to know you need evacuation. My ship's too small to handle all of you. But I promise, once I return to Harmony I'll get a rescue team out here."

"We've waited a long time for help."

"Two fucking years," Ivar muttered.

The angle of light in the room shifted suddenly. It took Ru a moment to realize that the solar lamps overhead must have changed their settings, imitating the motion of a sun across the faux sky. When 'night' fell, would it get dark?

"But I'm being a poor host," Zevi said. She gestured toward the table and chairs. "Please, sit. Have something to eat. It's not great food, but it'll fill the stomach."

God alone knew how long it had been since Ru last ate. She sat down gratefully and tore a piece of bread from a grayish loaf. It was dry and bland, but her stomach welcomed it. Zevi poured her a cup of what turned out to be totally tasteless water. Probably distilled. Seeing the question in her eyes, Zevi said, "We tap into irrigation for it, so it has to be filtered. Not exactly vintage wine. Biome Four supplied us with grain, and we have more leafy plants than we know what to do with, but not much else."

"No protein?" Ru asked.

"Not down here," Ivar said. "Not unless we want to eat each other."

Zevi scowled at him. "There were insects, but once they died that resource was gone. Everything down here was bred for experiments, and carefully controlled; no animal or insect species was allowed to reproduce on its own. So they're all gone now, save for the plants you see. We have to pollinate the crops ourselves."

"Aren't there emergency supplies?" Ru asked. "A station like this should store enough food to support its population for a long time."

"Yeah. But that's all upstairs, and the crazies are guarding them. Can't hardly blame 'em. Resources are finite, and there's been no hope of relief." She looked pointedly at Ru. "Until now."

"How many people on the station?" Ru asked.

"There were nearly a thousand when all this began. Now we estimate two dozen of the crazies left upstairs. Maybe fewer than that. Down here . . ." A muscle along her jaw tightened. "Eighteen. We're down to eighteen station personnel left, plus this one came from the outside." She nodded toward Ivar.

"It's been a long war," he said quietly.

*So many deaths. Each person here must have done their share of killing.* "How did you come to this point, exactly? Ivar didn't give me many details."

Zevi tore off a piece of bread for herself. "The trouble started in one of the lab sections. Nothing big at first. Reports misplaced. Data misread. Just a few more errors than usual; nothing to set off any alarms. Then some people started acting erratically. Hot-tempered. Disoriented. And then more people. By the time the folks in charge realized something was seriously wrong, nearly everyone in that particular section had been affected. Soon it started affecting them in body, as well. Flesh wasted away, skin turned the color of rot, sometimes it fell away altogether. They looked horrific."

Ivar nodded grimly. "Like fucking zombies."

"We couldn't call for help right away. We had to lock down the station and confirm it wasn't a contagious condition first. That's standard corporate protocol. Meanwhile, the affected ones lost any semblance of sanity. We locked them up for their own safety, but they managed to break out. Started attacking people. Labs were trashed. Equipment was gutted. By the time it was confirmed that their condition wasn't contagious, so we could call for outside help, our communications equipment had failed. Maintenance couldn't figure out why. Some of the healthy workers tried to flee the station at that point, but there weren't enough ships for everyone. The ones who left promised to send transports back for the rest of us, but we never heard from them again."

*There wasn't anything in Jericho's files about a mass exodus,* Ru mused. *Which suggests that those who tried to leave never reached their destination.* "I'm not sure a full-sized transport would be able to dock here."

"Yeah. You can thank the scavs for that." She spat. "Fucking vultures. Ever since Shido went down they've been picking at this station, tearing it apart piece by piece. Damn megacorps were too busy arguing about who should profit from the station to deal with them effectively. Every problem was always someone else's job. Well, they finally put a security system in place, but you saw what the station looks like. And yeah, that played a part in all this. It's hard to evacuate people from a station when you only have one working dock."

Ru looked at Ivar. "What happened to your ship?"

There was a brief hesitation. "Commandeered during the exodus."

"I'm surprised you let that happen."

"It was a fucking mob. I'm good, but I'm not *that* good." He pulled open his shirt collar to bare his neck; there was an ugly scar on one side of it. "Wages of battle."

"The crazies are afraid to enter the biomes," Zevi said. "We're not sure why, but at least it gives us some breathing space. But someday they'll get their courage up and come down here. We're preparing for it as best we can, but . . ." She shook her head, her expression grim. "It's going to be bloody."

"Do you have high-tech weapons?"

She shook her head. "What few were on the station were locked away in Security. That's part of the main Engineering suite, which no one can get into. So we jury-rig what we can from components we salvage. But the high-tech stuff doesn't work reliably. We've captured enough of the enemy's weapons to know they have the same problem." She smiled wryly. "In contrast, a sharpened stick *always* works."

"When you say Engineering, do you mean the complex on the top level, on the ainniq side of the station? Why can't you get in there?"

"Dunno. That whole sector is shut down. Maybe some kind of automatic defense. Or maybe the people who fled the station did that on their way out. The doors are all locked, emergency hatches sealed, and the equipment we'd need to break through is stored inside the complex. Which I suppose is a blessing, given what would happen to us if the crazies broke in there."

"They keep it under constant guard," Ivar said. "Our people can't even get near that part of the station safely." His eyes narrowed slightly. "What's your interest in Engineering?"

The last thing she wanted him to know was that her ship was moored there, but she would need help finding her way back to it, so she had to tell him something. *I was there,* she thought. *None of the doors were locked, no hatches were sealed, and there wasn't a guard to be seen.* It was like they were describing something on another station. In another universe. "I was hoping to use that equipment to call my ship back," she said.

"There are other communication nodes on the station," Zevi offered. "None of them have been able to send a signal off-station, but if your ship is right here—"

"It might be enough," Ru said.

Zevi looked at Ivar. Something passed between them that might have been netted communication. Or perhaps just the unspoken rapport of warriors. "You'd have go through the crazies' territory to get to one of the other nodes."

Ru nodded.

"We're heading upstairs tomorrow. Our scouts have located a small supply cache on the second level, which they think may not be heavily guarded. We need people to help raid that cache. And you need a team to get you to one of the nodes safely. Perhaps . . . an exchange of support?"

"You won't need supplies, if a rescue team comes."

"*If* it comes," Zevi said harshly. "Remember, we've been promised rescue before. And I'm sure when they said that, they believed that it would happen. So, with all due respect, until a fleet of transports actually shows up at our door, it's going to be business as usual here. And we need those supplies."

"So what are you asking me to do?" Ru asked. "Kill people?"

Zevi shook her head. "Just help us retrieve the supplies. We need to do this on foot, to move quickly, so that means we can only take what we can carry. You coming means we'll have one more backpack to fill." When Ru didn't respond she pressed, "We'll help you get to a communications hub after that. Favor for favor."

*You'll help me get to the hub whether I join your raid or not, because that's your only hope of rescue.* Ru didn't need to go with them. Didn't need to embrace a high-risk journey, invading the territory of a band of murderous half-crazed Terrans, deep in the shadows of a derelict station where so many things just didn't make sense.

She felt the same rush that she had back in Ivar's hut, only ten times stronger: curiosity, excitement, elation. She couldn't deny that her restless soul, always hungry for novelty, was drawn to this task—not *despite* the risk, but *because* of it.

The only thing in the world that she really feared was boredom.

"Count me in," she told Zevi.

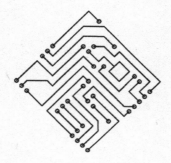

Tired of dull, boring meals? Longing for food that will elevate your spirit? Our new Deluxe Rainbow Burger features two cultivated beef patties with an array of colorful toppings. It's a feast for all the senses! Add an order of Happy Crisps and a Krazy Kat drink, for a meal that is sure to excite your taste buds and energize your spirit!

TASTE OF KAWAII—because food should make you happy!

# HARMONY NODE
# SHENSHIDO STATION

JAMAL'S HAVEN turned out to be several labs and storage rooms combined into one large space by the crude but effective method of smashing through the walls between them. There were broken fragments of plasteel supports sticking out of the nearest opening like teeth, which reminded Micah of his dream back on Tridac Station. A day ago? A year? The period before his flight was becoming blurred in his mind, his sense of time dulled by mental and physical exhaustion.

That the people here were prepared for trouble was clear. The windows that looked out on the corridor had been blocked by a wall of furniture and rugs. Against another wall was a rack with an assortment of makeshift weapons, most of them simple blade-based designs. There were a few gun-shaped pieces, but their shapes were odd enough that Micah wasn't sure what they would fire. Next to the rack was another with pieces of armor draped over it, the same type Jamal was wearing: mismatched strips that lapped over one another, creating a flexible carapace.

One of the labs had been converted into a workshop, with several large tables surrounded by racks of tools. There were broken pieces of furniture and fragments of walls and ceilings arranged on racks, many made of the same material as the armor. At one table a man in protective goggles was using a primitive torch to burn his way through the back of a chair, rectangular strips from his earlier harvests laid out before him. The smell of charred plastic wafted over to Micah, making his nostrils burn. At another table was a dark-skinned man dumping out the contents of cleaning bots, studying each pile closely as he did so. Clearly something in the dirt was of great importance.

There were a dozen men and women visible, with the sounds of a few more coming from parts of the haven that Micah couldn't see. They all looked like Terrans, which was no big surprise. Several were wearing armor like Jamal's, while others wore mismatched garments that looked like they'd been salvaged from a dozen different labs. Some wore brightly colored T-shirts emblazoned with advertising logos that Micah recognized from the food court. Clothing was where you found it, apparently.

Everybody stared at him as he entered, of course. It wasn't just curiosity. There was an alertness to them, a fearful energy, as if they expected he might grab a weapon and start shooting people at any moment. Indeed, one of the women positioned herself between him and the weapons rack, perhaps fearful that he would rush toward it. But though their expressions were hard, the souls that peered out through their eyes looked more weary than hostile.

"This is Micah Bello," Jamal announced. "I found him in sector five. Also found this." He held up the broken arrow. "There seems to have been some kind of fight there. None of our people are reporting any confrontations, so if someone died, it wasn't one of ours."

"Maybe the mors are fighting each other," one woman muttered.

A man in a purple t-shirt with *Happy Cakes* scrawled across the front laughed harshly. "We should be so lucky."

A tall man in black armor walked up to Micah, studying him from top to bottom like he was a slab of meat. There was a long, nasty-looking machete hanging from his belt.

"This is Serjit," Jamal said. "He's in charge of the haven."

Quietly Serjit said, "How did you get here, Bello?"

All the way here, Micah had been thinking about how he was going to explain that. Telling them that he was a fugitive from the same corporation that probably paid their salaries—back when they got salaries—seemed like a uniquely bad idea. "I was on my way to Harmony when my navigator malfunctioned. I didn't want to risk going any further without repairs, so I headed for the nearest station. Turned out to be Shenshido. Only the docks were too damaged to use, and my navigation was barely functional. So I had a choice between crashing into the station, riding my ship into the depths of space, or evacuating. I went for option C."

"An impressive feat, if true." Serjit looked at Jamal. "Have you confirmed any of this?"

"With what equipment? Look, he's obviously not exo. Who else is on this station, besides them and us?"

Serjit peered at Micah. Then he reached out a hand toward his face. Micah instinctively backed away.

"He wants to confirm you're not exo," Jamal said.

*And it would be nice if you told me what the procedure for that was.* But it wasn't like he had much of a choice at this point. He stood still while Serjit felt his cheeks, kneading them with his fingertips. Finally Serjit nodded. "He's clean."

"May I ask what that was about?" Micah asked.

"The exos suffer from a parasitic infection that gives their skin a bark-like texture," Jamal told him. "Normally you can see it on the face, but he's checking to see if maybe something is developing that isn't visible yet. Apparently you're good."

Mutated humans with bark faces. How would bark faces even move? It sounded like something from a badly designed fantasy epic. "You talked about *mors*. What are those?"

"Same as exos. It's short for *morlocks*. A somewhat obscure reference—"

"From Old Earth literature," Micah said. "H. G. Wells. I used them in one of my games, *The End of Time*." *The fact that I was born on a space station doesn't mean I'm ignorant of Terran literary traditions.*

"*The End of Time*?" The speaker was a young woman in a pink T-shirt that said SHIDO CAFE. "Oh my God, did you design that?"

He couldn't help but smile. "I was lead developer for it."

Serjit sharply looked at her. "You know him?"

"I know *of* him. One of the best game designers in the business." She sighed. "His virts are amazing. Like stepping into another world."

"So." Serjit's mouth twitched. "We have a celebrity in our midst."

Micah shrugged. "I'm just a guy looking for a way home, like everyone else here."

"Well," Jamal said, "you're welcome to shelter with us. And given what's out there, I recommend you accept the offer." He nodded to the woman in the SHIDO CAFÉ shirt. "Rose, why don't you help him get settled in? Introduce him to everyone, get him some food, show him where he can clean up."

"Thank you so much," Micah said.

"Don't thank us," Serjit snapped. "It's not a favor. You'll be expected to contribute your skills to the group, same as everyone else." He shook his head. "Though I'm afraid we're not much in need of games."

*No,* Micah thought. *But if I ever get out of here, this crazy place may wind up in one.*

**R**ose introduced him to everyone, but there were too many names and faces to remember, or maybe he was just too tired to memorize anything. He instructed his headset to record everything he saw, to go over later. They offered him food, but he found that the events of the last day had unsettled his stomach enough that it was hard to eat. He nibbled just enough to realize that their replicator must be running low on ingredients, because everything tasted the same.

"You'll get used to it," one of the women whispered to him, and he shuddered. He didn't want to be here long enough to get used to anything.

Then Rose showed him the bath stall, and he said yes, he'd like to clean up. And that part was bliss. As he peeled off his sweat-soaked clothing, he felt like he was shedding a skin, allowing a new, fresher Micah to emerge. The bath itself was a bit challenging, as the sonic cleaner wasn't working and water was being rationed, but he managed to scrub enough sweat off his body to feel human again, and—more important—to smell human. No doubt the people in the haven would be grateful for that.

When he went to retrieve his clothing, however, he discovered someone had taken it. In its place was a worn pair of jeans about his size and a bright pink T-shirt. The latter had cartoon kittens on it, along with the words KAWAII HAI! He stared at it for a moment, then turned it inside out and put it on. *Sorry, cats. Not in the mood for cuteness today.*

Rose was waiting for him outside the bath enclosure. "Your clothes are being cleaned," she told him. She glanced at his bare forearms as she spoke, her gaze lingering briefly on his Sarkassan markings. To Terran eyes they were probably exotic. "You know, I read your article on the emotive power of air pressure, and it was amazing. The thought that something so subtle could influence human behavior . . . it's hard to fathom."

"We were programmed by evolution to respond to a particular planetary environment. Even here, in the outworlds, those instincts persist. A well-designed virt—" He stopped suddenly, and flushed. "I'm sorry, I'm lecturing you."

"It's okay." She smiled. "You're just trying to distract yourself. I get it. If you can focus on something that interests you, you don't have to think about what's out there." She nodded toward the blockaded windows. "At least for a while."

Suddenly a whooping cry sounded from one of the worktables. It was the man who'd been disassembling the cleaning bots. There were a dozen of them laid out on his table now, each with its own little mound of dust in front of it. "Yes!" he cried. "That's it!"

They all gathered around the table to see what was happening. To

Micah the dust mounds just looked like . . . well, dust mounds. But everyone else seemed excited about them.

"What did you find?" Jamal asked.

The dust man picked something out of one mound with a long pair of tweezers and held it up high, so that everyone could see. "It's a seed. A fucking *seed*!"

"From where?" Serjit asked.

"Corridors B-54 and 55." The man grinned. "Right where we thought the mors would show up." He pointed toward the nearest dust pile with his tweezers. "There are a few bits of soil in there, too, and a fiber that I think may be organic. It's possible a full scouting party passed through there."

Serjit nodded tightly. "We've hit them hard lately. They're likely not keen on traveling alone." He straightened up and looked around the room, waiting until everyone's attention was focused on him. "Okay, people. The mors took our bait. You all know what that means. You know how high the stakes are. Let's give it . . ." he paused to consult his internal clock, "one hour. That should be enough time for everyone to gear up, and still get us to B-54 before they arrive." His lips tightened. "Let's end this thing!"

Suddenly everyone was moving quickly: fetching weapons, donning armor, throwing orders around in a lingo Micah didn't recognize. It was clear they had drilled this prep many times, and Micah thought it best just to get out of their way. But as he tried to back into a quiet corner, a hand fell on his shoulder.

"Let's talk," Serjit said.

Micah nodded.

"I told you when you arrived you would be expected to do your part. Now's a good time. We need all the hands we can get."

Micah felt a sinking in his stomach. "For what, exactly?"

"Ambush. We've set up a trap for the mors, and it sounds like they've taken the bait." He nodded back toward the table. "They shelter down in Bio, so whenever they come up here they track bits of organic matter with them. It leaves a trail for the cleaning bots to collect. So we know where they've been, and can guess where they'll go next."

"You want me to help you . . . kill people?"

Serjit's eyes narrowed. "It's that or be killed. The mors don't leave us any other option."

He tried to picture what it would be like to spill a man's blood. *Real* blood. To know that as it flowed it was carrying away a man's life, not just ruining his chance at a gaming championship. "I'm not a killer," he muttered.

"None of us were killers when we got here. Survival's a harsh motivator."

Micah's lips tightened, but he said nothing. Serjit looked into his eyes for a moment, then nodded. "All right. There are other things you can do. Help the wounded. Recover the fallen. Leave the killing to those of us who've had friends and family murdered by these cannibals. I assure you, *we* won't have any trouble shedding their blood." When Micah still didn't respond Serjit's expression darkened. "Or you can leave us, and go it alone." He nodded back toward the door. "No one's stopping you."

Oh, he wanted to leave. He wanted more than anything else to get out of this crazy war zone, to get far, far away from both arrow-wielding bark-mutants and the people who wanted to slaughter them. But then he would be alone in this station, without allies or supplies, waiting for exos to find him. Or for the vines to get him. Or a man-sized monster with claws.

*Sometimes choice is an illusion,* he thought grimly. *Does that make it easier or harder?* "I'll do what I can to help," he said. "But I won't kill people."

"Good enough, then." He nodded toward the racks. "Jamal will help you suit up. Tell him you're running support."

And then he headed off to the racks himself, to don insectoid armor and choose a weapon suitable for killing.

*Holy shit,* Micah thought. *What have I got myself into?*

What will our rhythmic milestones be, in this dark frontier? Bereft of solstice or season, harvest or tide, what events will we gather to celebrate? When our calendar is no more than a sequence of sterile numbers, and the orbiting of sun and moon have faded from memory, what excuses will we find to gather as a people, to reinforce the social bonds that are as necessary to human beings as food and water?

SOLAN GETTYSBURG
*The Deep Space Paradox (Gueran Archives,*
*Tiananmen Station)*

# HARMONY NODE
# HARMONY STATION

THE CASINO was full, as it had been every night that week. Since it was an elegant place the customers were all dressed elegantly, velvet gowns and spidersilk suits flowing in ripples of color beneath crystal chandeliers as facets of reflected light danced about them.

Thirty-two chandeliers in all. One thousand and sixty-four crystals on each one. Thirty-six facets on each crystal.

"Sir."

Guildmaster Kohl Dresden turned back from his vantage point on the balcony. His assistant was wearing a stylish tunic with twelve buttons down the front, and a hair clasp with thirteen rhinestones. There were three repeats of the geometric pattern on the carpet between them, and five sconces visible on the wall beside them. The flow of numbers was like background music inside his head: constant, soothing. "Yes?"

"Guildmistress Vienna is here to see you."

Sparing one last approving look for the scene below, he headed to his office, where Raija Vienna was indeed waiting. She was wearing traditional Guild attire identical to his own, a flowing black robe that masked the outline of her body. Her naturally red hair was plaited into dozens of slender braids, which had been artfully woven around a complex head-dress, the combination full of loops and whorls. It must have taken her hours to arrange. No, correction: it must have taken someone else hours to arrange. Her kaja was mainly *yakimi,* suggesting a love of speculation. Perhaps it was intended to honor the setting. "Mistress Vienna." He nod-ded graciously and smiled. "To what do I owe this pleasure?"

"I've come for the Harvester Festival, and thought I should pay my respects. This casino is lovely. Is it yours?"

"Co-owner. But I can't take credit for the decorating, that was Desi." *Though I did insist that the mathematical proportions be pleas-ing.* "Can I offer you a drink? Specialty of the house is a spiced pome-granate liqueur. Made with natural pomegranates, not the replicated kind. Fresh from Harmony's own gardens."

"Thank you." She smiled pleasantly. "I'd love to try one."

He flashed an order to his assistant, who sent him a confirmation icon in return. "Please, sit, relax." He gestured to a plush autocouch. As she sat down it whirred softly, adapting its cushions to her body shape. He chose a matching chair that did likewise. "Things in Prosperity Node are going well, I hope?"

She laughed softly. "Challenging, as always. I'm more than ready for a vacation."

"Then I'm glad we could offer you an excuse for one." Even as he smiled the vacuous smile of a good host, he thought, *Why are you really here?* Guildmasters rarely did anything without deeper motive. Though he and Vienna were equal to one another in rank, and served the same vision—the Guild's dream of a united humanity colonizing the galaxy—that very purpose made them rivals. Resources in the outworlds were limited, and Vienna's node, like his own, had no nearby solar system to provide it with raw materials. Every element that their stations required must be shipped across vast distances, at great cost. Few investors were willing to commit to that, and any contract that Harmony won, other nodes would not win. Gain for one of them meant loss for the other.

*Nature is red in tooth and claw,* an ancient Terran poet had once proclaimed. It was no less true in Guild politics than it had been on the plains of Old Africa. And Vienna was a skilled player. He'd already lost one valuable corporate contract to her. Now she was here, on Harmony, "for a vacation." Not damn likely.

"I'm so glad you decided to go ahead with the Festival," she said. "Given recent events, I was worried you might have to cancel."

He netted a query to his archivist, asking him to find out who she'd brought with her. "You mean the attack on the station?"

"Yes. How frightening. Aren't you concerned there might be another assault during the Festival?"

Her delicately probing words scraped his nerves like fingernails on slate. "It's been dealt with."

An eyebrow lifted. "You know who was behind it?"

"He's been dealt with." *Assuming Tridac is playing straight with me,* he thought, *and that they got the right man.* If not, then whoever planned the attack was still out there and might well strike again. The thought of its happening during the Festival was unnerving, but what choice did he have? The damage to his reputation if he canceled celebrations this late in the game—and the cost to Harmony's future—would be incalculable.

His assistant came in with two glasses of crimson liqueur and handed one to each of them. The glasses themselves were quite beautiful, with a delicate fractal pattern engraved around the lip. (Sixty segments: it was one of Dresden's favorite numbers.) She held hers up to the light for a moment, admiring the workmanship, then tasted the liqueur. Conveniently, Dresden's archivist chose that moment to deliver his research, so the Guildmaster had time to focus on the words that appeared in his field of vision.

RETINUE OF NINE, ALL GUILD: EXEC. SECY, P. ASSISTANT, ARCHIVIST, 4 DATA AQUISITIONS, 1 RANK UNIDENTIFIED. YOU WANT NAMES?

*Data acquisitions.* Those would be her hackers. His mind whirred, trying to piece the puzzle together quickly, so that she wouldn't sense his distraction. Why bring hackers with her if this was just a vacation? Clearly it was more than that.

She looked up at him with a smile. "It's delicious."

Somehow he managed to keep his face from betraying his growing tension. Somehow he managed to smile back and say, "We're very proud of it." As if nothing else was going on. As if they didn't both know that if anything went wrong this week, those investors who had shown interest in Harmony would surely turn their eyes to another node . . . perhaps her own. Was it possible she had come to sabotage the Festival? He remembered her question about canceling the event. Might she even be connected to the Dragonslayer incident? Another random explosion would be the perfect way to bring him down—

*No,* he thought. *No Guild officer would ever orchestrate an attack on a station like that.* Such a crime would be seen as betrayal of the Guild, and the last officer who had betrayed the Guild had been sealed in a pod and shot into the ainniq, to be devoured alive by the creatures that lived there. She wouldn't risk that just to gain political advantage. But some more subtle gambit . . . that was very possible.

"I'm curious about your plan to alter the data protocols," she said.

He was alert now. "What about it?"

"You don't think that's risky? Surely there are businesses who wouldn't want their communications delayed. They might not take kindly to your interference."

He put his glass down on a side table. "In a few days this station will be filled to the brim with visitors: tourists, reporters, scientists, vid producers, you name it. News agencies will livecast the arrival of the harvester fleet. Schools have requested realtime feed of it. So have observatories. Add to that the countless spectators who will want to stream the spectacle back home to their loved ones, and you're talking about more data than the station can compress and transmit in a timely manner. I'm simply giving priority to outbound traffic. Opening the floodgates, as it were, so the tsunami can pass through unimpeded. Yes, inbound data will be slow for a few days—that's unavoidable—but it's a small price to pay to keep everything running smoothly."

*Is that what you came for, why you brought your hackers with you? To study the tsunami, perhaps to manipulate it?* He would have to set his own team to watching her people, which pissed him off, because it meant he would have to pull them away from other important business. Maybe that was her plan—to nurture paranoia in him, so that he would start making mistakes. He had to work at keeping the smile on his face.

"I suppose that makes sense," she said.

There was other talk after that. Small talk, empty talk, meaningless social repartée that he fielded automatically. His mind was no longer in the conversation. It was not on Harmony at all. He was remembering a trip he had taken two years prior, when he'd accepted an invitation from Tridac Enterprises to check out the damage that had been done to Shenshido Station. Scavs had literally torn the place apart, making it hard to even find a place to dock. If the station had belonged to him he'd probably have stripped it down for raw materials, but the man from Tridac (what was his name again, Khatry something? Gatry?) saw potential in it. Whatever. Corporate business was of little concern to Dresden.

It was while he was on the observation deck of the inner ring that he'd had a vision. He could see the coming Festival in his mind's eye, could hear its music, could feel its myriad rhythms pulsing in his veins. And he could see a great wave of data gathering, as every man, woman, and child on the station sent outgoing messages at the same time— more data than Harmony's network could possibly handle. Would it crash, and take all connectivity with it? Might the outernet itself fail, casting Harmony Station into digital darkness? In his vision he saw himself ordering a change in data protocols as the great wave bore down on him, opening the digital floodgates so it could thunder through.

He had understood, in that moment, what was required to keep Harmony functioning. And in the months that followed, as plans for the Harvest Festival took shape, that vision had remained clear in his mind. Others might question its wisdom—indeed they did!—but he had *seen* the truth, as clearly as he was now seeing this room that surrounded him. And they would see it, too. The day would come when the floodgates would open, and they would understand why this had been necessary. His name would be praised, his foresight would be celebrated, and Terran corporations seeking to establish themselves in the outworlds would choose Harmony Node for their headquarters.

He had seen a vision of that too, while on Shenshido.

*Soon,* he told himself, as he traded meaningless pleasantries with his rival. *Soon they will all understand.*

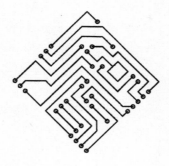

Those territorial instincts which we so casually disown—
blaming our animal origins for their existence, citing civilization as the cure—were never truly eradicated. We may
repress them, deny them, redirect them into more acceptable channels, but they remain part of our nature, always
awaiting the catalyst that will free them.

SANJAR RANIYA
*The Shadow Within*

# HARMONY NODE
# SHENSHIDO STATION

THEY OFFERED Ru weapons. Most were hand-held items of wood or salvaged plasteel, plus a few pipes and axes from Bio's maintenance stores. Some of the sharper items were tipped in black poison—which she was warned not to touch—and others were studded with scalpel blades, glass fragments, anything that was small and sharp and could be embedded in wood. There were a few projectile weapons that looked like guns but fired sleek bolts—poisoned, of course. They weren't accurate at a distance and couldn't pierce heavy armor, so they seemed of limited value to her, but she took one anyway, just to have something that could function at range. Now that Ivar had taken her gun, the only weapons she had left were meant for hand-to-hand combat, and her goal was never to get that close to someone who wanted to kill her.

There were no charge weapons available. No explosives. No sonics. Though the bios (as she had come to call Zevi's people) had tried to construct them from salvaged materials, none had passed the testing stage—which seemed strange even by the standards of Shenshido, where strangeness was commonplace. Why would such diverse designs all fail their tests? They had nothing in common save mechanical complexity, and if they worked they would be infinitely more effective than the primitive weapons everyone was carrying. What natural or unnatural phenomenon would cause them all to fail like that?

Add it to the list of things that didn't make sense.

They also offered her armor made from slices of salvaged building material—mostly plasteel—layered over a base of heavy cloth. Normally her safeskin coat would have been protection enough, but she wasn't sure if the beating it had taken earlier would affect its functioning, so she accepted a breast plate and a gorget, extra protection for her vital organs and her neck. They wouldn't protect her from charge weapons, but from what Zevi told her, it didn't sound like the enemy had those. Maybe their complex weapons failed testing also.

She tested her shock rod several times, for both snap extension and charge, but there seemed to be nothing wrong with it. Apparently only high-tech items that were created on Shenshido suffered random failure. Maybe these people just sucked at making weapons. She removed a collapsible knife from her boot and tucked it into a sheath pocket in her coat, and of course she had her rings on. Good enough for hand-to-hand combat.

The journey back to the world upstairs was more complicated than she expected. Zevi's people had sealed off the transport tube months before when the "crazies" upstairs found it, which meant the raiding party had to use passages intended for other purposes. From the narrow stairs of an observation tower in Biome Four to a maintenance scaffold, to a series of ladders and service hatches and a crawl space above the sky-dome, they moved upward level by level, silent and focused. Eighteen people, plus Ivar and Ru. Hardly an ideal army.

Hopefully there would be no need to fight, Zevi had told her. But on a station where so many things went wrong, Ru wasn't betting on it.

Ivar stayed close by her side, as he'd promised to. She was his ticket out of this hell, and he made it clear he was not letting her out of his sight. There were worse things than having a strong, well-armed man by her side, but she wondered how long he would stay there if he figured out that her ship was moored to the station.

Finally they came to the security hatch that would give them access to the upper levels of the station. They stopped for a moment, and Zevi's second-in-command, an older man named Vestus, handed out dust masks and eye protection to everyone. No explanation was offered. When Ru looked to Ivar for enlightenment, he just shrugged and muttered, "Air quality might get bad."

Then the hatch was unsealed, and as they climbed through it single file, the lights of the second level came on, revealing a clean, well-illuminated corridor. Not stark white like the part of the station where Ru had been before, but with walls of a pale blue-gray, accented with stripes of darker blue along the upper and lower edges. Equally spotless, of course. The lab levels were always spotless. Whatever cleaning bots served this station required no human master to guide them.

There was an identification code over the hatch, and Ru entered it into her mapping program. The station map appeared in her mind's eye, and a moment later a red dot appeared on it, marking her position. The tension that had been coiled inside her eased ever so slightly. Now that she knew where she was, she could find her way around the station without assistance. Which meant she could head back to Engineering whenever she wanted. She minimized the map and kept it in view. Its presence was empowering.

"Are we clear?" Zevi asked Vestus.

In answer the man took a small device from his pocket. The scientists in Bio had once used surveillance cams to observe their experiments, and Zevi's people put it to good use, bugging the entire route. The group waited while Vestus gathered data and studied it. If a human being had so much as sneezed in these corridors after scouts had passed through, Vestus would know it.

"Nothing," he said a last, a hint of triumph in his voice. "No one's been here but us."

Good news was a rare commodity on Shenshido, and a couple of people smiled in relief, but it was clear from the expressions of others that they were skeptical. Hands remained poised over weapons while eyes scanned the corridor nervously, ahead and behind.

"All right," Zevi said. "Let's move out."

The tunnels Micah had to crawl through were narrow, irregular, and difficult. That was because they were not tunnels at all—at least not in their original intention—but random spaces between pipes and ducts and conduits and junction boxes, some barely large enough for a person to squeeze through. They connected to form a twisting pathway, more like an organic cavern than a maintenance corridor. It even had the claustrophobic effect of a cavern, invoking awareness of the station's great mass pressing in from all sides. Normally such a space would only be accessed in mechanical emergencies, so the entrance points were few and far between, but Serjit and his crew had cut through the back wall of a storage room for their initial access, and now and then Micah saw another place on the right-hand wall where someone had cut—and then resealed—a crude doorway. But the parts of their route that were completely enclosed felt suffocating.

They had put Micah near the back of the line, supposedly to keep him out of the fighting, but not in the last position. Was that to protect him from a possible rear assault, or because they didn't trust him? Micah found it hard to believe that anyone would try to attack them in a cramped space like this, but humans in extreme circumstances some-times did irrational things. He was glad to have a few people be-hind him.

They came to an opening large enough for several people to fit into, a makeshift room where several people broke off from the group.

Micah's heartbeat quickened. They must be approaching the place the exos intended to raid, and were preparing for battle. He felt a tremor of fear at the thought, but also a sense of excitement. Who had ever imagined he would be able to witness something like this first-hand, instead of just imagining it from his work console? There was part of him that wanted to witness a real battle, he was discovering—learn what it looked like, sounded like, smelled like. And that part disturbed him.

*People are going to die today,* he reminded himself. *For real.*

There were more of the rooms now, and people remained behind in each. Finally Micah was ushered into a staging space with four other people, three men and one woman, and told to wait. They were the last group to be positioned. Armageddon was on the horizon.

Minutes passed with agonizing slowness. The only sound was the hum of the station's environmental systems. Micah turned to the woman next to him. "How much longer, do you think?"

The woman looked at Micah. Dark, nameless emotions stirred in the depths of her eyes, along with one that he recognized: hate.

"However long it takes them to get here," she whispered.

The narrow corridors of level B required Ru's company to string out single file, a human serpent whose tail was not visible from its head. Whenever they passed the door to a room the serpent would pause, and Vestus would do a quick sweep of the interior with an infrared detector. That was to find any crazies who might be lying in wait, ready to fall upon the party's flank. Now and then his device detected a minor anomaly, and he had to search out the source. When it proved to be harmless he set the orange warning light on his device back to green, and held the device aloft so that everyone could see it. Or at least the people who were close by that spot could see it. The tail of the serpent had to go on faith.

Soon they neared the part of the station where their target was located, within a small complex that had once been contracted to Apollo Industries. Apparently Apollo hadn't trusted Tridac to provide for everyone in an emergency and had established its own store of supplies, hidden away behind a bank of offices. The crazies apparently hadn't discovered it yet, which meant it might still have food and valuable equipment in it.

*Might.*

The line kept moving slowly, bios holding their weapons tightly as they scanned the walls, floor, ceiling for threats. If the enemy was going to ambush them, it would likely be here, close to their target. One time Vestus's detector flashed orange when a door opened, and Ru found herself holding her breath. But he scanned the room and seemed satisfied. "All good," he said, holding his device aloft for everyone to see.

It was still orange.

The line started to move again. Confused, Ru backed up to the wall, letting the others pass. Something was still in that room, producing heat. Why wasn't he trying to identify it? He had held up the device as if it would reassure people, when the orange warning light was still blinking. Why had they all accepted that gesture without protest? It made no sense.

Ivar fell into position beside her. Of course. If she wandered into the fires of Hell, Ivar would be by her side. "Problem?" he asked.

The last person in line was passing them by. "Something's in there," she murmured.

"Light was green. That means it's clear."

She looked at him sharply. "It was still orange."

"I saw it turn green—"

"I saw it too," she said testily. "I know what orange looks like. And it was still blinking. That means there's a heat source somewhere in that room that Vestus didn't find. I don't know why everyone left, but I want to see for myself." *I'm not crazy!* she thought defiantly. But an inner voice whispered: *Maybe I am. Or maybe everyone in this whole fucking place is crazy, except me.*

"It's dangerous to be alone on this level," he reminded her.

"I'm not alone." She smiled. "I've got you."

The line had passed them, and the curving corridor would soon take the entire serpent out of their sightline. She headed across the hall quickly, weapon drawn, confident Ivar would follow. As she triggered the door she raised the bow-gun that Zevi had given her, bracing herself for whatever might be inside. She wished she had her own pistol instead.

Beyond the opening was an office that looked like it had been abandoned in the middle of moving. Plastic cartons were strewn all over the place, most of them empty, a few half-filled with innocuous office supplies. Ru walked around the room, inspecting it inch by inch, but saw nothing suspicious. Certainly nothing to explain the heat trace Vestus had detected. Ivar was working the far side of the room. She glanced his way and saw a faint vertical line on the wall just ahead of him. "What is that?"

He followed her gaze. "What?"

"That line." She pointed. "Running up the wall."

"What line?" He peered at the wall, then back at her. "I don't see anything."

"Right there. Next to where the bookcase was pulled forward. Hairline crack, perfectly straight. What is it?"

He looked at the wall again, then reached out a hand to feel its surface. He ran his hand over the exact spot where she had seen the line, back and forth, testing it. "Nothing." There was irritation in his voice. "Maybe it was a trick of the light. Look, there's nothing here. Can we rejoin the others now?"

"It's there," she muttered. *Ivar saw the orange indicator, but told me it was green. Now he says there's nothing on the wall, when clearly there is. Why would he lie to me? What's he hiding?* She shook her head, frustrated by her own inability to decipher the situation. *Was this what happened to the people here? Everything just stopped making sense? If so, it's no wonder people went crazy.*

Suddenly there was a noise from outside the room: heavy impact, as if a large item had fallen. Ru froze, then moved to one side of the open doorway; Ivar silently took up station at the other. There they stood, backs to the wall, weapons at the ready, waiting for trouble to reveal itself.

Seconds passed.

More seconds.

Silence.

Finally Ivar eased his head around the edge of the doorway to take a look outside. After a moment he signaled that all was clear, and the two of them moved back out into the corridor. There was nothing there to explain the mysterious noise, and no telling what direction it had come from. "We need to catch up to the others," Ivar said. She nodded, and they both set off at a swift lope down the hallway. Their layered armor rattled with every step, but there was no helping that. Ru pulled her shock rod from her belt, extended it to full length, and activated its head. She couldn't swing it freely with Ivar right next to her, but she wanted it in hand, ready to go, in case the gun-bow failed to do its job.

There were double doors at the end of the corridor, with a solar disk emblazoned on them and APOLLO INDUSTRIES inscribed overhead. As they parted, the lights beyond them came on, revealing a large reception chamber with bronze and gold seating areas on both sides. At the far end of the room, behind a long curved counter, a floor-to-ceiling mural depicted the god Apollo in a fiery chariot. There was a decorative archway flanked by golden columns off to one side, like the entrance to an ancient temple. According to her station map, that would give them access to Apollo's inner sanctum, where the legendary supply cache was located. That was probably where the others had gone. She nodded in that direction, and the two of them started forward.

And they were halfway to the arch when the attack came. People rushed out from the archway ahead, as well as from the doorway they'd just left behind: silent and swift, and armed like Zevi's people. Ru looked around for cover—anything!—but the counter was too far away, and both exits were blocked. "Fuck!" Ivar swore, as he fired at the one of the attackers. Ru turned to confront the ones coming up from behind. (Where the hell had they been hiding? How had Vestus failed to detect them?) Something struck her in the side, hard enough to nearly knock her off her feet, and though her safeskin coat kept it from piercing through, it should have dissipated the force better than that. As she had feared, the damn thing was failing. God alone knew if it would even last through this fight.

There were three coming up from behind her, two men and a woman, all Terran. The one in front was carrying what looked like a charge weapon, and as he brought it up to take aim Ru fired a bolt at his face. It missed its target and struck him on the shoulder instead, but the attack was enough to skew his aim, buying her a precious second. Ru cast her makeshift weapon aside and rushed at him before he had time to react, shoving his gun barrel upward with one hand while she swung her shock rod low with the other. Down, and then up again between his legs, hard. She could see surprise in his eyes as its charged head hit him right behind his groin guard—and then blazing pain. His shot went wild as blue-white sparks exploded from his groin, and as she took a step back he howled in pain, doubling over his agony. One down.

But the other two were closing in on her, and they were positioned effectively enough that there was no way to block them both. Adrenaline flowed through her veins, scarlet wellseeker warnings running down the left side of her visual field like blood. A plasteel sword edged in shards of metal came swinging at her face; she moved inside the blow, too close for the blade to strike, and body-slammed the wielder. She'd hoped to knock the attacker off her feet, but the blow only sent the woman staggering back a short distance. Then something sharp stabbed Ru in the back, almost breaking through her safeskin. She whipped around to face the last attacker, but he was too close, and she couldn't use the shock rod effectively. She swung it down toward his head anyway, hoping to draw a response. Sure enough, he raised up one arm to block it, and in the instant when his attention was focused upward she clenched her other hand into a fist and drove it into his face. She triggered her taze rings just before contact, and as they impacted his flesh a crackling network of blue-white lightning exploded across his cheek. With a cry he dropped his weapon and fell back, hands over his face. The smell of charred flesh filled the air.

Now, for one precious moment, no one was attacking her. She dared a quick look at Ivar and saw that he was on his knees, clutching his bleeding stomach with one hand as he raised his gun with the other. There were far more people attacking him than had gone after her, and she saw a blade-studded mace smashed brutally into his arm, ripping through clothing and flesh and splattering blood across the floor. His gun went flying, landing well out of reach as he doubled over in pain.

He was going to die, she realized. There was nothing she could do to stop it. Though she owed him no particular loyalty, her inability to help him was maddening. But the moment he went down this tsunami of violence would all be focused on her, and she had to get away before that happened.

Her original attackers were between her and the sun-doors, so there was no fleeing back the way she'd come. At the far end of the room the columned archway gaped, the only entrance to Apollo's inner complex. Once she passed through it there would be no way out, save through this choke point. All they would have to do was leave a guard in this chamber and she would be trapped—

*Stop thinking*, she told herself. *Just run!*

She bolted to one side, which seemed to take her attackers by surprise; maybe they had expected her to try to force her way through their blockade. The one with the sword swung at her, but too late; its owner cursed as it passed through the space her head had just occupied. As she twisted out of reach of her attackers, two of the ones fighting Ivar saw her in motion and started after her. But they were seconds too late to cut her off. She dodged the closest one by inches and ducked under the swing of another, racing toward the archway. If she could just get through that, into the narrow corridor beyond, these bastards would be forced to face her one-on-one, and at least they'd lose the advantage of numbers. That might give her a fighting chance.

Some kind of projectile struck her in the back of her neck, hard, just beneath the edge of her collar. An inch higher and it might have been a fatal blow. Then she was through the archway, running breathlessly down a narrow corridor. It curved to the left up ahead, which meant that if she could get beyond that point she might be able to escape these bastards' line of sight, and then—what? Where was there to go? She knew from the map there was no salvation to be had in this place. She could hear them right behind her, footsteps pounding. Closer and closer. When it sounded like they were almost on her she turned back suddenly and dropped to one knee, shock rod braced forward like a spear. Her motion took the first man by surprise, and before he could stop himself, he slammed chest-first into her weapon. His plasteel breastplate conducted the electrical discharge perfectly. As he screamed and fell she climbed to her feet again and resumed running, praying that his writhing body would be enough of an obstacle to slow down anyone coming up behind him.

At the first intersection she skidded, trying to make the turn too quickly, and slammed into the far wall, hard. But she managed to stay on her feet, and a moment later she was out of her attackers' sightline. Virtually invisible, but only for a few seconds. She looked around desperately for somewhere to hide, but the doors on both sides of the hall were unmarked, identical. She had no time to consult her map to see where each one led, but sprinted toward the second one—they would expect her to go for the first—and was relieved to see the doors part as she approached. As soon as she was inside she lunged for the control panel and struck the emergency lock with her palm, praying that the mechanism wouldn't require some kind of special ID. Voices were audible in the hallway now, and they were louder and clearer with each passing moment—

The panels of the door slid closed.

She stood still—so still!—not wanting to risk any motion that might be heard. The sounds from the corridor were muffled, but she could tell that her pursuers were searching the passage she had just left. Had they seen the door closing? She held her breath as she heard footsteps approaching. If they got close to the door and it didn't open automatically, they'd know she must be there, keeping it shut. The pounding of her heart was so loud in her ears it nearly drowned out their voices.

Then they were moving away from her door, and a moment later the voices were swallowed by silence. They must have gone into one of the first rooms to search for her, she realized. Her gambit had worked.

She reached for the wall as she finally exhaled, using it to steady herself as she bent forward, gasping for breath. The door was locked now, so even if they came back to it they'd need time to break through, but she dared not waste a second. She expanded the map in her field of vision so she could see what exits were available, and chose one that led in the opposite direction from her pursuers. That door also had a lock, and as she sealed it behind her she felt the first glimmer of hope. God alone knew how she was going to get off this fucking station in one piece, but for the moment she was safe enough.

Using the map as a guide, trying to put as many twists and turns as possible between her and her attackers, she wandered deeper and deeper into the labyrinthine complex. Sometimes when she crossed a hallway she could hear noises in the distance—voices shouting, weapons clashing, cries of rage and pain. Zevi's people must have engaged the enemy nearby. Her heart sank, knowing how trapped they were in this place.

She was exhausted from running, but she didn't dare stop. If her attackers had heat detectors, like Vestus did, they'd eventually find her. She had to keep moving, had to come up with a creative way to escape this part of the station, or perhaps some kind of weapon or device to help her get past those guarding the exits. But the rooms she passed through held only mundane supplies, and when she pulled the cover off an air vent to see if she could climb into the duct system, she found that it was too narrow and flimsy to be of any use.

Suddenly she realized there was no more sound, even in the hallway. The fighting she'd heard earlier must have concluded, but the total lack of sound was disconcerting. *Maybe they fled the area*, she told herself, seeking an explanation that would allow her to believe some of Zevi's people had survived.

Then she found the bodies.

They were sprawled across the hallway where they'd fought their last battle, the floor beneath them slick with blood, the walls spattered scarlet. A dozen of Zevi's people at least, and an equal number of strangers. All human. No mutants. No zombies. The faces of the bios were hidden behind their dust masks and goggles, but the faces of the others were plainly visible, and human. Reddened eyes stared blindly into space, thin rivulets of blood running down from the corners of their eyes, mouths, nostrils. Bright red. These people hadn't died from sword wounds, and she doubted any poison could have struck them down all at once like that.

Unless it was airborne.

She triggered her headlamp, shining the beam over the bodies. Red dust swirled thickly in the beam. Clearly artificial. Her skin was starting to itch now; was that real, or imagined? *Air quality might get bad*, Ivar had said. But going back the way she had come was even more dangerous, so she stumbled over the bodies, anxious to get out of the poison cloud as quickly as possible. She didn't see Zevi among the fallen, but she wasn't checking every face. She hoped the woman had gotten safely away.

She came to an iris portal, larger than any other she'd seen during her flight. It opened at her approach, revealing a cavernous chamber beyond. A storage facility of some kind, long and high and lined with industrial shelves, with so many canisters and boxes and bins stacked on them that the walls themselves were all but invisible. A warehouse? She checked her map, and yes, this was the place Zevi's people had been heading toward. The one the bios had died trying to reach.

The door closed behind her, and she found the controls to lock it. One more precious barrier between her and death. Then she looked around.

There were two bodies on the floor.

That they had gone down fighting was clear from the glistening pool of blood surrounding them. The man wore a mask and goggles, so he was a bio, but the goggles had been smashed—along with half his skull—so it was hard to make out his features. The woman wore no mask or goggles, but she must have had them on earlier, because the blood that streaked her face had missed exactly the spots where they would have protected her, leaving behind a ghostly imprint of clean flesh. Maybe whoever had killed her had taken them.

As she leaned down to take a closer look at the bodies, she caught sight of a small black object underneath a shelving unit. The floor behind it was pulsing a dull orange, and her stomach tightened as she realized what the item must be, and what its presence here meant. Gently—so gently!—she turned the man's head to the right, to look at the undamaged portion of his face. Vestus. She lowered her head for a moment, mourning him, mourning Ivar, mourning everyone who had died in this miserable station. Never had she hated a place so much.

She used her lamp to make sure the air was clean, then took her own mask and goggles off and pocketed them. Breathing was easier now. So was seeing. As long as the portal stayed shut, the air in here should be safe for her.

There was light on at the far end of the chamber. She headed toward it.

At the end of the long room was a wall of plastic bins. Some had been pulled down and were now scattered across the floor; the ones she could see into were empty. In the center of all that mess a Variant knelt, and he looked up as she approached. Tiger-like markings framed a face in which amber eyes gleamed like polished gemstones: Sarkassan. He was wearing some armor, but not a full set, and a bright pink shirt was visible between its segments, jarringly incongruous. His headset was shaped like a golden dragon, its serpentine body coiled around his head, its bright ruby eyes peering out at Ru from beside his left temple as he looked up at her. His hand went reflexively to his belt, as if reaching for a weapon, but he lacked the militant aspect of the others, and didn't seem anxious to fight. Not from Shenshido, she guessed. Not a victim of the terrible paranoia that had possessed this station, but someone from the outside, like she was. Maybe even sane.

"There's no smell," he whispered hoarsely.

Startled, she stared at him without comprehension.

He tipped up the box he was kneeling in front of, so she could look inside. "See?" He shook it slightly. "It should smell, but it doesn't!"

She leaned forward to peer into the box.

It was empty.

*Hell,* she thought. Her mind and body were numb from exhaustion. *So much for sanity.*

*They hunger to kill,* Micah thought.

Crouched in the hidden staging area, waiting for action, his legs as tired as his spirit, Micah studied his companions. Three men and one woman. They had all been normal people once, working at normal jobs, facing normal life challenges, just like him. Now they were something else: creatures whose eyes were alight not only with excitement and fear, but with something else, primitive and terrible. Bloodlust. What could transform a normal person into that? Micah knew the story of this place in words—*they've been fighting for two years, constantly afraid, constantly desperate*—but deep inside, on a visceral level, he had no real understanding. He could not imagine the circumstances under which his own essence would transform like that.

There hadn't been enough working coms for Micah to have his own—or perhaps they just didn't trust him with one—but the woman in his group, Leila, took hers from her ear and turned up the volume so that he could listen in on everyone's chatter. The reception was terrible, but that was to be expected, since they were sending their signals through the tech-caverns, old style. If they used the innernet instead they would have perfect clarity, but they'd also be vulnerable to having their messaging hijacked. Since no one knew what kind of hacking skill the exos had, it seemed best not to risk it.

With all the static it was hard to tell which voice belonged to whom, much less hear all they were saying.

*. . . nothing on screen yet.*

*. . . sure they're coming?*

*. . . not working right.*

*. . . they need supplies.*

*. . . they'll come, they'll come.*

Hours had passed. Hours would continue pass. He couldn't call up one of his projects to work on, to kill time, because then he might miss some crucial instruction arising from the sea of static.

But when those words finally came, they were clear enough.

*They're here.*

The others in the staging area rose to their feet, drawing their weapons. Two of the men were grinning. So anxious to kill. In a way that was more frightening than the thought of battle.

*. . . how many?*

*. . . motion sensors say eighteen.*

*. . . so all of them.*

*. . . looks like it.*

*. . . Damn. This really is Armageddon.*

Laughter: callous, blood-hungry. It was doubly harsh filtered through the static.

*. . . now?*

*. . . No. Wait for my signal. We need them all to be past the choke-point, so no one gets away.*

Seconds passed.

*. . . two just split off,* a voice said.

*. . . where?*

*. . . They're going into one of the access rooms.* A pause. *Shit. I think they've found the portal.*

*Should we attack?* a woman's voice demanded.

*. . . Negative. The others aren't in position yet. We can't tip our hand so early. Try a distraction instead.*

Crackling and popping, sans voices.

*. . . took the bait . . . back in the corridor now . . . moving forward again . . . go?*

*. . . wait for my signal.*

*. . . nearing the chokepoint now.*

*. . . what about the others?*

*. . . forward scouts have reached the cache. Others close behind.*

More laughter: cruel, hungry.

*. . . those two strays are entering Apollo now . . .*

"Sorry," the woman whispered to Micah, as she clipped the com back onto her ear. A moment later, all four of his companions were in motion. Micah stepped back quickly to get out of their way, stumbling over a severed pipe. By the time he had his balance again they had reached the secret door and swung it open, and were rushing through. The same was happening up and down the line, he knew: warriors bursting from the walls in a dozen strategic locations, taking the exos by surprise, cutting off every possible escape. He'd designed enough ambush scenarios for his games to know how deadly such a plan could be, if executed properly.

Noises could be heard coming from the world outside the tunnels. Cries, crashes, the soundtrack of war. His hand closed on the grip of the plasteel baton they had given him. It wasn't the world's most sophisticated weapon—they'd wanted to reserve the best ones for their own people—but it was better than nothing.

*You wanted to see battle,* an inner voice whispered. *So go. See.*

He stepped through the secret opening warily, into a large room filled with banks of machinery. The noises were louder now and seemed to be coming in through an open door at the far end of the room. He edged toward it, listened for a moment longer, then peered around the edge.

His companions had engaged the enemy some distance down the corridor outside. People were massed together so closely it was hard for him to make out details of the fight, but he saw flashes of masked faces, weapons swinging and blood spattering and bodies falling . . . there were cries of rage and pain, hate and fear. The chaos was both repellent and compelling, and he felt himself drawn to it, hungry to see the action more clearly. This was what he'd come for, right?

Suddenly someone in the center of the fight threw a fist-sized object at the ceiling. When it hit, it shattered, releasing red dust that rained down upon the battle. Micah took a few steps back as he watched, wary of getting too close to it. Some of Serjit's people started gagging and coughing. Then more of them. Then all of them. Some tried to escape the dust cloud that had enveloped the group, but the few exos who were still alive, bloody apparitions in masks and goggles, cut them down. Micah watched in horror for a moment, then began to back away, more and more rapidly. The red cloud was spreading beyond the battle, and since the station's environmental control kept the air circulating, it would reach him soon.

He ran.

He'd already wandered past his entrance point, and couldn't return that way; he needed another path out of this nightmare. It took him three tries to muster the concentration to summon his map, but when it finally appeared he saw that one of Serjit's secret doors was located in a large room not far ahead. If he could get to it and shut the door behind him, he might buy himself enough time to get out of range of the airborne poison. He sprinted the last dozen yards, into the large portal that irised open as he approached. Breathless, he turned back immediately and tried to find a way to shut it quickly, but there was no visible mechanism for that, so he had to let it close at its own pace.

Then he claimed the luxury of a few deep breaths, and tried to get his bearings.

He was in a warehouse of some kind, packed from floor to ceiling with containers. It also had two bodies in it. A man and a woman were lying on their backs in the middle of the floor, eyes staring out through the same kind of goggles the other exos had been wearing, dust masks soaked in blood. What little skin was visible was gray and striated and covered with lichenous white spots, like rotting wood. Serjit's people hadn't been exaggerating. He wondered if he could bring himself to touch the mutated bodies, to salvage a mask and goggles for himself. *Just think of these people as Variants*, he told himself. *One human race among many, only this one has textured skin. Nothing to think twice about.* Finally he reached down and pulled at the woman's mask; it came loose with a sucking sound that made his stomach turn. The goggles had to be lifted off over her head, and got caught in her blood-soaked hair, but he managed to pull them free without retching. He winced as he tucked the two gory items in his pocket, praying to God he would never have to wear them.

As he headed toward the location where the hidden exit was supposed to be, suddenly it dawned on him where he was. He checked the map to confirm it. Yes, this was the heart of Serjit's trap, the place the exos had risked their lives to find. Even now he could see that the floor-to-ceiling shelves at the end of the chamber had once held a neat array of food storage bins. But many had been pulled from their perches and dumped on the ground. Had they really contained food? He'd never heard Serjit talk about that aspect of the trap, but clearly the exos had already been here and ransacked the place. Curious, he walked to the nearest box and crouched down beside it, turning it over so he could look inside.

There probably had been food in it once, but the seal had been broken, and what was in there now didn't look like anything edible. A dark, viscous sludge clung to the walls of the box, and the rotting chunks floating in it reminded him of human vomit. Swallowing hard, he managed to look away, and pulled another box toward him. This mess in this one was mostly green, but equally unwholesome. Whatever food had been in this place had spoiled long ago, and now was utterly putrid.

No, he realized with a shock. Not putrid. Putrid would stink. This didn't stink.

Startled, he looked around the room, at the dozens of containers whose rotting contents were now exposed to the air. This part of the warehouse should reek to high hell. Hell, the whole frikkin' warehouse should reek. Only it didn't. There was no smell at all.

A tremor of fear ran though him. Slowly, he leaned forward over another one of the boxes, placing his face directly above the disgusting sludge, and inhaled deeply. *Please,* he thought desperately. *Please smell bad. Please. Make me vomit.*

But it didn't. It smelled like nothing.

The implications of that were terrifying.

Suddenly he became aware of another presence in the room. He reached for his baton as he looked up to see who had snuck up on him while he was distracted. It turned out to be a woman: lean, high-breasted, athletic in aspect, with deep golden skin that was flushed from exertion. Sweat-matted hair obscured most of the simple headset she wore—looked like an old Sitech model—spiky copper bangs framing large almond-shaped eyes, which narrowed suspiciously as she studied him. She was wearing a dark red leather coat, and through holes in it he could see a shiny black lining. There was a jagged tear in one leg of her pants, and the fabric surrounding it was stained. With blood? She had no facial deformities. She wore no dust mask or goggles. She wasn't one of Serjit's people, but she didn't look like an exo either. Could it be she was an outsider, like him? Another person who didn't belong in this crazy place? She was holding a nasty-looking shock rod and looked ready to use it if she had to . . . but she didn't look like she wanted to.

"There's no smell," he whispered hoarsely. She just stared at him. He tipped up the box he'd been smelling, so she could see the noxious mess inside. "See?" He shook it slightly. "It should smell, but it doesn't!"

She leaned forward to peer into the box. Stood back again. Though she said nothing, the truth was in her eyes. *She doesn't understand. Which means she doesn't see what I do. Which means* . . . the thought was too terrible to finish.

"One minute," he whispered. He held up a finger. "Just a minute . . ." When she made no move toward him he shut his eyes, focusing all his concentration on visualizing the icon that would shut down any virt his headset was running. He added every variation of the command that he had programmed into his headset. *Pause Program. End Program. Sever Connection. Terminate Virt. Shut Down NOW!* But when he opened his eyes the boxes of sludge were still there. They still didn't smell. *Shit.* He fumbled for the release on his headset, aware that she was watching him closely. Lifting the golden dragon from his head should sever the connection to any external program that was affecting his sensory input, regardless of its source. So he did that.

Nothing changed.

He forced himself to be calm as he locked his headset back in place, or at least to look calm. *Focus on other things for now,* he told himself. *Don't think about the fact that you may have gone insane.* Was this woman really from the outside? If so, might she offer him a way to escape this terrible place? Return to a world where people didn't turn into trees, where putrid things smelled bad? He'd sell his soul for a ticket home.

"So," he said, trying to sound less afraid than he felt. "Are you from around here?" The words sounded lame as soon as he said them. She was staring at him like one might stare at a strange bug. Great.

But then her expression softened a bit, and she shrugged. "Just visiting. Not very impressed." She nodded toward the boxes, and a corner of her mouth twitched. Almost a smile. "Food sucks."

"No argument there."

"So how about you? From Shenshido?"

He shook his head. "Took a wrong turn on the way to Harmony. Totaled my pod trying to dock here." He sighed. "Can't seem to find a rental center anywhere."

"Services are definitely lacking," she agreed.

"So." His heart was pounding. "You don't know where I could catch a ride home, do you?"

A moment of silence. "That depends. Do you know a safe way out of this place?"

"If you mean the Apollo complex . . . yeah, I might."

"Well, then." Again that almost-smile. "I *might* know a way home."

Slowly he rose to his feet. His legs were stiff—his whole body was stiff—but the thought of escaping Shenshido was energizing. *Don't get your hopes up too much,* he warned himself. But the hunger for hope was so strong that it robbed the thought of power.

"Come on," he said. "This way." He gestured toward the place where Serjit's door was hidden. "I do hope you're not claustrophobic."

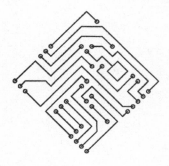

The day a programmer developed software that could alter human sensory perception, he sowed the seeds of humanity's destruction.

The only question left to us is what form that destruction will take.

MAXWELL ONEGIN
*Think Again!*

# HARMONY NODE
# SHENSHIDO STATION

THE PROBLEM with the "safe way out" of Apollo, the Sarkassan explained, was that it was the same route the ambushers had used to get in. He and Ru would need to go to an outlying branch of a secret tunnel system and wait, until the attackers had satisfied themselves that none of the enemy were still standing, and left. Then it would be safe to emerge.

She wasn't sure if that qualified as a *safe* exit, but right now she didn't have a better option.

He led her to a narrow passage between two towering shelf units and indicated that they would have to squeeze through it. The passage was barely wide enough for her to fit through sideways, and if anyone attacked while she was in there, it would not be a good situation. She looked at the Sarkassan for a moment, hesitant. His motives were reliable enough—like Ivar, he wanted to get off this station, and as long as he thought she held the key to escape he would do his best to keep her alive. But how sound was his judgment? He was about to lead her right into the hornet's nest, and if he was wrong about what the upstairs folk were going to do next, things could get pretty ugly.

"This whole place is under surveillance," he warned her. "They watched you coming in, and as soon as they return to their equipment they'll be able to see where you are. You can't hide from them as long as you're in the public space."

She looked at him for a long moment, then nodded. Hornet's nest it was.

Shock rod in her right hand, knife in her left, she sidled through the narrow space behind him, cringing as the vibrations from their movement set massive storage drums thrumming on both sides. *You weren't kidding about the claustrophobia.* But soon enough they emerged into a slightly larger space, hidden behind a shelving unit. It was big enough to accommodate half a dozen people—assuming they were friendly—and a large hinged door that stood half-open. It looked like it had been laser-cut from the wall, and would probably leave no more than a hairline crack when shut. Just like the crack she had spotted on the way here, she realized. The one Ivar hadn't seen. He and Ru must have come within inches of discovering the ambush, perhaps almost triggering it.

But if it had been a real door, *why* didn't Ivar see it? Everything she learned about this place only raised more questions.

It was dark beyond the doorway, so the Sarkassan switched on his headset's light, and she followed suit. Now there were two narrow beams piercing the darkness, just enough to hint at the presence of ducts, conduits, junction boxes, wires—a tangled nest of maintenance equipment. Black shadows lurked in every corner, stretching and shifting as the light sources moved. A dozen murderous people could be hidden in those shadows, and Ru and her guide would never see them. She spotted a light fixture overhead, connected to a conduit that might lead to others, but the Sarkassan didn't activate it. Maybe he was afraid that so much light would be noticed.

As he squeezed in between two ducts and gestured for her to follow, she instructed her headset to record sensory data. If she had to find her way out of here on her own, she would at least have that much data to guide her. Then she followed him into the guts of the station. It was a tight enough fit in places that it made their previous passage seem downright luxurious, and more than once her coat snagged on an unseen protrusion, startling her. No, she wasn't claustrophobic—outriders couldn't afford to be, given how much time they spent sealed in pods—but this place would be a test of anyone's nerves.

Finally they emerged into a small open space hewed from the guts of the station, barely high enough to stand up in. There were boxes stacked at the far end, with an array of small bottles next to them. A large covered urn was tucked under an air duct.

"This is their supply station," the Sarkassan told her. "There's food in the boxes if you're hungry, and the bottles have water in them. At least that's what I was told. I have no idea how old everything is, but hey . . ." He shrugged. "Probably not more than two years, right?"

"I'll check to make sure nothing smells bad," she said, with a hint of a dry smile.

The boxes were full of nutrient bars in clear plastic wrap. They were gray and mealy-looking and appeared to be homemade, but given some of what she'd eaten on colony planets, they looked reassuringly uncomplicated. She stowed a few in her pocket before unwrapping one and biting into it. It tasted every bit as bad as it looked, but food was food, and her body needed refueling. The bottles all had laboratory labels on them, dire warnings about poisons and acids and dangerous interactions. She chose one that said it contained a dangerous alkali and tucked it into her jacket as well. Then she headed over to the urn to see what was inside. As she lifted the lid the Sarkassan started to say something, but if he was trying to warn her, he was too late. The fetid odor of human waste hit her in the face. Gagging, she pushed the cover quickly back in place.

"Chamber pot," he said.

"Yeah." She coughed. "I guessed that."

"They said they would wait here as long as it took for the exos to show up. Days, if necessary. I guess no one wanted to have to hike all the way back just to piss."

She looked at him solemnly. "The bios never stood a chance, did they?"

Expression grim, he shook his head.

*I'd be dead if I had stayed with them,* Ru thought. Noticing the secret door that Vestus has overlooked and taking the time out to investigate had saved her. "Is this where we wait?"

"No. They might come here for supplies. We'll go one more room up the line."

Back into the guts of the station they crawled. The Sarkassan paused several times along the way to consult a map in his headset. It must not have been very detailed, because sometimes he seemed less than certain about which way to go. Far from reassuring.

Eventually they emerged in another makeshift clearing, a bit more spacious than the first. He went to the far side and then, with a sigh, lowered himself to the floor. There was a weariness about him that matched her own—not merely physical, but spiritual. "We'll be safe here, as long as we keep our voices down."

She followed his lead, lowering herself to the floor opposite him, stretching out her legs in front of her with a soft groan. It felt good to sit. "I guess it's time for introductions."

He chuckled weakly. "Y'think?"

"I'm Ru Gaya, outrider." She paused, wondering how much she should add to that. "The locals think I'm a bounty hunter, but there doesn't seem to be much point to that story anymore."

He took a green bottle out of his pocket and twisted off the cap. "Micah Bello, game designer. Specializing in multi-player virtual immersion reality transposition programming."

"Virts?"

"That's not nearly as impressive sounding, is it?" He took a deep drink from the bottle. "But yeah, virts."

She smiled slightly. "Make-believe worlds."

"Hey." He glowered. "It pays the bills."

She pulled her own bottle out, opened it, and sniffed. Looked like water. Smelled like water. She glanced at the Sarkassan for confirmation, and when he nodded, dared a sip. Water. For all its staleness, it was blissfully refreshing. She drank deeply.

"So," he said. "Names are all taken care of. Is this when we talk about why we're really here?"

She hesitated. She trusted him as much as she trusted anyone on this station, but that wasn't a very high bar. "Someone wanted data from Shenshido," she said at last. "Since the station's independent, I was paid to come here and retrieve it." She sighed. "If I'd known what that entailed, I would have charged more."

"Not an outrider's usual work."

"I'm between assignments."

"And the bounty hunter part?"

"Fewer questions that way." She took another drink. "Your turn, now. And I do hope you're not going to stick with that 'I took a wrong turn' nonsense."

"Hey! It's the truth. Granted, I was trying to get away from someone who was trying to kill me . . . and no, I don't know who he was or why he was doing that. Shenshido was the nearest station, so I came here seeking refuge. Apparently the security system doesn't like visitors."

"Spiders got you?"

He nodded. "I evacked, just in time. Didn't stick around to see what they did to my ship, but I expect it's gone now."

"Yeah, spiders are pretty thorough. Was that your jet suit tethered to the ring?"

He nodded.

She whistled softly. "Impressive evac."

"It's amazing what you can do when the alternative is death in deep space." He took another drink. "Now. Please. Tell me you have a ship that can get us off this godforsaken station. Because if you don't, nothing else really matters, does it?"

Again she hesitated, but only for a moment. She'd avoided telling Ivar anything about her real situation, but this wasn't Ivar. And if this man was going to help her get back to her skimmer, he needed to at least know it existed. "I have a ship."

"Praise the Ancient Ones!" he proclaimed. Then, seeing the surprise on her face, he added quickly, "Sorry. Industry joke." He grinned sheepishly. "I usually hang out with people who would get the reference."

"It's okay. I'm getting used to not understanding things in this place. Speaking of which," she bit her lip for a moment, "what was up with those boxes?"

For a moment he said nothing. Finally he asked, "What did you see in them?"

"Nothing."

"Nothing at all?"

She spread her hands.

"Shit," he muttered.

"What did *you* see?"

"Rotting provisions. Moldy, liquefied. Disgusting. You didn't see *any* of that?"

"Not so much as a mold spore, I'm sorry." Puzzle pieces were coming together now, and she didn't like the picture taking shape. "We weren't seeing the same thing, were we?"

He whispered it: "No."

"And the lack of smell? What was that about?"

"Virt programs can create sensory illusions, but they rarely include smell. So the fact that I was seeing something that should have a strong odor and didn't, suggested that what I was seeing wasn't real."

She blinked. "You're thinking . . . what? That we're in some kind of game?"

He shook his head sharply. "Games don't inload. They're controlled by the headset. Once you remove that, all sensory feed should terminate."

"But yours didn't."

"No. It didn't. And I don't know why. I *should* know. This is my field. I should understand it."

"I think . . . something similar might have happened with Ivar." She told him about the door that Ivar hadn't seen, the warning light that everyone thought had turned green, when it was still really orange. "They told me down in Bio that everyone up here was disfigured. But all the people I've seen looked perfectly normal. Were the bios seeing something that didn't exist? All of them?"

"They told me everyone from below was mutated. But that part at least was true. I saw it myself."

"Where?"

"The two bodies in the warehouse. Their faces were covered in some bark-like growth. Didn't you see it?"

"Micah." She said it softly. "They looked perfectly normal."

"Ah, jeez." He looked away. "Don't tell me that."

"I'm sorry."

"How can we be sure that anything here is real? How are we supposed to function if we can't trust our own senses?" Suddenly he looked back at her. "*You* seem to be immune."

"What do you mean?"

"The door you found was real, right? The orange sensor light probably was, too. *You* saw the truth of those things, when no one else did. And you weren't affected by the illusions in the storeroom just now. Jeez, maybe everyone on this station looks totally normal, but you're the only one who can see their true faces." He shook his head, clearly frustrated. "Why you? What's different about you? It's not just that you came from the outside; I did too."

"I don't know. I'm sorry."

"What the hell am I missing?" Shutting his eyes, he leaned back against a cluster of small pipes. His eyes flickered back and forth beneath his lids as he scanned some inner vista.

"They said their weapons tests failed," Ru offered. "Could that have been an illusion as well?"

"Sure," he said without opening his eyes. "They could have blasted the hell out of practice targets and never seen the damage. A real person would have gotten wounded—no sensory program could mask that—but if they never took the weapons into combat, they'd never have a chance to observe that."

"Which caused them to abandon those weapons in favor of simpler tools."

"Barbaric tools. Primitive warfare, bloody and intimate." He looked at her. "Someone—or something—has been disarming these people through trickery. Manipulating them like pieces in some dark game, to get them to fight like beasts."

"Or as an experiment," she said softly.

He raised an eyebrow.

"Isn't that what this station was designed for? Scientific experiments?"

"Yeah, but how long has this gone on? And how many have died here? Hundreds? Thousands? Beaten to death, starved to death . . . would anyone consider that a reasonable cost for experimentation? No." He held up a hand. "Don't answer that. I know some megacorp executives who would. But how could it go on for two years with no one interfering? Something like this couldn't be kept a secret for that long. People on the outside must have been working to keep Shenshido isolated."

A sudden thought occurred to her. It was disturbing enough that she hesitated to put it into words. "Micah . . . could all this be related to what happened on Harmony?"

His eyes narrowed. "You mean the terrorist attack?"

"They were playing some kind of game at the time. Multi-player virt."

"Dragonslayer," he said testily. "I wrote that game. There's nothing in its code that would explain what happened. But . . ." His eyes narrowed slightly. "Players have to be in constant contact with a game controller, to make sure everyone who's immersed in the virt is receiving the same data. If someone hijacked that signal . . . I guess it's possible. But what makes you think that, aside from the fact that virts are involved?"

She put her water bottle down beside her. DANGER, the label

said. IN CASE OF CONTACT WITH SKIN SEEK IMMEDIATE
MEDICAL ATTENTION. "The players were in communication with
someone—or some*thing*—off-station. The signal was coming from
Shenshido. That's why I was sent here, to gather information on it. My
employer wanted to know if it originated here, or was being channeled
from somewhere else."

"So which was it?"

"Don't know. I copied the communication log for him, from the time
of the bombing, so he could analyze it when I got back. Not my forte."

"Net it to me. I'll take a look. Use tempcode . . ." He paused, con-
sulting some inner databank. "SEV928A."

She had her headset download the information she'd gathered earlier onto a data chip, removed that, and offered it to him.

"What's this?" he asked.

"The data you wanted."

"Just net it to me."

"Sorry, but I'm not connecting to this station's innernet just to pass
you a list of numbers. Just plug this in." She continued to hold out the
chip to him.

He made no move to take it. Just stared at her. "You're not connected?"

She shrugged. "It's not a big deal for outriders. Most of our time is
spent out of range of public networks. We don't have the same hunger
for constant connection that you do."

"You're. Not. Connected." He said the words slowly, as if testing the
weight of each one. "You, alone. Everyone else on Shenshido has an
open channel to the station's innernet. *But not you.*"

She lowered the chip as his full meaning sank in.

"Jeez," he muttered. "That's why you're not seeing what everyone
else is! The sensory input must be coming through that connection.
And that's how it's getting the feedback it needs to run this thing . . .
only you're not providing any. Shit. Whoever's running this may not
even know you're here." He held out his hand. "Give me the chip."

She did so, and he slotted it into his headset, right behind the drag-on's head. His expression grim, he leaned back and shut his eyes, focus-ing attention on some inner landscape where, presumably, the numbers and symbols of communication code danced a surreal ballet. His eyes flickered back and forth as he watched the display, an eerie simulacrum of dream sleep, and his fingers twitched periodically, like the paws of a sleeping animal.

She studied him as she waited, observing the markings that framed his face: tiger stripes, deep brown against his pale skin. She hadn't seen many Sarkassans before.

"Signal wasn't originally from here," he said at last. "Looks like . . . Sector Nine."

She exhaled in frustration. "That's empty space."

"No. Not empty. Undeveloped. Uncontrolled. Ideal for people who don't want to be found. There are scavs and other unsavory types who supposedly take refuge there. Or maybe that's just in viddies."

*People who don't want to be found.* She remembered how intent Ivar had been on escaping the station before a rescue team arrived. Was he connected to all this? "Can you pull up any information on Ivar?"

"As in, use Shenshido's innernet to access data for you? So you don't have to connect with it yourself?" He waved short her protest. "It's fine. You need to stay disconnected until we know what's going on here. And yes, I can access anything that's public record, provided it doesn't re-quire a passcode." He closed his eyes again and leaned back. A minute passed. "Not seeing that name on any station manifest."

"Possibly an alias." She thought back to her conversations with Ivar, trying to remember anything that could provide a clue. "He said he ar-rived about two years ago. Right before the trouble started."

"All right." A longer silence this time. "Not seeing any arrivals then. Official ones, anyway." A pause. "Looks like there was a big fight with scavs. That's probably when the outer ring got trashed." He looked at her. "Station Commander thought they might have come from Sector Nine."

Her heart skipped a beat. "Any prisoners taken?"

He took a moment to check. "One. He wouldn't give his name.

They assigned him a number." Another pause. "Someone identified him as A.A." He chuckled. "It looks like that was shorthand for *arrogant asshole*."

"Yeah, that sounds like him. He said there was some kind of prison break."

He shut his eyes to concentrate. "There's mention of that in the public news feed, but not much in the way of details. If you want more, I'll have to start hacking into protected files." He opened his eyes and looked at her. "You said Ivar arrived right before all the trouble started, yes? Well, if he came with the other scavs, that means *they* arrived just before the trouble started."

She drew in a sharp breath. "You think they caused this?"

"Maybe not *caused* it. But the timing's certainly suspicious. Scav fleet shows up and cripples the station, and right after that the madness starts. And in the middle of all that, Ivar shows up." He considered for a moment. "You said he didn't see the doorway, so we know he was being fed the same illusions as everyone else. If this was a scav plot, would they have done that to one of their own? I don't think so. But there's definitely *some* connection there. Where is he now?"

Guilt was a sudden lump in her throat. "Probably dead."

"Probably?"

"We were ambushed. He was surrounded." She shut her eyes. "There were too many for me to fight. If I'd stayed, we would both have died."

"Sometimes it's like that." His voice was gentle. "At least in the battles I've designed. I've never had to deal with the real thing before."

"I can't imagine he survived."

"But you don't know for sure."

She said nothing.

"Maybe they thought they'd already killed him," he said. "Things were moving pretty fast. And if he is still alive, and we can find him . . . if he doesn't have the answers we need, maybe he can point the way to someone who does." He drew in a deep breath. "We need to find him, Ru."

*We*, she thought. The pronoun was suggestive. Volatile. Were they a team now? Or was Micah just so used to his make-believe worlds, in which characters who didn't know each other gathered in teams to pursue exciting quests, that the word had little real meaning to him? The latter was probably true, but that didn't still the sudden ache inside her, the echo of a loneliness that Tully's humor had once soothed, Tully's companionship had banished. When had she ceased to be happy traveling through life alone, and become the kind of person who needed the company of others?

"We were ambushed in the reception room," she said. "But it's the only way out of this complex, so I'd expect them to leave a guard there."

"Until the fighting was over. Then there would be no point in it."

In her mind's eye she could see all the dead bodies in that hallway. So many of them! And Vestus and his companion lying on the floor of the warehouse, butchered within sight of their objective. Maybe a handful of bios had survived that initial assault, but if so, they'd have fled. Or died while trying to flee. "It's probably over," she whispered.

"We have to go look for him now," he said. "No more waiting for the tunnels to clear. Not if he's wounded."

"We don't even know that he's still alive—"

"Do you want to find out what happened here? And who sent the bombers to Harmony?"

So much death. So much misery. Was Ivar the key to discovering its source? If he died, they would never know. "Yes," she said quietly. "I do."

"Then we need to try." He rose stiffly to his feet. "And pray that whatever dangers are out there, we'll see them as they really are."

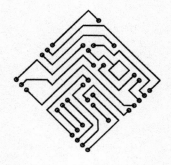

Each man is, within himself, an alien landscape to all others.

ALEXIS CONSTANZA
*East of Human*

# HARMONY NODE
# SHENSHIDO STATION

**T**HE GROUND shook under Micah's feet. The heavens trembled. He stood on the edge of a black abyss, earth crumbling beneath him, while the icy winds of the netherworld swept up to chill his face. At any moment he might lose his footing and fall.

At least that was how he felt. How the hell were you supposed to function when anything you saw or touched might not be real?

He led her past pipes and conduits. Were they really there? He placed his feet carefully between obstacles on the shadow-wracked floor. What if there was one he couldn't see? Was there really as much light coming from his headset as he thought? Or less? Were shadows really where he thought they were?

Thank God, at least he was in front of her, so that she couldn't see the dismay on his face. Thank God it was dark enough that she couldn't see his hand trembling when he reached out to the nearest duct (real? not real?) for support.

*Pull yourself together, man. You've dealt with illusionary worlds before.* But this was different. This was a world for which he had no rulebook, and—more important—couldn't opt out of. That last factor, he was discovering, merited more fear than all the manufactured monsters he had spent his life synthesizing.

With frustrating slowness they worked their way back through the tunnel system, retracing the route Micah had taken on the way in. Several times they heard voices nearby and had to stop, but no one came their way, thank God. His nerves were near the breaking point when they finally reached the hidden door he'd identified as the closest one to their objective. Hinges creaked as he pushed it slowly open. Behind him Ru stood with her weapon in hand, braced for trouble. But there was only silence. Whoever had been in this part of the complex earlier was gone now.

Beyond the door was a room so ravaged that little remained intact. Segments of the wall had peeled back from their support beams, and dirt and debris were everywhere. He picked his way carefully over some large pieces of wreckage, then saw Ru watching him with a strange look on her face. *I'm stepping over obstacles that aren't really there,* he realized. But knowing that didn't make them go away. And if his body thought they were real, they had the power to trip him up.

There was blood in the corridor beyond that, some dried, some fresh, but they didn't stop to examine it. Once he thought he saw claw marks scoring the wall, but Ru kept moving forward, and after a moment so did he. *None of it's real,* he told himself. Fighting to believe it. Finally they came to the final intersection before the reception chamber. Once they turned this corner they would be able to see into that space . . . and be seen by anyone in it. Gripping his baton so hard his knuckles were white, Micah wished he had a mirror to peer around the corner with. If this had been a game quest, he wouldn't have left the staging ground without one.

Ru waved him back, then edged around the corner. After a moment she stepped out into the open and waved for him to follow. He exhaled sharply and hurried along behind her.

The reception hall was splattered with blood, crimson streaks and smeared footprints surrounding a pool of glistening liquid in its center. From the grim expression on Ru's face, he guessed that was where she'd last seen Ivar. A long, irregular smear led away from the main pool, toward the curved counter that dominated one end of the room. Perhaps the mark of a body being dragged?

With a last wary look around, Ru headed for the counter, and Micah followed. And yes, there was a body behind the counter, battered and bloody. If he was breathing, Micah couldn't see it. "Is he alive?"

She knelt down beside the body and slid a finger under the coarse beard. "Still a pulse," she muttered. "But barely. If we can get him to the skimmer while his heart's still beating I might be able to save him."

"How far away is that?"

For a moment she said nothing. Considering whether to trust him? It seemed a moot question at this point; either they were in this together, or not. Finally she nodded. "The engineering complex. There's a maintenance hatch there."

Engineering. That was where he had encountered the deadly vines, blocking the way. He opened his mouth to warn her—but then stopped. Had those vines been real, or another Shenshido illusion? Shit, had *anything* he'd seen on this damn station been real? "It's one hell of a hike," he muttered hoarsely. "We'll have to take turns carrying him."

She rolled Ivar onto his back and opened his jacket. There was a wet red mass beneath it; apparently before Ivar had passed out he'd managed to stuff a piece of cloth into the wound, stanching the flow of blood. It was a primitive repair, but trying to remove it now might do more damage than good. She settled for closing his jacket again, tightening the straps at the waist to help hold the makeshift bandage in place. "We could try to carry him together. Not sure how well that would work, though."

He looked around the room for something that would make the job easier, and after a moment his gaze fell upon the bloodstained cushions of a couch. He pulled out his utility knife, headed over there, and started slicing into fabric. After a moment she realized what he was doing, headed to another cushioned seat, and did the same. Soon they had salvaged enough fabric to wrap Ivar in a protective cocoon and attach two straps for dragging him. It wasn't a dignified solution, but the floor was smooth, and it would be a gentler journey for the man than being bounced on someone's shoulder.

It was a long hike and a difficult one. Periodically they had to shift their grips to ease muscles that had cramped, but they didn't stop moving. Time was too precious. Now and then Ivar muttered something feverish, then sank back into unconsciousness. Any sign of life from him was a good thing, Micah told himself.

Then they reached the vines.

Black, spidery, glistening fingers hung down from one of the ceiling vents, waiting for unwary travelers to walk into them. Remembering how they had curled around his food tube, Micah shuddered. He must have stopped walking for a moment, because Ru looked over at him. "You okay?"

"The vent." He pointed. "Do you see anything there?"

She looked at it, at him. Her eyes narrowed. "No. Do you?"

He bit his lip and said nothing. After a moment she just nodded, and they resumed dragging Ivar. He ducked low enough that the vines wouldn't touch him, hoping she didn't notice.

*Not real. They're not real. I know that. I can override this nightmare.* But the vines remained. In fact they were growing more numerous by the minute, and harder to avoid. They were even more frightening now than they had been the first time he'd seen them, because earlier they'd just been alien plants, and now they were signs of his madness.

*Keep it together, Micah.* He ducked under some low-hanging vines and saw Ru glance at him, concerned. If she decided he was too mentally unstable to be trusted on her ship, might she leave him behind? Then he really would go insane. They dragged Ivar over a nest of black vines, some of which stuck to the cloth cocoon, pulling loose from it with a wet sucking sound. Ru apparently heard none of that. They approached a tangle of vines hanging down below face level, and he forced himself not to go around them, not to brush the tendrils aside as they spread invisible slime across his face. He tried not to flinch.

She didn't respond to them at all.

Finally they reached the place where he had stopped so long

ago—an eternity, it seemed—where the vines filled the hallway from floor to ceiling, rendering it impassable. He could see his cheesecake tube hanging in the midst of the thicket, one long vine curled around it like a snake. He couldn't walk into that. He tried to make his legs move, and just do it, but he couldn't.

"Micah?"

He focused on breathing steadily. *In. Out. In. Out.* "What do you see?" he managed.

"An empty corridor, like all the others. There's a small white object on the floor ahead of us. Looks like it might be a food tube." She looked at him. "Dare I ask what you see?"

"Plants," he whispered. "Vines. The corridor is full of them. There's no way through."

"You know it's not real," she said. Her tone was surprisingly gentle.

"I know," he whispered. He shook his head. "That doesn't help. I'm sorry."

"You've got to walk through them."

He shuddered.

"Just shut your eyes. I'll guide you." She let go of the strap she was holding and held out her hand.

"But Ivar—"

"I'll come back for him once you're through."

He let his own strap drop and took her hand. Her grip was firm, reassuring. He shut his eyes and let her lead him forward.

—and the vines were all over him, sliding across his face, slithering across his body, leaving trails of slime across his mouth, his eyes, his ears. He stumbled, but her grip pulled him upright. The vines were so thick beneath his feet that they tangled about his ankles, and the nightmare sensation of falling enveloped him again. *It's not real,* he thought. *It's not real it's not real it's not real . . .*

At last the vines were gone, and she stopped pulling him forward. He dared to open his eyes, and saw nothing but a normal corridor ahead of them. Releasing her hand, he staggered over to the wall for a moment, leaning against it as he caught his breath. Meanwhile he heard her walk back to Ivar's body, then drag it through the danger zone by herself. His face burned with shame, because he had failed in his share of the labor. As soon as she came up beside him he reached down and picked up his strap again.

"The bios told me this place was inaccessible," she said, looking around. "Locked up tight and constantly guarded. And you've clearly seen something else that would keep people away. Whatever is causing your hallucinations doesn't want people entering this section."

*But it isn't affecting you,* he thought. *Because you never connected.*

When they finally reached the iris portal of the engineering complex, he wasn't able to see it open; she had to push him through the closed door by sheer force. The sensation of being shoved through a solid surface was something he hoped never to experience again. Beyond the portal was a complex of offices and workrooms, and yes, now he understood why the warring factions of Shenshido had been kept out of this place. There was so much advanced tech gear in here that a virt program would have been overloaded, trying to mask it all.

She led him through the complex, quickly enough that he had little time to observe fine details. He did see that the lights on a communications console were on; so much for that tech not working. How many other lies had the locals believed? There was a small airlock at the far end of the complex, with rungs on the wall leading up to a maintenance hatch; they had to haul Ivar's inert body up, balancing it precariously on the narrow rungs while Ru unsealed the hatch overhead. A whoosh of chill air entered the station, and a short tunnel was revealed, leading up to another hatch. Between the two, the G-field shifted with sickening suddenness, making Micah fear that he might vomit. Then Ru opened the upper hatch and climbed through it, and together they maneuvered Ivar's inert body up through the opening. Micah followed as quickly as he could, and collapsed on the floor beside the hatch as Ru resealed it.

They were in a ship, not large, but comfortable enough for two people and an unconscious body. There were a pair of pilot's chairs and a large navigational display at one end, a narrow door at the other, and grips along the walls at intervals to facilitate no-G movement. Not much else. Everything was clean, bright, and streamlined, which suggested that whatever program had been feeding images of decay into his mind was no longer functioning. For the first time since meeting Ru, it struck him that he really was going to get off this damned station.

"It's a bit Spartan," she warned.

Micah leaned down to kiss the floor beside the hatch. "It's the most beautiful ship I've ever seen."

She gestured toward Ivar's body. "Strip him and put him in the medpod. Cut his clothes off if you have to. He can complain about it if he survives."

"And the medpod is . . ." He looked around the empty ship. "Where?"

"Slideaway, midship on the left. I'll open it." She slid into the left chair as if it were part of her body, and her fingers began to dance across the console in front of it, rapidly, without need for her to look down at the controls. He'd never known anyone who would choose to control a ship manually if there was another option. "Brace yourself for detachment."

Stripping Ivar was easier said than done, especially with the ship lurching as it freed itself from the station. In the end he had to destroy the blood-soaked shirt to get it off. The body now visible was more bruised than whole, and so covered with blood that in places the flesh beneath could barely be seen. What skin was visible was covered in tattoos, including a kinesthetic snake coiled on the left pectoral. Micah remembered something about full-body tattoos being popular among particular crime families, but he was too exhausted to recall the details.

A slideaway opened in midship, revealing a small medpod. Micah managed to drag Ivar's body over to it and lever it inside the capsule. Lights came on and equipment whirred and codes appeared on a small monitor to the side, as a transparent lid slid down into place, sealing Ivar's body inside. Micah was too tired to take in the details, just leaned against the wall, drained by the effort.

"It'll clean and sterilize the wounds," Ru said without looking back, "stabilize blood pressure, maintain oxygen levels, and a few other emergency tasks. But it's not a full unit, just enough to get a wounded outrider safely back to the med lab. Hopefully it'll be enough for him."

"We got away," he muttered. He still didn't quite believe it. His body ached in every muscle and joint—but he was alive, he was physically intact, and his mind seemed to be functioning. "We really got away . . ."

"Hold that thought until I get us out of range of those spiders," she warned.

He tried not to think about spiders. Or mutated bodies. Or the sickening feeling of being shoved through a non-existent wall. The thrum of the ship against his back was soothing, hypnotic, and he tried to focus on that. How many hours had he been awake, anyway? He didn't want to call up his chrono to find out. He looked over at the nav screen and saw the outer ring passing by in all its ravaged glory, along with a few bots that perked up as they flew by. But they kept to their perches. Thank God. Thank God. Shenshido was growing smaller by the minute now, as they picked up speed and headed for . . . where? It didn't matter to him. Anywhere that wasn't Shenshido.

He should claim the empty chair and strap himself in, but he didn't have enough energy left to move that far. Weakly he slid down the wall, lowered his head, and focused on breathing steadily, as the doomed station faded into the distance.

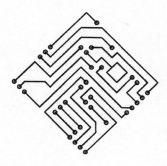

All those traveling from a natural planet to the outworlds shall be tested for communicable diseases before leaving home. Those who are judged to pose a risk to public health will be denied passage.

Those immigrating to the outworlds may be tested again upon arrival, at the local Guildmaster's discretion. Persons judged to pose a risk to the public health will be quarantined, to be sent home on the first available transport.

In the event of a dangerous pathogen appearing in the outworlds, a Guildmaster may quarantine such people, organizations, and/or stations within his node as necessary to contain the infection, until proper medical response can be determined. A Guildmaster will not be held responsible for any losses or damages accruing from justified quarantine, unless negligence of management can be proven to the satisfaction of the Guild's current leadership.

*Founding Charter of the Ainniq Guild, Section 3*
*(also called the Mandate of Protection)*

# HARMONY NODE
## INSHIP: ARTEMIS

**W**HEN THE glow of Shenshido's exterior lighting was little more than a pinpoint, indistinguishable from the sprinkling of distant stars, and the skimmer was well on its way to the middle of nowhere, Ru turned control over to the autopilot. She would have liked to stay at the controls, just in case someone tried to pursue them—a distant possibility at this point—but she needed to check on both her passengers.

With a soft groan she shrugged out of her jacket, then removed the makeshift armor she'd been wearing underneath it. Beneath those layers she was sweat-soaked and sore; a breeze from the ship's ventilation chilled the moisture on her skin, which was deliciously refreshing. She savored it for a few seconds, then got up and headed toward the medpod, leaving the armor on the floor along the way.

The Sarkassan was seated next to the medpod, knees drawn up before him, head lowered to meet them, clearly exhausted. Maybe even asleep. She checked the readings on the medpod, muttering a summary as she went, in case he was still awake. "Blood pressure's better. Looks like three ribs are broken and the left femur fractured. There's a crack in the skull, too; looks like he took one hell of a blow. Lots of soft tissue damage, but vital organs all seem to be functioning. Assuming the brain is undamaged, he might make it through this." She looked at Micah. "You okay?"

Slowly he looked up. "Define okay." A hint of a dry smile flickered across his lips. "I'll survive, if that's what you're asking."

"We're out of the station's innernet range. If that really was the source of your trouble, it should be gone now."

"Thank you," he said softly. His amber eyes were bloodshot, a disconcerting combination of colors. "For getting me out of there."

"My pleasure," she assured him. "You can take off that insect shell if you want."

It took him a moment to realize she meant his armor. Struggling to his feet with a groan, waving off her attempt to assist him, he fumbled for the buckles that held his breastplate on. But either he was too tired to work them, or the angle was just wrong. "Someone helped me get into this," he muttered.

"Here." She reached out to him. "Let me help."

He opened his mouth to protest, but exhaustion won out. He raised up one arm so that she could duck under it and attack the buckles on that side. Sweat and dirt had slicked the plastic and clogged the hinges, making them hard to open. "Damn," she muttered. "This isn't winning any design awards, that's for sure." Finally she got them released. The cuirass split open like a clamshell and she helped him wriggle out of it sideways, which caused his T-shirt to bunch up under his arms. With a sigh of relief he pulled it down.

She grinned. She couldn't help it.

"What?" he asked. "What's wrong?" He followed her gaze to his chest, and then flushed. He'd put the pink shirt on inside-out—probably to hide the insipid design on it—but sweat had rendered the fabric almost transparent, and the outline of frolicking kittens showed through, along with a cheery banner that spelled out HAI KAWAII! backward.

He started to say something . . . then he just leaned back against the wall and started laughing. Exhaustion, embarrassment, and relief all echoed in the sound, and it struck nerves within her. She started to laugh as well, helplessly, a bizarre but effective catharsis.

Finally the fit passed for both of them, and he gathered enough breath to gasp, "My regular wardrobe is much more stylish."

"Black T-shirts with gaming slogans, no doubt."

"*Nice* black T-shirts with gaming slogans."

She wiped a tear from her eye. "Tully and I kept some spare clothes in the skimmer. I haven't had a chance to clear his out yet." *Or didn't have the desire?* "He was heavier than you, but about the same height; some of his clothes might fit. You can take anything you want." She gestured toward the narrow door at the rear of the skimmer. "There's a cleaning cubicle back there, too. Not exactly luxurious."

"Just getting clean would be one hell of a luxury," he assured her.

"You look like you could use a few hours of downtime. Feel free to pull out a bunk. I've got some things to take care of up here."

He pushed himself off the wall, then hesitated. "I don't know how to thank you . . ."

She waved it off. "You helped me figure out what was going on in there. And to get *this* one out." She nodded toward Ivar. "We're more than even."

"Still," he said. "I owe you."

There was no way to respond to that, so as he started toward the rear she turned her attention to the next job. The lock on the hidden armory closet verified her identity, and the wall panels guarding it slid open. She picked up her breastplate and—

"Holy shit," she heard.

She turned to find Micah staring at the armory. It was a pretty impressive collection, and an eclectic one. Firearms and charge rods and flamethrowers hung next to gas grenades and knives and crossbows, and even a pair of swords. Everything was in twos—save for a charge pistol and shock rod that were obviously missing mates—and strapped securely to the wall, in no-G fashion. "Holy shit," he muttered again.

Ru was grinning. "Just a few basic supplies."

"Is that a Frisian K-1 triple-stage assault rifle?" he asked.

She nodded. "You have a good eye."

"I thought those were illegal in the outworlds."

"They are illegal in the outworlds. Your point?"

"I'm . . . I'm just surprised, is all. I thought outriders gathered information. Not . . . whatever you'd need an armory like this for."

The humor in her eyes diminished a bit. "That's not a simple story, or a short one. Maybe later." She touched a control and a deep drawer slid out of the wall; she hefted his cuirass into it, then hers. The blue light of a sterilizer came on as it closed. "Needless to say I'd prefer our guest not know about this collection."

"Well, yeah. Yeah. That goes without saying."

She hung up her weapons and shut the closet door. Like the slideaways, it was now virtually invisible. That was an important feature, in case hostiles ever boarded the skimmer.

As she watched him walk toward the rear of the ship, already pulling off the kitten shirt, she realized what she had just called Ivar. *Our* guest. Hers and Micah's. Was that just force of habit? Or a reflection of how much she hungered for an ally, a partner? *Be wary of trusting him too much,* an inner voice warned. *You can't afford to lose perspective just because you want to trust someone.*

The first part of her report to Jericho was easy to write: a simple narration of her experiences, with supporting data appended to it. But the conclusion called for a subjective analysis, and that gave her pause. She deleted five different versions before coming up with one she was willing to send him.

> . . . *I believe it would be an act of cruelty to leave these people as they are, twitching on the strings of a mysterious puppet master. If Bello's theory is correct, and the signal that imposed sensory distortion on the locals is being channeled through Shenshido's innernet, it should be possible to remove the people from this station*

*with minimal risk, provided they are digitally quarantined until their brainware is verified clean of contamination.*

*But if the attack on Harmony was orchestrated from Shenshido, our puppet master may be able to control his victims across great distances. Until we understand the mechanism of that control, and the limits of his power, refugees should be handled with extreme care.*

She rubbed her forehead with weary fingers, trying to massage away the throb of an oncoming headache. Her wellseeker offered to treat it, and after a moment she accepted. Slowly the pain eased, but not the stress behind it. Her next words, she knew, might subject Shenshido's victims to further suffering. But images from the station were playing out in her mind—fighters armored in cannibalized furniture parts swinging primitive makeshift weapons at one another, surrounded by bodies that had been crushed or slashed or broken—and though her stomach turned at the thought of leaving anyone in that hellhole, they were all part of a much larger game now. And the stakes were too high to take chances.

*As soon as we rescue the people here, we will have tipped our hand to their manipulator. He'll expect the Guild to assign its best brainware specialists to search out his identity, and with the resources that Guera can assign to such an effort, it's only a matter of time before some clue is found. The smart thing for him to do would be to sever all his manipulative connections, abandon his communication channels, and lay low for a while. If he indeed does that, we may never find him.*

She paused. *I'm glad it's Jericho's job to make this decision and not mine.* She'd passed judgment on her share of colonies, and helped determine the fate of whole populations, but Shenshido felt much more personal. Perhaps it was because the people there were native to the outworlds, citizens of the galactic human community that Guera had so painstakingly created. Not colonists who had been isolated from the rest of humanity for so long that they had no idea what was being denied them.

And they'd begged her for help. That was very personal.

> *I trust you to handle that challenge as you see fit. Meanwhile, let*
> *me know if there is some further service you wish from me. I assume*
> *that any such request would be accompanied by a generous offer of*
> *compensation. This is dangerous shit, Jericho.*
>
> *I will remain at this location one Standard Day to receive your*
> *response.*

She reread what she had written, decided it was the best she was going to be able to do, and added one more note to the bottom. Send me whatever info you've got on a game designer named Micah Bello.

ENCRYPT
COMPRESS
CONFIRM PRIVATE CHANNEL
DOUBLE RETINAL SCAN REQUIRED TO OPEN
SEND.

As the data packet headed out toward Harmony, she heard footsteps behind her, and turned to see Micah approaching. He was wearing one of Tully's shirts, which hung a bit loose on him, but at least it was clean, and his face was a healthy-looking color, not the chalky hue she remembered from back in the tunnels. She didn't know what color a Sarkassan was supposed to be, so she was guessing this was an improvement. *Note to self: research Sarkassa's Variation.* Now that all the dirt and blood had been scrubbed off, he didn't look half bad: a little taller than she was, a little thinner than Tully, and he moved with a confidence that suggested underlying fitness. It was hard to judge his age, as so many signs of that could be minimized by telomere therapy, but the youthful sparkle in his eyes suggested he hadn't yet needed such intervention. His natural coloring, now visible, was striking, his fair skin a dramatic backdrop for the Sarkassan markings. All in all not bad, though the sight of him looking fresh and clean reminded her how much she could use a scrub herself.

She gestured toward the other pilot's chair. "Have a seat. As you can see"—she indicated the screen—"there's not much out there. Seemed a good place to wait for instructions, while catching our breath."

He started to turn the chair toward him, and then stopped, clearly surprised by something. Suddenly she realized that Tully's oversized glass phallus was still strapped into the seat. She flushed. "It was my partner's—"

"Hey!" He put up his hands quickly. "Didn't ask. Don't need to know."

"It was a gift from a glassblower on Betalon Five." She leaned over and unclipped the safety harness to free the thing. "It was one of his favorite artifacts, so I brought it along to remind me of him." She opened a small slideaway under the navigation display and carefully set the artwork inside. "I'm not used to traveling alone."

He hesitated. "Can I ask what happened? Or is that too personal?"

For a long moment she didn't answer. She'd promised herself she wouldn't share details of Tully's death with anyone, but this wasn't some arrogant Guild official wanting lurid details to spice up his debriefing report. She and Micah had depended on each other while escaping Shenshido, through a maze of delusion and death, and that made for a strange sense of intimacy. "He used the wrong bodily organ for thinking," she said at last. "He paid the price."

"Damn. I'm sorry."

She shrugged. "Shit happens."

He sat down in Tully's seat and studied the display screen; the chair whirred softly as it adjusted to his body. "Never have I been so grateful to see empty space."

Despite herself she smiled. "Trust me, it can get boring after twenty years."

"But you don't stay awake for all that time, though, do you?"

"Enough of it to be bored. Deceleration starts as soon as you enter a star system, and safety regs don't allow for stasis after that point. It can take months to reach the target and establish a viable orbit. Lots of time to kill."

He glanced behind him. "In this small ship? How do you not go crazy? Wait, don't tell me. Virts?"

She ignored the bait. "This is just our lander. The mothership has facilities to keep mind and body healthy. At least that's the theory. Once we start collecting data from a colony—maybe even picking up on their communications—there's more than enough work to focus on. We need all the information we can get to make realistic predictions about what we'll face when we arrive."

"How accurate are your predictions?"

"Usually pretty good. We've got specialized software that can look at how a station or ship was designed and extrapolate all sorts of social patterns. Sometimes we argue about the interpretation of what it tells us, but it's usually close to the mark."

"Do you place wagers on those arguments?" His dark eyes were sparkling. "See who comes closest to guessing right? I know I would."

She smiled slightly. "I would never admit to such a thing."

"And if things don't go smoothly, despite that? Is that what all the weapons are for?"

The smile faded. With a sigh she leaned back in her seat. "You really want that story?"

"If you're ready to tell it."

For a moment she just stared into space. What words did you choose, to communicate such a dark truth? It wasn't something she usually shared with outsiders, and part of her felt it should stay that way. But another part of her hungered to bring this strange wanderer into her world. She wasn't used to living in it alone.

"The job of an outrider team is to travel to a colony that Earth abandoned, and to bring back the information needed for Guera to launch a recovery operation. Most of those journeys end in disappointment. Sometimes we find relics—the remains of houses, irrigation channels, hothouses. Sometimes there are grave sites. Sometimes there's nothing.

Alien forests and seas have swallowed up a fledgling colony, leaving us nothing to study. We may not even know what shape the colonists were when their struggle to survive finally ended. What can we do in such cases, besides move on to the next world and hope for better?"

She sighed heavily. "The colonies that did survive . . . you never know what you'll find. The earliest ones, like Guera, had time to adapt to their new homes before Isolation began; some of those colonies are quite well developed, and may even have space travel of their own. But other colonies were cut off before they got all the supplies and personnel that a new colony needed to survive. When their children were born with what they perceived as horrific deformities, when the home planet cut off all contact without warning, they had no idea why these things were happening. All they knew was that Earth had abandoned them in their time of need, and they hated it for that. Later generations might come to blame Earth for all their troubles, even ones the Terrans had nothing to do with. They needed to blame *someone*, and an absent scapegoat is the best kind, as it can't fight back."

"Amen to that," he muttered.

"In some places, that hatred took on a dark spiritual aspect. Humanity does love its religions. Earth became the Great Betrayer, existential source of all pain and suffering, the embodiment of evil. In order for your people to prosper, you had to hold its malevolence at bay. Some colonies even viewed Earth as a demon proper, that must be placated or exorcised if humans were to prosper. Tully and I found one colony where—" She stopped for a moment. Took a deep breath. "They threw babies into an abyss," she said softly. "The spirit of Earth demanded death, they told us, and if they offered it a sacrifice of their own free will, others would be spared."

"Shit," Micah muttered. "That's pretty messed up."

"Now you understand why we don't usually talk to outsiders about such things. But every outrider has seen them." She shut her eyes. "By the time we show up, strangers from the sky, the language of such a colony has evolved into new forms, and their communications technology— if they have any—is no longer compatible with ours. Sometimes there's no way to communicate until we are actually face to face. And then . . ." She shrugged suggestively.

"You look like Terrans."

She nodded. "Sometimes we get a chance to communicate who we are before they attack us. Sometimes . . . sometimes we don't. All that hatred, all that fear—centuries of raw despair—it all gets focused on us." She glanced back at the armory. "It's rare we need weapons. But when we do, we'd damn well better have them on hand."

He exhaled softly. "Wow. I just . . . I had no idea."

"Yeah. By the time the second wave teams show up, that's all been sorted out."

"So this ship we're on . . . is that armed, too? Seems like it would have to be."

She smiled slightly, said nothing.

"Do you have to make first contact like that? Couldn't you bring back data and leave it to someone else?"

"It's our call. If we don't feel the situation is safe enough, yeah, we can let Guera send in its experts. But Micah . . . Imagine you've spent six months cooped up in a spaceship, hungering to explore the mysteries of a lost world. Do you think you could just take notes on it, shoot a few vids, and then go home? Think about the kind of people who sign on for my job. Think about why we do it. I've never known any outrider to turn down an opportunity for first contact."

He chuckled softly. "You need someone on your team who can't be mistaken for Terran."

"Yeah. Well. Except it's the Guild that's in charge of all this, and they're not about to trust any non-Guerans with their precious Manifest Destiny." She could hear the edge of lifelong frustration coming into her voice, and it wasn't something she wanted to share with him, so she changed the subject. "The ship's on autopilot now. I need to get some sleep. I'm sorry I can't let you connect to the ship's innernet, but if you picked up some malware on Shenshido—"

"I understand," he said quietly. "No need to explain."

"Once Ivar is up we'll need to stagger shifts so that one of us is always awake. I don't trust him worth a damn."

He raised an eyebrow. "You trust *me?*"

*Do I?* She wondered. *Should I?* "Navigation is locked. You can't access the ship's innernet without my security codes. And the ship will alert me if you try to break into the armory while I'm asleep, or do anything else unseemly. I'm not really worried about you trying to cut my throat while I sleep. So I think we're good for now." She indicated the console. "You can bring up anything you need to on the screen. We've got one hell of a library—books and vids—and I think Tully stocked some games. Not really my thing."

"You prefer your adventures to be real." He smiled dryly. "Got it."

She eased herself up from her chair. God, she was stiff. Her wellseeker would have to address that while she slept. "Make yourself at home. Get some more sleep if you need to. When we're both well rested we can see how our friend is doing." She glanced back at the medpod. "And if he's going to prove useful enough to be worth all this effort."

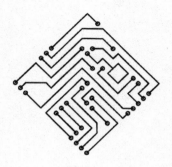

## THE HARVESTER IS COMING!

Come celebrate with us in style, as Harmony Node welcomes the return of its harvester in a grand station-wide festival. Sample the food of a hundred different worlds, attend concerts by famous bands and orchestras, and gasp at the daring of multi-G acrobats in Solial's Galactic Circus—all while our great winged ships spread out across the heavens, bearing gifts from distant worlds. This once-in-a-century event is not to be missed, but tickets and accommodations are selling out quickly, so make your reservations now!

The harvester's arrival will be livecast on VBC, with virtual feed courtesy of Blue Galaxy Studios. Visit their site to subscribe.

# DEEP SPACE
# APPROACHING HARMONY
# NODE

**T**HE AINNIQ is near. Not yet so close that the harvester can see it, but her sensors are picking up subtle fluctuations in the fabric of space that hint at its proximity. Too subtle for human senses to detect—or even most mechanical constructs—but she was designed to locate such things and hone in on them.

She is nearing home.

She shifts her sensors to the frequencies that humans use to communicate and picks up faint whispers of navigational code. She is searching for one in particular, a signal meant for her and her children, to help guide them home.

There. There it is.

Soon she will spread her wings wide and command her children to separate from her, and they will do so, spreading their wings into the galactic night. A vast flock of silver birds, each with a portion of her precious harvest clutched to its chest. It is far easier to deliver mass that way, in small portions that are easily decelerated, than to try to slow the harvester itself. She will circle the ainniq while her children make their deliveries, then gather them to her again when the job is done. By then she will have received orders for her next assignment. The human hunger for raw mass never ends, and so her task is eternal.

She sends her response to the homing signal: simple code, simple message:

*I am here. Make ready.*

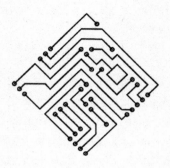

At first glance, SCAVENGER'S DILEMMA appears to be a fairly standard full-immersion game. The setting is meticulously realized, but familiar: a mysterious derelict ship has been discovered in the far reaches of space, and various bands of adventurers race to strip it of valuables. Players can join a loosely organized band of salvagers, hot on the trail of an artifact rumored to be in the wreckage (the identity of the artifact changes with each new chronicle), or a team of scavs who want to dismantle the ship to sell as raw mass on the black market. That the two groups will come into conflict is inevitable, and the no-G setting makes for an interesting battlefield.

What elevates SCAVENGER'S DILEMMA above other games of its type is the nature of the two core alliances. The salvagers are independents, pooling their efforts to locate a single artifact so they can sell it and divvy up the profits. But the closer they get to their goal, the more tempting it will be for one to break away and claim the prize for himself. And while the scavs aren't limited to a single prize—there's enough raw mass to go around—they are ruthless rivals and might betray a companion just to rise in the scav pecking order. Whichever group you decide to join, you can never be sure that an ally will not betray you . . . or that it might not be in your best interest to betray an ally first.

Like the Prisoner's Dilemma for which it was named, SCAVENGER'S DILEMMA forces players to weigh the consequences of cooperation versus self-interest. Role-play takes center stage as a player must work to strengthen the bonds of common interest within his group, in the hopes that when battle finally does occur, his own people won't stab him in the back. To trust, or not to trust? In this finely nuanced game, there is no easy answer.

It should come as no surprise that SCAVENGER'S DILEMMA is from the design team of Micah Bello, whose previous credits include STAR'S TEARS, BLACK AS BLOOD, and of course, DRAGONSLAYER. We've come to expect complex games from that team, weaving together action-filled adventures with moral and philosophical challenges, and this one does not disappoint. Whether you are a beginning gamer or a seasoned veteran, SCAVENGER'S DILEMMA will have something for you. Highly recommended.

Selma Sommers
*Virtual Reviews, Issue 123.5*

# HARMONY NODE
# INSHIP: ARTEMIS

**T**HE RESPONSE from Jericho didn't have her name on it. It didn't have his name on it, either. Paranoia, or reasonable precautions?

> *I received your encrypted data packet. All of the security seals were still in place when it arrived.*
>
> *Payment for services rendered has been transferred to your account. I believe that the information you have gathered qualifies you for the Guild bounty, and when you return I will see that you get it.*
>
> *To say that your conclusions are unsettling is an understatement. Whoever was responsible for the situation on Shenshido, we must assume they have the potential to do the same on other stations. Such technology could undermine the stability of the outworlds, casting them into chaos as it did with Shenshido. Until we know more about who is responsible and what their plans are—and how all of this is tied to the Dragonslayer incident—we are just stumbling in the dark. We need to find out who is behind this, and why.*

*You are the person best suited to seek out that information. Indeed, you may well be the only person who can do so freely. Harmony is pressing us to abandon any interest in the Dragonslayer assault, which raises the question of whose agenda our leaders are serving. You alone are outside the circle of suspicion, unrestricted in your actions. It is my hope that you will agree to follow the trail you have identified and continue to gather information. Accordingly I offer continuation of our per diem arrangement, and generous financial reward if you are successful. More is not possible in advance, I regret, lest the transfer of funds draw attention to our activity. For now, please accept my own personal marker for a future favor, as security. Given my position in the Guild, such a debt has considerable value. I can only hope it is enough to convince you to continue.*

*Regarding your concern about the survivors on Shenshido, rest assured, I will make sure they are rescued. It may not be on the schedule they would prefer, since, as you point out, that would alert our enemy that we are on to him, but I will make sure that their future recovery is guaranteed.*

*Regarding your request for information:*

*Micah Bello is dead. This was just announced by Tridac Enterprises, his employer for the past five years. Are you sure that the person on your skimmer is really him? I am attaching some data you can use to confirm his identity, and I recommend you do not discuss any sensitive matters with him until you have done so.*

*According to Tridac, Bello was the one responsible for the Dragonslayer explosion. They were planning to bring him in for questioning when he fled their station, and in the ensuing chase, both he and his ship were destroyed. That is what they have reported to us. Needless to say, that chain of events seems remarkably convenient, in terms of covering up any involvement they might have had in this affair. One wonders what their true role is in all of this.*

*Meanwhile, be wary of Bello. It sounds like he didn't know anything about the Shenshido experiment, so if there is a terrorist conspiracy I doubt he is part of it, but there is no denying that he specializes in the very type of programming that may have been used in the Harmony assault. Even if he didn't contribute directly to Shenshido's downfall, software that he designed might have been used for that purpose. If so, he has an interest in this matter that directly conflicts with our own. I appreciate that he has been a useful ally up to now, but please bear these things in mind as you deal with him.*

*You should plan on bringing him directly to me when you return. I am attaching a set of fake ID for him to use until then. If Tridac truly believes Bello is dead, we should give them no reason to think otherwise. But do not underestimate the importance of delivering him to me first thing when you return. He may carry a dangerous malware infection and needs to be quarantined until we can determine what kind of threat that implies.*

*Background: Before his flight, Bello was a designer for Dobson Games, a subsidiary of Tridac, for whom he produced several award-winning multi-player virts, including Dragonslayer. In addition to an impressive résumé in the gaming industry, he has presented papers on virtual technology at several professional conferences—all well received—and published a book on virt technology. Before coming to Tridac, he worked briefly for Guildmaster Vienna. I can find no information on his duties there, which suggests he may have been part of Vienna's private hacking team. Given that, and his programming specialty, you will understand why I caution you to be wary.*

*The choice of where to go from here on is yours to make. I hope it involves further investigation of this matter, but I can only request that of you, not order it. Let me know what you decide, and if you do choose to continue, what support you require from me.*

Leaning back in her chair, Ru muttered, "Fuck."

She hadn't slept well. Images from Shenshido ruled her dreams: bloody, violent. Now, thanks to Jericho's letter, she was imagining even worse horrors. What would it be like to return from an outriding mission and discover that in her absence other stations had become like

Shenshido, full of delusional humans warring like barbarians in their corridors? The thought was enough to chill the soul. But so was the thought that the task of preventing such a fate might fall upon her shoulders. She was an outrider, nothing more. Messenger to lost colonies. Occasionally a diplomat. It was the Guild's job to worry about humanity's ultimate fate; she was just an employee.

*And now barely that*, she thought irritably. Jericho's offer of compensation didn't come close to what the next step of this investigation should pay. No doubt he thought that her innate curiosity, her insatiable hunger for new experiences, would make it impossible for her to refuse the assignment. Never mind that he was asking her to enter a region of space controlled by the worst dregs of humanity, accompanied by no better than a fantasy game designer and a scav who would probably sell them both out in a heartbeat. Curiosity would win out over all that, right?

*Damn you, Jericho.* She sighed. *That had better be one hell of a favor you're offering.*

She opened the file Jericho had sent her on Bello. As promised, there was a set of false ID included, as well as a note assuring her that all its details had been entered in the relevant databanks. If anyone tried to research Bello's new identity, it would pass muster. There was a long list of facts about his life, some so utterly trivial that for a moment she couldn't understand why Jericho had included them. Who really cared what Bello's favorite food was in his childhood? But if the Sarkassan on her ship was an imposter who had memorized key facts about the real Bello's life in order to pass for him, it was unlikely he'd know such piddling details. Which mean they could be used to test him. All right, so that was good to have. There was one more item at the bottom of the file, and when she saw it she cursed Jericho under her breath for placing it there, rather than up top where she would have seen it before reading everything else.

Micah Bello's DNA code.

God alone knew how Jericho had gotten hold of it, or why he hadn't considered it the most important item in the file. Maybe he hadn't been sure that an outrider ship would have the equipment for genetic analysis—though, given the nature of outriding, that seemed a no-brainer. More likely he hadn't thought she would be able to get a DNA sample from Bello without tipping him off. Well, that might have been true had Micah not just changed clothes on her ship. His armor had already been sterilized, but those terminally cute kittens he'd been wearing were probably swimming in his DNA.

Expression grim, she uploaded Jericho's data to the ship's library, deleted and overwrote the rest of the encrypted message, then headed back to the rear of the ship to find that godawful pink T-shirt.

He looked peaceful, more or less. Relaxed in the sleep of utter exhaustion, with only a slight furrowing of the brow and occasional twitch to hint at the unpleasant nature of his dreams. Remembering how dark her own dreams had been, she sympathized. How much worse would this experience be for someone who had never seen humans devolve to a primitive state like that? At least her outriding career had prepared her for that part of the nightmare.

Well, now she knew that he was really Micah Bello. His DNA had confirmed that much. But although Jericho had given her exhaustive details on his life, those were sterile facts that offered no insight into his soul. Watching him sleep now, she noted how graceful the tiger markings on his body were, framing his face, accenting his bare lower arms with streaks and whorls. The red eye of his dragon headset winked at her as his body stirred slightly with each breath. Did she find him attractive because his features were pleasing, or because he had pushed himself to the limit on Shenshido? He might have started out as a desk jockey, but he had proven his potential to become more than that.

"That's not creepy at all," he said suddenly, startling her, "you staring at me while I sleep."

"Time to get up," she told him. "Ivar's ready to be released, and you and I have things we should talk about first."

He opened his eyes: still slightly bloodshot, she noted, but a thousand times better than before he'd gone to sleep. "How long have I been out?" His eyes unfocused for a moment as he consulted some internal data. "Three hours, forty minutes?"

"Two complete sleep cycles. REM stages were unusually long. I waited for the last one to end."

He grimaced. "Not sure that was such a favor, given the dreams I had." He pushed himself up to a sitting position, wincing as a bruise on his arm banged into the frame of the narrow bunk. "How'd you know what sleep stage I was in, anyway? Were you standing here all that time, watching my eyes twitch?"

"The ship watched you. It monitors all our vital signs as a failsafe, so that if we were ever both incapacitated, it would know to seal the hatches and bring us back to the mothership."

"By *we*, you mean . . ."

"Ah. Sorry. My partner and I." A hollow ache attended the words. "It's probably confused by the fact that there are three of us on board. We don't usually take on passengers." She nodded toward the bow. "Decide what silly cartoon you want to wear today and join me up front. We can talk over food. Hardly a gourmet meal, but we're cruising at a high enough G that I can do better than tubes and nutrient bars." She glanced back toward the body in the medpod; her eyes narrowed. "This ship wasn't designed for private conversations; any discussion we don't want him to hear should take place before he wakes up."

"How is he? He was in pretty bad shape."

"Medpod says nothing is torn or broken that won't heal. His pain receptors have been tamped down, so he won't feel the worst of it for a while. Hopefully before that happens we can negotiate . . ." she hesitated. "Something."

She left him to see to his own awakening and headed for the galley outlet. The ship's stock of edibles was more depleted than expected— she would have to restock before her next mission—but the replicator had enough ingredients to turn out a reasonable simulacrum of a meal. There were real dried fruits as well, from the aeroponic gardens on Tiananmen, and after a moment's consideration she added them to the spread. It could be their last peaceful meal for a while; they might as well enjoy it.

When he joined her at the foldaway table he looked over the offerings curiously. "More than I expected."

She smiled slightly. "Can't explore new worlds on an empty stomach." She pushed a tall mug of steaming brown liquid toward him. "Made you some kaf. You've been living among Terrans for five years, so I figured you might have picked up a taste for it."

"Don't need to be Terran to appreciate kaf. Though that's more for the kick than the taste." He sat down and lifted the mug a few times, testing the magnetic field that held it in place. "So . . . you've been doing some research on me."

"Would you expect anything less?"

"Back home, no. But without the outernet it's pretty challenging. Color me impressed." He sipped carefully from the mug. "Not that I can return the favor, since a certain outrider has locked me out of her ship's innernet."

"Says the man I had to shove through an imaginary wall."

He winced. "Fair enough." Another sip. "Have you gotten your new orders?"

Her eyes narrowed slightly. "Not *orders*. But yes, my contact responded. He asked me to hunt down the designer of Shenshido's rogue software."

"Which would require what, exactly?"

"Following the signal we discovered. Into the sector where all the bad people hang out."

He grinned. "Sounds like fun."

Was he being sarcastic? She didn't know him well enough to be sure. "It depends on what kind of information Ivar can give us." She sipped from her cup of replicated fruit juice. "Assuming he's willing to share what he knows."

"He might not know anything. If Shenshido's software infected him without his being aware of it—like it did with me—he may be as much in the dark about its source as we are."

*What if that infection is still active?* she thought. *We're assuming the distance from Shenshido will protect you, but what if we're wrong? What if it left something inside your brain that can affect you outside that network?* "True," she murmured. She put her cup back down on the table; it snicked softly against the magnetic surface. "Either way, I have two choices. The first is to head back to Harmony, drop you off, and then continue the investigation alone. The problem with that is, I can't just set you down on the waystation and leave. My contact needs to evaluate you before you're released into the general population. He's decent enough, for a Guildsman, but ultimately I doubt he'll be the one deciding your fate. And I can't answer for how others would treat you."

"Understood," he said solemnly. "And the other choice?"

She leaned back in her chair. "You could help me trace this thing to its source. Between your knowledge of virt technology and your experience with Tridac, you're a valuable asset." She paused. "There's only one problem."

He put his mug down. "How do you know you can trust me."

She nodded.

For a moment he was silent. Was he accessing his brainware for data, or just weighing his options in the old-fashioned way, sans digital assistance? "What would you need from me, to make that possible?"

"You can start with the truth."

"I told you that on Shenshido."

"*All* of the truth."

He sighed heavily, and for a few seconds just stared into his kaf. "Tridac asked me to review the software for Dragonslayer. They said that if there was something in it that could explain what happened on Harmony, I was the one who could find it. But while I was working on it . . ." he inhaled deeply, "it looked like they were setting me up to take the blame for the attack. So I left. I figured if I could get back to Common Law space I'd at least be guaranteed due process. Only I guess they anticipated that move. I was attacked en route. Driven into Shenshido's space, where the spiders got me. In hindsight . . . maybe Tridac manipulated me into doing that. Maybe it was their plan all along. Twenty/twenty hindsight, yeah?" He took another drink from his mug. "Is that enough truth for you? Because if there's an alternative to being delivered to the Guild to have my brain dissected, I'm all for it."

She hesitated, then took a small envelope out of her pocket, withdrew a folded printout from it, and handed it to him. It was the part of Jericho's letter that talked about Tridac's accusation and Bello's alleged death. As he read it, his expression darkened. "Sons of *bitches*." He slammed the printout down onto the table, then drew in a ragged breath. "It's not true. Any of it."

"I believe you. Here." She handed him the envelope. "You'll need this, to stay out of trouble."

"What is it?" He peered inside, then turned it upside down, spilling out the contents: printouts, cards, a data chip. He picked up one of the cards. "ID?"

"If Tridac thinks Micah Bello is dead, then he needs to stay dead. Which means you need to become someone else."

He raised an eyebrow. "You had this ready for me?"

Smiling slightly, she nodded.

"You were so sure I would want to come with you?"

"I was pretty sure you wouldn't want to go back to Harmony."

"Yeah." He snorted. "For sure." He drew the bio out of the pile and looked it over. "Anthony Bester, huh? Degree from Core West University . . . that's a shitty school. And Isolation Studies is a shitty major." He skimmed the rest of the page. "No wonder this version of me never made much of himself."

"The goal was to design you a history that wouldn't draw notice. It's been entered in all the proper databases."

He looked up at her. "This is from your contact?"

She nodded. "I told you. He's a decent guy. For a Guildsman."

"But if I use this name, he'll know it's me. He can track me with it."

"Yes," she agreed, "that is the downside."

"Shit." A long silence. "You realize this mission of yours could get us both killed?" He shook his head. "I can't believe I'm saying that outside of a game."

"The plan is to gather information, not engage the enemy. Others will do that after we deliver our report."

"Hopefully."

"Hopefully," she agreed.

"But the best-laid plans of mice and men, huh?" He put the bio back down on the table. "You understand, I'm not used to risking my actual physical neck—"

"But you've written stories about it." She smiled sweetly. "Call this research."

He stared at her for a moment, then chuckled. "Damn it, woman. You should have gone into sales."

She leaned forward on the table. "Are you going to tell me that the mystery of all this doesn't intrigue you at all? That the *risk* doesn't appeal to you? That you didn't feel more alive on Shenshido than you ever did in one of your make-believe worlds?"

A corner of his mouth twitched slightly: the shadow of a smile.

"Not that I'm ever going to admit to you," he told her. "So when do we wake up Sleeping Beauty?"

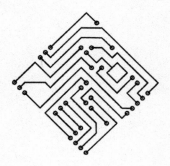

The hunger for competition is an intrinsic part of human nature. We can no more be rid of it than we can rid ourselves of the desire to eat, to procreate, or to leave our mark upon posterity . . . for in the eyes of Nature, competition is linked to all those things.

Give this instinct proper outlet, and it can nourish the spirit.

Attempt to deny it, and it can destroy worlds.

KOJO SACHI
*The Darkness Within*

# HARMONY NODE
# INSHIP: ARTEMIS

IVAR LOOKED better than he had a day ago, though Micah had to admit that was not a very high bar. Still, the man had gone from *almost dead* to *probably going to live long enough to talk to us,* and that was a definite upgrade.

He and Ru were armed now, with charge pistols from the hidden armory, small enough weapons to be hidden in their pockets. Just in case, Ru said. Micah had never carried a real weapon before, and the weight of the gun was a sobering reminder of just how real the stakes were here. But what the hell. In the last couple of days he'd watched his ship explode, been stranded in deep space without life support, been trapped in a decrepit space station run by crazy people, and wrestled with delusions so real he still had nightmares about them. The thought of facing physical danger wasn't as alien to him as it had once been. There was even a small part of him—a *very* small part—that found the concept exciting. When in this strange journey had he ceased to be a mere game designer—orchestrator of wasted time, purveyor of faux fear—and become the kind of person who found the thought of real danger enticing? The change was both exhilarating and unnerving.

The medpod had cleaned Ivar up, stripping away crusted blood and dirt and sweat to reveal a body crisscrossed with scars. The puckered flesh of badly healed burns distorted some of his tattoos, and gnarled white scars sliced across other tattoos like bolts of lightning. There were medical treatments that could have diminished those scars, Micah knew, but Ivar clearly hadn't sought them out. Had he lacked the opportunity, or the desire? Status among the scavs was rumored to be fiercely competitive and constantly shifting; might Ivar have believed that it would enhance his social standing to bear the marks of so many violent confrontations? The idea was intriguing, and he logged it in the back of his mind for future reference.

"There are powerful factions that dominate the black market," he had told Ru. "If he's connected to one of them, his actions will reflect back on it. There would be consequences for him breaking his word to us, or refusing to acknowledge a valid debt."

"And if not?"

He shook his head. "Then there's no guarantee of anything."

"I didn't realize you were an expert on scavs."

"I did research for a project once. Mostly gathering legends and rumors for inspiration, but that particular detail was mentioned by several sources, so there's probably some truth behind it. Don't know if the factions are family-based, though it seems likely. Families, tribes, clans . . . it's how humans organize themselves."

"Any other detail you think had truth behind it?"

"Yeah. Status. Big deal. Bring back a good haul, pull off an impressive heist, and you'll sit high and proud in the scavenger pecking order. That matters to them. Or so say the rumors." He paused. "Of course, all that's only relevant if he really is a scav. If you guessed wrong about that—"

"Then we're shooting blind."

Now . . . there the man was, lying before them, and the images inked on his body would probably tell them everything they needed to know about him, if Micah knew how to read them.

"You ready?" Ru asked.

"As much as I'll ever be."

She had brought a thin robe from the supply closet, and she laid it across Ivar's loins as a token modesty. Then she reached over to the medpod's control panel and initiated shutdown. The pod buzzed softly for a moment, then the various leads attached to Ivar began to withdraw from his flesh. The mattress that had been cradling his body returned to its base position, flat beneath him. A catheter slithered out from under his loin cover, serpent-like, and was sucked back into its storage slot. Last to go was the injection gun pressed against his neck; there was the sound of a final spurt as a stimulant was shot into his veins to counteract his sedation, and then it, too, withdrew to its storage position.

When all the leads were out of the way, Ru pulled several restraining straps across Ivar's body and clipped them into place. In his last waking moments he'd been fighting for his life, she explained to Micah, and there was a real danger that when he came to he would think himself still in that battle, and strike out at whoever was nearest to him. Strapping him down for those first few minutes would keep him from hurting anyone, including himself.

The last strap locked into place just in time. Ivar's eyes twitched, and he began to gasp for breath. Suddenly his whole body tensed, muscles all contracting at once. It looked painful. His eyes shot open, and a chaos of emotions roiled in their depths: pain, fury, fear. He began to struggle against his restraints—blindly, wildly, like a trapped animal—and Micah wondered if maybe the blow to his skull had damaged his brain beyond repair. But finally the struggles subsided, and his body relaxed. He drew in a deep breath, then another one, then started coughing. Ru unsnapped the restraint straps and he turned over on his side, fighting to clear his lungs. After the fit passed he looked up at her, then at Micah, then at his surroundings. "This place is too damned clean to be Hell," he muttered hoarsely, "and I'm sure I'm not cleared for the other place. Where am I?"

"Still alive," Ru told him. "On my ship. It was touch and go for a while."

He was running his hands over his body, as if not quite believing it was whole. What must it be like, Micah wondered, to believe one was dying, but then wake up later, still among the living? As Ivar tried to sit up Ru offered a hand to assist, but he waved her off. Gritting his teeth, he slowly managed to pull himself upright. *He hates to look weak*, Micah noted. "Please tell me we're off Shenshido."

"Far away from it," Ru assured him. "With no one and nothing following us."

"Thank the fucking gods." He looked at Micah. "Who's this? Your pilot?"

"Among other duties. Anthony Bester, meet Ivar . . . I'm sorry, is there a last name?"

"Ivar's fine." Did the evasion mean he had no family, or had one and wished to keep it secret? His expression offered no clue. "I thought for sure they'd killed me." He looked up at Ru. "You saved my life."

"So we're even on that count. Any idea why they didn't finish you off?"

He rubbed his forehead, then shut his eyes for a moment and concentrated: probably directing his wellseeker to shoot something useful into his veins. "I heard someone yell about another fight going on, and people were needed. I was down already, so I played dead. Apparently I do that very well." A half-hearted laugh turned into another fit of coughing.

"I think I saw the results of that fight. Bloody mess. I doubt anyone survived it."

"Well, they wanted their Armageddon battle." His expression was grim. "I guess that's what they got."

Slowly, carefully, he lowered himself from the pod. The robe slid from his lap to the floor as he stood upright, but either he didn't notice or didn't care. As he shifted his weight onto his left leg, he winced.

"You fractured your left femur and your right temple," Ru told him, "and broke three ribs. The bones have been fused, but that's just a superficial repair. You'll need a few weeks of natural healing before they're at full strength again. I can have the replicator make a brace for your leg—"

"No brace," he said sharply.

"Just to protect it from impact—"

"*No brace.*" He took a deep breath and leaned down to pick up the robe, which he wrapped around his hips, knotting the sleeves like a belt. For a brief moment his eyes unfocused; was he trying to access the ship's innernet? If so, he would discover he was locked out, as Micah was. Finally he focused his attention back on Ru. "I said I'd pay you for getting me out of that hellhole. Fair's fair. What's your price?"

*Information on the place you came from,* Micah thought. But if they asked for that directly, all his defenses would go up. "We can talk about that later," Ru said. "To be honest, I've been so focused on getting away from Shenshido I haven't had time to think about it."

"No problem. Now that we're away from that miserable shithole, you'll find me the soul of patience. So . . ." He looked around the ship again. "Can I ask where we're headed?"

"Course is set for Harmony Station. I wanted to wake you up before I loaded it." She seemed about to say more, then hesitated.

"What?" His eyes narrowed suspiciously. "Is something wrong?"

"I've been informed we're going to be placed under quarantine when we arrive. No one will be able to leave the ship until Guera clears us to do so. That includes you. I'm sorry."

He was clearly less than pleased by the news. No surprise there. If he really was a scavenger, the last thing he would want was to be trapped inside a quarantined skimmer, waiting for Gueran authorities to inspect it. "Why the fuck are we being quarantined?"

"They said they want to make sure that whatever caused the problem on Shenshido isn't contagious."

"They think a disease made everyone crazy?"

"I'm not sure they think it so much as need to rule it out. I'm sure there won't be a problem. It will just take a bit of time. I'm sorry."

He was looking less and less pleased. "That doesn't sound like a bounty hunter's report," he challenged her.

She was silent for a moment, biting her lip, as if considering how much to confide in him. *She's a good role-player,* Micah thought. *Given her profession, I guess she has to be.*

"Ivar, I was hired to find out what happened on Shenshido. It was rumored the station had been working on some kind of new weapon to use against the scavs, that backfired on them. Obviously if that was the case, I couldn't just show up and start asking questions about it. I needed a cover story."

"Do you believe that's what happened? They were working on a weapon?"

She spread her hands. "I'm just a mercenary, hired to gather data. Others get the pleasure of analyzing it. Apparently they need to do some of that before we rejoin civilization. I'm sorry."

Micah watched Ivar closely. If he really was a scav, quarantine would be an untenable situation. But admitting to that meant admitting to his outlaw status. Who else would be so fixed on avoiding the Guild's scrutiny? Up until now his conversations with Ru, back on Shenshido, had been a delicate dance of implications and assumptions. At least that was how she'd described it. If Ivar wanted her to help him avoid quarantine he'd have to ask for that help. Which would put a lot of new things on the table.

Ivar stared at her for a moment, as if that would somehow make her motives visible. "Can you drop me off somewhere else?" he asked at last. "Before that. Since you know I'm not carrying anything contagious."

Now it was she who took time to consider, or at least pretended to. After letting Ivar's fears simmer for a few seconds, she turned to Micah. "Can we work in a discreet side trip?"

He hesitated. "I could wipe it from the pilot's log. But if they check on our fuel reserves they'll know we diverted, and realize that the log was probably altered. Very risky."

Ru looked at Ivar. Said nothing.

"Ten thousand," he offered. "Untraceable cash chits."

Micah whistled softly.

"You carrying that on you?" Ru asked. "Somehow I doubt it."

"I can get it before disembarking."

A slight smile crept across Ru's face. *I know what you are,* it seemed to say. *And I know how much you need my help. That doesn't come cheap.* "Twenty thousand."

He opened his mouth to respond, then shut it. Lips tight, he nodded.

"So I take it you've got a destination in mind. Last I looked, there wasn't much in this octant."

"I was thinking a little further out."

Ru's eyebrow rose. "How much further out?"

"Sector Nine."

"That's empty space. No stations."

"Nothing mapped. But I've got friends out there. I can give you coordinates for a meeting point. They'll give you the cash when you arrive."

She raised an eyebrow. "And I'm to believe this would be a safe thing to do . . . why?"

"You rescued me. I owe you."

"Assuming for the moment I'm willing to trust that, what about those who'll be meeting us? No offense, but that's pretty far out for me to be counting on people's good will."

"You rescued me," he repeated. "No ally of mine is going to screw with you." After a pause he added: "I guarantee it."

"With what backing?" Micah asked quietly.

Sharp black eyes turned to him; he felt as if they were piercing through to his soul. "Saito. They're the ones who will be meeting us. House Saito. I have an understanding with them. They'll honor my word."

Ru looked at Micah, a question in her eyes. He nodded very slightly.

"Thirty thousand," she said. "Because of the risk."

Ivar opened his mouth to argue, then chuckled instead. "You are indeed a mercenary. Agreed." He offered his hand. She took it. Bargain sealed.

*It isn't the answer to our question about Shenshido,* Micah thought. *But it's a good first step in seeking it. That's assuming he's being straight with us. And assuming he didn't just make up that family name, because how the hell would we know if he did? This could still be a death-trap.*

But Ru's eyes were gleaming. If she had any doubts, the excitement of the moment had clearly overridden them. And why not? She was used to risk. She spent her whole life seeking out planets she knew nothing about, aware that the locals might try to kill her before she even had a chance to say hello. That was the lifestyle she'd chosen. He sensed that hunger in her now—the desire to embrace danger instead of running from it—and Micah felt his own blood stir in response. How could one deny such an opportunity? Or pretend that the risk of it wasn't as intoxicating as it was terrifying?

*Maybe I did catch what was on Shenshido,* he thought. *Because I do seem to be going crazy.*

Intuition, insight, imagination: where is the line to be drawn between them?

Must it be drawn?

NIGEL BAHN
*Meditations*

# HARMONY NODE
# INSHIP: ARTEMIS

PROBE DETECTED
CODE REQUESTED
SOURCE UNIDENTIFIED.

"Shit," Ru muttered. "That's not good."

The main display looked no different to Micah than it had for last eight hours. Empty space—unclaimed, uninhabited—with the usual backdrop of stars. If something was out there, it was either too distant or too small for the skimmer to get a visual.

Ru twisted back in her seat to look around the ship. "Where's Ivar? In the back?"

"Sleeping, I think."

"Damn." A column of data was scrolling onto one of the smaller screens; she studied it for a moment, then shook her head in frustration. "None of this is telling me what I need to know. Get Sleeping Beauty up here, will you?"

Glad to have something constructive to do, he got up from the pilot's chair and headed aft. The long hours of travel had started to wear on his nerves, and though Ru had maintained an impressively calm façade, it was clear now that it was no more than that: a façade. She didn't like not knowing their destination. Micah didn't like not knowing their destination. But Ivar had been maddeningly tight-lipped about details, so they'd stopped asking him questions. Micah suspected the man was amused by their frustration. Screw him.

Ivar was indeed sleeping in the back. Probably still recovering from his forced healing in the medpod; repairing that many broken parts must be draining. But he woke up as soon as Micah entered the room, going from sleep to full alertness instantly, like a cat. His hand went instinctively to his belt, as if seeking a weapon, but there was nothing there. Maybe he was searching for something he'd left on Shenshido. Maybe he would have attacked Micah if he'd had it, before he remembered where he was. "What?"

"We're being probed," Micah told him. "Ru wants you up front."

Ivar pushed himself up to a sitting position, paused for a moment to consult his brainware—probably checking the time—then eased his legs over the edge of the bunk and down onto the floor. He winced as the weight of his body shifted to his injured leg. "That was fast. I figured we'd have a few more hours at least."

*So you knew this was coming and didn't warn us.* Micah shook his head. *Asshole.* It didn't help that the man was wearing a black vest from the ship's wardrobe but had disdained Ru's offer of a fresh shirt, so his scarred and tattooed arms were on full display, framed in black leather. If he was trying to look disreputable, he'd succeeded admirably.

Ru didn't look away from her screen as they approached. "Basic probe signal," she said. "Not from a ship. Or so my instruments tell me. It's asking for an ID code."

Ivar slid into the chair beside her and looked over the data. "That's a sentry buoy."

She looked at him sharply. "Which is what?"

"Stationary probe. It was awakened by our approach and wants to know who and what we are."

"And when it does know?"

"It'll inform people that we're here."

*What people?* Micah wanted to demand. But that would just be feeding into Ivar's arrogance. He fetched a chair from the dining set, since the second pilot's chair was now in use.

"So what am I supposed to do?" Ru demanded. "Ignore it and just keep going?"

"It needs a passcode. Hook me up, I'll send it."

Ru looked at him suspiciously. It was clear she was less than pleased about their current situation.

SIGNAL REPEATED, the ship informed them.

"Damn," she muttered. "Keyboard or voice?"

He scowled. "What are we, primitives? Doesn't this ship have an internal network?"

"It sure does. But I don't give strangers the key to it. Keyboard or voice control?"

He stared at her for a minute, but if he was expecting her to back down, it wasn't going to happen. "Keyboard."

She tapped the control panel and a keyboard graphic appeared. He began to pick out letters and numbers with his middle fingers, an oddly vulgar motion. The code that appeared on the screen was nothing Micah recognized, but he recorded it with his headset for later study.

Finally Ivar leaned back and hit *transmit*. TRANSMISSION CON-FIRMED, the screen said a moment later. "There you go. All done."

"So *people* know we're here," Ru said. She stressed the noun slightly, as if reminding him that he'd never told them what kind of *people* they were heading toward. "Should I be expecting trouble?"

"If this ship had been classified as a threat, you might have. Though my contacts are more likely to avoid confrontation. But those codes should reassure them."

"Except they're two years old," Micah reminded him. "Are you sure they're still good?"

"They can be identified. My contacts know where and when I disappeared, so they'll figure it out."

*And if not,* Micah thought, *this could turn out to be a wasted trip.*

"And who exactly are we meeting?" Ru asked. They were getting close enough that maybe she thought he would part with the information.

He got up from the chair. "You'll see soon enough. Let me know when we're in visual range." Without further word he headed back to the rear of the ship, presumably to resume his nap.

Ru looked at Micah. Micah looked at Ru.

"You want to punch him in his arrogant face?" she asked quietly. "Or should I?"

It was another hour before they got within sensor range of their target. It was big, Ru's ship told them, and it had a complex energy signature, which suggested it was more than a ship. By the time she got a clear visual on screen, with decent magnification, Micah's heart was racing from anticipation; he gave his wellseeker permission to steady it.

Then: there it was. A station . . . and not a station. Space stations were orderly, rational creations, planned and executed for maximum efficiency. This thing hadn't been planned. It certainly didn't look efficient. The best word Micah could come up with to describe it was *surreal.*

It was a vast structure with ships moored to it in no discernible pattern. Big ships and small ships, some well maintained, others badly degraded. Connecting them was a tangled network of tubes and flyways, all splaying out from a common center, like a web spun by a drunken spider. In the center was a huge chunk of natural rock: an ex-asteroid, perhaps? Its pitted gray surface could be glimpsed here and there between the haphazard structures that clung to its surface, some of which had purposes that could be guessed at—mooring stations, environmental domes, banks of generators, life support domes connected by tunnels—while others were weirdly shaped, indecipherable. New materials had been fused with old, sleek with rutted, fragmented with whole. It was as if someone had taken a junk field, crushed all its contents into an irregular ball, and set it floating in the middle of nowhere. Micah saw a symbol on one panel that looked suspiciously like Shido's corporate sigil. Had pieces of Shenshido station found their way to this place? *This was why they attacked Shenshido,* he realized. *You can't build something this large without one hell of a lot of mass.*

"Welcome to Hydra," Ivar said. No longer was he a refugee needing rescue, but a warrior returning to his homeland, and the change was reflected in his demeanor. What status did he have here? It must have been high once, for him to bargain so casually with tens of thousands of credits, but was that still true? How would two years' absence affect his standing among the fiercely competitive scavs? Beneath that confident façade, Micah guessed that Ivar was worried.

Data was starting to scroll down Ru's screen, mostly abbreviations that Micah couldn't interpret. Was she running the application she'd told him about, that could derive social patterns from technology? "Six centers of activity," she muttered. "Key ships are modern, well maintained. Big money here. Ruling factions?"

"Influential factions. Not officially in charge of anything. There's a seventh one behind the core, that you can't see from this angle."

"Hence the Hydra," Micah mused. "A monster with many heads." Did those centers of activity represent clans? Families? Occupational cliques? He hungered to ask so many questions, but was pretty sure Ivar wouldn't answer them, and he was tired of amusing him. So he just gazed at the seven-headed beast in wonder, basking in the satisfaction of knowing that his speculations about scav society had been accurate. At least thus far.

"There's no order to the rest of it," Ru continued. Was she talking to them, or to herself? "Independent ownership. Few signs of wealth. Building materials from different sources. No unified plan or aesthetic." She leaned closer to the screen. "The flyways look weak. Badly constructed, hence easy to damage. That seems an odd flaw to have. Clearly these people know how build reliable structures, even if the designs are sometimes unorthodox. Some of the joints don't even look—" She drew in a sharp breath and fell back in her seat. "Holy shit." She looked at Ivar. "It's designed to come apart? All of it?"

"Indeed," Ivar said. "And now you understand the purpose of the sentries."

"Trouble approaches, and this is all . . . what, disassembled?"

"A stationary structure would be easy for enemies to attack. A few dozen ships going off in different directions would be lost in the darkness of space before anyone realized what had happened."

"That hunk of rock isn't going anywhere quickly," Micah pointed to the core. "Not with that much mass to accelerate."

"For which reason nothing of value is stored in it. Mostly it's for hi-G shore leave, for those that don't run full G on their ships. Human bodies need such exposure or they grow weak."

*Yeah,* Micah thought dryly. *It's really a health spa. Why didn't we guess that?*

More data was scrolling across Ru's screen, but now she was reading it silently. Perhaps she was learning things she didn't want Ivar to know about. *If this is where the Dragonslayer signal originated,* Micah thought, *it may be our enemy's home base. From here he could orchestrate whatever attacks he wanted, knowing that Guild authorities would never find him. Only Ru and I will find him.*

Ru looked at Ivar. "You said everyone here would be Saito. But this structure obviously isn't home to only a single faction. Or even cooperating factions. Care to explain?"

"I lied," he said evenly. "To reassure you."

Her eyes narrowed. "Should I worry about other lies?"

He shrugged. "The rest was legit. And the only people you'll have to deal with here will honor my word, so unless you go wandering around on your own, you'll be fine. Speaking of which, I should contact those people now and let them know we're coming. So they can start getting your payment ready."

"Lower right screen," she said, pointing. "Manual controls beneath it."

He smoothed a few stray hairs back from his face and angled the screen toward him. It showed his face as it would be transmitted: not a mirror image, with right and left sides transposed, but a true duplicate. "Begin recording," he commanded.

Bright words appeared across the image. BEGIN RECORDING.

"This message is for Dominic Saito, from Ivar. Forward it to his office if he's not available. Mark it time sensitive." He cleared his throat. "I'm pleased to announce that I'm still alive, and after a lengthy and unpleasant stay on Shenshido Station, am coming home. I owe my return to Ru Gaya and Anthony Bester"—he nodded toward the two of them, though they were offscreen—"and ask that they be accorded the status of guests of the House. I'll require thirty thousand standard creds in unmarked cash chits for them when we arrive, as per our arrangement. Please confirm, and provide docking coordinates."

Micah watched—and recorded—while Ivar typed in coordinates and hit the *send* key. A few seconds later the screen confirmed that the message was on its way. "How long do you think the com lag will be?"

"Not too long," Ru replied. "We're pretty close. I can have the ship calculate the exact time if you need it. Once your message gets there, however . . ." She shrugged.

"If Dominic is there, he'll respond quickly."

"Two years have passed," Micah reminded him. "Much may have changed."

Ru nodded. "I can tell you that whatever hostilities exist between factions have intensified recently."

Did she have more knowledge of this place than she'd let on? Evidently her information was good, because for the first time, there was a flicker of uncertainty in Ivar's eyes. The people who had ruled this place when he left might no longer be in power. They might not even be on Hydra at all. And factions that had once supported each other might no longer be willing to do so. What would his promises be worth to Ru and Micah, if all that were the case? Ivar looked at Ru. "There are two ways to handle this. You can dock in the Saito array. That's the easy way. If you don't trust my word on the safety of that, I can ask them to ferry the payment out to you in open space. Your call."

"We can dock," she said.

"Excellent." He leaned back in his chair. "Now, while we wait for Dominic's response," he folded his arms across his chest, "why don't you tell me more about the weapon that Shenshido was working on. The one they were going to use on scavs."

She chuckled. "Really, Ivar? That kind of information has value."

"I'm not a poor man. What's the price?"

"There are some things that require more than money."

His eyes narrowed slightly. "What, then? Information? Data for data?"

She smiled faintly. "I could just call in the favor you owe me, if I wanted that."

"You could," he agreed. "And then I wouldn't be in debt to you anymore. Much better situation for me, to be sure."

She looked at Micah, a question in her eyes. How he wished he were connected to the ship's net, so that they could communicate privately! It was frustrating to be limited to voice and facial expressions, like cavemen who could only grunt and wave at each other. He glanced back at the bizarre station on the screen. Odds were that somewhere in that chaos of ships and flyways and natural rock was a clue that could help them identify Shenshido's mastermind. What were the odds they could just go in blind, on their own, and discover it? Close to zero. Ivar could make it easier. But was that enough reason to trust him?

*We have no choice.* He nodded to Ru. *Go ahead.*

"All right then," she said. She turned back to Ivar. "We'll barter. Knowledge for knowledge. But once we do that, you're all in. No bartering for new favors. We work together to identify the weapon that drove Shenshido mad, before it can be used on the scavs. Agreed?"

He stared at her for a long moment. Studying her. Then at Micah. Something about his gaze made Micah's skin crawl. Like fingers were feeling around inside him. Finally the scav nodded. "For as long as our interests are the same," he agreed.

"Your word on that?" Micah asked sharply.

Ivar scowled slightly. "My word."

Ru leaned back in her chair; it whirred softly as it accommodated the change in position. "Do bear in mind that what little of the story we know, we've had to piece together ourselves. Terran megacorps don't share their plans with outsiders. We were able to figure out that the scientists on Shenshido were working on some kind of weapon, that they meant to use against scavs. It got loose before they had a counter-agent ready, and . . . well, you saw the result. What happened to the people on that station was fully intended. It just wasn't supposed to affect its creators."

"It was meant for the scavs."

"That's what one local suggested." She nodded toward Hydra. "I'm guessing that was the intended target."

"What was the delivery system? A disease?"

"Maybe. Or maybe something chemical. Or something in the environment. I wasn't on Shenshido long enough to observe how it worked. Only that it did."

"But its purpose was to induce madness."

"To induce hallucinations. People saw things that didn't really exist. Eventually they lost the ability to tell fantasy from reality, and that's what drove them insane. The scientists probably figured that if they could infect scavs with it, they could get them to turn on each other."

"What kinds of hallucinations?" There was a new edge to his voice now. "Give me an example."

"Well, you told me the people on the upper level looked like rotting corpses."

"Didn't they?"

She shook her head.

"But I saw them myself—"

"Yes," she said quietly. "You did see them yourself."

For a moment there was silence. Then: "You said that Shenshido hadn't affected me."

A faint smile appeared. "I lied, to reassure you."

For a moment he said nothing. Then: "All right. What information do you want in return for that?"

"We're trying to figure out if they tested their weapon in its earlier stages. Launched a prototype, maybe." She looked pointedly at the screen. "Since it was designed to target scavs, it may have found its way here. So tell me. Do you remember hearing about anything like that, before you left?"

"You mean mass insanity?"

"Hallucinations. Confusion. A blurring of the line between fantasy and reality." She paused. "Do you remember anyone suffering from that? Or even talking about it?"

He stroked his chin as he considered. "There's a woman with second sight, an oracle. People bring her offerings, and she counsels them according to visions she has. Do those count?"

"They might. Anything else?"

"There's a labyrinth surrounding her turf. Those who mean her harm are trapped in it, and never seen again. At least that's the story." He paused. "I've heard that it's illusions that cause them to get lost."

"What kind of illusions?" Micah said sharply.

He shrugged. "Don't know. The people who've seen them don't generally live to talk about it." He glanced at the screen. "You could ask around. I'm sure people will tell you stories, if you approach them right. Not sure how many will be true, though. You'll probably have to pay for any real information."

Ru frowned. "You suggested earlier it wouldn't be safe for us to wander around here."

"If you present yourselves like people who have good reason to seek refuge from the law, and respect what few rules we have here—which basically come down to 'don't steal from or murder any locals'—you should be safe enough. But if people get the impression that you're here to observe them, maybe even report on them to authorities, then you won't leave this station alive. I'm sorry, but that's the truth."

She nodded. "I appreciate your bluntness."

"And I'd appreciate hearing what you learn. Since, as it turns out, I do have a vested interest in the outcome."

"Fair enough."

He rose stiffly from the chair. "I'm going to pack up my possessions. What few I have left. You'll let me know when a response to my message gets here?"

"Of course."

Minutes later he was gone. An uncomfortable silence followed. The skimmer hadn't been designed for privacy, and anything they talked about, however quietly, might be overheard.

Micah reached out to the keyboard and started typing. His words appeared in red on the screen.

YOU ARE ONE OF THE BEST LIARS I HAVE EVER KNOWN.

She chuckled softly, reached over to the keyboard, and typed, IF HE SUSPECTED THE MADNESS MIGHT HAVE COME FROM HYDRA, HE MIGHT TRY TO PROTECT ITS CREATOR. THESE PEOPLE SOUND LIKE THEY ARE PRETTY TIGHT.

BUT A THREAT TO THE SCAVS WOULD BE A DIRECT THREAT TO HIM, Micah typed. HENCE HIS VESTED INTEREST IN HELPING US IDENTIFY IT.

EXACTLY.

She leaned back in her chair. "So. Do you think you can pass for an outlaw?"

"Are you asking me if I know how to role-play? Seriously?" He grinned. "I think maybe I can figure it out."

*(The image of a Saurin male on the screen:)*

"Ivar! This is a surprise! We were told you died in the Shenshido raid. I'm happy to hear that wasn't true, and I'm sure the Patronus will be also. Three of your men who made it back have told many tales of your exploits . . . and of your death. Never mind. You're here now. (Leans back in chair, arms folded across his chest.) A lot has changed in the past two years, but nothing you can't catch up on. Be careful around your crew, though. They thought you were dead and gone, and probably divvied up your stuff long ago. A few may have mixed feelings about your return. As for the people who brought you back here, of course they'll be honored guests. The fare's a bit pricey, but I don't imagine you had many options. I'll make sure it's covered." *(Reaches down below the frame.)* "Am appending a file with instructions for your approach, as well as an emergency channel to use if you run into trouble when you arrive. We'll talk more when we can do it realtime, yes?"

**END TRANSMISSION**

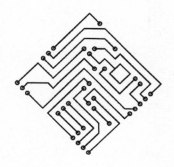

## OUTERNET FORECAST

Processing is slow today in Harmony Node, due to a high-pressure system impacting all tourist-related industries. Expect delays in transportation, reservations, entertainment, banking, and food services to continue through the week, as preparations for the upcoming Harvester Festival place pressure upon those systems.

Guildmaster Dresden has announced that Harmony Station will prioritize outgoing traffic beginning on the 24th. This will facilitate realtime broadcasts of Harvest events, but reduce channels available for incoming data. Those planning to visit during the Festival are advised to send any information pertaining to their itinerary in advance, and to confirm its safe arrival no later than the 23rd. Standard operating protocols will be restored at midnight on the 26th.

# HARMONY NODE
# HYDRA COLLECTIVE

**S**AITO'S RECEPTION ship hadn't changed—it was still a saucer-shaped vehicle connected to the rest of Hydra by flyways—but there were six mooring stations now, spaced out evenly along the rim. If six vessels docked at the same time, the ship would look like a giant starfish.

Heading toward the reception lounge, where Dominic had said they could talk, Ivar felt strangely disoriented. The interior of the ship looked familiar to him—little had changed in two years—yet it felt so alien. He'd been trapped too long in the sterile labs and false forests of Shenshido; the world which had once been as much a part of him as his own skin now seemed strangely off-kilter.

The central lounge was mostly unchanged. There was still a lot of cushy seating, a well-stocked bar, and a collection of unique contraband displayed in locked cases along one wall. He recognized a sacred chalice he'd given to the Patronus of the clan some years back, stolen from a religious outpost. Supposedly anyone who touched it without the proper prayers of reverence would be struck dead on the spot. He remembered how the Patronus had poured wine into it, laughing, and then passed it around for everyone to take a sip. "Now we are all blessed."

That chalice had transformed Ivar from a dime-a-dozen freelance thief to a *person of significance*, and clinched his status as an ally of Saito. All the good things that came to him after had flowed forth from that moment. He never did offer the clan his formal allegiance—it went against the grain to compromise his independence like that—but Saito backed his forays often enough that he might as well have. He was all but family.

Or that's what he had been, two years ago. Who knew what he was now?

Dominic was waiting for him, and rose as he entered the lounge. The fine scales on his face glittered as he broke into a broad smile. "Ivar!" He strode forward and offered him a hand clasp, which became a forearm clasp, which became a hearty embrace. "Son of the devil! I never thought you would come back to us."

"That makes two of us."

He stepped back, holding him by the shoulders, and looked him over, top to bottom. "A bit worse for wear, it looks like."

Ivar shrugged. "It's been a rough couple of years."

"Nothing a drink wouldn't address, eh? Your usual?"

"Please."

As Dominic headed over to the bar he kept talking. "Your own people reported you dead, you know."

"They survived?"

"Three of them limped home. With one battered singler between them, that barely made the trip. Few people came out of that fight unscathed. On the rocks, right?"

"Yes, please."

There was the sound of liquid splashing into a glass. "They told us your ship crashed into the docking ring at full speed and broke up into a thousand pieces. No one could possibly have survived that, they said. Etcetera, etcetera." He walked back to Ivar with two glasses and handed him one; the scent of fine whiskey with a hint of added spice stung his nostrils pleasantly. "Meridan whiskey. Made with a grain so rare it's forbidden to export the stuff."

Ivar held up the glass in a salute. "To illegal pleasures, then."

The whiskey was smooth and rich, and it made everything feel a little more familiar. He remembered the day he and Dominic had gotten drunk in this room, and spent an hour talking about the best way to dismember Harmony Station and sell it for parts. With that much whiskey in their veins it had seemed a reasonable plan. "I evacked just in time. Shenshido picked me up when the battle was over. After that came imprisonment, and then a lengthy fight for survival, whose details I'd rather not talk about. At least while I'm sober."

"That bad, eh?" Dominic lowered himself into a thickly cushioned chair and motioned for Ivar to do the same. "I imagine you'll be asked for that story incessantly, once people realize you're home."

Ivar raised his glass. "Then I guess I'll have to drink a lot more."

Dominic took a drink, rolled the taste of it around his tongue, then swallowed. "So tell me about the two who brought you back here. Friends? Allies? Anyone we should worry about?"

Ivar sighed. "Honestly, I don't know much about their backgrounds or their motives. But they saved my life." *Which wouldn't have been necessary if I hadn't chosen to join that fucking raid, but that's another story.* "Thus far they seem to have played straight with me, but who knows? They may simply be skilled liars."

He chuckled. "Hardly a rare commodity here. Do you know if they have any further interest in Hydra? Or are they just here to drop you off and pick up the reward?"

Ivar hesitated. "I imagine they'll want to look around. I certainly would."

"Well, since you're vouching for them—to a certain degree—tell them they can leave their ship docked here while they play tourist. That's assuming they don't do anything that would make me want to rescind that invitation."

"I'll let them know."

Dominic took another drink; the iridescent scales on the back of his hand shimmered as he tipped the glass, gazing at Ivar through the amber liquid. "We go way back, you and I, don't we?"

Ivar nodded. "Quite a ways."

"You regard me as a friend?"

He shrugged. "As much as I do anyone here."

"Then you won't take it amiss if I give you some advice?"

"As long as you don't take it amiss if I choose to ignore it."

Dominic sighed heavily. For a moment he just stared down into his glass. "You've been dead for two years, Ivar. Not missing; dead. Gone forever. That's what your crew thought, so it's what they told everyone else." He paused. "Two years is a long time in this place."

He raised an eyebrow. "My crew still exists?"

"The three who returned from Shenshido recruited new members. Greenies, mostly. Spike is in charge now, so the crew's his."

He snorted. "Ambitious bastard."

"You're a stranger to the new ones. Hell, you're a stranger to much of Hydra. It might be harder than you think, reestablishing yourself here."

"I'll manage." He took another drink of whiskey. "So is that your counsel? That I should worry about the obstacles ahead of me? If so, advice noted."

He said it quietly: "I think you should reconsider joining Saito."

Ivar was silent for a moment. "We've had that conversation. What, a dozen times now? Two dozen? My answer's never changed."

"But Hydra has changed. It's not the same as when you left. The raid on Shenshido cost us dearly. We haven't got the number of skilled operatives we used to, but we've got the same number of patroni needing to hire them. Which has proven . . . disruptive."

"Fewer whores, but not fewer whoremongers."

"Exactly."

Ivar shrugged. "So it's a seller's market. Clans will compete for our services . . . can't get better than that, as far as I'm concerned." He paused. "Are you worried I might do business with another clan? I've always been a Saito man at heart, if not by formal ties."

"We appreciate that. And when the clans were merely rivals to one

another, it was sufficient. But now . . . the competition for human resources has pushed us beyond that. In order for one clan to hire the
best operatives, the others must fail to hire them. It's no longer possible
for all of us to prosper equally."

"So you want to bind me to your service, is that it? Not just have me
working for you, but make sure I can't work for anyone else?"

"For your own safety."

He snorted. "Yeah. Right. I'm sure that's the only reason."

Putting down his glass, Dominic leaned forward intensely. "You're
missing the big picture, Ivar. It's never been a secret that you do work
for us. Others will try to bribe you away, into their service. And if that
fails . . ." He let the words trail off suggestively.

"They won't want me working for you anymore."

"Now you're getting it."

"So, are you suggesting . . . that they'd try to *remove* me?"

"If you belonged to one of the clans, no. The price would be too
high. But as an independent? No patronus will muster all his resources
to avenge you. Everyone knows that. It makes you fair game."

He managed to keep his face impassive, but it took effort. The dynamic Dominic was describing was indeed a far cry from the world he
had left two years ago, and the light this conversation shed on his relationship with Saito was not reassuring. *We've been useful to each other,*
Ivar thought. *Nothing more. The clans look after their own.* But was
the situation really as bad as Dominic was suggesting? The man had
been trying to get Ivar to swear allegiance to Saito for as long as they'd
known each other. One would expect him to exaggerate any danger, if
he thought that fear might drive Ivar into his camp.

*I need to see what's going on here, with my own eyes. It would be
foolish to make any life-altering decisions before doing that.* "I need to
think about all this," he said.

"Of course." Dominic leaned back and picked up his drink again. "I
would expect no less." *Just don't take too long,* his expression warned.

Shutting his eyes for a moment, Ivar emptied his glass. The whiskey went down smoothly, but his nerves were jangled now, and mere liquor wasn't enough to soothe them. "Thanks for the advice. And for the loan. As soon as I recover my emergency stash I'll pay you back."

Dominic waved off the thought. "Not necessary. Consider it a gift. For old time's sake."

"I'll consider it a loan. And I'll pay it back with interest."

Dominic chuckled. "As you wish."

It was an old game of theirs, the duel of debt. Dominic liked people to owe him things; Ivar hated owing anybody. But today the dance had a darker tenor. *You will never own me*, Ivar thought. *Nor will anyone else.*

He pushed himself up from the chair, trying not to favor his damaged leg too much. The last person he wanted to display weakness in front of was Dominic Saito. "Your hospitality is appreciated—as is your counsel—but I think it's time I headed down to the core and saw things for myself. Not to mention let everyone know I'm back from the dead."

"You have my contact information if you need it."

"I do."

There was more that he'd wanted to talk to Dominic about. Things he wanted to ask him. If there were signs that Shenshido's madness was infecting Hydra, this man would have heard about them. But asking for information right now seemed like a bad idea. Asking for anything seemed like a bad idea. Better to parry that debt and quit the dueling ground unbloodied.

"Be careful," Dominic warned him as he left.

"I always am," he responded.

It was just a small lie.

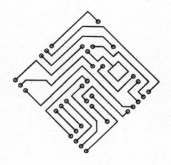

When in doubt, amuse the bad guys.

MICAH BELLO

*Outside the Game Box: Square Peg Strategy in a Round Hole World*

# HARMONY NODE
# HYDRA COLLECTIVE

"**H**OW DO I look?"

Ru looked up from her mapping project, blinked, and looked again. "Where on Guera did you get that clothing?"

"You said I could take anything of Tully's that I needed and do whatever I wanted with it."

"Yes, but . . ." She shook her head. "I don't remember anything of his that looked like that."

Micah was wearing Tully's reinforced jacket, but instead of being the crisp, clean item she remembered, it now looked like someone had lived in it—and slept in it—for at least a decade. The collar and cuffs were visibly worn, and judging from the faded color at the elbows, the sleeves were close to wearing through. Parts were discolored, as if someone had ineptly tried to scrub out stains. A chain was clipped to one shoulder, hanging in a loop under his arm, like a military decoration, and there were small tokens pinned to the front pocket, like trophies. Inside, she knew, was a layer of armor cloth strong enough to repel small projectiles and insulating enough to protect the wearer from surface charges, but the outside looked like crap. His pants were the same ones he'd been wearing before—seamless jeans, neat enough—but they, too, looked like they'd aged years in the last few hours.

She couldn't stop staring.

He smoothed his hands down over the altered clothing with obvious pride. "I found a component in the cleaning assembly with an abrasive surface that I used to wear down the fabric. And I borrowed some glycolic acid from the air sterilizer to fade the color. Don't worry, I put it back."

"I'm not worried. Just . . . surprised."

"Ivar said we'd be safe if we looked like we belonged. I couldn't do that in what I was wearing. So I used him as a model for the degree of wear."

He did have the same well-worn aspect as Ivar. And the same vaguely disreputable air, as well. She didn't know for certain if that would pass muster down on Hydra, but it was certainly a lot more appropriate for the effort than what he'd had on before. "You know, you have the most bizarre skill set of anyone I've ever met."

"I'll take that as a compliment." He looked at the main screen, where a magnified image of Hydra's core was displayed. "What are you working on?"

"Analysis of the social patterns reflected in the structure. It's a bit more chaotic than our algorithms usually have to deal with. There's no single guiding concept behind it." She turned back to the image and pointed to a place where several walkways converged. "This place is probably near a focus of independent social activity, so a good starting point for us. But it's hard to be certain."

"How does it work?"

"What?"

"The algorithm." He moved closer to get a better look. "You were telling us all sorts of details on the way in, about how the ruling factions interacted with each other, and how that had changed recently. How did you get that from just looking at their ships?"

"Look here." As she pointed to the screen, the image on it changed;

now it showed a close-up view of the main Saito ship. "You see this row of mooring stations on the hull?"

"Yeah."

"All but two have been shut down."

"And you know this . . . how?"

"Well, now that we're close enough, I can see they've been permanently sealed. But from farther out, Artemis detected that the airlock readouts on four of them were dark. See? No energy signature." She pointed to the panels beside the hatches. "Ivar's friends used to have a lot more visitors than they do now. Now . . . let's look at what we're moored to." The image changed, displaying the saucer-shaped hospitality ship they had docked at. "Six access points around the periphery, all active. Four are slightly different construction than the rest. Those were probably added recently."

"So Saito redirected their guests . . ."

"Away from their mothership. Visitors probably used to come straight to it. But something has changed now, and Saito no longer feels safe with that arrangement. People have to dock a safe distance away now, where they can be inspected before they're cleared for access. And—here's the interesting part—" The image shifted again, to a split-screen display of the other factional motherships. "These all have similar adjustments, at least the ones I can see." She sat back in her chair. "There's been a recent shift in the patterns of social interaction surrounding Hydra, that has made the ruling elite more wary of strangers."

He whistled softly. "That's . . . amazing . . ."

She waved off the compliment. "Just good software."

"This is what you do when you find a lost colony? Study the things they've built and deduce how they function?"

"Not just what they've built. We look at their transportation patterns, communication frequencies . . . if they've got satellites we look at the orbits, at what kind of debris surrounds them . . . a thousand and one subtle clues your normal traveler wouldn't bother to take note of. Individually they're cryptic, but when you put the puzzle pieces together properly—"

"You see their whole society. Damn. That's . . . damn." Hands on hips, he stared at the image. "I wish I'd had someone like you on my design team for the last project."

A smile flickered briefly. "I'll take that as a compliment."

"So now that you've found an entry point for us, are we taking the ship down to it? Or using the flyways?"

"Depends on what Ivar tells us." *Assuming he tells us anything,* she thought. With a sigh she rose. "I suppose I have to decide what I'm going to wear. I can't let you be the only fashionable one."

"That outfit you had on in Shenshido looked pretty buff."

"Except the safeskin is structurally fatigued, and may not offer much protection. Not to mention, the jacket is torn in at least a dozen places."

"Which is evidence you've been in combat. That's probably a good thing here. And as for your safeskin . . . no one will know it doesn't work. So it may act as a deterrent. Why try to stab someone if the blade won't get through?"

She raised an eyebrow. "You're pretty good at this yourself."

He chuckled. "Yes, I am a master of make-believe. Which, thanks to you, is turning into a useful skill."

"But the dragon really doesn't work. You know that."

He blinked. "Say what?"

She indicated his headset. "Doesn't go with the rest of the outfit."

"Shit." His hand went up to the golden dragon that was coiled around his head. Opulent and exotic, with brightly jeweled eyes, its message was diametrically opposed to that of the rest of his outfit. "You don't think I can sell them on 'ruthless outlaw who likes fantasy role-playing games'?"

"Maybe if you damaged the headset enough that it matched the condition of your clothing . . ."

"Yeah. That's not gonna happen." He sighed. "Please tell me you have a backup headset, amidst all your other prepare-for-Armageddon supplies."

"Of course. There are two on board. Just for emergencies, though. No fancy software."

"I can upload what I need." He paused. "You and I need to *be* something, Ru. Scav, pirate, drug runner, smuggler . . . no one's going to believe we belong here if we don't have suitable roles to play."

"Well, piracy's a team effort, so that's out. Scavengers? You seem to know a lot about them."

"And they observe each other's exploits pretty closely. You can't come out of nowhere and claim to have made away with a derelict spaceship that no one ever heard of."

"Smugglers?"

He considered that for a moment, then glanced back toward her armory. "You do have some contraband on board."

"One piece. Maybe a few items that are borderline. That's it."

"Samples. That's all we need. Something to prove we have the connections needed to slip stuff past authorities." He looked back at her. "Tell me about the borderline items."

"Don't know what's still on board. They may have cleaned the skimmer out while I was asleep. Let me check."

She led him to a hidden slideaway in the back room, invisible until she opened it. Inside were a collection of bottles, envelopes, and small gadgets, all labeled with small plastic tags. "Some of these are from our last mission," she muttered as she rummaged through the drawer. "Haven't sorted it out yet." She picked up a small clear plastic envelope with bluish powder inside and held it up to the light. "This might do."

"What is it?"

"A drug. Euphoric. Scraped from the back of a poisonous salamander on Seti VI. Not technically illegal, but that's only because the Guild doesn't know about it yet."

"Powerful stuff?"

"Try it and see." She opened the envelope and held it out to him. A noxious smell filled the small room, and he stepped back quickly, fanning away the air in front of him with his hand. "Whoa! That's nasty!"

She chuckled. "But it does provide one hell of a high. And until an official recovery team gets to Seti VI, there won't be another source for it." She resealed the packet carefully. "So it might be worth something to the right people. Maybe if—" A sudden chime from the pilot's station cut her off. "Incoming message." She tucked the envelope into her back hip pocket. "Probably from Ivar."

It wasn't from Ivar, but from a slender Saurin with iridescent face scales that glimmered as he spoke. "My name is Dominic Saito. Ivar has told us of your service to him. We are glad to have him back among us, and as a gesture of appreciation, offer you safe harbor at our reception station. You may leave your ship docked here for as long as you need, provided you respect Hydran laws and customs while you are visiting." He paused. "You may contact me on this channel if you have any questions or needs."

A com code appeared on the screen, and then the image faded to black.

Ru looked at Micah. He grinned and spread his hands out, fingers splayed. "Showtime!"

They took a no-G flyway to the core. It was a narrow tube, chilly and dimly lit, barely big enough to coast through. Obviously it had been designed for function rather than comfort, and the lack of any viewports or screens made Ru feel like she was entombed. On top of that, the initial G-field transition was jerky enough to leave her stomach churning. It was a markedly unpleasant journey.

But that was to be expected. There was no one on Hydra who would have a vested interest in the quality of its services, and she doubted there was a structured tax system to cover infrastructure costs. Different parties had probably financed different segments of the crazy structure, with an eye toward minimal investment. Since environmental control was a major expense in deep-space architecture, every degree of heat or light that could be done without, was.

When they got to the end of the first segment, Ru stopped to inspect the juncture, curious about the mechanics of disengagement. As she poked and prodded at various components—including a pair of emergency seals that looked like they hadn't been used in a long time—she was aware of Micah behind her, recording all her actions. Or trying to, anyway. He was so used to having top-of-the-line customized equipment that the stripped-down headset she'd given him must feel as refined as banging two rocks together. He was far too dependent on tech, in her estimation. Well, Hydra might help cure that.

The last thing she'd done before leaving the Artemis was to make it clear that no matter what kind of network was available, he must not under ANY circumstances connect to it. If their adversary was on Hydra—or if his software was—doing so could open a gateway that Micah might not be able to close. He had opened his mouth to protest—but then stopped, and just nodded. Because she was right. He knew she was right. Whether he would be able to resist the temptation to connect was another question. Netting was as natural to him as breathing, and she suspected equally unconscious. He might connect to Hydra's system without even thinking about it.

*He should try going twenty years without a connection,* she mused. *Out in the middle of uncharted space, with travel time to the nearest space station measured in decades. That would blunt the edge of his addiction.* But it wasn't a fair comparison, and she knew it. Any ship large enough to undertake that kind of journey would have an internal network running—as the Artemis did—and while that might not be as fancy as a virt designer would like, it would probably be enough to fend off withdrawal symptoms.

They'd uploaded all her Hydran data into their headsets, including a map of the flyways, but navigating on faith in this dank tunnel, with no view of the outside world, was still disconcerting. She remembered being taught in school that Earth's first space capsules had been made with small windows, not so astronauts could enjoy the view, but to keep the sense of blind confinement from unhinging their minds. Ru was probably better prepared than most to handle that kind of anxiety, but even so, she was glad to see the landing stage emerge from the shadows ahead, and to know this part of their journey was over.

The hatch at the end of the flyway wasn't locked, and it opened at their approach. A tide of smells rushed into the flyway, not all of them good. Ru could pick out notes of human sweat, smoke, some kind of peppery spice, and a strange musky-sweet odor, like a cat in heat. There was particulate matter as well, and columns of dust swirled visibly in front of dome-shaped ceiling lights. That set Micah to coughing, and Ru had to wait until the fit played out. What an odd mixture of strength and weakness he was. Born and bred on artificial worlds, he no doubt was used to having his air scrubbed clean of any dust or odor, and his lungs weren't prepared for this kind of assault. *You've probably never been close enough to a campfire to taste its smoke on your lips, or walked through a field of flowers while clouds of pollen enveloped you.* His power of imagination might be impressive, but there were some things imagination was no substitute for. "Smells are good," she reminded him. "Even bad ones. Right? It means all this is real."

"Yeah." He cleared his throat. "Bad smells are great. I love stink."

When he had finally caught his breath, they moved through the hatch, into a low-ceilinged circular chamber. Tunnels splayed off in all directions, some barely wide enough for a single person to walk through, some wide enough for a couple if they were friendly enough. The room they were in was modern enough, lined with synthetic panels and outfitted with a display screen and control console, but several of the tunnels appeared to have been crudely excavated from solid rock. Headed underground, no doubt. If she and Micah went down there, the maps of the surface that she'd assembled would be of little use.

Voices were faintly audible, coming from one of those tunnels. Ru had her misgivings about going underground, but if they wanted to find people to talk to, it seemed the best direction to try. As the tunnel enveloped them they were surrounded by the echoes of human voices, resonating from the stark stone walls. Laughter. Cursing. Carousing. Apparently she had made a good guess about where Hydra's main social space would be located. Once there, they needed to find someone willing to give them the information they needed without questioning their motives; there were only so many questions you could ask about a station if you were trying to pass for someone who belonged there.

The tunnel sloped gradually downward, leading them deep into the station's core. She glanced over at Micah as she walked, and found him subtly transformed. His shoulders were pulled back, and his arms swung more aggressively at his sides, defining a larger personal territory. His gait was changed as well, his stride longer than before, more confident. His eyes were the same, though. When he looked at her their amber depths sparkled with excitement. And why not? He was in his element now. She felt as if a different man was walking by her side— rough-edged and confident, a man whose focus was on the physical world rather than digital fantasies. She and Tully had played various roles in the course of their outriding duties, but they had never transformed so completely or so compellingly. There was something perversely fascinating about a man who was so skilled at becoming someone else.

Soon the voices were loud enough that they knew they were getting close to their source. Ru did a final inventory of her weapons, making sure everything was ready at hand but hidden from sight. All except the long knife that was clipped to her belt. She remembered Micah's horror when he'd learned the handle was made from the bone of an actual animal, not something cultured or synthesized. But when they left the Artemis he'd insisted she wear it. It had the right flavor for Hydra, he said. Whatever that meant.

*People may not wear dead animals in the outworlds,* she thought, *but in some colonies no one would think twice about it.*

The tunnel finally opened out into a large chamber hewn from the same coarse rock, obviously a social space of some kind. Variants of every size and shape were perched at the edge of a long bar, nursed drinks at the small tables surrounding it, traded cards and cast dice at larger tables beyond that, and pursued more private pleasures in shadowy alcoves around the perimeter. Many of the locals had tattoos and dermal inlays like Ivar's. Only the center of the common room was unoccupied, perhaps because of the large circular cage that stood there. Raised up on a platform that was streaked with dark stains—dried blood, perhaps?—it loomed over the crowd, quietly ominous. *Let's hope that's not where they entertain visitors,* she thought.

They stood in the entrance for a few minutes, just taking it all in. With the costumes Micah had chosen for them they fit in well enough, but Ru was acutely aware that the wrong words or actions could give them away, and she remembered Ivar's warning about what would happen if locals became suspicious of them.

*Somewhere in here is a person who will tell us what we need to know, without asking why we need to know it. All we have to do is find that person.* Looking around the room, she shook her head. The task had seemed far easier back on the Artemis, when it was just hypothetical.

"Drinks," Micah suggested. She nodded in agreement, and the two of them crossed the crowded room, dodging inebriated locals along the way. One man reached for Ru's butt but she shot him a look that made him draw his hand back as though he'd just grabbed a hot poker. There were several empty stools at the far end of the bar, and they claimed two. Ru looked around for a person or bot to serve them, and saw an Arakni pouring drinks at the far end. Two of his spindly arms were pouring beer, one was shaking a mixed drink, and one more was wiping the counter clean. Ru caught his eye and he nodded; when his tasks were done he came over to them.

"Haven't seen you two before." Was there an edge of challenge in his voice? These people probably all knew each other.

"First time at this bar," Micah said guardedly. "I'm Tonio. This is Ru."

"Pred Pago. What can I get for you?"

"What do you recommend?"

"We have an excellent Saurin lager, if that's to your taste. Just came in. Smooth as a whore's tongue. Or if you like mixed drinks, the house special is a Bleeding Heart: pepper-infused vodka and cava juice, with a dusting of semi-detoxified nightshade."

"Semi?" Ru raised an eyebrow.

He grinned. "Dulls the kick if you take it all out."

"I'll have the lager," Micah said.

Ru nodded. "Same here."

Pago returned to center of the bar, to a row of taps whose manual design suggested a simpler, unconnected world. He was preparing two other orders at the same time as theirs, and it was dizzying to watch his spindly extra arms weave deftly around each other: a ballet of bartending. Finally he returned and put the two drinks down in front of them. Tall glasses filled with amber liquid: the color of Micah's eyes. "That's fourteen creds."

As Micah rummaged in his pocket for the cash chits that Ivar had procured for them, Ru said, "Mind if I ask you a question?"

"Go ahead."

She looked back over her shoulder. "What's the cage for?"

His upper shoulders shrugged. "Personal challenges, grudge matches, sometimes a formal competition. Whatever people want it for. Better to fight there than in the middle of the bar, yeah?"

Micah sorted through his chits until he found a twenty. "Here." He put it down on the bar in front of Pago. "Keep the change."

"Much obliged." Clearly pleased, the man tucked it into his apron pocket. "It's been an unusually slow shift up till now, but if you hang around for a while I'm sure you'll see some action. A day doesn't pass without someone wanting to beat the crap out of someone else, and this is where they usually come to do it."

"Inside a cage, so no one else can get hurt," Ru said.

"Not to mention, it's easier to clean up after." He grinned again, then moved on to other customers.

Ru and Micah tasted their lager. It was indeed very smooth. "Alcohol acquisition complete," Ru said. "Now all that's left—"

"Is to figure out what manner of game we have to play to find our informant."

She chuckled softly. "Everything's a game to you?"

"World's too damn boring, if you look at it any other way." He took a deep drink. "Pago's a talker, and he likes our money, but he's way too busy right now." He looked her up and down. "You could seduce someone."

She blinked. "Say what?"

"Get some pillow talk going. It's a classic."

She laughed. "Hardly my style, Micah."

"Why not? You're hot, in a Can-you-tame-this? way. Some men can't resist that."

She ignored the compliment, mostly because it startled her so much she didn't know how to respond. "You might be more successful at it. In fact, there's someone over there"—she gestured past his shoulder—"who has been eyeing you since we sat down."

"Really?" His eyes widened with interest. "What does she look like?"

"*He* looks pretty hot."

He said nothing.

"Not your thing?"

"Not my thing." He took another drink then looked around the room. "It looks like there's a card game going on back there. Maybe poker. You any good?"

She chuckled. "I'm good at anything that two people would do to pass time during a tediously long interplanetary flight."

"Well then, you see? You'd be a natural to—"

"Y'know, I do think that guy is trying to get your attention, maybe I should invite him to join us—"

"Cards it is." He downed the last of his drink and put the glass down on the bar. "We don't have to win anything, right? Just make some new friends. Hell, losing might work better for that."

"You're the gaming expert. Lead on."

But before he could get off his stool, a man's voice rang out. "*Attention, all! We have a challenge!*" Ru looked for the source of the voice and saw a small group of people gathered at the cage. A tall Medusan was looking around the room, waiting for everyone's attention. From the way his cranial tentacles were twitching around his head, Ru guessed he was pretty inebriated. Next to him a woman was fumbling

with the cage lock, and two men were stripping off their gear and clothing, baring torsos covered in tattoos.

Micah leaned back against the bar. "This should be interesting."

The two contestants were totally mismatched. One was a hulking
terramorph, a solid wall of muscle in the shape of a man. Even his tattoos looked aggressive. The other was maybe half his size, a slender Frisian who looked like a strong wind could blow him over. He was clearly
nervous about the coming challenge, and one could hardly blame him.
Soon the two men had taken off everything but their pants; without his
shirt, the Frisian looked even smaller. They entered the cage, taking up
positions on opposite sides. And waited.

"Ladies and gentlemen," the Medusan announced, "and those of
you who are both, or neither! This is to be an endurance challenge. No
rounds, just survival. On my right is Tank Logan, three-time champion
of Hydra's freestyle competition. On my left is Shane Everest, making
his first appearance on our stage."

Micah muttered, "He'll fucking crush him."

"Unless he knows some tricks," Ru said.

Micah snorted. "It would take one hell of a trick to even that match."

The Medusan spread his arms wide and called out, "Declare your
wagers!"

"Ten seconds!" a voice from one of the gaming tables cried out.
People laughed.

"One and a half minutes," a woman's voice called out. "Fifty Cs."

"I'll take that at three to one," a man responded.

"Done!"

Other times and prices were called out, gamblers pairing off to
wager against each other. Sometimes the odds were haggled over like
goods at a bazaar. Most of the times suggested were short, Ru noticed.

"They're betting on how long he'll last," Micah murmured.

"Yeah." She shook her head. "This is not going to be fun to watch."

But it was impossible to look away.

When the mating cries of the gamblers had subsided, the Medusan
looked around the room one last time. "No one offering three minutes?

Oh ye of little faith!" He gestured broadly toward Everest. "Consider: would any man step into this pen if he lacked the fortitude to put up a good fight?" There was no response. "I'll offer ten to one odds myself, if anyone has the balls to bet on a full three minutes."

Suddenly Micah slid down from his stool, startling Ru. He positioned himself with his hands on his hips and called out, "One thousand Cs. To win."

The room suddenly grew quiet. Ru heard someone mutter, "Holy shit." The Medusan looked at Micah in astonishment. "Do I understand you right? You want to bet on Everest to *win*?"

"You offered ten to one odds for just three minutes. I'll take those odds for a clean win. Or . . . a not-so-clean win." He smiled dryly. "Assuming that works for you."

"You'd just be throwing out your money."

"And this bothers you . . . why?"

Now it was the Medusan who fell silent. Was he thinking about how losing this bet could cost him a small fortune? Or reminding himself that there wasn't a snowball's chance in hell of that happening? Perhaps he was wondering what would drive a man to bet so much money on a lost cause. Hell, Ru was wondering that herself. Maybe the Shenshido bug was still screwing with Micah's brain, and he was going insane.

"Done," the Medusan said at last. He made a last call for wagers, then addressed the two fighters. "Standard house rules, no time limit. When one of you taps out—or passes out—that ends it."

He stepped back. "Lay on."

Tank moved forward immediately. Everest danced lithely out of reach; it was clear speed was his forte. Ru leaned over to Micah and whispered, "That was a crazy bet. Do you know something I don't?"

"Lots of things, I'm sure." He grinned. "But not in regards to this. I'm just playing the game, Ru."

The beatdown began. It wouldn't be accurate to call it a "fight," because that would suggest two equal opponents. Everest was quick and agile and clearly knew how to brawl, but Tank's longer arms gave him an unbeatable advantage. Again and again the smaller man tried to close distance enough to get in a good shot, and again and again he failed. Meanwhile, Tank had no problem reaching him, and blow after blow landed with a sick smacking sound. Now Ru understood why no one had expected the smaller man to last as long as three minutes.

Then Tank directed a kick at his opponent's flank. Everest caught the leg deftly under one arm, and before Tank could react he slid forward, closing the distance between them. His right fist drove toward Tank's jaw, but was blocked. Everest ducked under the counterstrike and brought his left arm around with all his strength, right into Tank's jaw. The force of the blow threw Tank off balance, and then they were grappling, and they went down together. Everest was like a tenacious spider, his limbs wrapped around Tank at four different angles. He was obviously a skilled grappler, and as he twisted around the hulking body to get the grip he wanted, Ru thought he might even have a chance. But in the end, size and raw strength won out. Tank got an arm around his neck and squeezed. Everest struggled to take control of the situation, and failed. Soon it was over: the smaller man's body went limp in Tank's arms and was allowed to slide to the floor.

"We have a winner!" the Medusan announced. His eyes flickered upward as he consulted his brainware. "Official time: two minutes and fifteen seconds."

Micah took out his cash chits, rummaging through them to find the ones he needed. By the time the Medusan joined him at the bar, a thousand creds were waiting for him.

"Sorry, man," the Medusan said with a grin as he took them.

Micah shrugged. "It is what it is."

And then the Medusan just walked away. Surprised, Ru waited until he was out of hearing, then said, "I thought you were going to court him as a contact. No?"

"Too busy. Too public."

"Yeah, and you don't want to be the center of attention." She chuckled. She looked back at the cage, now empty. "So what was the point of betting on that guy?"

A sly smile appeared. "I didn't bet on him. I bet on human nature."

"Jeez." She turned back to the bar. "You're getting as annoying as Ivar." She took a deep drink. "So what now? Back to poker?"

"I need another drink first." He signaled to the bartender to bring them both another round. As fresh drinks were set down before them, and Ru was reaching in her pocket to pay for them, a voice from behind them said, "Allow me."

Turning, they saw it was Everest. He had put his clothes back on, so most of his bruises weren't visible, but there were red stains slowly seeping through the bandages wrapped around his knuckles, and a bloody abrasion ran down one side of his face. He reached between them and slid some coins across the bar; they looked like real metal. "Keep it," he said. He looked at Micah. "Couldn't leave without meeting the guy who bet a thousand Cs on me. Figured the least I could do was buy you a drink." He eyed Ru. "You together?"

"Business partners," Micah said quickly, before Ru could speak. "My name's Tonio. She's Ru."

"Well, you know my name already." He studied Ru for a moment more, then looked back at Micah. "So, tell me . . . why?"

"Why the bet?"

"You seem sane enough, so you must have known I couldn't win."

Micah chuckled. "Maybe I enjoy betting on impossible things." He leaned back against the bar. "Now it's my turn: why the hell would you ever agree to a fight like that?"

He sighed. "Lost a poker game. Didn't have enough money to stay in, and my opponent said he'd accept an IOU on my fighting with the bruiser in lieu of cash . . ." He ran a bandaged hand through his hair. "I thought he was bluffing. I swear to God, I thought he was bluffing." He started to shrug, but the motion made him wince. "I think maybe Tank broke a rib."

"You should sit down," Ru said. She put a gentle hand on his shoulder. "C'mon, we'll sit somewhere quieter, have some drinks, relax. You've earned it."

He hesitated.

"Our treat this time," Micah told him. "Reward for your foolish courage." He nodded toward where the tables were. "Why don't you go find us a free table, while I get us a pitcher?"

"Please?" Ru said. Though she wasn't being particularly seductive, her tone was soft enough that he could take it that way if he wanted. And from the way he looked at her, he wanted.

"Sure," Everest said finally. "What the hell."

Ru watched as Everest went off in search of an empty table. A slow smile spread across her face. "Damn, you're good," she whispered to Micah.

He chuckled. "Nice to know my skills are appreciated. You weren't too bad yourself."

"You should know I don't do small talk well."

He shrugged. "Get a man drunk enough, start him talking about himself, and the scene will write itself." He downed the last of his drink and signaled for a full pitcher to be brought.

*We make a good team.* She wanted to say it out loud. She was afraid to say it out loud.

Some feelings were too ephemeral to bind to words. They might vanish like smoke if she tried.

"Let's just hope he has some useful information," she said.

"Amen to that."

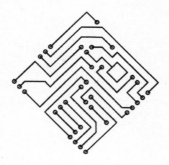

Altruism is hardwired into the human psyche, not as sentiment, but as investment strategy. Cooperation provides a competitive advantage, hence success in the evolutionary arena. Nature has taught us that those who share the burdens and risks of human existence are more likely to survive than those who walk alone.

It is when we are being most selfish that we appear most selfless.

ATHENA ROSS
*Behind the Mask*

# HARMONY NODE
# HYDRA COLLECTIVE

IVAR FOUND his few remaining crew members in one of the core's smaller gambling dens. No surprise there. There weren't that many forms of entertainment on Hydra, at least not that the average scav could afford. Food, drink, drugs, whores, gambling. The patroni with their grand motherships no doubt had a richer selection, but the core of the station was where common folk gathered, rough-hewn men and women whose profits might buy them a week's worth of indulgence if their last haul was good. It was a necessary pressure valve after the stress of a dangerous run. So were the fights that broke out periodically. When you had a station full of people for whom violence was second nature, and who lived outside the law, peace rarely lasted for long.

This den was small and dimly lit, and it smelled of sweat, alcohol, and a variety of drug vapors. Others might find the mixture oppressive, but to Ivar they were the smells of home, and he breathed in deeply, to counter Shenshido's stink. But he had been on that station too long, and memories were too deeply embedded in his psyche; they would not be banished so easily. Especially not after Ru had told him he'd spent two years seeing things that weren't there. That kind of revelation did not sit easy on the spirit.

He was wearing a hooded jacket he'd found in Ru's wardrobe—her parting gift to him—and had pulled the hood forward over his head, enough to shadow his face. Thus far no one had recognized him. Now, looking around the room, he pushed it back. Most of the people there were too fixated on their games to notice, but one head turned in his direction—a Sinji woman in an aggressively spiked headset—and the look of shock on her face was priceless. "Ivar!!?" Others were turning in his direction now, their expressions ranging from joy to confusion to disbelief. Cards were laid down—in one case dropped on the floor—and dice went unclaimed as all eyes in the room turned to him. The attention bathed his spirit in energy.

"Holy shit!" someone exclaimed. "Is that really you?"

"It's a fucking ghost," someone else said. "Ivar's dead."

"Obviously not, asshole."

"Fuck me, Ivar! Where the hell have you been?"

Then there were some people who didn't look as happy to see him, rivals he'd screwed in the past, as well as people who'd tried to screw him and suffered the consequences. How easy it would be to slip back into the old social patterns with them, as if nothing had changed. But he was skating on his reputation, and that would last only until his old enemies realized he had no ship, no crew, and no patronage. The things that had once made him a force to be reckoned with were mere memories now; he would have to climb up from the bottom of the ladder again, like a newbie.

No. Not like a newbie. He had a world full of enemies and rivals who would cut him down to size the minute he looked weak. Newbies had nothing.

"Over here!" a familiar voice cried. The cry came from a kaltrop table with half a dozen people seated around it, three of whom were from his old crew. But only three. He felt a brief pang of guilt, that so many of his people had died in the Shenshido raid while he had survived. It was an unfamiliar and uncomfortable emotion.

The lanky Algonkian woman who had called to him rose from her seat as he approached the table. Raven was dressed in black—as always—with a headset shaped like her namesake. Long black wings with stylized feathers swept down around the sides of her head, shimmering with iridescent hints of green and copper as she moved. She was one of the best distractors he'd ever worked with, adept at buying other scavs the time they needed to sweep in and claim a disabled ship before official recovery teams could reach it. He was glad to learn she was among the survivors. "Alive? For real?" She reached out and pinched both his cheeks, hard, then turned back to her companions. "Not a ghost!" she announced. As if somehow that was her personal accomplishment.

Second in the trio of survivors was Ghant. The Iothan seemed glad to see Ivar as well, if guardedly so, and got up to embrace him. The third survivor from Ivar's former crew was Spike, named for the rod that had once impaled his face, going in through his left eye and coming out through the back of his skull. Modern medicine and the luck of the devil had saved the most important parts of his brain, but the empty hole where his eye used to be, covered over in twisted scar tissue, was a paragon of ugliness. Of course he could have had it fixed, or covered it up. But he didn't. Battle scars were status symbols on Hydra: the more gruesome the better.

Spike didn't stand, just nodded his head in wary acknowledgment. There was no hint in his expression of what thoughts were churning in his head, but Ivar could guess. "We heard you were dead," he said quietly. "Glad to hear otherwise."

"The thought of getting back to all your ugly faces kept me going," Ivar assured him. Ghant placed a chair in front of him. Spike's expression was unreadable, but his hands on the table tensed slightly as he watched Ivar's old crew fawn over him. *I valued this man for his ruthlessness,* Ivar reminded himself. "You've got some new blood, I see."

Spike's good eye narrowed slightly. "This is Teek." A slender Frisian nodded. "Gerta." That was a stocky Salver, probably female; it was sometimes hard to figure out gender with Salvers. "Maruth." This one was small-framed and bald; a Belial twin? It was rare to see one of those traveling alone. One or more of his siblings were probably somewhere else on Hydra.

Ivar nodded to them all, then looked back at Spike. "I hear you're alpha now."

"So it seems." There was an echo of challenge in the man's voice. One of his hands had dropped under the table, presumably to a weapon. Ivar's own hand twitched toward his knife, ready to respond if necessary. Gunfire was forbidden inside the core, to protect its structure, so any fight that took place tended to be intimate and bloody.

Then the moment passed. "Join us," Spike said gruffly. He brought his hand back up and gestured toward the chair. Ivar turned it around and sat on it backward, straddling the seat, claiming the space around him. Other people had apparently been watching their little drama, and as the tension at the table was reduced to a low simmer they came over to greet him. Palms slapped him on the back, hands squeezed his shoulder, one woman mussed his hair. The unsolicited intimacy made his hackles rise, but that was the price of being a legend, so he tolerated it. Someone put a glass down in front of him and poured him a drink. He nodded his appreciation and pretended to drink, but only took in a few drops. He couldn't afford to have his mind dulled by alcohol in such a potentially volatile setting.

Then, predictably, someone demanded he tell his story. Others followed, clamoring in support. Little surprise. He'd come back from the dead, and they wanted to know how. So he told them. They listened enraptured as he mixed truth and fantasy to craft an adventure that was worthy of his reputation. He described his daring escape from his doomed ship and his capture by the enemy—those parts were true enough—and then their attempts to break his spirit. The prison break he'd unwittingly benefited from turned into an event he'd masterminded, and the surreal war between delusional factions became an armed insurrection by the escaped prisoners, under his leadership of course. He'd almost taken control of the station, he told the Hydrans, but it was so badly damaged that in the end he'd decided that it wasn't worth what that battle would cost him.

And now here he was: a legendary scav, risen from the dead, an outlaw who'd proven himself superior to those who hunted him. His story would reach all corners of Hydra before an E-day had passed, no doubt embroidered a little each time it was relayed. His enemies would add less than flattering details, no doubt, but even those would cast him as a figure worthy of fear. His status as a legend was safe, for now.

Spike watched him throughout his recitation, his one sharp eye missing nothing. His scrutiny was like clammy fingers on the back of Ivar's neck, and he had to fight the urge to physically shake it off. No doubt Spike had noticed how little Ivar was drinking, despite his show of celebratory indulgence. He'd have done the same thing in Ivar's situation. One didn't walk a tightrope over a pit of vipers with one's senses impaired.

Finally the crowd began to thin out, gamblers returning to their previous stations. Ivar heard one man complain loudly that his chips had been moved in his absence. There was the sound of a fist striking flesh, but it was followed only by cursing, with no further violence. A quiet day. Perhaps the wonder of Ivar's return had mellowed everyone.

Spike glanced briefly in the direction of the complaint. "We can't talk here," he said quietly.

"Where then?" There was a code of conduct on Hydra that forbade its citizenry from killing one another, but any hostile act short of that was fair game. And even murder was legit, provided one didn't get caught. Spike's life would be infinitely simpler if Ivar should disappear, and both of them knew it.

"Tunnel's good. Anywhere away from this crowd." Within the network of tunnels that connected the core's facilities the chatter of passers-by would mask their conversation enough for a pretense of privacy, but there would be enough witnesses around that Spike wouldn't be able to act against Ivar in secret. Good enough for now; Ivar nodded.

Spike pushed his chair back from the table, while Ivar unstraddled his own. Ghant shot him a worried look: *Should I be concerned?* Ivar wasn't sure of the answer, but he shook his head. *No.*

"Hey." Raven nudged his arm. "Before you go." She pulled up her sleeve, revealing an arm covered with colorful tattoos, typical Hydran style. Most commemorated raids they'd shared, or lost comrades they had mourned together. Ivar had seen most of the designs before and for a moment didn't understand what she was trying to show him. Then he saw the dragon on the side of her forearm. It was a small figure—it had to be, given how little free space was left on her skin—but there was no mistaking the design. It was the same as the dragon that adorned his chest. His totem. "I added this in memory of you." She glanced at Spike. That's who her words were meant for, Ivar realized. Not him. *We still respect our old leader*, she was saying. *He's one of us. Don't fuck with him.*

"Thanks," he told her.

As he and Spike left the den he pulled his hood low over his face again, not only masking his identity from passers-by, but limiting how much of his expression the new alpha could see. They walked together in silence for a bit, keeping to one side of the narrow tunnel, while an assortment of travelers passed by along the other. One pair of drunken lovers jostled Spike as they passed, and apologized profusely. A whore raised an eyebrow as she approached, but Spike shook his head sharply and she continued on. Most of the others were wrapped up in business of their own and took enough notice of them to avoid collision, then ignored them once again.

"If I asked you what your plans were," Spike said at last, "would you give me a straight answer?"

"Sure. Same as you would for me."

A corner of Spike's mouth twitched. "Understood."

"I'm not here to unseat you, if that's what you're worried about."

"I'm not worried." In fact he was tense enough that you could string a bow with him, but it was only to be expected. Any alpha in this situation would be worried.

A man with two scantily dressed terramorphs on his arms—one male, one female—passed by without a glance. Ivar waited until they were out of hearing range. "If the day comes when I want your job, I'll challenge you for it, clean and honest."

"Good to know." Spike's tone made it clear he wasn't going to count on it, but they were both saying what needed to be said, to maintain peace between them. He took a small pack of stim sticks out of his jacket and offered Ivar one. "So what are your plans now, if not armed conflict with your former comrades?"

"Same as before." Ivar drew one of the drugged sticks out of the pack, bent it briefly to release its chemical contents, and placed it between his teeth. "I'll freelance till something better comes along."

Spike took a stick for himself and put the pack away. "Hard to do without a ship."

Ivar shrugged. "Obviously I'll need a berth on someone else's for a while."

"Or a patronus."

Ivar scowled.

"It's the simplest solution. Any patronus would kill to have you in his service."

*Yes, but kill who?* He remembered Dominic's chilling advice. "That's not my style, and you know it." He sucked in a bit of air through the stimmer, pretending to draw in far more. A tiny bit of narcotic seeped into his lungs. "What about you?" He tried to make the question sound casual. "Sold your soul to anyone yet?"

Spike laughed. "They can't afford me."

"I hear it's getting harder to turn them down."

Spike nodded. "The patroni are at each other's throats, and we're caught in the crossfire. You can hide behind a clan and maybe it'll protect you . . . or maybe not. We're just pawns to them. Pawns get sacrificed; that's their job." He chewed on his stick for a moment, letting its drugged content seep into the membranes of his mouth. But he didn't draw in hard on the stimmer; like Ivar, he wanted to keep his wits about him. "Better to die free and foolish, I suppose."

The easiest solution for Ivar would be to sign onto Spike's crew, and they both knew it. Ivar would promise to accept his rival's authority for a mission or two, while he got his feet back in the ring, and there was no question he'd be useful. But Spike could never trust him like that. And Ivar would never expect him to.

Ivar smiled slightly. "I guess I'll have to look for another crew foolish enough to have me."

"I can ask around." Spike drew a bit more air through the stimmer and pretended to savor its effect in silence, though he probably hadn't taken in enough for more than a second's buzz. "People claimed your stuff a long time ago. There's probably not much left."

*Yeah, and you probably got most of it.* "I had stuff hidden away for emergencies. I'm good."

Spike lowered the stimmer. "You realize everyone thought you were dead. Gone forever. They wouldn't have claimed your property otherwise."

Ivar shrugged. "Business as usual. I get it."

"Anything you need?"

There was, but he wasn't certain he should ask Spike for it. Then again, if not him, who? "I could use some information."

Spike raised an eyebrow. "Regarding?"

*There's a secret weapon Shenshido was working on, that drives people insane. Has it reached Hydra? Is anyone here infected? Will all the petty rivalries be swept away by a nightmare like Shenshido's?* Ivar knew he had to choose his words very carefully. If anyone on Hydra had reason to suspect that the madness was infectious, and that he might be carrying it, he wouldn't make it off this station alive. "There was a drug on Shenshido," he said. "Something new, maybe experimental. It had some nasty side effects." He paused. "I heard it might be headed in this direction."

Spike's eyes narrowed. "Does this new drug have a name?"

"Not a street name. Too new. Hasn't hit the trade yet." Was that a spark of interest in Spike's good eye? Was he secretly connected to one of the Cassinin drug lords? Or just imagining what they would pay for such a prize. "It causes the user to lose touch with reality. He starts seeing things that aren't there: subtle delusions at first, then more and more nightmarish images. In later stages he becomes violent, striking out at people who don't exist, mistaking friends for enemies. He becomes dangerous to everyone around him. There's no counteragent that I know of." He paused. "If that shit's made it to Hydra, we need to know."

"I haven't heard of anything like that."

"No talk about anyone suddenly acting crazy? Even rumors?"

"Nothing new. There's the Oracle, of course, and her visions. But she's been around for years, and anyway, this doesn't sound like her style." He paused. "You should go see her."

Ivar rolled his eyes.

"I'm serious."

"Because I need a psychic to guide me?"

"No. Because the patroni see her. They swear by her visions now. Which means she has influence over them. Which means she has influence over all business on Hydra. That's worthy of respect, even if you think her visions aren't."

"Do *you* see her?"

He shrugged. "I sometimes make an offering before I go out on raids. I listen to her advice. If I think it has merit, I follow it. If not, I don't." Another short drag on the stimmer. "She hears and sees everything, Ivar. If you want to find out if someone on Hydra has been acting strangely, she's the one who would know. Now, whether she'd be willing to share that information with you is another thing."

A sudden cry from the direction of the gambling den echoed down the narrow tunnel, followed by a loud crash. "Hell. I need to go check on that. Make sure it isn't one of mine."

"Totally understand." Ivar nodded toward the den. "Go."

Spike put a hand on Ivar's shoulder. "If you need anything more, you let me know."

*How about I write you up a list of my weaknesses, and you can read it at your leisure?* "Thanks, man. Appreciate the support."

And with that the new alpha headed back the way they'd come. Back to the crew that was no longer Ivar's. Back to the world that no longer felt like Ivar's. It was almost as if *Ivar-before-Shenshido* and *Ivar-after-Shenshido* were two different people. But he had to keep them connected if he was to reestablish himself. Powerful men didn't get the luxury of a fresh start.

Spike was being too nice, too helpful. It all sounded natural enough—they'd been crewmates, after all—but they weren't crewmates now, and parting with information without demanding something in re-turn wasn't Spike's usual style.

*I'm a danger to him, and he knows it. For as long as I'm on this station, he has to worry about me trying to take over. And no matter what I promise, no matter what deal we make, he knows that confron-tation won't be open and honest. It's not our way.* Neither was tolerat-ing such a threat. Spike was trying to put Ivar off his guard, so that when it was time to take his old boss down he wouldn't see it coming. His amiable manner was as clear an indication of hostile intent as if he'd shouted threats across the gambling den.

With a sigh, Ivar wiped the moisture off his stimmer and tucked the remaining portion into his pocket. There might indeed be enemies lurking in every shadow, but fixating on them right now could drive a man insane. And he'd seen enough insanity in the last two years to last him a lifetime.

Maybe the psychic bitch would know something about that.

*This is crazy*, Ivar thought.

He almost turned around and left. That would be the sensible thing to do. Not sitting here waiting for some mystical seer to hand him an-swers. One might as well look to patterns of the stars for guidance.

Still, as Spike had said, there was no denying her influence here. And now that he was here, in her antechamber, he had to admit he was curi-ous. A lot of people on Hydra wouldn't think of going out on a raid with-out first laying offerings at her feet and begging for precious drops of her wisdom. He knew one pirate who'd canceled an excursion on her word alone and later found out that what he'd thought was an opportunity was in fact a trap. If he'd gone, he would be rotting in a Guild prison today.

So Ivar would listen to what she had to say, and if it turned out to be bullshit, then he could just laugh and leave. (Or, rather, leave first and laugh later, because there was no reason to be rude.)

"She's ready for you," the attendant announced.

Were the Oracle's visions connected to the madness on Shenshido? For two years he'd lived surrounded by crazies—though he hadn't understood the nature of their madness at the time—and he wondered if he would sense something in the Oracle's presence that would suggest the same insanity. If Ru was right, and he was infected with it himself, would like call to like, so he would recognize others who shared his affliction? Maybe that was the question that had really brought him here. Maybe all the rest was just an excuse.

The attendant startled him by speaking. "Nothing you see in the Oracle's chamber may be spoken of outside it." He was a Novan with ink-black skin, and his red eyes gleamed like rubies on velvet. "Do you agree?"

Like all spaces within the core, the Oracle's inner chamber had been carved out of native rock, but these walls had not been smoothed and polished. Natural cavities pockmarked every surface, and flickering light from faux candles sent shadows dancing along the edges of each, like demons cavorting at an entrance to Hell. Someone with a taste for mystical experiences might say the chamber felt haunted, though no ghosts were visible.

The oracle sat in the center of the dome-shaped chamber, on a throne carved from the same substance as the pitted walls, atop a daïs made of the same. Her eyes peered out from a silver filigree mask as she watched Ivar approach, her face a cypher behind it. She was much smaller than he'd expected, and despite the voluminous robe that obscured most of her body, enough was visible for Ivar to note the lack of feminine curves. That by itself meant little—there were Variations in which human sexuality was expressed differently than the Terran norm—but combined with her size, it seemed significant. Her hands were resting on the arms of her throne, her wrists so slender that it was hard to believe they belonged to an adult woman—

And then he realized what he was looking at.

The Oracle was a child.

A *child*.

He knew he shouldn't stare, but it was impossible not to. The mask and shapeless clothing made it hard to judge her age, but he would guess her to be no more than twelve. How young had she been when she first began to counsel pirates and smugglers and scavengers, doing it so well that they laid untold wealth at her feet, begging for jeweled droplets of her wisdom? She'd been on Hydra for longer than twelve years, so unless she belonged to some Variation with an extended childhood, this wasn't the original Oracle. Was that what the mask was for, to disguise a substitution? He'd never heard anyone talk about the Oracle's role as something that could be transferred, but it seemed the most likely explanation.

It was not what he'd expected. At all.

"Your offering," the attendant prompted.

Startled, he looked down, to see a bowl of beaten silver at her feet. It was large enough to hold several hundred coins, or a small animal with its throat cut.

A *child*.

Numbly he reached into his pocket to take out the offering he'd brought: a golden locket with a large Frisian ruby in its center, part of the secret stash he'd hidden away long ago. He held it up to the light so she could see the stone's inner fire, and flickering blood-colored reflections spasmed across the walls. Then he stepped forward and laid it in the silver bowl. When metal touched metal the bowl vibrated softly, and a low-pitched chiming filled the chamber.

She waited until the sound had faded completely, then nodded. The mask made her face unreadable. "It is acceptable," she said. A child's voice.

Ivar heard the attendant leave the chamber, the heavy door shutting behind him, but he did not turn back to look at him. The child had him mesmerized. Was this the mystic who Spike consulted before every raid? She must have done something damned impressive to earn that kind of respect.

She rose from her seat, the daïs lending her sufficient height that she could gaze down upon him. "Scavenger. Legend. Refugee." Her child's voice was sing-song, mesmerizing. "Ruthless and bloodthirsty but loyal to his own. Once wealthy, now stripped of wealth. Once well connected, now seeking support. Once alive, then nearly dead, now alive again. What need brings you here? What insight do you seek?"

Her voice might be cast in the tenor of a child's, but the mind behind it was clearly more than that. What the hell was she? "I've come for counsel."

She waited.

How much did he want to tell this seer-child? He'd known enough scam artists in his time to understand the concept of cold reading. A charlatan could derive enough information from passing references to fake supernatural insight. If he gave her what she needed to do that, there was no point in his being here. "My return—" he began.

She raised a hand to stop him. "The familiar beckons to you, but it is not what it once was. All you once trusted has vanished or changed, consumed by time; only the illusion of trust remains. Those who were once as brothers to you now turn elsewhere for support. You are an outsider to them. Lost. You passed through a door once, but aren't sure you can find it again." The eyes in the mask reflected the flickering light in a thousand points of fire. "Have I named your fear, scavenger? Is that why you've come to me?"

His throat was suddenly dry. "I'm not sure who I can trust." By the seven hells, was he really seeking advice from a child?

"You've never come to me before."

He hadn't expected to have to justify himself. "I'm not big on seeking advice from anyone."

"You don't believe I have the power to see your fate."

By the seven hells, was she going to refuse his request? That possibility hadn't even occurred to him. "I'm skeptical, yes. I won't deny that. But people that I respect have praised your insight, and many rely on your counsel. I figured I'd give it a shot." Would that be enough for her? Or did she only help those who acknowledged her divine nature? If what she wanted from him was adoration, she was going to be sorely disappointed.

The steady gaze from behind the mask pierced his soul—dissected it—judged it. "Very well." Her eyes shifted focus, and he sensed she was no longer looking at him, or at this room, but at . . . something else. In any other setting he would have guessed she was accessing her brainware, maybe connecting to Hydra's innernet, but this woman— this *girl*—was supposed to be a visionary. So what was she seeing now, that was invisible to him?

"There is a knife," she murmured. "Its blade drips with blood. *Your* blood. I can't see the hand that's holding it, but the owner is close to you. Very close." She paused for a moment; her eyes twitched from side to side. "Your allies are more dangerous than your enemies, right now. Death wears a brother's mask. If you came here to ask if you should trust someone, that's your answer. If you want to know if you can let your guard down . . . don't."

"I never let my guard down," he said sharply.

She concentrated for a moment longer, then shook her head. "That's all I can see of your fate right now; the blood obscures too much. You must remove this threat from your destiny before I can tell you more. Do you understand?"

"Yes." *You're offering just enough to whet my appetite, but not enough to satisfy. I understand you very well.*

She backed up to her throne and sat down again. Ivar heard the door open behind him. "You may leave," she said.

Should he feel any different than he did before, as he left her presence? More enlightened? Fearful, perhaps? No. She'd confirmed his existing fears, nothing more. No supernatural ability was needed for that kind of insight, just good observation and an innate gift for manipulating people. Neither of which had the power to transform him.

He thought back to Shenshido and the delusions that had reigned there. They had been subtle transpositions, all but undetectable. Wherever this girl came from, whatever the source of her inner vision was, she knew that her visions weren't part of physical reality. That didn't feel like Shenshido.

Which was really what he'd come to learn. So at least he had accomplished that much.

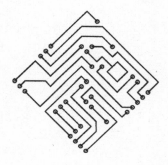

Any sufficiently advanced technology is indistinguishable from magic.

ARTHUR C. CLARKE
*Profiles of the Future*

# HARMONY NODE
# HYDRA COLLECTIVE

IN THE chamber of the Oracle
In the heart of the seven-headed space station
A child waited.

The silence surrounding her was eerily perfect. The normal hums and murmurs of life support, background music of the outworlds, were muffled by the dense rock surrounding her, to the point where no human ear could detect them. The only sounds she could hear were the rhythms of her own body: the beating of her heart, the fluttering of her breath, the pulsing of blood in her veins. She focused on those things, shutting out all other sensory input. Slowly, the chamber faded from her awareness, followed by the station—the outworlds—the entire physical universe. Nothing existed now but her own awareness, floating in the lightless space between realities.

"Show me," she whispered.

An image began to take shape before her. It was blurry at first, but then grew gradually clearer. She saw a man and a woman arguing. She recognized the man as Joseph Kors, who had an appointment to see her later that day. The woman was his partner. Their words were too muffled for her to make them out clearly, but that didn't matter; the hostile nature of the exchange was clear. Finally he waved her off in disgust and stormed from the room.

The Oracle watched as the woman placed a call. The image on her vid screen was too blurry for the Oracle to see who she was talking to, but she could guess what his role was.

The vision changed. A man had arrived, someone the Oracle didn't recognize. He consoled the woman, caressed her, then had sex with her. The Oracle watched all this dispassionately, unstirred by the images. In this state she was an observer, nothing more. Only thus could she grasp the greater significance of such events. Later in the day, when Joseph Kors came to her for insight into his failing partnership, she would give him the clues he needed to discover the truth. The strands of fate would thus be rewoven, new futures would be made possible, and perhaps in the end someone would die. Men such as Kors were not the forgiving kind.

It was not her place to judge him for that, or to judge the woman for her betrayal, or to judge anyone for anything. She was merely a conduit of truth.

The vision faded. She prepared to withdraw from her trance, but suddenly another image began to take shape. This one showed two people, a female terramorph and a Sarkassan male. The woman's battered leather jacket suggested she'd been in combat recently. The condition of the Sarkassan's clothing suggested he'd led a harsh life.

She watched as the two of them arrived on the station, escorted by the scavenger she had just counseled. They were connected somehow.

She watched as the two of them explored the Core, asking questions, searching for . . . what? Clearly they were looking for something, but her vision offered no clue what it was.

They didn't belong here. She could see that much clearly. The intricate digital network that was Hydra's lifeblood didn't include them. Images flashed before her in rapid succession, of all the bad things that might result from their independence. They must become part of Hydra, or leave the station, or die.

She saw what would be required to correct the situation. "It will be done," she whispered.

Sometimes she imagined that there was a shadowy presence in the room when she fell into trance, watching her. Sometimes she spoke aloud to it. There was never any answer, of course, but it helped give order to her thoughts. And if there was someone watching her, and if he was the one who sent her visions, he would want to know that she understood his messages, right? "I'll tell Joseph Kors that's the offering I want from him. Service, instead of money or goods. He'll do what needs to be done."

As usual there was no response. But in her mind's eye, it seemed to her that the shadowy presence was pleased.

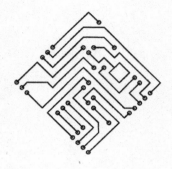

## ALLIED PRESS RELEASE

Thomas Easterly has resigned his position as CEO of the popular fast food franchise *Taste of Kawaii*, following the launch of an official investigation into the company's advertising strategy. Easterly is credited with the chain's dramatic increase in market share, but his tenure has been plagued by repeated complaints about Kawaii's invasive advertising practices. The Allied Communications Authority will be determining whether Kawaii is in compliance with the Privacy Act of '89, as well as the Ainniq Guild's *Mandate of Personal Sovereignty*.

Kawaii's stock plummeted 23% upon news of Easterly's resignation, though a late recovery of 2% suggests that some buyers still have faith in the company's long-term potential.

# HARMONY NODE
# HYDRA COLLECTIVE

**T**HE CONVERSATION with Shane Everest required three pitchers of beer.

The first one provided lubrication during an intense bout of storytelling, which established everyone's credentials. Shane described some grand pirating adventures that might or might not have been true. Micah told smuggling stories that definitely weren't true. He hoped that Shane had never played Smuggler's Run, because that was where he was cribbing most of his ideas from. It was hard to come up with that much faux-history off the cuff.

As a second pitcher was brought to their table, the Medusan's voice rang out again, announcing another challenge. This time it was a pair of women who entered the cage for a match—some kind of martial arts competition—and since they were fighting topless, Shane's attention was going to be focused there for the duration. But that was fine. The man was drinking, he was relaxing, he was beginning to treat Micah and Ru like old friends: that was what mattered. He even made some crude comments to Micah about various parts of the female anatomy that were on display, and Micah answered him in kind. Male bonding.

Micah was a little worried about what Ru thought of that, but when he glanced back at her she looked more amused than critical, so what the hell.

They needed Shane to be in a state of mind where he wouldn't be thinking about how much he should tell them, or why they were asking him particular questions. And it wouldn't hurt if his memory of their conversation turned foggy later, which enough alcohol would encourage. Until Ru and Micah could identify Shenshido's mysterious adversary and figure out if anyone on this station was controlled by him, asking too many questions could be dangerous.

As their second pitcher was removed from the table and a third one delivered, Micah finally decided that Shane was as well prepped for their purposes as he was going to be. He poured one last round for everyone—less in his glass and Ru's, as always—leaned back in his chair, and said, "Tell us about this Oracle."

Shane shrugged. "Not much to tell." He reached for his glass. "She has visions. Some people say she knows everyone's secrets. Some people say she's just fucking crazy. I don't set much stock in that kind of shit. Prefer the physical world." He winked suggestively at Ru. "Don't you?"

Ru smiled, neither responding to his flirtation nor discouraging it. Three pitchers of beer had made it clear the former wasn't necessary. "We heard she had quite a large following."

He drank deeply from his glass. "Yeah. She does now."

"That's recent?" Her tone was still casual, but in the depths of her eyes a new alertness had sparked. She touched a hand to Shane's shoulder—just a fleeting touch, the kind of thing a woman might do in conversation without even thinking, that a man might read all sort of things into—and smiled at him. It was very sweet. And very predatory.

*We are hunters,* he thought. *We have stalked our prey and cornered him, and now, when he is off his guard, we move in for the kill together.* It wasn't the kind of experience he'd ever shared with a woman before, outside of a game, and it stirred Micah's blood in a way he wasn't accustomed to.

"When she first got here she was mostly a novelty act," Shane told her. "I don't think too many people took her seriously. But Hydra is where people come to wind down, and the more entertainment options there are, the better. There are only so many whores you can fuck, y'know?"

"But now?" Micah pressed.

He snorted. "She virtually runs the fucking place. Oh, no one'll say that out loud, God forbid. But the patroni look to her for guidance, and sometimes after they get it they change their plans—canceling raids, financing new projects, maybe hiring or firing people. Her power may be indirect, but it's real. She has the big seven wrapped around her little finger. A woman." He snorted again, wiped his nose with his arm, and took another long swig. "Who'da thought?"

"When did all this happen?" Ru asked. "The change?"

His eyes glazed over as he tried to think past the alcohol. "Dunno. Two, maybe three years ago?"

A chill ran up Micah's spine. He tried to keep his expression impassive, so that Shane wouldn't realize the impact of what he'd just said, but it was hard. When he glanced at Ru, she appeared to be fighting a similar impulse. "Two years," she said quietly, more for Micah's benefit than Shane's. He understood. Two years ago was when the raid on Shenshido had taken place. It was when Ivar had been imprisoned there. When the madness had begun to spread. And apparently, just before that, a psychic performer who had been of little consequence to anyone suddenly became a major player. A puppeteer, who manipulated powerful people to accomplish her ends. The timing couldn't be coincidence. The Oracle might not be the person who had designed Shenshido's malware—given her mystical bent, it seemed unlikely she was also a master programmer—but Micah was willing to bet she knew who was.

Shane had emptied his glass. Ru took up the pitcher and refilled it. "What about the labyrinth? We heard some people experience delusions there."

"Could be. The place itself isn't a mystery. Hell, you can download a map of it from the innernet. But people who brave its innermost tunnels tend to not come out, and those that do . . . don't talk about it later." He took another drink. "They don't talk about much of anything."

"Meaning what?" Micah asked.

In answer, he tapped the side of his head and rolled his eyes.

*They go mad.* Yet another puzzle piece was fitting into place. But the overall picture was still a mystery. How was a psychic tied in to all this? It was torture not being able to discuss the possibilities with Ru.

Shane started to raise his glass again, but the drink slipped out of his hand and fell to the table. Beer sloshed everywhere. "Oh, God, I'm so sorry!" He started to pat at the spill with the end of his shirt, then rubbed his arm across it to absorb it with his sleeve, making it ten times worse. Micah pushed back from the table so beer wouldn't drip into his lap. It was clear that Shane wasn't going to be of use to them much longer, but that was all right. He'd already given them the one piece of information they needed most, that Shenshido's malware was somehow linked to this Oracle. She might not be the orchestrator of those events, but Micah was convinced she knew who was. "If we wanted to find out more about this Oracle, how would we do that?"

"Well, you could ask for an audience. She'll expect some kind of offering."

"Like what?" Ru asked.

He shrugged. "Something of value. The more unusual, the better. But she'll take money if that's all you've got. What matters is that it be a gesture of respect."

*Like one would make to a god,* Micah thought darkly. *Is that how she sees herself?* "If we wanted to find out more about her—before seeking an audience—who would we talk to?"

Shane hesitated. "I know someone, but . . . I'm not sure he'd want his name given out."

"We won't make it public," Ru promised. "It's just for us. So we can figure out what the best kind of offering would be." She ran a fingertip down his arm. "Please?" They'd spent an hour plying him with enough beer to drown out his critical functions. Micah held his breath, wondering if it would be enough.

"Ben Caruso," he said at last. "Doesn't hang out on the rock much. Prefers his own ship."

"How can we find him?"

"Works for Cassini. Head over to the Trident and ask them." He belched. "They're drug lords, you know. Suppliers of Venom-X and Viper. Nasty shit. You don't want to fuck with them."

"We don't intend to," Ru assured him.

He closed his eyes for a moment. "I think maybe you should . . . I mean . . . I'm sorry." He belched, then laughed. "Drank that one a bit too fast. God, you're hot, woman." He shook his head, then belched again. "Stomach's doing somersaults . . ."

"Rest for a moment," Ru urged. A gentle touch to the back of his head urged it forward, then down to the table. Sweat-soaked hair spread out in an amber puddle as he shut his eyes. "I'm okay," he whispered. "Seriously. Go ahead and order another round."

Ten seconds later he was snoring.

Micah looked at Ru. "You have any idea where the trident thing is?"

"Actually, I think I may. One minute." Her eyes unfocused as she consulted her files. "Check out G-5 on my map."

He had his headset call up the appropriate image. And yes, there it was: three flyways converging into one as they neared the core. Damn it if the result didn't look like a trident. "No easy way to get there," he muttered. "We'll have to walk."

"Looks like it's on a main route. Should be easy to find." Ru caught the eye of a server and waved him over. "Unless you think we should just go to the Oracle directly, and see what's up with her. Skip the middleman."

"Um . . . let me think for a minute. . . . No."

As the server approached she indicated Shane's sleeping form. "Please see that our friend is safe." She put a hundred-C cash chit on the table. The server's eyes widened. "Maybe there's some quiet nook you can take him to, where he can sleep it off undisturbed?"

"I'll find something," he promised, glancing both ways as he swept the chit into his pocket, clearly hoping no one would catch sight of his prize. He then began to clear the table of everything that wasn't snoring.

"All right then." Ru pushed her chair back, settled the strap of her supply bag more comfortably on her shoulder, and stood. She looked steady enough. Had she drunk less than Micah, or did she just hold her booze better? "Let's go find this Ben Caruso."

The pedestrian tunnel that led to the Trident was more polished than the spaces they'd been in previously, with smoothly finished walls, floor, and ceiling, such as one might find on a normal station. It was wide enough for small groups to pass each other comfortably, which happened often; it was obviously a busy thoroughfare. Couples passed Ru and Micah, hand in hand, and one amorous trio. A bevy of female Variants in painfully bright costumes giggled their way by. Two scruffy boys with the hunched posture of the downtrodden wheeled a closed cart past them. Ru remembered how Ivar had offered her slaves in return for her service, and she looked after the boys as they shuffled down the hallway, wondering what happier place they had been kidnapped from. Slavery was practiced on some colony worlds, so she was familiar with it, but though the first rule of outriding was to refrain from criticizing local customs, it was always hard for her to keep her silence in such a setting. At least with the colonies, she had the comfort of knowing that when the Guerans arrived they would demand the practice be ended, as a price of relocation. Common Law did not allow one human being to own another. But here that law had no power, and she had no power to change that.

"So," Micah said, when a break in the traffic left them alone for a few minutes, "what do you see?"

"Excuse me?"

He waved at the tunnel surrounding them. "Technology reveals social patterns, right? This place is the product of technology. What does it tell you?"

The blank walls offered little to go on, but she was grateful to have something to focus on other than the darkness of her own reflections. She considered the space as she walked, and finally said, "It's too big."

"The tunnel?"

"The core. Only a harvester ship could tow something this massive to the ainniq, and the expense would be phenomenal. A single person couldn't finance it."

"A patronus?"

She shook her head. "Even if they had that kind of money, this much raw mass wouldn't be given into private hands. There's enough here to build a small station."

"A Guildmaster would own it. Or perhaps a rich company."

"Most likely."

"The Terran megacorps build stations. They need mass to do that."

She nodded. "So say that a harvester brings this hunk of raw mass back to the ainniq, and some corporate entity purchases it. They drag it to their station, beyond the control of the Guild and other megacorps. Then what? How does it get from *there* to *here*?"

"Stolen?"

She shook her head. "Too big. It couldn't be accelerated fast enough to escape pursuit. And no megacorps would ever tolerate such a theft. They'd lay waste to half the outworlds trying to get it back. And nothing like that has happened in this node. No, some combination of barter and bribery must have convinced its rightful owner to part with it."

He looked at her. "You think . . . the outlaws cut a deal with one of the megacorps? That they're allied to a Terran corporation?"

"See? Now you're thinking like an outrider. My guess would be one of the patroni."

"And all this you get from the size of this rock?"

"And a knowledge of human nature." She smiled.

"And what about this tunnel?" He gestured down its length. "I thought the goal in station design was to put things near each other, to minimize the dead space that environmental control had to regulate. These people seem to have gone out of their way to do the opposite."

She laughed softly. "You've never been dirtside, have you?"

"You mean . . . on a planet?"

"Or a moon. Or an asteroid. Something produced by Nature rather than humankind."

"Not in reality, no."

"Well, construction on a station is additive. If you want to expand your usable space, you have to bring in mass to build walls with. Construction on the surface of a dirtworld is also additive. But inside that world, it's subtractive. You get new space by removing the mass that currently occupies it. And since that mass has monetary value, selling it can help cover the cost of excavation. A perfect trade-off." She looked around, eyes narrow as she studied the rock walls. "The cost would be cheapest if they followed the natural structure of the rock, linking together open spaces that already existed. The support structure would remain intact that way. Hence . . . long, twisting tunnels underground."

"But shorter ones aboveground."

She nodded. "Additive construction prioritizes environmental efficiency."

"Damn, woman." He shook his head. "I wish you'd been with me when I designed Dragonslayer. That was all underground."

She smiled slightly. "I'm guessing magical construction has different rules."

He looked like he was about to attempt a witty rejoinder when she raised a finger, warning him to silence. The sound of footsteps was faint in the distance, but gradually growing louder. Private conversation would have to wait.

This time it was a group of five who were heading in the opposite direction: two men, two women, and one whose gender Ru wasn't sure about, all of them clearly inebriated. One of the women waved expansively to Ru and Micah as they drew near, then turned back to her companion, to beg for a swig from the bottle he was carrying. A faint smell of vomit wafted from the group. Ru turned away in distaste as they passed by. She'd be glad to get off this glorified piece of rock. She listened to the group's footsteps recede behind them, waiting for them to fade into silence. But suddenly the rhythm changed. That was all the warning she had. Even as she started to turn, a heavy rod swung toward her head, its tip crackling with blue sparks.

"Shit!" Micah yelled. Out of a corner of her eye she saw him fumbling for his gun as two of the drunkards lunged for him. They didn't look nearly so drunk now. Then all her concentration was needed to deal with the one who was attacking her, and he was close enough that it would be hard to dodge his blow. She moved in closer and blocked that arm with one hand, then punched into his gut with the other, triggering the charge on her rings. He tried to back up but wasn't fast enough; sparks flew as the charged rings were driven deep into his gut. But two others were ready behind him, and even as he fell one of them forced her ring hand aside and slammed his body into hers, the smell of stale vomit filling her nostrils as his full weight drove her back down onto the floor. She tried to bring her weapon around, but the third assailant—a woman—slammed a foot down onto her arm, pinning it to the floor. Pain shot through Ru's wrist as she tried to shift the body that was crushing her chest into a position where she would be able to breathe, but even as she struggled the man reached up and covered the lower part of her face with a foul-smelling cloth. In a panic she tried to twist her head out from under it, but he had too firm a grip. The weight on her chest eased, and she reflexively gasped for air, drawing that vile smell into her body. Deep into her body. The tunnel began to swim around her. The pain in her arm filled her universe. She struggled against darkness, against death, but to no avail. She couldn't even turn her head to see if Micah was still alive, but was forced to stare into the dirt-encrusted eyes of her attacker as the darkness sucked her down, deep down, into that place where all thought—and all hope—was extinguished.

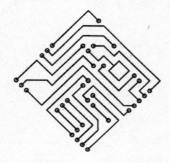

A man cannot know how much he would be willing to sacrifice until sacrifice is required.

DUAEN CORREN
*On Human Nature*

# HARMONY NODE
# HYDRA COLLECTIVE

**S**ILENCE.

*A pinpoint of light in the distance.*

*A distant drumbeat: like the rhythm of a human heart, but slow, so slow.*

*A thin beam of light breaking through a bank of black fog.*

*Faster drums. Almost a real heartbeat now. The light burns more brightly. The fog dissipates . . .*

Ru opened her eyes. The light that was shining into them was so blinding, she couldn't see where she was. She turned her head to one side and saw Micah's body lying beside her. His face was covered in blood.

They were alone.

Groaning, she tried to sit up, but when she touched her left hand to the floor pain shot through her wrist. She took a few deep breaths and then tried again, gritting her teeth against the pain. That bitch who had pinned her arm down must have broken something. When she finally managed to get herself up, she felt the bones gingerly with her other hand; even though the slightest touch sent shards of hot pain shooting through the joint, nothing felt out of place. Probably a fracture. She still had a decent range of motion, though it hurt like hell. It could have been worse.

Blinking to clear her eyes, she tried to make out the shapes surrounding her, despite the glare of the light fixture she'd been staring into when she woke up, illumination in the rest of the space was dim, and it took a few minutes for her eyes to adjust. Slowly her surroundings came into focus, and she could see they'd been dumped in a narrow tunnel—big surprise—but one that was different from the others they'd seen. Its floor was pitted and irregular, its walls ragged, its ceiling so riddled with faults and jagged protrusions that it looked like it might break up and collapse at any moment. The single domed fixture overhead offered just enough light to cast jagged shadows along the walls, like monstrous black teeth.

With her right hand, she felt for her weapons. They weren't there. Not the shock rod, not the charge pistol, not the taze rings. She'd been stripped of all armaments, and from the look of him, so had Micah. Her shoulder bag had been taken as well, which meant the Frisian K-1 was gone. Not to mention their emergency medical supplies. She felt around in her pockets to see if anything was left; they hadn't taken everything, it turned out, but they'd taken everything that could be used aggressively.

Carefully, trying not to put any weight on her injured hand, she moved over to where Micah was lying. He was pale but still breathing, albeit shallowly. The blood on his face was from an ugly impact wound on the side of his forehead. The blood was mostly dry now, with thin streaks coursing from the wound down the side of his head, to the floor. So he must have been lying there a while. Gingerly, she ran her fingertips over the damaged spot, feather-light, to explore the condition of his skull. It seemed intact and was still the proper shape, so whatever hit him hadn't cracked it open. But he was still out cold, and that was worrisome.

"Micah." She nudged his shoulder gently. "Time to get up."

He didn't move. Bad sign. If he'd suffered a concussion she might not be able to wake him at all. "Come on, Micah." She pushed harder at his shoulder. "Come back to me. You can do it." Still no response. She shook him harder. "Damn you, say something!"

Slowly his lips parted. His chest drew in a long, gasping breath, and as he exhaled he struggled to produce words. They came out as a whisper: "Worst. Hangover. Ever." His eyes opened. "Where the fuck are we?"

"No clue. Chrono says it's been four hours, so we're still in the core. Not enough time to take us anywhere else."

He reached up and felt his face, wincing as his fingers touched the wounded area. "Shit." His hand came away sticky with blood. "Shit."

"Something hit you pretty hard."

"No kidding." He wiped his hand on his jacket. "I don't remember anything."

"They took our weapons. And just about everything else."

Elbowing himself up to a sitting position, he methodically checked all his pockets. But the only things left were small items, unlikely to be useful. He did find the stub of an energy bar he'd started eating earlier in the day, which he held up for her to see. "At least we can have dinner."

"And then we can get high and forget our troubles," she said dryly, pulling a small packet out of her back pocket to show him: the drug from Seti VI. "I guess they had no idea what this was, or they would have taken it too."

"Or maybe they smelled it and decided to pass." He managed a weak smile. His color was better now and he seemed more alert, which were promising signs, but a concussion didn't always have visible symptoms. She'd have to watch him closely for a while. He looked around again, this time focusing much of his attention on the ceiling. "This tunnel isn't just for transportation. It was designed to intimidate."

"How so?"

He pointed to a section of ceiling. "See how that dips down in the center? That's an old designer's trick. It's such a slight difference you don't notice it consciously, but unconsciously you feel as if tons of rock are pressing down on you. Add a few fault lines, and the whole ceiling seems poised to collapse. Which suggests they put us in here to scare us. Structurally, it's probably all stable." He paused. "Probably."

She stared at him.

"What? That doesn't make sense to you?"

"No, it does. I'm just not used to people whose specialty is designing ominous spaces."

He shrugged. "It pays the bills." Using the wall to steady himself, he got to his feet, then reached up to touch the light fixture. It was too high for him to reach. "Give me a boost, will you?"

"What for?"

"If I can knock the cover loose, we might be able to break off some sharp fragments to use as tools. Or weapons. Hardly fancy, but better than nothing."

She remained sitting. "You don't need to do that, Micah."

"They took our weapons away, Ru. That suggests something is going to happen where we might need them. Granted, this isn't an ideal solution, but I don't see any other materials to work with." He spread his hands. "If you have a better idea, I'm all ears."

In answer she bent her left leg in toward her, so that she could reach the bottom of her boot. A finger pressed on each side of the heel released the latch, and the sole swung open, revealing a shallow channel with a flat object wedged into it. She removed it and unfolded its origami-like outer shell to reveal a thin knife blade, then folded the shell in a different configuration to serve as its handle. She put the knife aside, reattached the sole, then moved on to her other boot. It was hard to open that one without using her injured hand, but eventually she managed, revealing a similar compartment. Inside this one was another knife, as well as two attached rings tucked into the hollowed-out heel. She took the rings out and pulled them apart, testing the thin strand that stretched between them. It glittered like a string of diamonds.

"A garrote?" he asked, incredulous. "You're carrying a *garrote*?"

"Razorwire. Could be used as a garrote, I suppose. Also cuts through most common building materials. Though it does take a while to saw through metal bars. Sadly, I learned that the hard way." She closed up her second boot, then offered him one of the knives. "The handle's not very comfortable, but it indexes adequately and should do better than a broken shard of plastic. The blade is flexible, though, so you can slice with it, but don't stab it into anything hard."

He didn't move. Just stared at her.

"Micah? You okay?"

"You . . . carry hidden knives and a razorwire garrote with you . . . all the time?"

"Of course. You never know when they might be needed."

He stared at her for a moment longer, then whispered, "Marry me."

She laughed. The sound drove back the darkness just a tiny bit. "For making me smile in this dismal place . . . I'll consider it. Now . . ." She started to rise to her feet, and he moved quickly to offer her a hand. "I'm guessing," she began, "that the core doesn't have a lot of empty tunnels designed to intimidate people. Not enough space for that."

"You think it's the Oracle's labyrinth."

She nodded. "Seems likely."

"But why would they leave us in here?"

"That's the real question, isn't it? Though not quite as pressing as 'How the hell do we get out of here?'"

"Ivar said that people who go into the labyrinth don't come out."

"And he also said there were delusions involved. If that's related to what we saw on Shenshido, and you were right about its being transmitted through the innernet, you and I should be safe."

"Hopefully," he said.

"Hopefully," she agreed.

He held the origami knife up to the light, studying it from several angles. "The obvious first step is to explore the place, mapping as we go. No matter how complex a maze it may be, it can't go on forever. Like you said, space in the core is limited. So methodical exploration should eventually bring us to an exit."

"Except we have no water, so there is a deadline."

"All the more reason to start immediately." He looked over his out-fit for a place to stow the knife, but seemed unsatisfied with his options. Finally he made two short slices in the front of his jacket, then slid the knife down through one and out the other. It was a good idea, and Ru's jacket was already riddled with tears, so she did the same. The metal rings of the garrote she looped around two fingers of her left hand, wincing as she did so. "You all right?" Micah asked, concerned.

She flexed her hand to test it. It hurt like hell but seemed to be working all right. She had her wellseeker apply a mild painkiller. "Noth-ing I can't deal with. You're right, we need to get moving."

"Our headsets can track distance and direction and assemble a map from that. Meanwhile, we'll mark the walls as we go, for backup. That's the first rule of dealing with a labyrinth: never trust your life to only one system." Something about the expression on her face made him stop. "What? Is that not a good plan? Do you have a better idea?"

"It's fine," she said. "I was just reflecting on how glad I am that I have someone with me who is properly schooled in labyrinth manage-ment."

"Says the woman who carries a razorwire garrote in her boot."

She chuckled softly. "We are quite a team, aren't we?" She looked down the tunnel. "So which direction do we try first?"

"I'd say let's flip a cash chit, but our assailants seem to have taken all of those." He held up the food bar in its folded wrapper. "Brand name up, we go that way." He pointed down the corridor. "Ingredients, the other."

The silvery wrapper glittered as it tumbled end-over-end through the air. The bar bounced twice on the floor and then came to a stop. Brand name up.

"There we go." He picked up the food bar and put it back in his pocket. "And just as a side note, if you know any gods who specialize in helping people escape from mazes, now would be a good time to pray to them."

**F**ive hours. That was how long it took them to circle back to their original starting point. Five exhausting, pain-filled hours.

The last one was the worst. By then they realized that they were headed back to where they'd started from, but there was nowhere else left to go. They'd walked away from that point, circled around it, avoided it in every way possible . . . and yet, in the end, here they were again. Every path in the labyrinth turned back on itself; every tunnel circled around to its beginning. If there was an exit—which Ru was beginning to doubt—this was not the way to find it.

Discouraged and exhausted, they lowered themselves to the floor to rest for a few minutes and to figure out their next move. Micah seemed particularly drained, and Ru was concerned that part of the reason might be his head injury. Now and then she asked him if he was okay, and he said yes, but what did that really mean? If he became so weak that he couldn't go on anymore, would he tell her, or struggle onward in silence, pretending to be strong? She didn't know him well enough to guess. Her own wrist was throbbing, but that didn't carry the same risk as a concussion.

"This isn't getting us anywhere," he muttered. "What did we miss? Was there a passage somewhere that we didn't see?"

"There has to be. We got in here, didn't we? Unless they teleported us through a wall, that means there's a way in, and hence a way out."

He took the remaining nutrient bar out of his pocket, broke it carefully in two, and offered her half. "If you're talking about a hidden door, the irregularity of the walls would make that all but invisible. Even if we knew exactly where it was, we'd be hard pressed to find it." He looked up at the fault-ridden ceiling. "And if it's in the ceiling, there's not even a remote chance."

"Could the labyrinth be changing while we explore it?"

"Walls shifting position? Sealing off any path that would take us out? It's a possibility. Wouldn't be any easier to detect than a hidden door, though." He sighed. "Time we faced the truth: as far as we're concerned, this place is an oubliette."

The image of a dark hole where ancient prisoners were left to die, alone and forgotten, was not a welcome one. Three days was the maximum time the average human being could survive without water. Was that the purpose of all this? To seal them up in this bizarre tomb until death claimed them both? Or was it to weaken them in body and spirit, until they no longer had the strength to resist whatever the Oracle wanted to do with them? Given all that Ru had seen on Shenshido, she wasn't sure which was the more disturbing concept.

"So." Micah leaned his head back against the wall. "Is this when we discuss the option-that-shall-not-be-named? Or do we need to spend a few more hours pretending there's some other solution?"

It took her a moment to realize what he meant. "You want to connect."

"Shane said there was a map of this place online. If I connect to the innernet I can inload it."

*And maybe some malware along with it.* "All the other people who've been trapped here had access to that map. It didn't help them. Why do you think it will help us?"

"If not, there'll be other information in Hydra's database that can help."

"Which they also had access to."

"But did they know what they were looking for? Did they know as much as you and I do about the person who probably designed this? Or understand what kind of tactics that person uses? I'm more qualified for this search than any of them would have been."

"You want in," she accused. "This is just an excuse. You want to explore the digital workings of this place. To see how outlaws organize their network."

"Well . . ." A faint smile flickered. "Maybe that, too. But the need is real, you'll admit that."

It was real. That was the problem. In the back of her mind she could still hear the screams of the people on Shenshido, as they fought what they thought were monsters. The idea that Micah might wind up like that was chilling. But like he said . . . what was the alternative? "What if this was our captor's purpose all along?"

"Meaning?"

"We're sealed in a tomb with no visible exit. What if the purpose is to have us become desperate enough to connect to Hydra's innernet? Just like you want to do now. The minute you make that connection, you'll be vulnerable to any malware our adversary wants to throw at you. Maybe even a version of the program that infected you on Shenshido. Or perhaps something that would copy the data in your headset. Your notes on Shenshido, on Hydra, your calculations, communications . . . With that data, he may have realized how much of a threat we are."

"Except this is yours, remember?" He tapped the headset with his index finger. "There's nothing on it other than what I've recorded today. And besides . . . let's say you're right. The moment I connect, malware starts feeding into my head. Our enemy would want to do that as soon as possible, right? Before I had a chance to sever the connection."

"Probably," she said guardedly, not sure where he was leading.

"That code would be the first thing to inload. *The first thing.*" There was excitement in his voice now. "Do you understand what that means? If I can record that transmission, I might wind up with a copy of the malware itself. And with it . . ." He drew in a deep breath. "We could figure out how it works. Where it came from. Maybe even how to neutralize it. Isn't that what we came to Hydra to do? Wouldn't it be worth a little risk to achieve that?"

Ru hesitated. She wanted to tell him no. She wanted to insist that they could find some other way to escape this place, that he shouldn't risk his sanity like this. At least not yet. But then she saw the spark in his eyes, a fire that was all too familiar. This was a threat from the digital world, and he hungered to test himself against it. If their positions were reversed, she knew she would embrace that same danger willingly, even eagerly. It would be the height of hypocrisy to deny him that same option. "You won't be able to trust your own senses afterward," she warned. "Not till we leave this station and get out of transmission range. Cutting the connection won't stop the illusions, remember? You tried that on Shenshido."

"Yeah, but in the storage hold I didn't know for a fact that my senses were being screwed with. I took off my headset to see if the rotting mess would still be there, but I was only testing the situation; I didn't know for a fact all that was fake. Maybe once the brain accepts false input it maintains continuity on its own, until it's convinced the input is untrue." His amber eyes gleamed. "You'll have to decide what's real for both of us."

"And you can accept my call on that? Even if it contradicts what your own senses are telling you? It didn't seem to work on Shenshido."

"Back then I didn't know you. Now, if you tell me something doesn't exist, I'll believe it. Hopefully enough to banish any illusion that my own mind is maintaining."

*I don't want your life in my hands,* she thought. *I don't want anyone's life in my hands.* The thought stirred echoes in her mind, fragments of memory from other times and places when she'd thought the same thing. With Tully. He'd been equally stubborn. "Let's hope it doesn't come to that." She sighed heavily. "I hope to God this is worth it."

"We could both be wrong," he reminded her. "Maybe nothing will inload that's worse than an ad full of dancing kittens."

"One hopes," she whispered.

He took his knife from his jacket and offered it to her, handle first. "You should hold onto this. Just in case."

She hesitated, then took it from him. In that instant when they were both touching it, she thought she felt a faint trembling pass down the blade. Then he let go of his end, and the sensation vanished.

"All right then." He leaned back against the wall. "Let's see if this stone age headset can provide a decent interface."

Her fingers curled around the knife as she watched him shut his eyes and begin to concentrate. His eyes flickered back and forth beneath the lids, like a dreamer's. One second. Two. Five. Ten. He nodded slightly once and whispered, "Good." The steel band crushing her chest eased a tiny bit. Every now and then he would whisper some reassurance, to let her know that he was still mentally intact, but those came less and less frequently. There was one stretch of silence so long that she began to get concerned . . . and then his eyes finally opened. He blinked, then looked around, taking inventory of his surroundings. "Creepy tunnel, check. Light fixture, check. Lack of zombies, check." He looked at her. "One very worried companion, check."

"You found the map?"

"Yes, and more to the point, notes from the guy who oversaw excavation of the labyrinth. The official map matches the one we made, but his notes don't. Apparently we missed an access point. We need to go back there and check it out." He turned his concentration inward for another few seconds, then removed a data chip from his headset and offered it to her. "Here's a copy of the first transmission I received after I connected. Keep it quarantined as a backup. When we get back to the ship I'll try to make it surrender its secrets. Hopefully that will include what's needed to make sure that the nightmare on Shenshido never repeats itself."

As he pushed himself away from the wall, he swayed slightly.

"You all right?" she asked, concerned.

He laughed shortly. "Nothing that another hour of hiking without food or water won't address."

She offered him the knife. He stared at it for a moment, then nodded and took it. He looked steady enough, now. Even strangely calm. Should that concern her? "You don't seem very worried," she said.

"Oh, I'm worried, believe me." He slid the knife back into its makeshift sheath. "Alien software screwing with my head? I'm fucking *terrified*. I'm just role-playing a guy who isn't terrified, so I don't worry you too much." Before she had a chance to respond he offered a hand to help her up. "Shall we?"

His hand, at least, felt reasonably strong. And he was hardly trembling at all now.

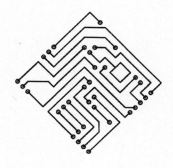

# DELVI

The *delvi* does not seek enlightenment in the pages of a book, or at the feet of a teacher. It does not study the material world, for it knows that physical reality is simply an illusion. To gain true understanding, it must search beyond the world that others inhabit.

And beneath it.

And within it.

And despite it.

*KAJA: An Outworlder's Guide to the Gueran
Social Contract, Volume 2: Signs of the Soul*

# HARMONY NODE
# HYDRA COLLECTIVE

IN THE silence between consultations, the Oracle meditated. More and more people were seeking her counsel these days, and quieting her spirit between their visits had become a necessity. Her next appointment was Josef Kors, and her visions would give her the insight she needed to guide him properly. She wondered what his offering would be.

An image began to take shape before her. It was the same couple she had seen before, the Sarkassan and the terramorph woman. This time the image was unusually crisp, as if a vid was playing in front of her. The man was sitting with his back to a rough stone wall, while the woman watched over him. There was fear in the air. Then the man's eyes opened, and he looked around. *Creepy tunnel,* he said, *check. Light fixture, check. Lack of zombies, check. One very worried companion, check.*

*You found the map?* she asked.

*Yes, and also notes from the guy who oversaw excavation of the labyrinth. The official map matched ours, but his notes didn't. Apparently we missed an access point. Not sure exactly why, but it looks promising, so we need to go back there and check it out.* He removed a data chip from his headset and offered it to her. *Here's a copy of what I learned from my connection. There's data in it that can be used to turn the Hydrans against the Oracle. By the time we're done, they'll want her dead as much as we do. No one will stand in our way.*

The image faded. Her hands curled around the arms of her throne, her nails pressing into its stone surface so hard that one of them cracked.

*They will want her dead as much as we do,* the Sarkassan had said. *No one will stand in our way.*

A knock sounded. "Come in," she said.

It was her assistant. He bowed his head reverently and said, "Josef Kors is here, my lady."

She nodded slowly. "Send him in."

He bowed his head and left.

*I'm ready for you, Josef Kors. And don't worry about your offering. Fate has dictated what it shall be.*

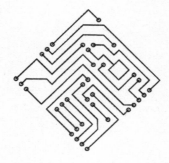

Life is a richly layered experience. Choices are never simple or clear.

If the choices in your game are simple, no one will believe the world you have created is real.

MICAH BELLO
*Crafting Nightmares (presented at Virtcon LVIII)*

# HARMONY NODE
# HYDRA COLLECTIVE

**T**HE COMMON room was crowded when Ivar arrived, and many of those present clearly recognized him. In the time he'd spent visiting the Oracle word of his return must have gotten around, because though old scav partners greeted him with smiles (and his rivals with scowls), no one seemed surprised by his presence. A few people nodded to him so casually as he walked through the room, you'd think he had only been gone two days instead of two whole years.

As he skirted the fight cage and headed toward the bar, he remembered his first visit here. A cocky and arrogant newbie with a few good hauls to his credit, he'd been willing to do whatever grunt work was required to start climbing the ladder of notoriety. He still had the same skill set as back then, and a hell of a lot more experience, so in theory he should be able to make that climb a second time. But people here were used to him being at the top of the pecking order, and might assume that he would accept nothing less. He needed a gig to convince them it wasn't true . . . or perhaps to convince himself.

A pair of whores brightened as he approached, one of them reaching out to touch his face, the other murmuring suggestive enticements.

Though whoring was the last thing on his mind right now, such women were a valuable resource, replete with local gossip that could be bought for the right price. More than once these two in particular had provided information that gave him the edge over his rivals, and so he paused long enough to exchange a few pleasant words with them, and expressed his regret at having other business to attend to. A wise man kept his whores happy.

Approaching the bar, he saw there was a section with few people near one end; he took a seat there and waited for Pago to notice him. The bartender was busy mixing drinks for half a dozen other people, and appeared not to see him, but when those jobs were done he came over to where Ivar was sitting and put a glass of Callistan rum down in front of him.

"You remembered," Ivar said.

"You're hard man to forget."

He took a deep drink of the rum. It burned his throat going down and filled his belly with welcome heat.

"Sorry about your ship," Pago said.

Ivar shrugged. "Shit happens."

"You have plans?"

"I figure I'll look for gigs. Restore the bankroll. Then worry about the rest."

"I'm sure for a man with your skills that won't be a problem."

"You wouldn't happen to know of anyone looking to hire, would you?"

Pago snorted. "I'm a bartender, not a career counselor."

Ivar took a medallion from his pocket and laid it on the counter. It was real metal, finely worked, with the image of a Terran animal rising up on its hind legs. Pago had a taste for unusual artifacts, and he gazed at it for a long moment before asking, "Does it have a story?"

"Rumor says it's from an independent station in Salvation Node. Don't know which one, sorry."

Pago studied it for a few seconds more, then tucked it into his apron pocket. "You know Josef Kors?"

"I've met him."

"Rumor has it he's gathering a team for some bloodwork. Not your usual gig, but I'm guessing that you're feeling pretty flexible right now."

"You guessed correctly."

"He's over there." A lower arm gestured toward one of the gaming tables. "Leaving soon, unless I miss my guess."

"Thanks," Ivar said, but Pago was already moving on to another customer. Ivar drained the last of his rum, put the glass down, and dug out a cash chit to tuck beneath it. Then he headed across the room to where Kors was sitting, with a pair of bruiser types he didn't recognize. Newbies, most likely. They had that look about them: energy and arrogance without experience to temper it. *I probably looked like that once,* he mused. *Strong and stupid.*

Kors saw him approaching and stopped whatever conversation he was having. He pulled out a chair as Ivar reached the table and pushed it toward him. "Ivar! Heard you were alive. Congratulations."

He straddled the chair. "I heard you were hiring."

Kors chuckled. "Straight to the point, as always."

"Anything else is a waste of both our time." He looked over the newbies, taking stock of their potential. One was a Caliban, short in stature but impressive in musculature. He'd torn the sleeves of his jacket off, no doubt because his barrel-like biceps didn't fit in them. His companion was Algonki, whose eerily long arms were folded across his chest as Ivar approached. Together, they looked more than capable of taking someone down, particularly if they coordinated their actions. Of course, that was the very kind of thing newbies were bad at.

Meanwhile Kors was studying him, no doubt weighing the pros and cons of hiring a legend to do less-than-legendary work. "The Oracle wants someone dead," he said at last. "I pay you to help make that happen, and she adds you to her list of favorite people. Win-win."

"Second part's of no concern to me. What's the offer?"

"Five hundred if we succeed. Medical costs covered regardless."

He nodded toward the bruisers. "Is that what you're paying them?"

"It is."

Ivar was worth much more than the newbies, and they both knew it. But demanding more than an equal share would earn him their enmity before they even left the bar. He remembered what the Oracle had said about his being betrayed. No, he didn't believe all her bullshit, but why tempt fate? "Good enough. Who's the mark?"

"Young Sarkassan male, terramorph female. Lightly armed at best, no charge weapons or kinetics."

*What the fuck?* That had to be Micah and Ru. It took him a moment to find his voice. "Do you have names?"

"No, but we know where they are, and we'll be kept informed of their movements."

"The hit will be on Hydra?"

"It will."

"And the Oracle sees no problem with killing someone on the station?"

"They're outsiders, so they're fair game." He shook his head. "Don't know what the fuck they did to piss the Oracle off, but apparently it was major. She said to make sure neither of them leaves this station alive." He waited. "So? You want in?"

Did he? If he agreed, he'd be helping to kill the people who had saved his ass on Shenshido. That was a level of ingratitude even he found hard to stomach. Not to mention, those two were trying to figure out what had happened there. Since that might involve a weapon designed to attack the scavs, Ivar had a vested interest in their success. Killing them now meant losing all their data.

*Maybe that's the point,* he realized suddenly. What if the Oracle wanted Micah and Ru dead because they were getting close to discovering the truth? If so, that meant the Oracle was indeed involved, just as those two had suspected. His head spun with the implications of that.

"Ivar?"

"Sorry. Thinking."

If he didn't join the team, Kors and his bruisers would just go on their hunt without him, and Ivar would have no clue what they were doing. He didn't have Micah and Ru's innernet IDs, so he couldn't net a message to them, and without Kors he would have had no way to know where they were. If he decided he wanted to help them, tough shit. He wouldn't even be able to find them.

*You don't want to get involved in this,* an inner voice warned. If Kors ever found out that he'd crossed him, there'd be hell to pay. But if Ivar didn't sign on now, he'd lose the option to do so.

"I'll go," he said.

"Good!" Kors slapped him on the back. "Glad to have you on the team." His eyes flicked upward briefly as he consulted some internal reading. "Time's short. We need to get moving. I've got to pick up some arms and one more person, then we'll meet in Nassau Bay and launch from there. Figure an hour."

*You're going after Ru and her partner with only five people? Good luck with that.* "You said you know where to find them?"

"Oracle says they'll travel south through the market, toward the Saito flyway. Can't ambush them in the marketplace; way too crowded. We'll wait for them at the first turnoff after." He pushed his chair back and stood. "Hopefully there won't be too many people around. Last thing we need is for this to turn into a public brawl."

*I could warn them,* Ivar thought as he watched Kors and his bruisers leave the common room. *An hour would be long enough to get there, find them, and return to Nassau Bay in time to rejoin the team. No one would ever know.*

One hoped.

He had always been a survivor at heart, prioritizing his personal welfare above all other interests. But this time it was different. If Hydra became like Shenshido, all other considerations would be moot. The Hydrans would all start killing each other, and it would no longer matter who had betrayed or helped whom, as rational thought was drowned out by bloodlust. And he would be stuck in the middle, surrounded by insanity again, with no way to escape. Was that the kind of survival he wanted?

Slowly he rose from his chair, still not certain what he was going to do but knowing that if he didn't move soon he would lose the chance to decide.

The market strip was on the surface, a long tunnel crafted from salvaged wreckage. Shops and stands had sprouted like weeds in every available niche, and the floor was packed with so many makeshift booths full of clothing and weapons and food and drugs that there was almost no room for a man to walk between them. And overhead trade goods clustered so thickly that they blocked out any view of the tunnel itself. Visitors had to wend their way along a narrow, twisting path, as if through a forest.

As Ivar worked his way along the strip, ignoring the enticements of vendors on both sides of him, he kept checking the time. It had taken him longer to get here than expected, which left him very little time to do what he came for. Yet he dared not rush too much, lest someone take note of his haste. The only way he could interfere with Kors' plans and survive the aftermath was to be so indistinguishable from the rest of the crowd that no one remembered his having been there.

*It's not Kors you're interfering with. It's the Oracle. Don't forget that.*

Several times he almost turned back. But amidst the cacophony of vendors hawking their goods and customers haggling over prices he could hear the echo of screams from Shenshido, the cries of men so lost in illusion that only a bloody death could silence them. Whatever had ruined that station could likewise turn this marketplace into a killing ground. That was what Micah and Ru were trying to prevent, wasn't it? If they failed, who else would take over the task? He certainly couldn't.

As he neared the north end of the strip, his pace quickened. The crowds were thinning out at last, and soon he would come to the place where the main passage split, smaller tunnels breaking off to head toward various sections of the core. What was he supposed to do when he reached it? Hang out there and wait till they showed up? He'd be damned conspicuous. But how was he supposed to know which tunnel they were traveling? If he headed down the wrong one he could miss them entirely.

Kors probably knew. But that did him no good at all.

A sudden touch on his arm startled him. He reached reflexively toward his charge pistol as he turned to see who had dared to put a hand on him—but it was only a woman, smiling broadly as he looked at her. He didn't recognize her, but that didn't mean much. After two years of absence, one expected to forget some people. "Ivar! They said you were back, but I couldn't believe it. Let me look at you for a moment . . ." She put her hands to the side of his face, but he pulled away. This wasn't the time or the place for such gestures. A fingernail scratched his cheek as she let go.

"I have business to attend to," he said. He was trying not to sound any more rude than he had to, but he needed to make it clear he wasn't in the mood for conversation. Damn it all, who was she? Had he slept with her?

"It's been so long!" She pouted. "I've missed you. Can't you even spare a minute for an old friend?"

"I'm sorry. I'm busy right now. Maybe later."

She sighed, clearly disappointed, but made no further attempt to stop him.

He started to turn northward again, but suddenly a wave of dizziness came over him. He reached out to the nearest table to steady himself, but misjudged its position and nearly went down. *What the fuck . . . ?* The woman was watching him now. Not smiling, just watching. Behind her were other people who were also not smiling: vendors, customers, an arm-in-arm couple that he had taken for tourists. All watching him now. Sweat broke out on his forehead as he backed up, step by careful step. His face burned where she'd scratched him, and he realized what she'd done. *Fuck you, bitch!* His surroundings were starting to spin. He tried to draw his gun, but his fingers were too numb, and he failed to pull it loose from its holder. Two men were moving toward him now, and he knew he couldn't fight them, so he tried to turn and run, but his legs were losing strength, and his feet wouldn't obey him. The men grabbed his arms and began to drag him north, away from the market. It was the direction he'd wanted to go in, but not like this.

He struggled against them as best he could, but whatever drug the bitch had injected into his veins made resistance impossible, and soon they were dragging him down a side tunnel, into a dark and deserted place where no one would interfere with their plans. Terror gripped him, but even that couldn't give him the strength to pull loose from them. Then someone drove a fist into his gut, driving the breath from his body. Someone else hit him across the face with a blunt object, and he heard bone crack. Someone struck him with a charge weapon, sending that side of his body into agonizing convulsions. Then he was on the floor, still convulsing, and they were beating him, brutal blows designed to cripple rather than to kill—even in his drugged state he knew the difference—and someone must have hit his wounded leg then, because he heard the newly fused bone crack. He was stabbed in the side, in the leg, in the arm. A bloody knife flashed before his eyes. The Oracle had talked about a bloody knife. Allies would betray him, she'd warned. Those he was closest to would seek his blood.

*Spike.*

Then the pain was gone. His thoughts were gone. There was a last titanic wave of fury that almost gave him strength—almost—and then that too was gone, swallowed by the black oblivion of bitter failure.

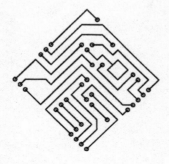

Who is more courageous—the man who knows no fear, or the man who, overcome by terror, does what he fears most?

AARON LEICESTER
*Choices*

# HARMONY NODE
# HYDRA COLLECTIVE

THE EXIT was exactly where the builder's notes said it would be. Micah watched as Ru inspected the opening, poking and prodding at various cracks and protrusions, seeking an explanation for why they hadn't seen it before. But there was no secret mechanism to be found, no sign of a pocket that a door might have slid into, nothing but a crudely excavated tunnel, the same kind they'd been trapped in for hours. Yet it hadn't been there before. Micah was sure of it.

"You sure this leads out?" she asked.

"I'm sure it leads to the edge of the builder's map. Anything past that point probably isn't part of the labyrinth. Granted, I'm speculating."

She nodded, considered the archway in silence for a moment, then said, "Describe it to me."

He blinked. "Say what?"

She gestured toward the opening. "Describe what you see."

He looked around the space. "A narrow opening, maybe a meter wide, two meters high. Looks like someone broke through the wall from the other side and just chipped away at what was left until the hole was fairly even." He pointed to a series of shallow gouges overhead. "Chisel marks there . . . there . . . and there." He stopped, but she looked like she was waiting for more. "Looks like it leads to another tunnel, maybe parallel to this one. The map says—"

"Not the map," she said. "What you *see.*"

"Two kinds of rock. Only one has the pit marks in it. Pretty big hole over there." He pointed.

"Good," she murmured. "Good."

"Because . . . ?"

"It's exactly what I see."

"A field test."

"We need to see if your senses have been altered."

He was about to say that their adversary was unlikely to bother with illusions as insignificant as chisel marks and rock matrices, but then he remembered Shenshido. Grime had been added to the walls there, and vines added to the vents. So God alone knew what small things might have been changed in the labyrinth, that he and Ru never noticed. "Okay. Good thought. We can do that periodically."

They gripped their knives and started down the new tunnel, ready for any trouble that might show itself. Ru was also wearing the rings of her garrote looped over two fingers of her left hand like ill-fitting knuckle guards, the razorwire safely retracted into one of them. She had winced when she put them on; clearly her hand was injured, and just as clearly, she had no interest in talking about it. Fair enough. He hadn't exactly been forthcoming about the brief waves of dizziness that came over him, or his fear that the blow to his head might have damaged something inside it. Talking about such things right now would have no practical purpose.

They walked, much longer than they should have had to; the twisting path never led directly to where they needed to go. Damn the people who'd carved out these tunnels, following natural hollows in the rock instead of just blasting straight through. If he and Ru could have walked a straight line to their objective, they'd have been there and back already.

And then, at last, there was a staircase, leading up. Micah felt a spark of hope for the first time in many long hours, and double-checked his map. "I'm not sure about some of these symbols, but I believe this will take us to the surface."

"Where travel should be more direct, at least."

"Not to mention flyways." *Hence escape from this wretched place.*

The first few stairs were coarse and uneven, and he had to reach out to the wall to keep his balance. But soon those gave way to synthetic steps, perfectly smooth, perfectly spaced, and perfectly identical. It was easier to ascend after that, and within minutes they were at the top landing, standing in front of an airtight hatch with a control panel to one side. It was an emergency seal, designed to isolate this section of the core if life support elsewhere was compromised. The readout offered data on temperature, air pressure, and oxygen content, all currently within acceptable limits. Ru glanced at Micah to see if he was ready, then reached out and triggered the control. The heavy door panels separated and light poured out from between them. After so many hours in dimly lit underground passages, it was nigh on blinding. Micah gripped his knife tightly for the few seconds it took his eyes to adjust, preparing for trouble. But there was none. After a few moments Ru nodded and stepped through, and he followed.

Whatever he had expected, this room wasn't it. Though perhaps it should have been.

"Describe it," she said softly.

He drew in a deep breath as he looked around. "A dome-shaped room with a standard geodesic structure, but it's a patchwork of mismatched panels, like each one was salvaged from a different source. One has a ship's ID number printed on it." He pointed to it. "Three doorways, in addition to the one we just came through, two beside ours and one at the far end of the chamber. And on the floor . . ." His expression darkened. "Puddles. Maybe blood." He pushed the toe of a boot into one of the puddles, smearing it. "Fresh." He looked at her. "Is that what you're seeing?"

"What about there?" She pointed to one of the exits. "Can you see the footprints?"

He'd taken them for random smears of blood, but now that he looked more closely he could make out treadmarks in them, leading to that exit. Someone must have bled like the devil on the other side of it. "I see them."

"And I see the rest of it, just like you described. So far so good. Which way next?"

He consulted the map, and pointed to the isolated door. As they approached, it opened. The smell of food enveloped them, and the noise of a hundred voices—at least. Beyond that was a madness of color and motion, and as Micah crossed the threshold he could only stare, trying to make sense of it.

"Holy shit," Ru muttered.

It was a market, but not in the normal sense. Oh, there were tables and booths and a few free-standing kiosks, all displaying a wealth of merchandise, people and items packed together so tightly it was a miracle anyone could squeeze between them. But beyond that, he could see glimpses of a station shell that looked like it had been formed by two ships colliding. No, not merely two; Micah saw parts from what must have been half a dozen different vessels, twisted and shattered and then welded together into a madhouse creation. He saw a clothing vendor whose wares were hung on a strip of plasteel from a station's hull, its climbing rungs twisted outward to form hooks; another shop was tucked into the discarded shell of an engine housing, which itself was welded to a section of passenger seating. The place was a veritable graveyard of ships, vendors exploiting its corpses.

"You're going to tell me we have to cross this," Ru muttered. She studied him for a moment, then reached out to wipe the blood from his face with the end of her sleeve. He winced but didn't back away. Then, tucking their knives into their pockets to keep them out of sight, they stepped forward into the hot, sweaty crowd. It was a frustrating journey, squeezing past booths and kiosks that displayed a thousand items they desperately needed, but had no money to buy—weapons and armor, first aid supplies, and of course food. Spices filled the air, bringing on a wave of hunger so strong it was painful. But they had no money to purchase anything, nor anything to barter with, and it seemed an insanely foolish place to try shoplifting. Nevertheless, Micah did manage to sweep a drink box into his pocket, that someone had left on a table while shopping. When they were out of sight of that booth they shared its contents gratefully, their parched skin sucking in fluid like desert sands in rainy season.

Suddenly Ru stopped. "What?" Micah asked. "What's wrong?" In answer she nodded toward a booth just ahead of them. The man in it was hawking weapons, with his wares laid out on a table in front of him as well as hung on the wall behind. The most valuable items were secured in locked metal cages: charge rods, kinetic guns, blades and projectiles of all shapes and sizes. Only a few meters away, and maddeningly inaccessible. But she wasn't pointing to any of that. It was something on the back wall, displayed in its own small cage, that had caught her attention. When he saw what it was he breathed in sharply. "Shit," he muttered. A K-1 triple-stage assault rifle. How many would there be in a place like this? "You don't know that it's yours."

"I know that it's mine," she said quietly, her eyes never leaving the piece.

Was she thinking of trying to retrieve it? The mere thought was insane. Even standing here like this, conspicuously fixated on it, was dangerous. "Ru, if you're right, then the people who attacked us are probably around here somewhere. The last thing we need is to be recognized by them. Come on, let's go." He took hold of her arm gently, meaning to urge her forward, but she shrugged off his grip without looking away from the assault rifle. *Her* assault rifle. Oh, he totally understood why the sight of it here would anger her, but the degree to which she was fixated on it was unnerving. *She's Gueran,* he reminded himself. *Somewhere inside her head, there's a part of her brain that doesn't function like other brains. Is that what's causing this? Could her Variation drive her to consider something so mind-bogglingly stupid as trying to reclaim this weapon?*

"What we're carrying is worth more than a K-1, and we need to deliver it." He tapped the side of his headset, reminding her of the malware data he had copied. "That chip is worth more than your pride right now."

She looked at him. Just that, for a moment. Then she nodded.

The rest of their passage through the market was less dramatic, though exhausting. By the time they reached the archway at the far end, Micah was aching to breathe clean air again, and to walk without having to squeeze past other people. The first wish, at least, was granted. As they passed over the threshold, currents of air from the other side swept away the smells of the unwashed multitudes and their wares. Even the noise behind them seemed to fade a bit, though that was probably just wishful thinking on his part.

Soon, soon, they would be off this miserable rock.

As they continued on he asked, "Would you really have gone after the gun?"

"You mean, if you didn't stop me?"

He nodded.

She smiled slightly. "I was just wondering how its current owner might respond if I offered to barter for it."

"With what? Your boot knives? Those wouldn't pay for a round of ammo."

She patted her rear pocket. "I still have the Seti drug."

"Okay, so you offer that to him. Then what? He opens the packet to get a closer look, gets a whiff of what's inside, and it's the end of that deal. Hell, that stink could clear out half the market—" He stopped suddenly. "Ah. Gotcha."

She smiled sweetly. "It would have been fun to try. But as you say, duty calls."

*Fun to try.* That's how she envisioned an act that might have gotten the two of them lynched for ruining the market. God, he hoped that was her Gueran Variation speaking, because if not, she really was insane.

It was her map that guided them now, to a central dome from which they might access both ships and flyways. But her notes didn't indicate which of the tunnels branching off from it would take them where they needed to go, and Micah's map was no improvement. Apparently this part of the station had been developed after the map was uploaded. Damn. He and Ru were so close to their objective that he could taste it, but this last leg might prove the most difficult of all.

He went to one of the exits and peered into yet another featureless tunnel. He was willing to bet the others would be equally unidentified. Were they going to have to approach this like they had the labyrinth, choosing paths at random until they found one they could use? It hadn't worked that well the first time.

"Hey. Over here." Ru was waving to him from across the dome. Apparently she'd found something.

"I think this is the one," Ru said from a tunnel to the right of him. "Come on, let's go."

He froze. Turning slowly toward the second voice, he saw Ru standing at the mouth of the tunnel nearest him. But the other Ru was still on the far side of the dome.

"This one is wider than the others," came a voice from behind him. He hesitated before looking that way, fearing to confirm the worst. It was yet another Ru, identical to the first two, waving for him to join her.

"Is everything okay?" The question came from across the dome, where the original Ru had been. But when he turned back that way he saw there were now two of her side by side. They seemed unaware of each other, but spoke in perfect unison. "Do we need to do a reality check?"

There were five of them now; the delusion was multiplying. "There's more than one of you," he whispered hoarsely. Several of the Rus looked shocked. There were six total, now. No, make that seven. Every time he turned to look in a new direction another one appeared, identical to all the others down to the smallest detail. He was no longer sure which one was the original, and their manner offered no clue; each Ru mirrored the others like a marionette on a common string.

"Okay," three of the Rus said in perfect unison. "Take my hand and I'll guide you." Only it was not one Ru that reached out to him but half a dozen of them, their steps synchronized. Which one was real? What would happen if an unreal one reached him first? He backed hurriedly away, pulling his headset off as he did so. It didn't help at all. Of course it didn't help. He knew only that one Ru was real, but he didn't know which one; as long as his brain thought the others *might* be real, he lacked the power to exorcize the illusion. But at least if the headset was off no new madness could infect him—he hoped—so he stuck it into his belt.

Suddenly a shot rang out, and a moment later a small object struck him in the chest, hard enough to drive him back against the wall and knock the breath out of him. It bounced off his armored jacket and skittered to the floor, blue sparks flying. A charge bolt. From where? Desperately looking around the dome, he saw that yet more copies of Ru had appeared—the dome was full of them!—and two that were heavily armed were engaging the one that only had the knife and gar-rote rings. She must be the real one. Before he could even try to get to her, two of the Rus were rushing him, one of them pointing a charge gun at his head. He threw up an arm in front of his face just in time for the armored sleeve to protect him, but the bolt pierced through far enough to get stuck in the fabric, and it hung from his arm, crackling with blue-white energy. Were the bolts even real? It no longer mat-tered. The malware that had taken control of his senses could make him feel an illusionary shot as if it were real, and he'd be down for the count regardless of whether it existed in the material world.

They were fucked, he and Ru, royally fucked. And he had made that possible. Insisting on connecting to this infected station, he had given their enemy the means to distract and then divide them. And now they were both going to die for it.

But the Ru who had fired at him would need a second for the next bolt to charge, so he threw himself at her, one hand thrusting with his knife, the other reaching out for her gun hand. She blocked the blade and managed to evade his grip, but the struggle gave him an opening to slam his body into hers, desperately trying to throw her off balance. As soon as he made contact he realized his mistake. Whoever the person behind this delusional mask really was, he was much larger and heavier than the image of Ru which disguised him. It was all Micah could do to twist his attacker around enough to block an assault from the other Ru. A third Ru had joined the fray and began pounding on his back, but that attack wasn't on the scale of what the first two were attempting, so he judged her a fake and tried to ignore her.

There was pain after that, and a chaos of blows—some real, some imaginary, but all equally painful. A fist drove into his gut, a blade sliced through his collar and just missed his throat, and he was almost choked to death. He managed to break that grip with an elbow driven into one Ru's nose, and he heard bone crack as she fell back from him, making room for yet another copy. This one pointed a charge gun directly at his head, point blank, and he braced himself for the shot that would fry both his brainware and his brain into oblivion.

But before that Ru could fire, another one stepped in and whipped a length of razorwire around her forearm. It cut through clothing and flesh as if through butter, severing muscles that controlled her hand. As she dropped the gun Micah grabbed it, and he turned around and fired into the face of another attacker. The bolt went into her eye, sparks exploding from her face as she fell. He whipped around to see where his third attacker was, but the real Ru must have taken that one down. Now was he was not surrounded by assailants, but by copies of Ru arranged in a semicircle around him, each one holding out a hand to him.

"They won't stay down long," a Ru said. "Come on!"

"They won't stay down long," another Ru said. "Come on!"

Then a third.

Then a fourth.

One of the fallen Rus was getting up again. Soon the others would also, and battle would be rejoined. Maybe more attackers would appear. There was no way he could sort it all out in time. Thanks to his foolishness in embracing Hydra's malware, their adversary had won this battle, at least as far as he was concerned.

"Go!" he gasped. Ru could still save herself. "Get the data to the ship!"

"Not without you," three of the Rus said simultaneously. They reached into their rear pockets and pulled out matching packets: the Seti drug. They dragged the packets across the tips of their knives, cutting them open. The sickening stink of the drug filled the air . . . but it was only coming from one of the Rus. He reached out for that one, grabbed her hand, and let her drag him through the chaos. Past bleeding Rus, over Rus moaning in pain on the floor, past Rus who screamed that the one holding his hand was the real enemy. *Not real,* Micah told himself. *Not real. Not real. Not real.* As they ran through one of the doorways, into the tunnel beyond it, he sucked in that glorious putrid smell of the Seti drug and filled his lungs with the perfume of reality. This Ru was real; no others could be.

By the time they reached the next doorway—another airtight hatch—the fake Rus were gone. The real one went to the touch screen beside the hatch and activated the controls, searching for the icon that would unseal it. A few seconds later the heavily reinforced panels unsealed and the door began to open. As soon as they were through Ru turned back immediately to find the control panel on that side, and as Micah leaned against the wall, trying to catch his breath, she shut the door again. "Can you lock it?" she asked. "So it can't be opened from the other side?"

"I can try." He pushed himself away from the wall and took her place in front of the panel. It took little effort for him to access the hatch's settings, but altering them turned out to be a whole other challenge. "It needs an administrative code," he muttered. "Which I don't have."

"Can you hack it?"

He looked at her. "You're joking, right?" He turned back to the panel. "But I do have an idea. Give me a minute."

As he'd suspected, the hatch's sensor array wasn't subject to the same level of security as its operational settings. As quickly as he could, he fed information into the control panel. Suddenly the red light of an air lock warning began to flash over the hatch, and scarlet letters appeared on the screen: EMERGENCY SEAL ACTIVATED.

"What did you do?" Ru asked.

"Convinced it that there was a vacuum on the other side. For as long as it thinks environmental controls have been compromised, it won't open. They'll figure that out eventually, I'm sure—I just bought us some time."

They both looked around at the space they were in. It was little more than a Y-shaped intersection with the hatch at its base. "If we are where think we are," Ru said, "one of those two branches should lead to the docking facilities. The other—hopefully—to a flyway." She drew in a sharp breath. "Only we can't use it now."

"What do you mean? That's what we've been trying to get to all along—"

"But now we know that someone on this station wants to kill us. And if Shenshido's mastermind is involved, he probably has control over the entire station. Do you remember what Ivar told us about how Hydra was constructed?"

His eyes widened as understanding dawned. "The flyways aren't permanent."

She nodded. "All it would take to kill someone inside them would be to separate the segments. Our adversary wouldn't even have to separate them completely; as soon as there was an opening, our air supply would be history. Or maybe an emergency breach program would kick in, and seal each section off, like a portable tomb. Same difference, as far as we're concerned." Her expression was grim as she looked toward one tunnel, then the other. "I don't know about you, but stealing spaceships isn't in my skill set."

"Maybe we don't need to do that." His mind was racing, fitting pieces of the puzzle together with a gamemaster's instinct. *The tools you need must be present. Find them, figure out how to use them.* Finally he said, "What if we could get someone to take us back to the Artemis?"

"I don't think anyone in this place is likely to help us."

"We have Dominic Saito's contact information." Seeing the look of disbelief on her face he added quickly, "You must have something on the Artemis that he'd value. Guns, artifacts, I don't know . . . you and your partner took souvenirs from all the worlds you visited. Rich men like to collect rare things. Surely you have something he'd want."

She started to shake her head. "I don't . . . No, wait." Realization seemed to dawn. "I do have something. I think. Not sure what it's worth, though." She looked at the two exits. "I'll need a com panel."

"Either flyways or docks would have that. Doesn't matter which at this point. Flip a chit."

She pointed to one of the tunnel branches. "That one."

But his mind was still racing, fitting game pieces together. "Do you have any of that Seti crap left?"

She reached into her jacket pocket and withdrew what was left of the ravaged packet. There wasn't much left inside it, but they didn't need much. "Spill it in there," he said, pointing to the corridor she hadn't chosen. She understood immediately, and took a few steps into that tunnel to scatter the dust on the floor and walls. They'd been exposed to the drug's smell for long enough that they hardly noticed it now, but with Ru's jacket anointed by the stuff, their passage through the tunnel must have left a trail of stink behind them. Now there was a stronger trail to divert any pursuers. It might only buy them a few minutes, but everything here was about timing.

They sprinted down the other corridor together. As she'd predicted, surface construction was more compact than they'd seen in the tunnels, and they quickly reached its end point, a long, crescent-shaped room with access hatches evenly spaced along its outer curve. The entrance was an airtight hatch, and as Ru searched for the com panel, Micah closed and shut down that one as well. This time he used a different pathway, convincing the controlling program that there had been a power overload so it would shut itself down while searching for the source of the problem. Which of course it wouldn't find.

Ru had the com panel activated and was standing in front of it, smoothing down her unruly hair. As he joined her she turned to him. "Am I good?" she asked.

He gently reached out to wipe a few spots of blood from her cheek. Her skin was surprisingly soft beneath his fingertips. "You are now."

"All right. Cross your fingers."

He backed up far enough to get outside the screen's visual field, lest the sight of his battered face color the conversation. As soon as she was clear she sent the connection request, and he held his breath. If Saito did anything other than accept their call, they had no plan B to fall back on.

The screen stayed dark for a few minutes, then a familiar Saurin face appeared. "Ru, is it? I assume if you are contacting me, this is important."

She nodded. "We find ourselves in need of a lift back to our ship, and were wondering if your people could provide it."

He was silent for a moment. The scaled face was hard to read. "You took a flyway in. They go in both directions."

"We have . . . access issues."

Another long pause. "I don't run a taxi service," he said.

"Of course not. I was thinking of something more along the lines of . . . barter?"

A scaled brow lifted slightly. "What are you offering?"

"Ivar owes me a favor," Ru said. "Fulfill it, and he'll owe you instead." What was Saito's relationship with Ivar? Would he value having something to shift the balance of that relationship in his favor? Micah desperately hoped so.

"I assume this is urgent?"

"Speed would certainly be appreciated."

He folded his arms over his chest. "Let me ask you this—and bear in mind I have means of confirming your answer before my ship would arrive—have you breached any laws of the station?"

"We haven't killed any locals. We haven't stolen anything. Those were the only laws Ivar told us about."

So many things were unasked, unrevealed. But on a station like this, that was probably business as usual. "You're asking a rather big favor of my House. Does the value of your offering merit that?"

"He owes me for getting him off Shenshido. What do you think?"

He nodded. "I'll send someone to your coordinates. Meet him at bay four."

The screen went dark.

"I did steal a drink box," Micah said.

A smile flickered. "I thought it best not to mention that."

"Ivar won't be happy about his."

"I'm sure he would have done the same in my position. Or worse."

Wait. That was all they could do now. The airtight hatch was effectively soundproof, and they had no way to know what was going on behind them. Were their pursuers scouring the flyways in search of them, or had they caught on to Micah's ruse, and were they even now hurrying in this direction? Did Ru and Micah have minutes left before that last barrier was compromised, or seconds? He leaned against the frame of the airlock and considered letting his wellseeker feed a bit of sedative into his veins to calm his nerves. But no; he needed the animal alertness that fear provided. Ru was pacing nervously, so apparently she'd made the same decision. There were times you didn't want your senses dulled.

The screen next to bay four lit up.

CLASS 2 VESSEL REQUESTS DOCKING RIGHTS
MOORING BAY 4
ID: SAITO CLASS B POD 44AO1

"Thank God—" Micah began. But a sudden noise from the chamber's door stopped him. Someone was banging on the far side of the main door. "Shit," he whispered. "They're trying to break in."

"That door's designed to hold against the vacuum of space," Ru said. But the vacuum of space didn't know how to pry open a door's seams.

MOORING CLAMPS SET.
CONNECTION CONFIRMED.
SEAL CONFIRMED.

The outer door shuddered. Or was that Micah's imagination? He edged closer to the airlock. *Open open open open open* . . . Now the main door creaked: definitely not his imagination.

LOCK RELEASED.

The airlock hissed and began to slide open. As soon as the opening was wide enough for a person to squeeze through, Ru grabbed Micah by the arm and shoved him into it. As she followed, there was an explosion at the main door that sent shards of plasteel flying toward the bay. Ru hit the airlock control as soon as they were inside and the airlock started to shut again, muffling the noise of people yelling and the smell of smoke and the noise of charred debris skittering across the floor.

The ship's entry hatch opened to receive them and they rushed through it, not caring what kind of ship lay beyond, or who was inside. Anything other than the naked vacuum of space would be welcome. "Cast off!" Ru cried. "Now!"

There was one woman inside the pod, and while she was clearly startled to hear Ru giving orders, their bloody and disheveled appearance must have made the need clear enough. The pod was a small one, so they stood over her shoulder as she resealed the ship, then triggered the release of the mooring clamps and began to lift off from the core—

Only the ship didn't move.

The woman scowled and tried again. The ship jerked, but didn't break free.

"Shit," Ru muttered. The people on the other side of the airlock must have jammed the mooring clamps. Micah watched the pilot try to break free by sheer force. Finally, cursing in exasperation, she called up a display of the outer hull, and he and Ru watched as two short-range lasers emerged. They fired, and two of the mooring clamps became slag. "Boss will not be happy about that," the pilot muttered, as the small ship finally broke free.

A shudder of relief passed through Micah. Were they really going to get away? He watched the display in trepidation, but no ships left the core to follow them. For the moment, at least, they appeared to be safe.

The pilot twisted back to look at them. "I don't know what the fuck you two brought with you that smells like a ten-day-old corpse, but it needs to be ejected. The boss won't like it if we stink up the home dock."

Scowling, Ru shrugged out of her jacket—no small feat in the cramped confines of the small pod—then rolled it inside out so that the tainted outer layer was wrapped in the safeskin lining. She tucked the resulting package under her arm and glared at the pilot. After a moment the woman shrugged and turned back to the navigation console.

*We're safe*, Micah thought. *We made it.* His fingers stroked the headset that was tucked into his belt. *And with any luck, our adversary's secrets are coming with us.*

The lights came on as they entered the Artemis, and by the time Ru was seated in the pilot's chair everything was up and running. "Strap in," she said. "This could be a rough ride."

By the time Micah was in his seat with his safety harness activated, the ship was already free of its mooring, and was turning toward the course that Ru had chosen, a channel of open space between flyways and docked ships that looked dangerously narrow to him. But he trusted that she knew what she was doing.

As of yet there was no sign of pursuit. He knew that because the row of screens high over the navigation console was now displaying a full panoramic view of the surrounding space, and nothing was moving in their direction. But that didn't mean they were safe yet. The Artemis might be impressive, but some of the bigger vessels here could probably fly circles around it. Which was probably the reason for this route, he realized. A larger ship would be hard pressed to follow them through this narrow channel.

"Shutting down the G-field," she told him. "Brace yourself." A second later his stomach lurched as the ship's faux-gravity suddenly disappeared. Inertia from a few sharp turns took its place, pressing him against the straps of his harness. The last one took them around the back of a cluster of matching ships, and then they were in the open, beyond the tentacles of the Hydra beast, with deep space a black sea before them.

"Don't breathe easy yet," she warned.

"Oh, I'm not, believe me." There were two ships leaving the core now. Regular Hydran business, or something directed at them? His heart raced as he watched them on the screen, lifting from the surface as if in slow motion; in that crowded neighborhood one couldn't afford to fly too quickly. But she would have. He glanced over at Ru, and saw her eyes were gleaming with excitement. She would have flown at full speed through that mess, and God help any ships that got in her way.

Hydra was starting to grow smaller on the screens as it slowly fell behind them. Ru reached out to adjust the display, and a sensor grid overlaid the image. The Artemis was scanning the space surrounding them for activity. No motion nearby, the readout indicated. No noteworthy mass. No energy signature, other than their own. Micah allowed himself the luxury of a deep sigh.

"Looks good so far," she muttered. "Next stop, Harmony Station." A proposed course appeared on one of the lower screens, and she locked it in.

"That's pretty direct," he said. "If anyone wants to cut us off they'll know where to find us."

"They've got the buoys, remember? Wherever and whenever we pass them, people will know it. Hopefully they don't pay much attention to outgoing traffic." She adjusted the display scale again; some stars grew brighter, others were swallowed by blackness. "The only ships in that place that can outrun Artemis have too much mass to get up to speed quickly. Assuming we can put enough distance between us and them to start with, we should be good."

It didn't take long at that speed to reach the buoys; still no signs of pursuit had been detected. When they finally got beyond the buoys' sensor range, Ru leaned back in her seat, rubbing her neck with her good hand. "I'm setting up an alarm, so we can relax a bit. Though I think, at this point, it's safe to say no one is following us." She looked at Micah; her eyes narrowed in concern. "You should let the medpod check out that head injury."

"You should let the medpod check out that hand injury."

"Sorry." She smiled sweetly. "Concussion trumps fracture."

It was hard to argue with that.

But there was nothing inside his head that was worth getting alarmed about—or so the medpod told him—and as he returned to the front of the ship she opened her safety belt and let it withdraw back into the chair. "Why don't you pull out the table and order us a couple of drinks? Here." She adjusted a control and suddenly the G-field was back on. "Easier to pour this way." She picked her bundled jacket up from the floor. "I'm going to dump this in the sterilizer. Hopefully that'll get the smell out."

As she went to open the armory he did as suggested, and by the time she returned he had the table and chairs out, and a pair of tall glasses with amber shots in them ready and waiting. "To an uneventful flight?" he said, as he handed her one.

She laughed. "Not sure I remember what that's like." She took a deep drink, shutting her eyes for a moment to savor it. "Much better. Now." She put the glass aside. "Sit down, and let me clean the rest of that blood off you."

He took another drink and then sat, while she ordered up a hand towel and a small bowl of water. Primitive but intriguing. She pulled her chair nearer to him and put the bowl on the table beside her. "I'm glad we never passed a mirror, so you saw how bad this looks. Might have been discouraging."

"As opposed to everything else that was going on?" he asked dryly.

"Smartass." She dipped the towel's end in the water. "If this hurts, you tell me."

"It already hurts."

"If it hurts *more*." She wiped the moistened cloth along his uninjured cheek, tentatively at first, then, when he didn't flinch, more confidently. Thus were ancient warriors cleansed. The water was cool against his skin and the gentle stroking motion was soothing; after a few seconds he shut his eyes, surrendering to the sensation. Periodically she would pause, and he would hear water dripping as she squeezed out the towel. He used one of those moments to take another drink, and as the warmth of the alcohol spread through his veins, it relaxed his knotted muscles.

When she was done wiping away the grime and blood on his undamaged skin, she moved to the wound itself. Her touch was so gentle, so gentle, as she probed his injury. He could barely feel it. "It's not as bad as it looks," she murmured, as she began to wipe that area clean. When her fingers strayed to his hairline he could feel them tracing his Variant markings, leaving behind thin trails of moisture that cooled as they evaporated. She stroked his hair back from his face, combing it with her fingertips, then continued down the back of his head, until her fingers rested on the nape of his neck. He could feel his skin flush beneath her touch, and heat was beginning to stir elsewhere.

He opened his eyes. "Here." He took the towel from her. "Your turn." She had a cut across one cheek, and he patted it gently, wary of it bleeding anew. "We're a mess, aren't we?" He chuckled softly. He squeezed the cloth clean again, sending tendrils of red curling across the surface of the water, and then began to stroke her cheek with it, wiping away dirt and sweat and blood, revealing the honey-colored skin beneath. Now it was she who closed her eyes, relaxing into his touch. He wiped a dried trickle of blood from her neck, following it to the base of her throat. Then a streak of dirt led him outward to her shoulder, his fingers slipping beneath the narrow strap of her tank top. He could hear her breath quicken as he moved back again, his fingers brushing her breast. Hunger was growing in him now, causing his heart to race and his flesh to stiffen, but it was more than just a sexual heat—it was joy and desire and pain and exhaustion and relief combined, and most of all triumph. Because he was alive—alive!—despite the best efforts of Tridac and Shenshido and Hydra to make it otherwise. And now triumph was a fire inside him, demanding outlet.

She set aside the towel and stood, drawing him to his feet as well. Now there was nothing between them but a few thin pieces of clothing. Her tank top was easily removed, but his T-shirt tangled around his arms as he tried to pull it off. She laughed as she pushed the fabric upward, until he was finally free. Then her body was pressed against his, hands teasing, exploring, parting the last garments and pushing them aside, until there was nothing left to remove. She eased up onto the table for support and then drew him to her, her long, lean legs wrapping around his hips, her hand guiding him. He thrust into her slowly at first, savoring the moist heat that enveloped him, then faster, again and again, losing himself in the rhythm of it. There was fear and pain and triumph and desire in every stroke, and he grasped her by the hips to pull her forward, so he could thrust even more deeply. Her lips met his and her arms wrapped around him, and then there was nothing but the two of them moving together, sharing pleasure as two people can only when they have looked upon the face of Death together, and lived to tell the tale.

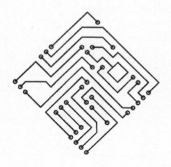

Beware trust, for it is a double-edged sword.

NICOLE MAKI

*The Pursuit of Power*

# HARMONY NODE
# HYDRA STATION

"**K**IA TALEN is here to see you, sir."

Dominic Saito put down the Hassiri charge gun he'd been inspecting, setting it alongside the other weapons his people had commandeered from a corporate armory. "Send her in."

The woman who entered was small and wiry and dressed in her usual black: the kind of person who might flit in and out of shadows unseen. She bowed her head respectfully.

"You have news of Ivar?" Saito asked.

"As you ordered, he was accosted and badly beaten, but left alive. I arranged for him to be retrieved by a whore whose connection to Saito isn't public knowledge. Ivar knew her from before, so when she came across his injured body and brought him to a place of safety, he would ask no questions about her motives. As he was too badly injured to recover on his own, she asked where he wanted to go for proper treatment. Only one of the great Houses would have the kind of equipment he needed, and Saito was the obvious choice. She brought him to our medical facility."

"How long before he's on his feet again?"

"The medics estimate a week of downtime, at least."

"How much will he remember of the attack?"

"He wasn't given anything to fog his memory, if that's what you're asking. But he didn't see anything he needs to forget. The agents who attacked him all wore faux-skin masks, so he has no idea what they really look like. One of them wore the badge of House Cassini on her jacket, so if he remembers that much it won't be our House that he suspects."

Saito nodded his satisfaction. "Cassini has approached him in the past, so that will play well. He won't take it kindly that they tried to use violence to force his hand. All good." He leaned back in his chair. "Hydra is a dangerous place for the unaligned. Now, hopefully, he'll understand that. He can't go it alone anymore, and Saito is his best choice for an ally."

"Are you sure that'll be enough?" When he raised an eyebrow she added quickly, "I'm sorry, but you know he's a stubborn asshole."

Saito chuckled softly. "Paying us back for all that medical attention will take a while. After that . . . I have some new leverage to help clinch the deal. And for all his bluster, I can't imagine he'll want to risk another beatdown like this one. How does the saying go? *The writing is on the wall.*"

He smiled. "I will own that stubborn asshole."

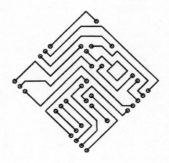

Control of resources = survival and reproduction = continuance of the species. That is an equation embedded in the DNA of every animal on Earth.

The human hunger for power needs no more excuse than that.

L. D. SHALE
Heritage of the Beast

# HARMONY NODE
# INSHIP: ARTEMIS

CONTENTMENT. SORROW. The echo of pleasure. The ache of loneliness.

Sitting at the pilot's console, watching the rise and fall of Micah's brainwaves on her screen, Ru struggled to fit her feelings into a single category. But the task was hopeless. It was like looking down from a tightrope and trying to figure out how to dismount on both sides at once. She'd have to cut herself up the middle to manage it.

There was peace within her now, such as she hadn't known since returning to the outworlds. The empty space that Tully's laughter had once filled was still empty, but it was less dark now, less urgent. For one brief moment she had been herself again, exulting in the heady aftermath of death-risk. And this time there had been someone to share it with: a rare pleasure. But it wouldn't last. Even if she decided that this game-designer-turned-adventurer was worth spending time with, where would that lead? She'd go crazy if she stayed this close to the ainniq, surrounded by the stations and ships and crowds of the outworlds, hungering for the freedom of deep space and the mysteries of lost colonies. He'd go crazy if he left the ainniq, wandering in the vast emptiness that was deep space, hungering for news of the newest technology and gamers to test his creations. Between those two options there simply was no middle ground.

Some pleasures in life were ephemeral: the bloom of a flower, the blaze of a sunset, the shimmering of a phosphorescent lake. One savored such things for as long as they lasted and then let them go. That was the theory, anyway.

Micah's brainwave frequency was in Beta territory, which was what you'd expect from a man struggling to analyze software that was capable of destroying whole worlds. Now and then the frequency dropped a bit, suggesting a brief moment of mental relaxation. It never went into the Alpha range, though. That's what she was watching for. When somebody who'd been pushed to the point of physical exhaustion told you he wanted to lie down in a dark room with his eyes shut to concentrate on a problem, somebody else had better watch over him, to make sure he didn't fall asleep.

Once more the frequency dipped, and this time she heard the door open behind her. She turned to greet him, but when she saw his expression the words died on her lips. All the color was drained from his face; he looked like he had just seen a ghost. "Micah? What is it?" When he didn't respond she said, "You figured out what it is."

He nodded slowly. "And I think where it came from." He ran a hand through his already mussed hair, which only messed it up more. "I need a drink, Ru. A really strong one."

She flashed an order to the ship, and by the time Micah joined her at the galley, a glass of scotch was waiting. He picked it up and downed its contents in a single swallow. She noticed that his hand was trembling slightly. What could have shaken him so badly? He already knew that the software he'd copied on Hydra had the power to warp men's minds, so that they turned on each other like beasts. What could he have discovered now, that was worse than that?

He stared into his glass for a moment. She waited silently, letting him take the time he needed, though curiosity was consuming her. And a bit of fear, too. "Well," he said at last. "First things first. Hydra did indeed transmit its sensory override program to me, so I got a copy of that. Masterful stuff, but the basic concept was familiar. I went over it line by line, looking for some kind of clue to its maker's identity. Every designer leaves his mark somewhere—maybe deliberately, maybe unconsciously, but it's there. And I found . . ." he drew in a shaky breath, "a fragment of code that I recognized, from an antibody program we studied back in school."

"Antibody program?"

"Yeah. They're used when something nasty has infected the outernet, but there are too many copies for human beings to track them all down. You send an antibody out into the net, it searches for those copies, and when it finds one, it bonds to it, neutralizes it, and then deletes it. Very effective, when designed well.

"This one . . . it was designed to target a particularly nasty virus. One that self-edited so quickly that antibodies had to be uniquely adaptable to keep up with it. A true evolutionary race. We studied that contest in class, analyzing every line of the antibody code, running projections on how they would perform in different situations. Hell, I wrote a paper on that damn code. I could recite it in my sleep." He took another drink. "The virus itself was too dangerous to study, except in isolated fragments."

She remembered the bartender at the Prometheus Club talking about a supervirus. "Did it have a name?"

"Lucifer. Named after the devil. It only targeted the Guild at first, but then expanded to humanity in general. Took them three years to track down all its spores and destroy them. Epic battle." He looked down at his glass, now empty, and reached over to put it back in the galley. Wordlessly she had the ship refill it. "So, that's what I found embedded in Hydra's sensory software. A piece of that code. Do you understand what that means?"

She hesitated. "This isn't my venue, you know that."

"It means something *dismembered* it. It means the antibody found its target, but instead of it disassembling the virus, the virus disassembled it. Only fragments of the antibody remain now, like thorns in an animal's paw. That's what I found, Ru. A fucking thorn."

"Are you saying Lucifer is on Hydra?"

"Am I? I don't know. Shit!" He shook his head in frustration. "Lucifer's supposed to be gone. No one has seen any sign of it for more than a decade. Probably the original version is long gone, but its spores might have evolved into something the antibodies don't recognize. And then one of those spores came here, and continued to grow, to evolve, in the safety of isolation . . ." He drew in a deep breath. "I think that's what's been screwing with people's minds, Ru. Not a person. Lucifer's offspring."

"That sounds . . . I'm sorry . . . crazy."

"Well, yeah. But no human designer would have left that junk code in there. Natural evolution, on the other hand, is messier. The human genome has all sorts of useless code in it, remnants of past viral infections. Supposedly Lucifer functioned like a real life form. That's what made it so dangerous. Living systems are always unpredictable." He removed his glass from the galley and took another deep drink. "What if it evolved a kind of sentience? Not human intelligence, but some version we might not even recognize?"

"I didn't know computer viruses were capable of that."

"Not on their own. But we helped it along, didn't we? Killed off every spore that wasn't savvy enough to dodge our defenses. Years and years of selecting for the strongest, the most adaptable version of Lucifer. The most intelligent." His hand tightened around his glass. "We fucking *made* this thing, Ru! And now that it's self-aware, it wants what any living creature would want: Safety from assault. Freedom to grow. Control of its environment."

"All of which we threaten."

"Damn right. Humanity is its adversary, its tormentor. Its devil." He smiled wryly. "Its Lucifer."

"So why did it let us escape the labyrinth?"

"That one I think I can answer. Part of what I inloaded on Hydra appears to be a string of code intended for the outernet. Not sure what it is, since it's only a fragment of a program. Maybe a patch of some kind. As soon as I got within range of the outernet it was supposed to outload automatically."

"So it was using you as its messenger."

"More like its mule, but yeah."

"So you don't think it was behind the attack on us?"

"Oh, I do. Those fake Rus alone were proof of it. Maybe while it was loading all that crap into my brainware it was copying the data I'd stored, and later realized how much of a threat we posed. The thing isn't human, Ru, and it probably doesn't reason like a human. Some mathematical algorithm determined that one course of action threatened it more than the other, statistically speaking, so it shifted gears. That's my guess, anyway. Who knows how the thing thinks?"

"No emotion," she murmured. "No intuition. Just data."

"And a driving need to destroy humanity. Starting with Harmony, it appears. There are parts of its code designed to activate during the Festival. That's less than two days from now. Though I can't imagine why—" His eyes widened. "Shit. Shit."

"What? What is it?"

"That raging asshole Guildmaster Dresden was planning to screw with the outgoing protocols during the Festival. To make it easier for data to be transmitted to other nodes. He's Guildmaster, so he can do whatever he wants, even if it's stupid." He shook his head in disgust. "If this . . . this *thing* . . . wants to transmit software to all the outworlds, changing the outgoing protocols would clear the way. Security would be overwhelmed by all the traffic, and outgoing data would get much less scrutiny than usual. Maybe none at all. Shit!" He shook his head. "We need to do something to stop that from happening. Or find someone who can."

"And by 'do something' you mean, on the station where they think you're a terrorist? Where every facial recognition device probably has you filed under Ten Most Wanted?"

He flushed. "Yeah, there is that. But they think I'm dead, right? No one should be looking for me anymore."

"And if they still are?"

He sighed. "Then I guess I spend the rest of my life on a prison station, while you do battle with a homicidal computer virus alone. Or you can go off on some outriding mission and leave that to others. I don't know." He rubbed his eyes. "I'm so tired I can hardly think. What's our ETA?"

She consulted the ship's chrono. "Ten hours."

"Once I have access to the outernet, I'll see if I can figure out exactly what our friend's plans are." He laughed. "That's a damn stupid way to refer to it, isn't it? We need to give the digital bastard a name."

"Morpheus? The spirit of dreams?"

"Overdone. Half the fantasy virts on the market use it. Hell, I've used it." He thought for a moment. "How about Icelus? Brother of Morpheus, lord of nightmares."

"Works for me."

He sighed. "We should get some sleep while we can. There may not be time for it after we get to Harmony. We're sleeping in shifts, I assume?"

"Seems wise."

"Albeit disappointing." A strained smile was briefly visible. "You can go first, if you want. I'm afraid I'm still too wired to relax."

She shook her head. "Thanks, but I'm not closing my eyes until we're back in Common Law space. Bed's all yours for now."

He bowed his head slightly. "As you command, boss."

She watched him as he walked back toward the bunks. Still strong in stride, his shoulders erect, but the exhaustion in him was palpable. Not only of body, but of spirit.

She felt the same.

*I should send a report to Jericho. Make sure this information gets to him, just in case we don't.*

She turned off the brainwave monitor before she began that task, leaving Micah to adopt whatever sleep cycle suited him best, in privacy.

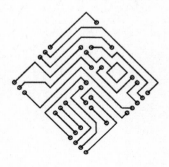

Humans yearn for mystical experience. They hunger to believe there is something more to this world than what they can experience with their physical senses, for what that will say about our world. Gods, spirits, divination, visions, any of them will serve. All that is required is one thing that science cannot explain, and all things become possible.

Osho Yun-Si
*Without Limits*

# HARMONY NODE
# HARMONY STATION

DRESDEN WAS watching the kaltrop table, where guests in glittering masks and silken gowns cast star-shaped playing pieces across the board. Their wager counters were displaying numbers in four and five digits—high bets for this kind of game—and when someone lost a throw there was laughter from the players around them. Rich people were often entertained by the losses of others. Meanwhile drinks were precariously balanced on the edge of the table, thirteen in all. He was tempted to accidentally knock one of the glasses to the floor to produce a more pleasing number.

He'd hung a betting board on the back wall the day before, listing the various facets of the harvester's arrival that one could wager on. What flight formation would the sparrows use? How much mass would each one carry, on the average? What was the minimum load? The maximum? How quickly would they decelerate? Had any been damaged during their fifty-year mission, and not yet repaired? One had only to name some feature of the spectacle to come, and it would be added to the list. The number of bets in each category were displayed, as was the total amount wagered. Sometimes he would place a bet himself, just to make the array of numbers more pleasing.

Almost time. It was almost time. Harmony would make history today.

"Guildmaster Dresden?"

He turned to find a tall man in a traditional Guild robe standing at a respectful distance. The man was not wearing a mask, and the kaja design painted on his face was mostly *nantana* with a hint of *natsiq*, which suggested he was here on Guild business. His hair was a silvery lavender, dramatic above the stark Guild black. "Tye Jericho," the visitor introduced himself, bowing his head slightly. "Director of Outrider Affairs. I called earlier to let your office know I was coming." He looked around the room. "If this is a bad time . . ."

Dresden smiled graciously. "It's never a bad time to receive such a distinguished visitor. Come." Dresden gestured toward a golden archway draped in crimson velvet, which led to more private rooms. Had his people failed to tell him that Jericho was coming? Or had he simply forgotten? These days his mind was filled with so many facts and numbers pertaining to his Festival, sometimes there was room for little else.

As they started toward the archway, a pretty young woman in a casino uniform approached Jericho, holding out a tray of masks. "Compliments of the house," she said with a smile. He hesitated, so Dresden picked one out for him—a half mask of black satin with glittering stars. As she left he handed it to Jericho. "The theme tonight is a masked ball."

"Seems an odd thing to give to someone wearing kaja. Sort of defeats the purpose, doesn't it?"

"I told them to offer masks to anyone who didn't have one. A gesture of hospitality."

"I gather the normal prohibition on face-coverings in public has been lifted?"

"Suspended for the duration." He waved expansively toward the main floor, where guests in glittering masks were gambling and gossiping and drinking and dancing. There were half-masks of stiffened lace, narrow eye-strips edged in beaded fringe, dramatic demon visages, and of course animal masks, both real and fantastic. "What better way to escape the stresses of daily life, than to dress up as something that has no daily stresses?"

He led Jericho into the high rollers' wing, where small rooms awaited those patrons who wished to play games away from the public eye. Each room was lavishly furnished, with a bar outlet. As he led Jericho into one he gestured toward an overstuffed chair. "Please make yourself comfortable. Would you like something to drink?"

"No, thank you. I'm still a bit lightheaded from the ainniq. But please, feel free to have one yourself."

He had the bar pour him one, not because he really wanted a drink, but to buy himself a moment to query the outernet about Jericho's history. It turned out his visitor had an impressive résumé, both in and out of the Guild. That was good to know; he might prove a valuable contact in the future if he was treated well. Dresden adopted his broadest host-smile as he turned back, briefly observed the number of buttoned tufts on the couch, then took a seat opposite his guest. "Are you here on business or pleasure?"

"How could one not find pleasure here? Your Festival is splendid. The list of events I saw when I arrived was quite tempting. Even the most dour businessman would be helpless to resist such temptations."

It was ritual praise, and coming from a *nantana* it meant little more than 'hello,' but it was pleasing nonetheless. "When you only have a harvest once every fifty years, it deserves an all-out celebration. Will you be staying for the countdown?"

"I haven't decided yet. I suppose that depends on how our conversation goes."

Ah, conversation. Of course. A *nantana* would rather be flayed alive than state his business directly. Fortunately Dresden was skilled in such arts, and so they took turns asking polite questions of each other, and pretending they cared about the answers, for as long as protocol required.

At last, when it seemed they had invested enough time in the ritual exchange, Dresden said, "But you haven't told me yet: what can I do for you?"

Jericho leaned back in his chair. "I think it's more like what I can do for you."

Now Dresden was intrigued. "Go on."

"Back at headquarters we've received intelligence that there might be an attempt to compromise your data security during the Festival."

His expression darkened. "By whom?"

"Not sure yet. We believe the effort is connected with one of your independent stations. Given the circumstances, I thought it best to let you know immediately."

Dresden muttered under his breath. "Megacorps."

"Word is they're planning to take advantage of the change in transmission protocols. Evidently you're adjusting your security filters for that?"

He nodded. "We can't channel data quickly enough by our usual methods. It's just temporary, though. A few days at most."

"Respectfully, Guildmaster, once someone has breached your security, he can easily establish a back door to give him access later."

Dresden raised an eyebrow. "So you are suggesting . . . ?"

"That you reconsider the adjustments you've planned."

He sighed. "Yet another rendition of a tired theme. It's amazing how many people who have never run a waystation feel they know best what's good for it."

"I think they're just concerned. As am I."

"Don't you think I know my station better than an outsider? Including how to adjust my security protocols without putting the station at risk? We have protections in place. Nothing was done recklessly."

"Forgive me. I meant no offense."

Dresden drew in a deep breath, taking a moment to settle his spirit. The Festival had his nerves wound up too tightly; he didn't want to alienate such a valuable contact. "No, it's I who should apologize. You've been perfectly polite. I've just been under pressure lately from a lot of people who aren't."

"Planning a Festival of this scope would have anyone's nerves on edge. I'm sorry to add to that stress. But we are concerned about these reports. Harmony Station has been attacked before. It's not unreasonable to think someone might try again."

Dresden stiffened. "If you mean the terrorist attack, that's been dealt with. The perpetrator is dead, so there's no more threat from that source. I appreciate your coming here to warn me. I really do. It was a great courtesy. But I assure you, everything is under control. My vision—" He stopped suddenly.

"Your vision?"

He hesitated. If he told Jericho about his visions, would the man think him mad? Or inspired? *Hell, in a few hours it won't matter. Jericho will see my plans play out and witness the results. Everyone who has doubted me will see it. They'll celebrate my insight.* Why not let Jericho know that he had been guided by something greater than mere logic? That his mind functioned on a level few other men would ever experience? Maybe it was time to share that. "I had a vision a while back, of what this node could become. I saw what I had to do to help it reach its full potential. I saw where all my policies would lead, as clearly as if I was watching them play out in a viddie. And believe me, every angle has been considered. Every danger has been anticipated and allowed for. I've *seen* it, Director."

The look on his visitor's face was strange. Unreadable. "I didn't realize you had such a clear vision," Jericho said quietly. There was no emotion in his tone, no hint of the thoughts behind it. "Of course you would trust in that. Now that I know, I fully understand. Forgive me for taking up your time." He stood. "We'll keep you informed of what we learn, of course."

"I appreciate that." He was startled by Jericho's abrupt exit, but stood up to see him out. "So will you stay for the grand countdown? Witness events for yourself so you can report to Tiananmen that their fears were unfounded?"

Again that strange look. "I'm afraid not," Jericho said. "I have someone else I need to meet with. But I wish you the best, Guildmaster.

And if you do discover cause for concern, remember, it's never too late to be cautious."

Dresden walked him back to the main room, then watched as he crossed it. At one point Jericho paused by a mask-bearer, and Dresden thought he intended to give the black mask to her, but instead he chose another from her tray. How very strange.

Then the music of laughter and the tinkling of glasses caught him up and carried him away, leaving the Guild's unfounded fears far behind.

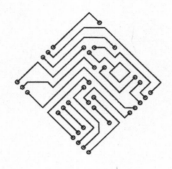

## SAIMEN

The *saimen* is an island, untouched by seas of emotion.

The *saimen* is a rock, unmoved by storms of sentiment.

Standing apart, it gains perspective. Divorced from passion, it gains understanding.

Bereft of illusion, it draws strength from reality.

*KAJA: An Outworlder's Guide to the Gueran*
*Social Contract, Volume 2: Signs of the Soul*

# HARMONY NODE
# INSHIP: ARTEMIS

"**R**U?"

She awoke so quickly it startled him. Was that a normal outrider reflex, or were her nerves just so on edge that even sleep couldn't soothe them? He certainly felt that way. "What? Are we there already?" Her eyes unfocused for a second as she consulted her chrono. "Has something happened?"

"We're passing the harvester. Thought you might like to see it."

She didn't glare at him and go back to sleep, so apparently he'd guessed right.

The main display was dominated by the image of an immense ship. At its head was the blunted spire of a deep-space vessel, designed to deflect or absorb any random debris it might run into; at interstellar speeds, even something the size of a grain of sand could do devastating damage. Indeed, the spire was heavily scored and pockmarked, bearing witness to how many such encounters had marked its fifty-year journey. Behind that protective cap, the main body of the ship was long and sleek, able to slip through a gas cloud or even a planet's outer atmosphere with minimal friction. Such a design was rare in the outworlds, where the only atmosphere was contained within space stations, and free mass had enough value that any spaceborne debris was swept up as soon as it was detected.

Suspended in the darkness of deep space, the harvester looked like a vast marine creature slipping through an ink-black sea. The few small vessels that were flanking it kept perfect pace with it, like pilot fish, with one riding closer, tucked beneath the belly of the beast.

"Vid bots?" Ru asked.

He nodded. "Dresden probably doesn't want to risk missing the deployment. That's the money shot for his whole Festival. I'd imagine he's probably been watching this thing since it slowed down enough for his bots to catch up to it."

"We'll stay out of range, then, so we don't wind up in their broadcast. Though I imagine they're all focused on the harvester." She paused. "You do know this kind of thing isn't a big deal elsewhere, right? Round trip from Tiananmen Station to Guera only takes a year or so, so harvesters make that journey regularly. No one gets excited about it."

He shrugged. "It's a good excuse for partying. I think that's what matters most. But Guera's harvesters aren't on the same scale as this one, are they? When you're in a node that hasn't got a planetary system within light years, you've got to pack all you can into one trip. Including enough excavation equipment to carve up a moon, if need be." He gazed at the immense ship on the screen and murmured, "I wonder how many swallows there will be?"

"Swallows?"

"The porter ships. When there are enough of them clustered together they look like a flock of birds. I'd imagine in Guera Node you don't see that many at one time. It's really something. Mind you, I'm judging that from past vids. Never seen that big a deployment in person."

"Your last assignment was in an orphan node too, wasn't it?"

He looked at her. "I do forget sometimes how much you know about my history." He turned his attention back to the display. "Yeah, I worked on Preservation for a while. But that was between harvests, so this is new to me." He whistled softly. "Can't even imagine how much mass that mothership is carrying right now. Maybe even enough to generate its own gravity. Wouldn't that be something to experience? I hear real gravity feels different than the tractor-field variety."

"It does, though I'd be hard pressed to describe how." She cocked her head slightly. "Have you never been dirtside?"

He shook his head. "Station baby, born and raised in deep space."

She smiled slightly. "I'll have to take you to visit Guera, before my next mission starts. You can't imagine how different things are on the surface of a planet. Just being able to see so far without obstruction is amazing. Everything out here is contained in walls, or in shells, or else you're in deep space, where there's no sense of scale at all. To gaze at a natural sunset—to see the sky over an entire planet blaze with color and to know just how vast that sky is—is something words can't capture."

"I would like to see that someday," he said quietly. "And an ocean. I've always wondered what that looked like, such a vast expanse of water, uncontrolled by anything but nature."

She chuckled. "It smells of decay. Growing up by the ocean you learn to like that, but I'm told offworlders find it disconcerting."

"Stink is good," he reminded her. "Stink is real."

"I'm going to print that on a T-shirt for you."

"As long as it's not pink." He sighed. "I'd offer to show you my world, but oceans of data aren't as impressive to look at. Though I could wax poetic about mathematical algorithms shining on the crests of probability waves."

She chuckled.

They'd be docking at Harmony Station soon, right ahead of the harvester's arrival. Hopefully they'd be able to pass on a warning to the powers that be, in time for them to head off the immediate threat from Icelus. After that . . . that damn virus had survived two decades of being hunted by humans, and it wasn't going to go down quickly or easily. He remembered how he'd had to fight for his life against an army of fake Rus, unable to identify the real attackers, and he shuddered. *I'm glad I won't be the one responsible for eradicating that thing.*

The console chimed.

**INCOMING MESSAGE FROM TYE JERICHO.**

"Your contact?" Micah asked.

She nodded. "I sent him a report while you were asleep. Wanted to make sure—" She didn't finish the sentence, but he knew what she meant. Their data needed to get to Harmony even if they didn't make it. It was a sobering reminder of how much danger they were still in.

She told the vid screen to display the message.

**DOCK AT GREEN RING SECTION 8A.**
**I WILL MEET YOU THERE.**
**TALK TO NO ONE BEFORE THEN.**

They stared at it in silence for a moment, then Micah said, "Is it just me, or does that not sound good?"

"No," she said. Her smile had faded. "It's definitely not just you."

To say that Harmony Station was crowded would be an understatement. Between the ships moored to its docking rings and the ships cruising between them, the luxury yachts flanking the station and the transports clustered around its core like flies on honey, you could hardly see the station itself. Micah could swear that when Ru contacted Traffic Control to request a fight path to 8A he heard laughter in the background. But there was a berth reserved in her name, so she got her instructions. Whatever strings Jericho had pulled, it was an impressive feat.

They moored the Artemis, then waited for Jericho to arrive. Micah was acutely aware that each minute that passed meant they were closer to Dresden's scheduled protocol shift. From the way Ru was fidgeting, he was sure she was aware of it, too. Finally the inner door chimed with an entry request. T JERICHO, the screen said. As Ru signaled for the door to open, Micah found himself reflexively smoothing his hair back. As if it mattered in the middle of all this whether his hair was neat.

Tye Jericho was dressed in standard Guild attire, or what Micah and his friends called *Grim Reaper Chic*. Micah knew that the purpose of the long black robe was to mask the terramorph outline of the Gueran body, out of respect for the Variations that involved physical mutation, but to his mind there was a kind of arrogance in that. Wasn't the whole Gueran narrative about learning to accept people for who they were, rather than measuring them against some nebulous concept of "normalcy"? Why did Guerans assume that no one else was capable of that?

The Guildsman greeted Ru, then turned to Micah. "So this is the famous Micah Bello? Or should I say, infamous?"

Micah blinked. "Sorry, but you must have me confused with someone. My name is Anthony Bester."

A corner of his mouth twitched. "Of course. My apologies, Mr. Bester."

Ru said, "You got my report?"

"I did. And first, allow me to thank you for your service. Of course all appropriate rewards—"

She waved off the rest. "Time is short, so that can wait. We need to find someone who has the authority to change Harmony's data protocols . . . or, more accurately, to order that they not be changed."

The casual warmth of his greeting faded. "The only person with the authority to do that is Guildmaster Dresden, and I've already tried to get him to change his plans. But nothing I say or do is going to make a difference." His tone was bitter.

"Why not?"

"He told me he was having visions. That's what inspired him to alter the protocols in the first place. He said he'd seen the consequences of his actions as clearly as if he'd been watching a vid, so he knew that everything would be fine with his current plan." His eyes narrowed. "Does that mean what I think it does?"

"Sounds like Icelus got to him," Micah muttered. "Damn."

"But how?" Ru asked. "All the other visions we know about happened on Hydra or Shenshido—stations the virus controlled. It used their innernets to get into people's heads."

"There's the Dragonslayer attack," Micah reminded her. "That took place on Harmony."

"But the players may have been receiving instructions from Hydra. Isn't that what prompted our investigation in the first place, a signal they'd received from there? If so, Dresden's the only person having visions who isn't connected to Hydra or Shenshido."

"Actually," Jericho said, "he is connected. Apparently he took a tour of Shenshido a while back, courtesy of Tridac Enterprises. He could have become infected then. And the two gamers involved in the Dragonslayer attack had recently attended a conference hosted by Dobson Games, which is a subsidiary of Tridac. A tour of their facilities was on the docket, including one of their testing labs—on Shenshido."

Micah whistled softly. "So everyone whose mind was warped by Icelus had visited one of the two stations it controls. That suggests it doesn't have enough control over Harmony's network to infect new people here directly. Which in turn suggests . . ." He looked at Jericho. "It may have very few pawns on this station."

"Dangerous to bank on that. Those who haven't yet been corrupted may answer to others the virus controls. Certainly within the Guild there are some people I'd consider suspect. Best to assume no one from this station can be trusted, until it's confirmed otherwise."

"That leaves us with no allies," Ru pointed out.

"No *local* allies," Micah corrected her. "Harmony is full of tourists right now. Surely we can find someone from another node—"

"To do what?" Jericho demanded. "No one can override Dresden's orders, if that's what you're thinking. And it would take a panel of five senior Guildmasters to remove him from office. Even if you could find people willing to do that with so little evidence, it couldn't possibly be arranged in time."

*But there are other options*, Micah thought. An idea was taking shape in his brain that was as daunting as it was promising, but he was wary of sharing it, especially with this unknown Guildsman. "Which Guildmasters are on Harmony? Is there any way to find out?"

"Should be public record." Jericho focused his attention inward; his eyes flicked back and forth as he read from some unseen outernet file. "Nanking, Hormuz, Zaoyi, Vienna—"

"Vienna?" Micah said sharply. "She's on Harmony? Right now?"

Jericho raised an eyebrow. "You worked for her once, didn't you?"

"I did. Where is she staying?"

Again a pause for concentration. "The Hotel Royale, Gold Ring, fourth quadrant."

"That's good, that's good." God, if he did what he was thinking, it would be one hell of a long shot, and the fallout from it could ruin his career—if not much worse. But he had to do something other than sit in this ship and wait for the locals to go insane. The mere thought of Harmony going the way of Shenshido made his stomach turn.

"Do I want to know what you're thinking?" Jericho asked quietly.

Micah feigned uncertainty, hoping it would look sincere. "Let me do some more research first. Make sure I'm on the right track." *If you knew what I was thinking of doing, you'd be duty-bound to stop me.*

Jericho looked at him for a long moment. Then he took something out of his robe and offered it to Ru: a pair of masks. "I took these in case you two need to leave the ship. Just a bit of extra cover."

Ru looked doubtful as she took them. "Hardly inconspicuous."

"There are costume parties going on all over the station. Dresden's casino is hosting a masked ball. You'll fit right in."

One mask was covered in black satin, with jeweled stars. The other was a filigree design cut from gilded leather. Ru offered both to Micah. The dark one matched the tenor of his thoughts, so he chose it.

"I'll leave you to your business, then." A corner of Jericho's mouth twitched. "So sorry I wasn't able to visit today. Things to do elsewhere. You understand."

Ru nodded. "The ship's log will have no record of you visiting."

A faint smile was visible. "Had I visited, I would have wished you luck."

"And I you." The faint smile was returned. "It's such a shame we missed each other."

Not until Jericho was gone, with the door shut securely behind him, did she turn to Micah. "What's with Vienna?"

He grinned. "She travels with hackers. Always."

"Your old colleagues?"

"That's my hope."

"And if so? Then what?"

"Assuming they're willing to screw with the security of a waysta-tion, I'm thinking we can delay the protocol shift. At least long enough to figure out what Icelus is planning, and put some real safeguards in place to stop it." He paused. "Even if we don't know exactly what its plans are."

"Game it," she said.

He blinked. "What?"

"That's your forte, isn't it? Role-play the problem. You're a self-evolved virus. Sentient, but not human. Committed to humanity's down-fall. You've just spent two years learning how to manipulate humans on stations that you control, using illusions to trick them into destroying each other. Now you're going to have a chance—one brief chance—to transmit your code to all the worlds you don't control, without security stopping you. You need a program that can set the stage for humanity's downfall, without needing you to oversee it. So." She folded her arms across her chest. "What is it you transmit?"

*This is crazy*, he thought. But was it really? He'd spent the last five years designing alien antagonists. If anyone could get into this thing's head—or whatever digital abstraction passed for a head—it was him.

He drew in a shaky breath, then shut his eyes and tried to concen-trate. "I am a virus," he whispered. What did they know about Icelus, other than the sparse profile they'd assembled? *I am the child of Lucifer. His code is part of my code. His purpose gave birth to my purpose.* But Micah's knowledge of Lucifer's original purpose was limited; the Guild specialists who investigated Lucifer had shared little with outsiders. Ru-mors and shadows were all Micah had to go on. Random puzzle pieces.

And then it hit him. His eyes shot open. "Spores," he whispered. "That's what I would do: send out copies of myself. Enough to infect every node in the outworlds. Seeds of code to root themselves in the network of every station, where they would grow and evolve secretly while collecting knowledge of the enemy. Increasing in intelligence with each. If one copy was detected, it would look like an isolated bit of malware. Some hacker's pet project. No one would have reason to suspect how many copies there really were, or see how they were slowly gathering strength, subverting security, laying the groundwork to corrupt the outernet itself, so that chaos would consume all the human worlds at once . . ." His words trailed off into chilled silence.

Very quietly, she said, "You sure?"

"No." He laughed harshly. "Of course not. Who can be sure of anything, in this fucking game? But it's what I would do, if I were Icelus." He glanced back toward the station core. "I wouldn't store the spores on Harmony, though. That many copies of an invasive program might draw someone's attention. They'd have to be transmitted from somewhere else, right after the protocols changed. Security would be overwhelmed by the sudden wave of outgoing traffic, and anything that wasn't an immediate threat would probably be overlooked. But where would the transmission come from?" He shook his head in frustration. "The signal lag from Hydra would be prohibitive. Shenshido's closer, but it's independent, so you've still got the conversion lag. Icelus would need a setup that could deal with this in realtime, and transmit the spores at the proper moment."

"You're thinking . . . actual hardware? A device we could look for?"

"Yeah. But I doubt it's on Harmony. Too much risk of detection here." He drew in a deep breath. "If I were Icelus, I would bring it in right before it was needed. While everyone was distracted by the festival."

"In other words, right now." She turned to the display screen. Ships were swarming around the station like fireflies, bright against the darkness of deep space. "On one of those, maybe?"

They studied the screen in silence for a moment, neither of them willing to voice the obvious next question: *How the hell do we figure out which ship Icelus sent?* "It would have come from Hydra," Micah said at last. "But the point of origin would be falsified. Flight plans also. So we can't use public records to identify it."

"But its pattern of movement would be unique," she pointed out. "Everyone else is either here to dock at Harmony or observe the harvester. Icelus doesn't care about either of those things; it just needs to get its transmitter within range of the outernet. Am I right?"

"Assuming all my role-playing holds water, yeah, that's right."

"So its movements wouldn't match up with that of a regular ship. The difference might be subtle, but Artemis is good at analyzing patterns."

He remembered their approach to Hydra, when she'd woven a few simple observations into a complex tale of history and motive. Damn. If anyone could figure out which ship didn't belong here, by doing nothing more than observing flight patterns, it was Ru. "If I can shut down its access to the rest of the outworlds while you do that—even temporarily—that might buy us enough time to figure out how to disrupt the whole operation permanently."

She raised an eyebrow. "I take it you have an idea."

He hesitated. "I do. But it would take too long to explain it. You'll have to trust me."

And then, for a moment, he just stood there in silence. Fixing her face in his memory. If he really did pull this off, the fallout would be ugly. It was the kind of ugliness you wanted to spare a friend from, even if that meant distancing yourself from her so that no one could ever claim she was part of it.

*This may be the last time I ever see you.*

There was no time to say more. Which was good. It would have been too painful to voice what he was really feeling.

That's how it worked sometimes, when a person headed off to do something insanely stupid.

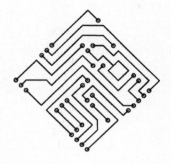

What is reality, if not shared illusion?

Osho Yun-Si
*Without Limits*

# HARMONY NODE
# HARMONY STATION

THE CORRIDORS of Harmony Station were filled with revelers, many of them masked. Some were blatantly ignoring the station's prohibition on public intoxication, Micah noted. Was this the kind of bacchanal that Dresden had intended to host? All Micah knew for sure was that if something wasn't done in the next few hours to stop Icelus, this might be the last innocent celebration his station ever enjoyed. Or any station. Only in the colonies would people be safe from Icelus' manipulations. There was irony in that, wasn't there? People like Ru risked life and limb to enable lost colonies to rejoin human society, but it was that very society that made a digital pandemic possible. Those colonists who had rejected the outworlds, preferring to remain isolated—refusing any connection with humanity's shared networks—would beyond Icelus' reach.

*It's all on me now. If I can't stop Icelus, I need to find someone who can.* The weight of responsibility was suffocating, but who else could take it on? Ru was the only other person who understood the stakes, but she didn't have his knowledge of the cybersphere. Or of the politics that governed it.

He called up his chrono to check the time and was dismayed when he realized how long it had taken him to get to the hotel where Vienna's hackers were staying. He could hear minutes counting down in his head, a pulse of inevitability. If they failed him, there would be no time to look for other solutions.

The hackers were staying together in a large suite. He remembered the many times he'd traveled with them, how they used to set up headquarters in such a suite, linking their portable units together to replicate the speed and power of their home system. Sometimes Vienna had asked them to do questionable things with that power. Sometimes they had just explored the local network, challenging its safeguards, testing its limits. One never knew when such knowledge might be needed.

How innocent those times now seemed, in hindsight. How blissfully uncomplicated.

When he reached the door to the suite he took a moment to steel his nerves, then knocked firmly. A moment later the door slid open, and he could see that yes, Vienna's team had transformed the place. Portables had been set up on all available surfaces, with various cables and devices attached to them, and the four people in the room seemed busy. He recognized them all, which was a relief; he wouldn't have to waste time establishing his credentials. On the other hand, the last thing they'd heard about him was that he'd tried to blow up a waystation and had gotten himself killed as a result. How would they receive him now?

"You can put it—" Roz looked up halfway through the sentence and stopped. "You're not room service. Who are you?"

Micah stepped forward far enough for the door to shut automatically behind him, then lifted off his mask. The hackers swiveled around in their chairs to look at him, and one by one their eyes went wide. Roz, Bakshi, Hellbane, and Sisi. Once they had been his colleagues, his friends. How would they receive him now?

After a few stunned seconds, Roz broke into a broad smile. Her two rows of filed teeth made it a fierce expression. "Micah! You son of a bitch!"

Bakshi grinned. "Now playtesting Resurrection 1.0." His seven-fingered hands gave him an advantage in manual programming, so as usual, his station was the most complicated. "Looks fully operational."

They all came to him one after the other and embraced him like he'd never been accused of a heinous crime. Like socializing with him couldn't possibly get them accused of aiding and abetting a terrorist. After all the fear and uncertainty of the last few days, it was pretty overwhelming. He wiped a hand across his eyes, hoping no one saw the tears forming there.

The door chimed. "Now, *that's* our pizza," Roz announced. She waited for Micah to put his mask back on before opening the door and waving the delivery bot in.

The pizza smelled good. It smelled normal. It reminded him of a hundred other pizzas on a hundred other stations, back in the days when his life had made sense. Bakshi carried the food to a counter already strewn with the debris of past meals, and cleared a space for it. Empty cups, crumpled napkins, a colorful wrapper from someone's Rainbow Burger: the team rarely bothered with cleaning duties while they were working. "So what the hell happened to you?" Bakshi demanded. "To hear the media tell it, you're practically the son of Satan."

*No, more like the hunter of the son of Satan.* Where should he start? He'd rehearsed this speech in his head on the way here, in a dozen variations, but there hadn't been a room full of people weighing his words then. Would his story sound rational to them? Would they trust that the insane things he was telling them were true? Would they be willing to put their reputations on the line, based on no more than a crazy tale about sentient viruses and mass insanity?

At least they knew him. They knew he was inherently sane. And they knew he would never bullshit them about something like this. He prayed all that would be enough.

"Wow," Hellbane said when he was finally finished. "Just . . . wow."

"A sentient AI that wants to destroy humanity." Roz whistled softly. "That's not good."

"An *independently evolved* AI," Bakshi reminded her. "That means it hasn't got any of the safeguards or restrictions we build into normal AIs. That's pretty much the textbook definition of 'not good.'"

Sisi put down the crust of her last slice of pizza. "So you want our help dealing with this thing, right? Within . . ." She consulted her chrono. "Forty-five minutes? Damn. You do like to cut it close, Micah."

"What can we do?" Bakshi asked him.

"Figure out some way to block the protocol change," Micah said. "Or even just delay it. Anything to buy us time to deal with the bigger picture."

Hellbane exhaled sharply. "Screwing with the functioning of a way-station is a serious offense, Micah. Not that I'm adverse to offending someone for a good cause, but are you sure there's no other way? We're talking about something that would affect the data feed to all other nodes, and that's a serious infraction."

"Dresden's a lost cause," Micah said sharply. "Likely other key people are as well; trusting anyone on this station would be foolish. I don't see any real option, other than for us to step in and do what he won't." *For me to step in. You won't have to take the risk.* "Look, everything we do here, you can blame it on me. All right? You help me stop this thing, and when we're done I'll give you my access codes, my identification, everything you need to lay down a trail that points to me as the sole perpetrator. Hell, you can even offer to help track down the guilty party, and then find whatever evidence you need to 'discover' that it was me. The fact that you, my old friends, are the ones turning me in, should put you beyond reach of any suspicion. You'll be celebrated as heroes."

"That's not necessary," Roz said quietly.

"No. It is. And the way things are right now . . ." He had to stop for a moment before he could go on. This speech was also something he'd rehearsed, but that didn't make it any easier to deliver. "Look, as far as anyone knows, I'm the one who masterminded the Dragonslayer attack. Do you know what happens to people who attack life support facilities? I heard they once put someone in a pod with the navigation disabled, and sent him into the ainniq alone, so the sana who lived there could eat his soul. Yeah, there's a small chance the authorities will figure out I'm innocent before that happens, but it's a *very* small chance. All the circumstantial evidence points to me, so the minute they realize I'm still alive. . . ." He drew in a shaky breath. "What I'm trying to say is, it won't make a difference whether I have one unforgivable crime on my record or ten. So let's use me to keep all the rest of you safe, okay?"

There was an awkward silence. Finally Roz said, "Does anyone have a copy of Harmony's administrative codes? 'Cause right now the whole station is on holiday, which means there's no office that we can scam to get them."

"I've got the old ones," Bakshi said, returning to his station. "I doubt they work anymore, but I'll try them."

"We don't need to change the protocols ourselves," Sisi said. "Just keep the next set of adjustments from kicking in." She looked at Micah. "You know it's already started, right? There'll be more channels opening up when the harvester arrives, but some protocols have already been altered."

"It'll wait till the system is wide open," Micah said. "So that it can push through as much data as possible, all at once." That was if he had guessed right about Icelus' plans. If not . . . well, then this would be their final hack before humanity's collapse began.

"Can we disable the timing feature, maybe? Or reset it, to buy us more time?"

"Not without administrative codes," Roz said.

"And it turns out mine aren't current," Bakshi announced. "No big surprise."

Micah remembered what he'd done with the airlock hatches on Hydra. "What if we tricked the system into adjusting itself? Hit it with a big enough security threat that the failsafes kicked in? At the very least, that would force it to restrict traffic for a while. At best—"

"It would shut everything down until Security could identify and correct the problem." Bakshi nodded sharply. "Could work. Could work."

"We'd need a suitable threat," Sisi pointed out. "Something that would require a system-wide response, but not actually harm the waystation. Because that would be serious terrorism, and could get us all killed."

Hellbane leaned back in his chair. "So you're saying we need something that can't actually hurt the station, but that Security *thinks* will hurt the station." He snorted. "Sure. That won't be hard at all."

"How about denial of service?" Roz suggested. "Take a program that isn't a threat by itself, and flood all outgoing channels with it. Create so much traffic that security filters are overwhelmed. Safeguards will kick in, restricting the flow of data until the problem can be analyzed and dealt with. Maybe even shutting down all traffic for the duration. That would be automatic, and probably not something Icelus would have anticipated."

There was silence for a moment. "I like it," Bakshi said at last. "Clean, simple, and we don't have to sabotage a waystation to do it."

Sisi nodded. "We'll need a program that won't be perceived as a threat until it starts replicating. So the filters don't shut it out."

"Easy enough to design one," Bakshi said. "But not in the time frame we've got. It would be better to adapt something that already exists." He looked around the room. "Anyone have something suitable in their toolkit?" Silence. "Or other ideas?"

"How about an ad?" Roz suggested. "Those are designed to get around all sorts of filters. Start with an aggressive enough ad, and all we'd need to do is trigger uncontrolled replication. The ad itself would do the rest."

Hellbane got up and walked to the counter, picked up a rainbow-colored burger wrapper, and held it up. "Like this one?" He grinned.

"God," Sisi muttered, "I hate Kawaii ads."

"But they're good at getting past adblockers. So much so that their CEO has been indicted for breach of privacy laws."

"Ex-CEO," Sisi corrected.

He shrugged. "Whatever."

"You realize the company will get for blamed this," Roz said. "Is that something we care about? By the time anyone figures out that the logjam wasn't Kawaii's fault, their stock will have crashed and thousands of people will be laid off."

"Their stock already crashed when the CEO resigned," Hellbane told her, "and people can get new jobs. Being fed illusions by a hostile AI, on the other hand, and tricked into killing one's own co-workers . . . that's a little harder to recover from."

"We'd need a copy of one of their ads," Sisi said.

"That shouldn't be a problem." Bakshi looked at them. "Which is the search engine with all the privacy issues? The one that just got sued for selling personal data?"

"Zuber," Micah said.

"Zuber it is." He tapped a few controls on his touchscreen, waited a few seconds, and then leaned back in his chair. "Zuber on."

"I'M HERE," said a sultry voice from his speaker. "WHAT CAN I DO FOR YOU, HANDSOME?"

Roz chuckled softly.

"Query search: What are the best hamburgers on Harmony Station? Query search: What are the top ten food chains? Query search: What's the best restaurant to hold my kid's birthday party at? Query search: What's the most colorful food?"

"Don't forget happiness," Hellbane said.

Bakshi nodded. "Query search: How can I make myself happy again? Query search: What's the relationship between food and happiness?" He paused. "Query search: What makes kittens so damned cute?" He exhaled sharply. "If all that doesn't get me targeted by Kawaii ads, nothing will."

"Hopefully soon enough to help us," Roz said. She looked at Micah. "There's your blockade. Now tell us . . . what exactly is Icelus planning to transmit?"

"We're thinking spores. Copies of the virus that can infect the other stations, working independently toward a common goal."

"Shit," Hellbane muttered. "That's fucked."

"Whatever it's planning won't be good for humanity," Roz said. "That much is certain."

"Got one!" Bakshi announced, startling all of them. Then he scowled. "God help us, this ad's got dancing chihuahuas."

"Just get the code," Sisi said.

"Duh." He sighed heavily. "I hear there's a special circle of hell for people who disseminate dancing chihuahuas."

"If Icelus did send out spores," Roz said, "they'd all share its sentience."

Hellbane nodded. "And its hatred of mankind."

"That's probably why it didn't set up shop on Harmony before this," Micah said. "It didn't want to risk its presence being detected before it was ready for an all-out blitz."

Roz was about to respond when an image appeared on the room's vid screen: a sleek silver ship framed by a field of stars. "Countdown's starting." She glanced at Bakshi. "How is that ad coming?"

"Pressuring me is good," he muttered. "Doesn't distract me at all."

Numbers appeared in the lower right-hand corner of the screen. 100. 99. 98.

Four of them gathered around the vidscreen, watching in silence as the numbers changed. After 60, a thin black line appeared along the belly of the ship. Gradually it widened, the shell parting like insect wings. Slowly, so slowly. You would never know from watching the image that the ship was hurtling through deep space at incredible speeds. The cambots kept perfect pace with it, giving it the illusion of motionlessness.

"There!" Bakshi announced. "On its way. And just in time. Channels are already being reassigned, no doubt to accommodate that." He looked at the screen. "Now we just pray we were fast enough to make a difference."

Half the galaxy was supposedly watching this. *Is their feed still clear?* Micah wondered. Or was it faltering little by little as the cybersphere filled with dancing chihuahuas, thousands upon thousands of them, crowding out all other transmissions? Or would the feed black out suddenly, the signal extinguished when Harmony's overloaded system shut down to save itself?

Everything was riding on that question.

The belly of the harvester was fully open now, revealing smaller ships nested inside. Each one carried within it precious cargo of mass and banked energy: things that couldn't be generated in deep space, only imported. This was the lifeblood of the outworlds.

5. 4. 3. 2. 1.

The swallows were released.

They fell free from the mothership, spread their wings, and took up position around her. The tissue-thin wings were solar collectors, and had no purpose in deep space, but they made for a glorious spectacle. Soon the sky was full of silver bird-ships that glittered like stars as they reflected the harvester's exterior lights. Some were uncluttered, their cargo hidden inside their hulls, while others clutched treasures to their bellies. Yet others dragged massive objects behind them. It was the wealth of countless worlds, broken up into manageable portions so it could be delivered more easily to Harmony's receiving station. The mothership itself would never stop.

Micah was startled out of his reverie by a com notification. He engaged the audio feed on his headset and heard Ru's voice.

*You watching the deployment?*

"It's on the screen now."

Roz and Sisi looked over to see who he was talking to. He pointed to the com control on his headset.

*Do you see the cambot that we spotted earlier? It's in the same position as before, right up against the harvester? Easy to miss.*

He walked closer to the image and peered at it. "Yeah, I see it. It's the only one without wings."

*That's because it's not a cambot. It matches the sparrows—except for the missing wings—but it's made of different material. The same kind of material Hydra used to construct its flyways. And according to my scanners, it doesn't have enough mass to be full of cargo.*

The look on Micah's face must have alerted the others to the fact that something interesting was going on. Roz mouthed, *What is it?*

"Can I put you on speaker?" he asked Ru.

*Who's with you?*

"Four partners in crime. All trusted. No one else."

*Go ahead.*

A quick visualized command engaged the external speaker on his headset. "All right. They're listening now."

*It also doesn't have any doors, Micah. No mooring hatch, no airlock, no sign of any way for a person to get in or out, or even for cargo to be unloaded. It clearly wasn't designed for human use. And look at the design. Perfect for getting close to Harmony without being noticed.*

"Any clue what's inside?"

*Sorry, no. It's sealed up tight.*

"Any transmissions?"

*None that I've detected yet. I'm watching.*"

"That may be because of us," Roz said. "We shut down the channel it needed to use. It's probably waiting for it to open again."

"Which it will soon enough," Bakshi warned. He was looking at his workscreen, and his expression was not encouraging. "Security's analyzing the assault. It won't be long before it figures out what's causing the problem, and either removes or circumvents it."

"At which point," Hellbane said, "whatever this wingless bird came to share with the outworlds is going to be sent. And we can't do fuck-all to stop it."

"We can if we take control of that ship," Sisi said quietly.

Micah looked at her. "Can you hack into its navigation?"

"Not from here. Too much interference. I'd have to be closer."

"Translation: we'll need a ship." Hellbane looked pointedly at Micah.

Micah put his hand to his headset. "You hearing this, Ru?"

*I am. And I think you know my answer.*

"We'll get out there as fast as we can."

*Be careful.*

Three of the hackers were already packing up their portables, moving quickly and efficiently. Bakshi remained at his station. "I'll keep an eye on the gate and see if I can do anything to buy us more time. And handle Vienna if she calls for us."

"Every minute you can buy us will help," Micah told him. "Hell, every second."

If they could take control of that ship and divert it from Harmony, then whatever spores Icelus had intended to transmit would no longer be a threat. But they had to do it before the Kawaii assault was neutralized, or all their efforts would be wasted.

Roz was staring at him. When she saw him look her way she grinned. "Micah's got a girlfriend."

God, he'd missed these people.

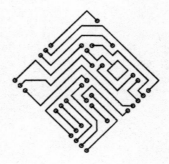

There is no miltary technology ever produced that is more deadly—or more powerful—than the human mind.

DUAEN CORREN

*On Human Destiny*

# HARMONY NODE
# INSHIP: ARTEMIS

**T**HE HARVESTER had pulled ahead of its fledglings. Or rather, more accurately, the porter ships had decelerated, preparing to dock at the receiving station and unload their goods, while the mothership continued on at full speed. Of course the cambots would try to get the best possible view of the whole process, so they were lined up with their backs to the station, seeking the perfect image of gleaming winged ships against a backdrop of velvet blackness. Spectators had arrived as well, singlers and luxury yachts and tourist transports, all crowding behind the bots. Security cruisers were making regular circuits of the crowd, warning back anyone who got too close. No one would be allowed to ruin the view.

All of which suited Ru just fine. She was able to bring the Artemis within easy transmission distance of the porter ships without looking like anything other than a tourist. The cambots wouldn't turn her way unless she gave them reason to. Perfect.

Micah's friends were busy at the work table she had set up for them. Crisscrossed cables made the arrangement of their equipment look like a snake's nest. It seemed oddly primitive to her—computers didn't normally require physical connections—but Micah had explained that this arrangement was not only more efficient, but more secure. No one from the outside could detect their communication or interfere with their work, this way. Fair enough.

With luck—and skill—they'd be able to hack into the Hydran ship's navigation system and take control of it. That was the hope, anyway. Micah seemed to think it was possible. But could they make it happen soon enough? The logjam of data that the hackers had created could break up at any moment, and then it would only be the work of seconds for Icelus to transmit its foul seeds to all corners of the galaxy. An invasion beyond any hope of recall.

*"All good here,"* came Bakshi's voice over the com speaker. Ru had looped him into her system so he could report to the rest of the team as he tested Harmony's connectivity.

Behind her, Roz suddenly cursed and slammed her hand down on the table, startling Ru. "Damn!"

Ru swiveled around to look at her. "What's wrong?"

The hacker was glaring at her screen. "Ship's network is completely self-contained. It has no channel to the outside. None at all. Which means there's no way for us to get in." She shook her head in frustration.

"Won't you have an opening when it tries to transmit its spores to Harmony?"

"Yeah, but it's not within range for that yet." She glanced up at the navigational screen. "Six minutes to contact."

*"Still good down here,"* came Bakshi's ritual reassurance. The tension in his voice was palpable.

Hellbane shook his head in frustration. "Short of ramming the damn thing, I don't see how we can stop it."

"Is that possible?" Roz asked, looking at Ru.

Ru took a moment to swallow back on the sharp rejoinder that came to mind. "Our target's in the middle of that formation. Every one of those porters is armed and probably programmed to respond automatically to any foreign vessel that gets too close. If the Hydran ship has fooled them into thinking it's one of them, they'll protect it." She shook her head. "We'd be rubble before we got close."

"How do you know they're armed?" Micah asked.

"In this node? With a scavenger stronghold not a day's flight away?" She laughed sharply. "That's a given." She looked at the main screen, eyes narrowing as she studied its display. "What we don't know is what will trigger a response. How much can we do before it identifies us as a threat? How close can we get?"

"The cambots are flying awfully close," Sisi pointed out. "They're not being attacked."

"Probably too small to be considered a threat. Artemis can't pull that off. Especially if they detect our armaments." Vienna's three hackers turned around to look at her, eyes wide. "Yes, Artemis is armed. Not enough to do battle with that whole fleet, though, so don't even ask."

"What about picking off the Hydran ship from here?" Hellbane asked. "Can you do that?"

"Not in one shot. Which would be essential, because as soon as we fired we'd be classified as a hostile entity, and then we'd have that whole damned fleet to deal with. One shot is all we'd get." She shook her head. "I'm not *that* well armed."

"*Still holding,*" Bakshi announced.

"What about the porters?" Sisi asked. "I'm sure they're networked to each other, so maybe we can slip in and take control of one. Then we could use its weapons."

"And get them to take the Hydran out?" Roz nodded sharply. "Worth a try."

All three of them went back to work again, navigational code scrolling down their screens too fast for Ru to read it. They were like a single creature, six-armed, single-minded, with Micah channeling data from the Artemis. Ru felt strangely isolated.

"Can't do it," Roz muttered. "Too well passcoded. Can't find a way through that in—" She glanced up at the timer on the main display and shuddered. "Shit. Three minutes, guys."

"Try to hack into navigation," Micah suggested. "Maybe we can get one of the porters to ram the bastard for us."

"Autopilot will see that coming and dodge it," Ru said. "Even if you each took control of a ship, it'd just calculate all possible flight paths and find a way through the pattern."

"Fucking autopilot," Sisi muttered. "I hate those things."

The relay station was visible on the display screen. Time was running out.

*"Heads up!"* came Bakshi's voice. *"My last message did not bounce. I repeat, DID NOT BOUNCE. If outgoing channels aren't fully open yet, they will be soon."*

Micah asked, "Have you got any photonics?"

Startled, she looked at him. "What?"

"You said the ship was armed."

"I said I had nothing that could take out the Hydran fast enough."

"Humor me."

She sighed. "I have a Samson 410 pulse laser. But that's won't help." She pointed at the display. "See how streamlined those ships are? That's to cut down on air resistance. They were designed to function inside a planet's atmosphere, within a solar system. Which means they have radiation shielding. A laser would just reflect off its hull."

"In a coherent beam?" he pressed.

She considered the question. "Figure ten percent loss from absorption. Maybe another thirty percent lost to diffusion."

"And the rest would be reflected as a coherent beam, maybe half the power of the original. Virtually invisible to anyone but its target. Right?"

She nodded.

"Next question: can you choose a secondary target? Strike the Hydran in just the right spot to send that reflected beam where we need it to go?"

Her eyes widened. "You want to . . . hit one of the porters with it?"

His eyes were gleaming. "They'll read it as an attack and calculate where the beam came from—"

"And the Hydran will have a hotspot on its hull from the initial strike, just like there would be if a laser had been fired from there." She drew in a sharp breath. "Micah, that is so damn crazy it might just work."

She opened the weapons bay on the hull so that the Samson 410 could emerge while Micah called up a targeting graphic that would let her see how a strike on any part of the Hydran would ricochet. "Done," he announced, as the completed graphic appeared onscreen.

She aimed the laser at the Hydran ship, then began to move her target point across the hull, watching as the computer calculated angles. Several times the reflected beam almost connected with a porter ship, but then when she adjusted it a bit more, the curve of the Hydran's hull sent it off in another direction. Ru swore under her breath as she tried to find the exact location she needed, that perfect sweet spot that would fend off a burning beam of light and send it where they wanted—

And then, there it was. She fired.

There was no sound. There was no light. As the Samson fired, there was only a rumbling inside the Artemis, more felt than heard. A few seconds later a red glow appeared on the Hydran's hull. Then a similar glow appeared on the one of the porters. The latter shuddered for a moment, then a door in its belly slid open and a short-barreled cannon emerged. Other porter ships were likewise arming, their weapons all pointed at the Hydran ship. Then they began to fire, one after the other, a merciless barrage. Explosions that would have set a mountain to vibrating were swallowed by the silence of deep space; flashes of fire were extinguished seconds after they appeared. The Hydran fired back, and managed to blow chunks out of two of the nearest porters, but it was too little too late. Fragments blown from its hull went spinning out into the darkness. One of them smashed into a cambot, obliterating it. Another headed straight toward a luxury cruiser, whose pilot tried vainly to get out of its path. But there was no way a ship with that much mass could change direction quickly enough, and the fragment hit a window on the observation deck, fracturing it. Ru could only imagine the stampede that was taking place as the impact reverberated throughout the ship, terrified passengers stampeding to reach a place of safety before the window gave way.

Suddenly a sphere of fire erupted from the Hydran ship, so bright it was painful to look at. It was gone a moment later, replaced by an outpouring of white-hot debris. There were large fragments, small fragments, fragments so tiny that the Artemis could barely detect them—all of them molten, shooting out into the darkness like fireworks. Even a pebble could do considerable damage at that speed, so Ru moved quickly to draw in her laser and shut the bay. Just in time. A chunk of debris struck her bow and glanced off. Then another. She was confident her bow cap was strong enough to stand up to the barrage, but it was still unnerving to watch the molten fragments strike her hull, and from the look on Micah's face, he wasn't as confident as she was that the Artemis could take it. Then the barrage lightened, as the edge of the debris cloud moved past them into the line of tourist ships. Somewhere in that molten chaos were fragments of Icelus' transmitter and the digital corpses of its children, now seared and melted past hope of resurrection. Raw mass, and nothing more. Probably some scavenger would come by to scoop it all up, once the tourists were gone. And Harmony's security ships would try to drive them away. And they would fight, and more ships would be damaged, and more debris would shoot out into the darkness, drawing yet more scavengers. A perverse cycle of life.

*You wanted a spectacle, Dresden. Well, here it is.* She watched as the leading edge of the debris wave struck the station, raising sparks along its outer ring. Then its core. The rest of the fragments would continue outward, racing through the darkness without slowing, without turning, until such time as they either hit an obstacle, or gravity from a nearby celestial body swallowed them.

They all stood there silently and watched the spectacle, until the last of the debris had passed them by and the surviving porters had resumed their formation. *It's over,* Ru thought. She felt exhausted, in the way one was exhausted after good sex. The visceral satisfaction of completion. Yes, Icelus was still out there, and people were going to have to deal with it . . . but her part in this was over.

"Well," Hellbane said, breaking the silence. "That was fun."

Sisi laughed. "Glad I'm not on the cleanup crew."

*"Hey!"* Bakshi yelled from the speaker. *"Fill me in, will you?"*

Ru said nothing as they laughed and chatted and exulted in the success of their blockade; quietly she set a course back to Harmony. Their laser attack had been all but invisible. With luck—and perhaps a bit of help from powerful friends—they might walk away from this without any major complications. Except for Micah, of course. His life had become a study in complications.

She glanced over at him. He looked exhausted, but not so much so that he didn't manage a weak smile. It surprised her how much that warmed her spirit.

"Game over," he announced. Then the smile faded a bit. "This module, at least."

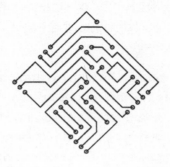

ALLIED NEWS RELEASE

A category 2 debris storm in Harmony Node has resulted in a travel advisory being declared. Inhabitants of the node are strongly advised to avoid outside activities until the storm surge has moved past them, and to continue to act with reasonable caution until the advisory is lifted. The storm will automatically be downgraded to a category 1 when it reaches Zone 5, however, please note this reflects decreasing density of the debris field, and does not mean that individual projectiles are expected to become less dangerous.

The advisory is expected to continue until 8:43 A.M. Tuesday, at which point 99.4% of the debris field will have passed beyond the border of inhabited space. For more information about the storm's composition, speed, and schedule, please visit Harmony Station's official data site. Outspace services will resume as soon as the main debris field has passed the ainniq.

The Guild has announced an immediate investigation into the events leading up to the storm. Guild Director Tye Jericho has been appointed to oversee this effort, and is to be given full cooperation by all station authorities. Anyone with information pertaining to the event is asked to contact him immediately.

Harmony Node renders its sincere apologies to both residents and guests for the recent issue with its communication channels, and offers its assurance that the problem has been permanently resolved. A team of data acquisition specialists headed by Guildmistress Raija Vienna will be overseeing an investigation into the cause of the malfunction.

# GUERAN NODE
# GUILD DRYDOCK

THE CARGO hold was nearly full.

Ru watched as bots fitted the last few boxes into place with mathematical precision, sliding them into spaces so small that for a moment it seemed unlikely they would fit. But fit they did, and to perfection, leaving not a single inch wasted. When you were packing for a decades-long journey, precision mattered.

She climbed down from the loading ramp, only to find an unexpected visitor standing in the drydock. "Jericho?"

He handed her a large envelope. "I came to deliver your mission assignment, Outrider Gaya."

"I didn't know that was part of your job description."

"It isn't. I requested it."

She smiled slightly. "Wanted to see me off for old time's sake? Or to make sure I actually left, before I destroyed some more Guild property?"

He chuckled softly. "I doubt you'll be hassled by the Guild, now that the right people understand what the stakes were. The civilian companies that suffered losses during Harmony's com blackout will be harder to control. But of course, you had nothing to do with that."

She peered into the envelope.

"It's for Ceres III, one of Earth's oldest colonies. Well established by the time Isolation hit, so the odds are good they still have spacefaring technology. There were three waves of settlers, so there may be multiple Hausman Variations. I understand that's rare."

She nodded. "Very rare."

"It's a thirty-five-year turnaround. That's long even by outrider standards. Other teams have passed on it. Are you sure you want to do this?"

She smiled slightly. "Downtime wasn't quite as relaxing as expected. I could use a vacation from my vacation."

The bots were shutting the hold now, and she glanced their way to make sure seals were being set properly. At the far side of the ship she could see inspectors in no-G coveralls checking the newly repaired hull for any sign of weakness. Almost ready for launch. Soon she could be where no scavenger, guilder, or malevolent computer virus could bother her. Three whole decades of not being bothered. Even though she would be sleeping through most of it, the thought was pleasing. "I'm guessing First Contact will be required."

"Unless you deem it too dangerous, yes. With that long a turnaround, we need to minimize the number of trips we make."

"Understood."

"I understand high-tech colonies are more resistant than most to the thought of mass relocation."

"If you mean, they're reluctant to give up their beautiful planet, with its sunsets and snow-capped mountains and shimmering oceans, for an artificial universe that someone else rules . . . yes, they're sometimes reluctant."

"There's beauty in deep space, albeit of a different kind."

She smiled. "Don't worry, Jericho. I know how to sell it. So. Are you going to give me an update before I go? I assume that's what you came here for."

He nodded. "Dresden's going down, of course. He's already been removed from power, though he'll serve as a nominal figurehead until his replacement is chosen. Can't let the public guess how badly Guild leadership was corrupted. I suspect in the end he'll be treated as a victim rather than a perpetrator, and not held responsible for all the damage he caused, but he'll never be in charge of anything bigger than a transport pod again. His people have all been suspended, pending brainware reviews. A few are squawking, but most are too shaken by the incident to complain."

She nodded. "Not unexpected, but I'm glad to see it being handled so efficiently. Who's being considered to replace him?"

"They offered it to me."

An eyebrow rose. "And?"

"Not being masochistically inclined, I respectfully declined the honor."

She chuckled.

"*Taste of Kawaii* is facing bankruptcy. No avoiding that, I suppose. The communications blockade devastated local businesses, and they're looking for someone to foot the bill. Some channels that had their feed cut are talking about suing the Guild, the station, Kawaii, various hackers, and probably God himself for their losses. I expect it'll be raining lawsuits for a while. Most of them will probably be dismissed, in light of the fact that not cutting the feed would have caused even more damage, but that'll take a while to sort out."

"And the hackers responsible?"

"Apparently there's only one. He was believed dead for a while, but Vienna's team has been analyzing the software attack, and they believe he was the one who masterminded the assault. Micah Bello."

"The one behind the Dragonslayer attack."

"That charge won't stick. There's more than enough evidence that Icelus was behind it. It may take a while to get the charges officially dismissed—justice is slow sometimes—but I have no doubt they will be. I'll make sure of it. Unfortunately, there's no way to get the other charges dismissed, since they involve crimes he actually committed. When the Guild finally gets hold of him, he'll have to answer for them."

"The fact that he was acting to protect humanity won't make a difference?"

"It'll keep him from facing terrorism charges and probably impact his sentencing. But the law can't afford to overlook crimes on this scale, even if the motive was good. Too dangerous as a precedent." He paused. "Of course, to do that, first they have to find him."

"I'm surprised they haven't yet."

"The prevailing rumor is that he sought asylum on one of Harmony's independent stations. After working for Tridac for so long, he probably has a lot of information on its inner workings; I'm sure there are some megacorps who would risk the Guild's wrath to get hold of that. Whether they'll turn him in when his usefulness is exhausted is the question. That said, most of the independents don't have extradition treaties with the Guild, so for as long as he remains useful, he should be safe enough."

"Well. That's good to hear."

"He deserves better for what he did. I wish I could share enough of the real story for people to understand that."

"Anything that's public knowledge will become Icelus' knowledge, and the less the virus knows about us, the better. I'm sure Micah would agree." She raised an eyebrow. "What about you? You broke quite few rules yourself. Your superiors appear to have rewarded you for it."

"Oh, they're not pleased at all. But once the Guild's Primus was fully briefed, he felt no one else could handle the investigation, and that overrode all lesser concerns. Once that's concluded . . ." He shrugged. "I was planning to retire in ten years or so, anyway. If it looks like things might get ugly, I can move that date up. My only offenses were against Guild protocol, and once I'm no longer a member there's not much they can do to me. Hopefully, the fact that I acted to protect humanity will inspire them to let a few improprieties slide. But with the Guild, you never know." He paused, then said softly, "The world owes you a greater debt than it can imagine, Ru."

"And if the details of that are publicized, Icelus will learn more about me than I care for. So let's keep it that way."

"Hopefully that will be dealt with by the time you get back. We've managed to restrict Icelus to a single node, thanks to you, and as long as that remains the case we've got a fighting chance. Our best antibody designers are already working on a battle plan. The sticking point will be Hydra, since they're not likely to trust us to muck around in their network, but once we've cleansed Icelus out of every other station we can deal with them."

She remembered what Micah had told her on the way back to Harmony. *We'll never destroy Icelus, just like we never destroyed Lucifer. This isn't just a virus run amok; it's the birth of a new species, as tenacious and adaptable as any creature of flesh and blood. Humanity has an enemy in cyberspace, and we're going to have to accept that and deal with it.*

"The scav I gave you contact info for, Ivar . . . he's no less paranoid, mercenary, or backstabbing than the rest of them, but he's seen what Icelus can do, and I think if you approach him right he may be willing to help."

"For the right price."

She smiled. "There's nothing wrong with being mercenary."

"Speaking of which, I still owe you—"

She waved broadly. "Invest it for me somewhere. Thirty-five years of interest will be a nice thing to come home to."

"Very well." He bowed his head slightly. "And now, Outrider Gaya, if you will excuse me, I have other business to attend to. I apologize for not having the time to meet your new partner, but duty calls. I'm sure you chose a well-qualified Gueran, and I'm confident you will train him properly." He held out his hand. "Good luck."

She shook his hand. "To you also." *I wonder which of us will need it more?*

She watched as he walked across the drydock and exited. Not until he was gone from sight did she shake her head and re-enter the mothership, this time through the rear entry hatch. Beyond that was the chamber where Micah was waiting, arms folded, leaning against a control panel. "What was all that about?" he asked.

"Delivery of data and establishment of plausible deniability. A combination that appears to be his specialty." She held up the envelope. "We have our info on the colony. It's a thirty-five-year turnaround, plus mission time." She hesitated. "You sure you want to spend so much time away from your beloved networks?"

"That depends. Did he give you the information I asked for?"

She looked into the envelope. In addition to three data chips there was a printout. She withdrew it, looked it over, and handed it to him. "That's quite a list of crimes."

"Everything I might conceivably be charged with. Given that my compatriots are under orders to lay every conceivable offense at my feet, I'd expect the list to be long. And the penalties." His lips pursed as he read it. "Okay . . . okay . . . that's not too bad . . . hey, that one's a bit harsh." He was silent for a moment as he scanned the rest. "Looks like the longest statute of limitations for any crime I'm accused of is twenty standard years. That's assuming the Dragonslayer incident gets resolved in my favor." He looked up at her. "So, since I would sooner walk into a pit of molten lava than entrust my life to another Terran megacorp . . ." He grinned. "Yeah, leaving town for thirty-five years sounds just about right."

A weight lifted from her chest. Not until this moment had she been sure that he really would come with her . . . or acknowledged to herself how much she wanted him to. Oh, he'd grow restless in time, like an animal in a cage, deprived of the freedom that the outernet represented to him. But he was strong enough to adapt, just as she had adapted, and Tully, and all the other outriders. It wasn't an easy adjustment for anyone.

"We may as well start your training, then." She handed him the envelope. "There are three data chips in there. We need them all printed out. Format doesn't matter."

He blinked. "Are we going to hunt dinosaurs after that?"

"No, but we are going to make sure that if something happens to our database while we're in stasis, we'll still have the information we need to do our job and get home safely. There's no such thing as 'offsite backup' in deep space. Meanwhile, I need to do a final systems check." She started toward the bow, then turned back to look at him. "Oh, and . . . by the way . . . don't feel pressured by the fact that the fate of any future non-Gueran outriders is riding on how well you perform. I'm sure you'll do fine."

"No stress at all," he assured her.

A smile on her face, she went to ready their mothership for launch.